David Cortez, a decorated US Marine, is now on the run from his own government after escaping a top-secret CIA lab when an experimental medical procedure turned sour.

While lying low in Mexico, an assassin sent from British Intelligence tracks him down. However, Sonny from MI6, a British-Iranian with a cockney accent, offers David a choice: join his team, or be killed.

David chooses to work with Sonny, not only because he wants his life back, but because he feels a kinship with the man.

They're also both in the unique position of being the only living test subjects with alien DNA in their blood. Could that explain the strong attraction between them?

SPECIMEN

PRISM AGENTS, BOOK ONE

C. QUINCE

A NineStar Press Publication
www.ninestarpress.com

Specimen

First Edition, March 2025

ISBN: 978-1-64890-848-4

Also available in eBook, ISBN: 978-1-64890-847-7

CONTENT WARNING:

This book contains sexually explicit content, which may only be suitable for mature readers. Depictions of gun, gun violence, medical procedures, human genetic testing, and animal cruelty/testing.

For my dear B.

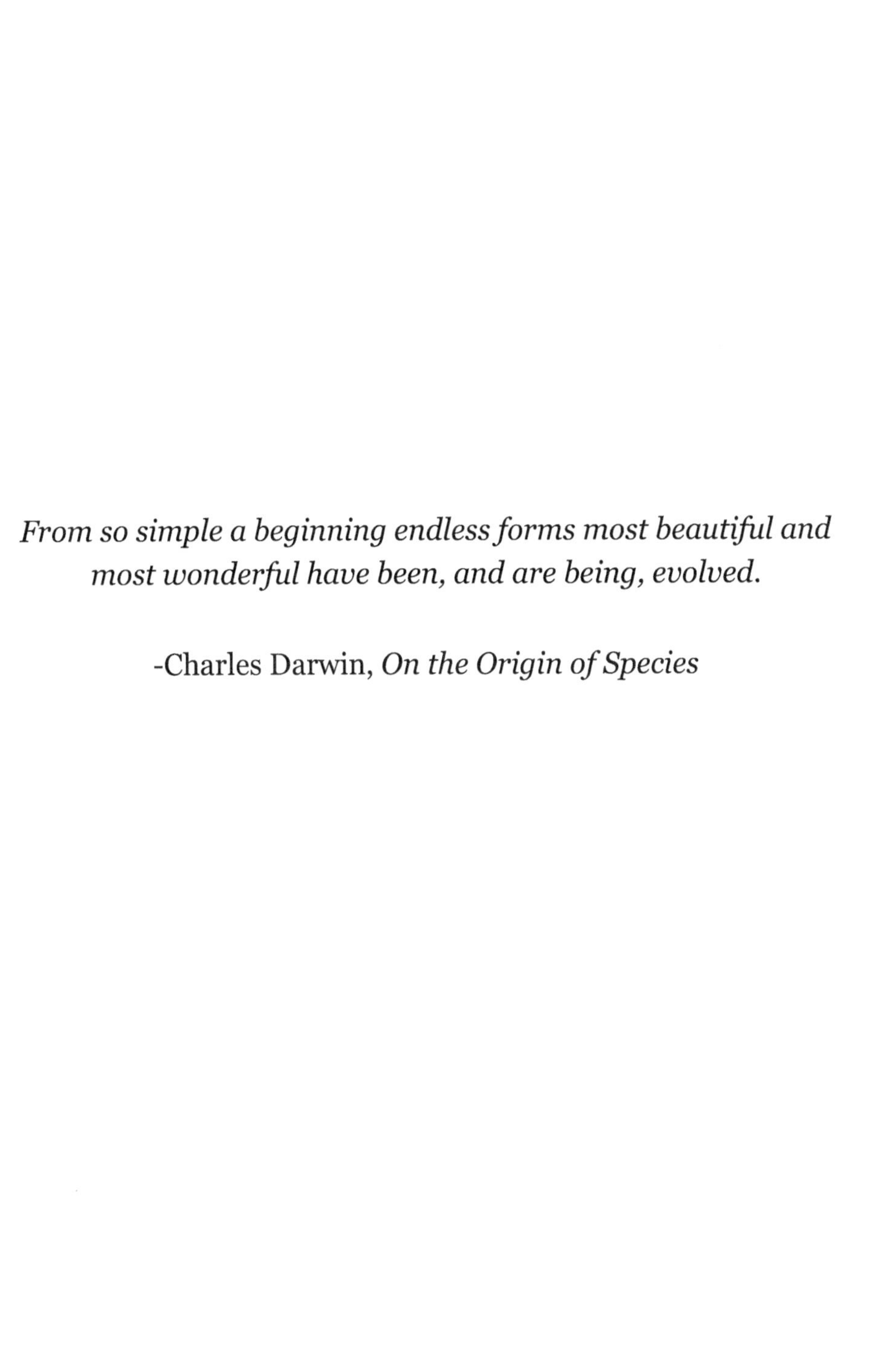

From so simple a beginning endless forms most beautiful and most wonderful have been, and are being, evolved.

-Charles Darwin, *On the Origin of Species*

Chapter One

Tijuana, Mexico

David was being followed.

He couldn't see who the tail was; every time David paused to do a little window shopping on the street and check his six in the window's reflection, the tail managed to hide. Whoever they were, they were good at slipping by undetected.

David wasn't sure who it was. Agency, probably, or another US-based shadowy government division. He should've picked Venezuela to lie low, but Mexico was his home, his heritage. He had lingered here longer than he should; he knew that, but he'd been so careful, using different names and cash only. He'd grown a beard to blend in and kept moving from place to place, never settling. David had been looking over his shoulder for six months. Now it seemed the bastards had finally caught up to him.

The sun was low in the sky, turning the clouds pink and

orange. Vendors in the busy street were out in full force, providing good cover. David calmly made his way down the street, not letting on that he knew he was being followed—but if his tail was worth their salt, they'd know that he knew.

If his tail was a US Government agency like David suspected they were, they wanted one of two things: One, they wanted to keep tabs on him. Two, they wanted to bring him in. The latter would involve kidnap in some form or other; then they'd transport him to a black site—a soundproofed lab where nobody would hear him scream.

David should know. He'd been through that scenario once, and once was enough. If they thought he would come in quietly after what they'd done to him, they had another thing coming.

In the early evening hubbub of Tijuana, David led his tail down side streets and off the beaten path. He knew this town like the back of his hand, and it gave him the advantage.

On an ill-lit street, popular with gang members from the local cartel, a neon bar sign flickered on and off over an open doorway. David ducked in there. Immediately inside the door was a set of steps descending into darkness. David hurried down. At the bottom of the stairs, another open doorway awaited him. David knew the bar; it was small, gloomy, lit only by neon, and it was popular with drug dealers. Today it was busy enough, with music playing loud, and David was able to slip in without attracting attention.

He planned to lie in wait and watch who came through the door after him, so he situated himself at the far end of the bar, facing the entrance. He ordered a light beer. The bartender opened a bottle and stuck a wedge of lime in the top before handing it over.

David took the beer but didn't drink yet. His eyes were

trained on the doorway. Nobody had followed him in, which meant they were hanging back.

If the shoe had been on the other foot and David was the one doing the tailing, he wouldn't have run straight into the unknown either. That meant this tail wasn't a local, much as he'd suspected.

David leaned on the bar more casually and poked the lime wedge down into the bottle so he could take a sip of beer. He happened to catch his own reflection in the mirror behind the bar. Illuminated by red neon light, David's tan skin looked darker than it usually did. He'd grown his hair out to ear length, the colour a mid-brown shade kissed by the sun. His full beard was a darker shade of brown. He looked like a local.

It was ironic; he'd spent his youth in California trying to look less Mexican, trying to fit in with the White kids in his grade. He'd lightened his hair with frosted tips for a while there—hair in the early '00s...not great. David was half Mexican on his father's side. His mother was Caucasian American from San Diego.

Now David had fled the US, he wanted to look more Mexican. He had felt shielded by his disguise so far, but maybe it was time for a new disguise. A new location.

Still no one had come through the door. That was nearly five minutes, a lifetime in surveillance work.

David was about to cut and run, when a figure appeared at the entrance. For a moment David tensed, but he soon saw that this figure was tiny. A short Mexican woman, and likely not his tail. She was the first of a group of local youths entering the bar. Two women, three men.

David relaxed some. These were Mexican kids. He could tell by looking at them; their dark hair, their complexions, and their clothes. The shoes gave it away: slides and sandals weren't exactly standard surveillance footwear. These were civilians.

As the lively group came further into the bar to order their drinks, David noticed that one pair of feet among them had on black boots.

Bingo.

That was his tail, the man at the back of the group. Likely he had waited for a group to enter the bar and tacked himself on. Clever.

David tried to see who it was, but all he caught was a dark head of hair and tan skin. Regular street clothes for Mexico, black boots aside; a short-sleeve shirt and dark pants. He could be from a cartel, for all David knew.

He couldn't get a good enough look before the guy peeled off from the group and melted away to the back section of the bar. That's where the cartels usually hung out.

Maybe no one was tailing him after all, and David was being paranoid. Six months on the run would do that to anybody. He was tired of looking over his shoulder, but he wouldn't sacrifice his freedom.

He took one more swig of beer, then left it on the bar along with some notes for payment. David headed for the gents' toilets.

On his way, he glanced at the mirror behind the bar to see if he was being followed. Amidst the bustle of the patrons, it was hard to tell, but he'd soon find out.

David had to go up another set of steps to reach the toilets. He ascended quickly, entered the tiny bathroom, and closed the door behind him. The urinals were vacant, ditto the single stall. Good timing.

David headed over to the window. He'd picked this bar for a reason. He knew he could sneak out this way.

Nobody had followed him into the bathroom yet, so he took

his chance. David climbed up on the ledge and peered out the open top window. Outside, the back alley was dark but empty.

Most people couldn't get out of this window; it was too narrow. But David wasn't most people. Balancing on one leg while holding the window open with his hand, David first carefully threaded one leg and arm through the thin slip of window. He had to roll his body over the pane and land his foot on the outer ledge, balancing like a circus act.

Once he'd done that, he had to hold his balance while threading his other arm and leg through. He made it out the window and followed the natural turn of his body, slowly flipping himself over. He landed down on the dusty ground in a crouch.

He hadn't made a sound during all this. David paused for a moment, listening for anyone in pursuit.

Nothing yet.

Either he was being paranoid and nobody was following him, or he was about to give his tail the slip. Caution had kept him alive and free this far. David decided to make a break for it. Nobody else was in the alley. He got up and took off at a jog to get back onto a vendor street.

David found a stall selling garish shirts and exchanged cash for one. Concealed among the street vendors, David watched the street corner while he quickly changed his shirt for the new one.

Nobody had followed him.

Shit, maybe he *was* paranoid.

David discarded his old shirt and walked away, doing up the buttons on his new one. He could've worn his white undershirt by itself, but he had plenty of scars on his skin from his time as a Marine that he didn't enjoy showing off.

He stopped by a taco vendor to grab something to eat. He'd be taking the long route home tonight, just in case, and he needed sustenance.

"Gracias," David said, as the friendly vendor handed over a loaded taco.

"¡Provecho!" he replied, moustache bristling as he grinned.

David loved Mexico. People were so friendly here and he always felt at home.

He took a bite out of his taco as he walked down the street. Once or twice, he checked behind him, but he sensed his tail was gone now—if he'd ever been there. But to be safe, David would pack up his things tonight and move to another city. He would miss Tijuana, but he had to stay several steps ahead.

He ate his taco and walked. David doubled back a couple times to check for a tail, and to grab another taco from a different street vendor—he needed a lot of food, being on the run. He also picked up a cup of freshly squeezed orange juice from the juice man's cart.

David had gotten to know all these vendors the past couple of months, and he'd miss seeing their friendly faces. Hopefully, they'd still be here when he came back around to Tijuana one day.

He tipped the juice vendor, because David knew he had three kids back at home. The guy was always chatting about them.

"Gracias, señor!" he said, smiling as he pocketed the money.

"De nada." David smiled back. These little interactions with vendors were often the most time he spent with other people. Being on the lam wasn't fun. He missed human connection. Avoiding everyone and being suspicious was wearing him down.

He took his OJ and walked away, slurping great gulps through the straw.

David happened to glance at an open alleyway as he passed. Force of habit. A man stood there, casually leaning against the corner wall and eating a taco, a taco from one of the same vendors

David used.

David hadn't seen this guy around before. He could be local, given his colouring. Or possibly another ethnicity. David was used to analysing strangers in the blink of an eye; another habit. He had to ascertain if someone was a local or not for his own safety. This guy had a dark head of stylish hair and some equally dark stubble on his face, and...well, he was cute. Very cute. David noticed that more than anything.

He had avoided getting close to anyone for months, given his situation, but no harm in looking. No harm in a flirty smile in passing. And the longer the other man held eye contact, the more chance there was he was into men too.

But David quickly realised this perhaps wasn't the case. Yes, this guy was watching David and holding eye contact, but something was off. He held up the taco he was eating, and he smirked at David as if to say, I can see why you like these so much.

Like he knew David, knew his movements.

David looked down. Black boots. The guy wore black boots. It was his tail from the bar. Well, this time David would confront him.

"Hey!" David said and began making his way across the street. Not an easy task with vendors, shoppers, and tourists in his path.

Meanwhile his tail slipped into the alleyway before David could reach him.

David got to the alley, and it was empty with only trash cans and two stray dogs sniffing around a piece of taco on the ground, and they quickly withdrew once they noticed David there.

Where had the man gone? Maybe ducked in a doorway or hid behind the trash bags? David felt torn. He should turn and run. He'd confirmed he had a tail, confirmed someone was following him. But David had a hunch this wasn't the Agency. Unless they'd wised up enough to send a flirty guy in David's direction.

Like a bee drawn to a flower, David entered the alley. He wanted to find this guy and question him. There was still a chance he could be one of the locals, but... David knew in his gut he was from outside Mexico. If he wasn't local, and he wasn't Agency, then what did he want?

David searched the alley cautiously but turned up nothing. The tail had vanished like a ghost. It riled David, because stealth skills like that were damn good, and he was competitive.

Well, clearly, he'd wanted to get David's attention, get under his skin, and let him know he was being watched. He'd been smug about it with that cocky smirk, but that cockiness was going to be his downfall.

If he wanted to tango, then David would play along. He'd make himself an easier target, lure the smug bastard out.

Then, David would strike.

Chapter Two

Nine months ago
New York City

David was still getting used to wearing a suit and dress shoes on the job instead of combat fatigues and boots.

Working security was a bit different to the marines, but essentially the goal was the same: do the job with integrity. Now David was covering US diplomats at international security briefings instead of sniping out in the field.

He'd thought this detail was the change of pace he needed. He'd lost more than half his unit during an IED explosion in Sudan the year prior. David and his spotter, Jaime, had escaped relatively unscathed, but the rest of their unit hadn't been so lucky.

They weren't just colleagues; those were David's brothers and sisters. He took their loss hard, felt responsible for not protecting them. At the suggestion of his CO, David took some time off. He'd gone to stay with his cousin, her husband, and their new baby in Mexico City. They needed the help with the new baby, but changing diapers wasn't really David's scene either. Trying to fit into civilian life was hard now. David was an oddly shaped peg that didn't fit anywhere.

When he went in for eval with his CO's office, they offered him the option of going into another unit or to take an honorary discharge. David took the discharge, because he couldn't join another unit that soon. He simply couldn't. He was pushing thirty and had been in the marines for over ten years by that point. He could do with a change of pace.

David took a road trip up to San Diego, his childhood home, not sure what to do with himself. He was at a loose end for weeks. So, when the offer came in from a buddy of his, another former marine, to work at his private security firm, David decided to give it a shot.

A lot of these private security guys were former US Special Forces like David. It was an opportunity to do similar work without doing the exact same job, and David put his all into it.

The diplomat his detail protected was a Black man in his early thirties, only a handful of years older than David. His name was Philip Sherman, and he was insightful, intelligent, and kind hearted. He was passionate about climate change, civil rights, ceasefires and peace treaties instead of wars and arms, and he wanted to make the rich pay more tax. Which was precisely why he needed extra security, as he'd received several death threats from every group with ill intent in the last two months alone.

Philip was to attend the diplomat's annual conference in New York, in preparation to inspire and mentor the new generation of diplomats and activists from around the world.

David had been with Philip's security detail for six weeks and was still considered the new guy. Things had been fine; a few false alarms and red flags here and there, but their package (Philip) made his engagements safely and without incident.

David couldn't have asked to protect anyone nicer. Philip was a great guy; he was married with three young kids back in DC. The night before the conference they were set up in Philip's hotel suite. He was doing some press interviews on video conference, eating snacks, and preparing notes for his keynote speech tomorrow.

A normal evening like any other. There hadn't been any threats made to Philip's life for over a week now.

That probably should've been their first sign of trouble.

David was on duty in the suite, dressed in his suit and tie. Philip often requested David to be in the room while the other guys waited outside. The two of them got along well.

When Phillip wrapped up his last call, he sat back in his chair and stretched. "I wouldn't mind some coffee," he mentioned. "Think I'll order in. Make the most of room service."

"You getting decaf?" David asked. He wouldn't mind some coffee himself.

"Yeah, decaf," Philip confirmed. "Or I'll be bouncing around the walls all night long."

The coffee was ordered, with a couple of croissants because they were Philip's weakness. When Philip's calls were all done, he settled in at the table with his notes and laptop to go over his speech. He used his cell phone to video call his wife and kids, who wanted to say goodnight to him before they went to bed.

While he was doing that, David went to answer the knock on the door. Room service had arrived.

Two more of the security detail were stationed outside the room, and they would perform the typical security checks for weapons or strange items on the member of staff and on the wheely cart. The knock meant they'd already done that, and room service was cleared to enter.

David opened the door. A man dressed in hotel staff uniform wheeled the cart of coffee inside. He didn't ask where they wanted it served, which David thought was unusual, but maybe this guy was new.

"Put it on the table," David advised. He escorted the man over to the table, and watched him transfer the pot of coffee, the silver topped plate housing the croissants, and the fine china cups with saucers onto the table.

The cups wobbled on their saucers when he did so. David noticed the man's hands tremble slightly as he handled them. When David looked more closely at the man, he detected a tiny bead of sweat on his temple.

It struck David as odd. Sure, it could be written off as a new guy being nervous or feeling hot in the stuffy uniform and hat he had to wear, but something felt off.

"Thank you," Philip said to him. "That's fine, you can leave it," he added, as the server had begun setting out a cup for Philip.

He nodded and quickly wheeled his empty cart out of there.

As soon as the door closed, David raised his wrist to speak into his comms to Control. "Have there been any new additions to hotel staff?" he asked softly.

"Not on file," came the reply in his earpiece. "I'll look into it."

"David, please relax," Philip told him. "Good thing we ordered decaf!" He chuckled in amusement and took it upon himself to pour out coffee into two of the cups.

He was probably right. David was being paranoid.

But, still, he decided to take the cup that the server had been trying to give to Philip. He let Philip have the other cup. Force of habit.

It was probably nothing. The hotel meticulously checked their food and the equipment used for diplomats every day.

David drank his coffee. So did Philip.

"Does it taste bitter?" David mentioned.

Philip shook his head. "No? Add more creamer."

David added more creamer. He should've realised something was wrong. Within fifteen minutes, David's throat had a funny taste. He felt hot under the collar, dizzy.

On his earpiece, Control said something about conducting a sweep of the hotel's service areas. They'd found a discarded uniform, suggesting that someone had snuck in and posed as staff to deliver the coffee.

David couldn't take the words in. He felt unwell.

"David?" Philip asked. "What's wrong?"

David clutched his throat. He couldn't speak. He was burning up.

"Oh, my God," Philip uttered, and made the call to alert security.

Soon, the hotel room was swarming with the full security detail. David was treated on the floor by the medic. It was all a blur to him as he faded in and out of consciousness.

He woke up in the bright lights of a hospital, feeling sick and struggling to breathe properly. Doctors leaned over him and explained that he'd been poisoned. The coffee had been laced with thallium sulphate.

All David thought was, thank God it had been him and not Philip. He'd never forgive himself if he'd lost anyone else on his watch.

He'd done his job.

Philip came to see him, held his hand. He looked upset.

David tried to tell him it was fine. Better this way. David had made his peace with dying in the line of duty a long time ago. Now he could die with honour and not with shame.

He was on IVs and laid up in hospital for days. He lost weight rapidly and clumps of his hair fell out. Days bled into weeks; David's condition deteriorated, but he somehow clung onto life. His mom came up from San Diego with his sister to visit him once. They were his only relatives in the US (and not even his favourites; everyone he liked was in Mexico).

David's sister asked him if he'd made a will. If David could've laughed then, he would have. If she was expecting money, she'd be disappointed. David had nothing to give. His meagre savings would barely cover a funeral.

His mom said they'd come visit him again, but the words were empty. David knew that even if they did make it up a second time, it would be too late. He had flashbacks of his mom screaming at him when he was a teenager informing her that he'd signed up. She'd hated his choice then, and he knew she still hated his choice now. Even though, technically, this incident had happened in private security, not the military. He knew she'd see it all as the same thing.

His spotter and his old CO came to see him: Jaime and Carl.

Jaime was real cut up. If...*when* David kicked the bucket, Jaime would be the only one of their old unit left alive. David felt bad about that, but Jaime was moving on with his life. He had a wife, and now a little baby girl. He would be okay. David told him not to sweat it.

Carl visited David a couple more times, a bleak expression on his face.

"Doctors told me it's a miracle you've lived this long," Carl mentioned. "You're a fighter, David."

David was on an oxygen mask all the time now. His throat was dry as the desert, but he managed to reply, "I'm good."

Carl still looked bleak. He exhaled slowly. "Listen, David… I have an old buddy in another division. He's got a contact there. This department runs experimental procedures. Medical testing. I could have a word with him, see if they can run some tests. Get you back on your feet."

David had already made his peace with being a lost cause. The doctors here had told him point blank he should expect to die from this poisoning.

"Sure," David rasped. "Why not?"

In hindsight, he should've said, "Hard pass."

Chapter Three

Present
Tijuana

The mystery bastard didn't take the bait for two whole nights, which ticked David off. He'd made himself an easy target alone in his trailer, inviting the stranger to come take a pop, but no dice.

David thought he saw a figure lurk outside his window early in the morning, but that could've been a shadow and his paranoia. Either way, his stalker wasn't taking the bait here. Maybe he'd guessed that David had plenty of firearms stashed inside the trailer, a veritable deathtrap on cinderblocks.

Plan B, then: David would present himself as a target in motion. He knew most hunters were more inclined to take that bait.

So, on the third evening, David packed an overnight bag and made a show of locking up his trailer. He took his pickup and drove out of Tijuana on Highway 2. David wanted to make tracks anyway and planned to check out a past job he'd had.

The sun had already set, tinting the twilight sky dusky pink. David drove up the highway, leaving the urban areas behind him and entering dry, rural hills. He had the radio on low, because he wanted to hear his surroundings. He checked his mirrors frequently for a tail, and it was easy to spot car headlights as it grew dark.

He wasn't sure if his tail was following or not. Each time David spotted lights in his rear-view mirror, the cars eventually turned off at exits while David kept driving.

Of course, it was entirely possible that his pickup had been bugged and they were able to follow at a greater distance. David had done a cursory check for car bombs each day but found nothing. Tracking bugs were smaller, and he could've missed one. Even more reason to ditch his car when he reached the depot.

David drove into the night, finally reaching the auto transport yard—slap bang in the middle of nowhere, with barren hills on either side of the highway.

David had done a few truck driving jobs, so he was on their drivers register—well, "Luis Rodriguez" was. All he had to do was pull into the yard and wait for a job.

He drove past the yard that housed the huge shipment containers up on stilts, and onto the entrance for vehicles. The area was lit up by a few floodlights that ran on noisy old generators, with a spot to park personal vehicles at the far end. David drove in there to park.

A few other drivers were here this time of night, but not many. A dozen at most. David parked his pickup and killed the engine. He planned to leave the keys in the ignition later and bid farewell to this truck for good.

"Adiós, pal," he murmured, patting the dashboard. This truck had served him well for four months and he'd grown attached to it.

David did a cursory look around the yard. The coast was clear. He took out a battered, navy-blue ball cap and slipped it on over his head, smoothing back his hair. He'd dressed in comfortable jeans, boots, and a T-shirt. He left the air-conditioned cab of his truck and stepped out into the night air, still warm even this late.

He went around to his passenger side and performed another visual check before he opened the door, then took his handgun from its hiding place. It was already loaded; David had done that before leaving. He checked the safety was on and tucked the black Sig Sauer P220 in the back of his jeans. Then he picked out a loose fit, short sleeve shirt from his overnight bag and put that on over his tank top to conceal the weapon.

He also had his trusty knife strapped to his left boot under his jeans cuff. David was ready for a fight, if a fight came to him.

He zipped up his bag and left the passenger door partially open. Someone would take it. David hoped the new owner would be good to her.

He carried his bag and walked across the dirt yard to the supervisor's hut. As always, there were drivers hanging around there, smoking, waiting for trucks to drive out. Mostly Mexicans. David recognised a couple of them, and they recognised him.

"Hola," they greeted casually.

"Hola," David replied. "Cómo estás? How are you?"

He made small talk with the drivers in Spanish for a few minutes. When the supervisor was free, David went in to put his name on the list. He had the fake ID, and since he'd already driven HGVs before, he was easily accepted again. He asked for long haul, didn't matter the destination.

The supervisor said there were some trucks going out at 4:00 AM that needed drivers. David was instructed to wait around. It was first come, first served here.

He stashed his bag in the office and went out into the yard. A small food truck was parked on the roadside, doing business for truckers and anyone who happened to be driving past. David walked over there for something to do. He'd grab a bite to eat, chat with the drivers to pass time.

In another life, David would've liked a quiet and low stress existence like this. But the grass was always greener. David missed being part of a team, missed having buddies watching his six.

And he sure missed flirting with cute men and women.

All the men here, the other drivers, were married men with kids. Straight as rulers. David chatted and nodded along to their stories of wives and children, but he didn't have a lot to add. That life wasn't for him.

He felt like he didn't fit in most places, always hiding some part of himself from people he met. He wanted to be accepted for who he was: a bisexual, Mexican-American vet, and escaped prisoner.

The food truck server handed him his loaded taco.

"Gracias," David said, and bit into it. As he was chewing his mouthful, he glanced out at the road as car headlights approached. Force of habit, checking out civilian vehicles. Not many came out this way.

The hairs on the back of his neck stood up when David saw this car had tinted windows, and it slowed down like it wanted to scope out who was at the food truck.

Even cartel bosses wouldn't be driving around out here, so this had to be his tail.

Game on.

*

David didn't finish all his taco. He tossed the last bits and the wrapper on the ground as a breadcrumb trail to lead his tail away from the truck stop itself, away from the civilians and the floodlights.

In the moonlight, David found a gap in the chain link fence and snuck into the container park. Out here it was dark, deserted, and there were plenty of places to lay an ambush.

David took out his gun and removed the safety. In gloomy shadow, he walked silently between the huge cargo boxes propped up on their stilt legs. The boxes created alleyways; a silent city where danger could lurk at every corner. David's plan was to draw his tail in deep, then strike. He didn't plan to kill, only injure. He had questions, and he wanted answers.

He found a good hiding spot between boxes and crouched down to wait. He gripped his gun securely with both hands. He was ready.

David listened, but he didn't hear anyone in pursuit. If they were too quiet for detection, he'd have to wait until he had a visual. Waiting sucked, but David fell back on his sniper training. He could lie in wait for hours.

Distantly, he heard one of the HVGs leave the park at the other end and drive off down the highway. Everything else was quiet.

David waited, on full alert.

His target was stealthy. David had to use his gut instinct on top of his other senses. He had a feeling the mystery guy was here in the lot with him—he had taken the bait. He also felt a certain tension in the air, the sort that came right before a fight. It was going down tonight, one way or another.

David waited. He didn't move a muscle. He was in a good spot; he simply had to wait for some confirmation of the target, then move in closer...

A sixth sense made him glance down at his chest. He saw the red dot there and knew instantly it was a sniper's mark painting him.

Son of a—

David propelled himself sideways into a roll, losing his hat in the process. The bullet meant for him whistled past mere inches away and lodged softly into the metal casing of the box behind him.

David looked up in the direction the bullet had come from, knowing that if it was one lone shooter he would have to reload his next shot. He had mere seconds to look, but David spotted him: up there on a container, several boxes away and silhouetted against the moon.

Got you.

He got up and took off at a run toward his opponent, weaving between boxes so the shooter couldn't get a clear shot at him.

That had been a close call. Too close.

David heard another bullet whip past quietly, followed by another five seconds later. They hit the ground and the metal boxes nearby but didn't hit him. He was too fast and good at weaving. When David got close enough, he pointed his gun up and broke his cover. Annoyingly, the shooter had vanished. Changed his position, no doubt.

David ran again, sprinting fast and easy. He ran alongside the boxes, looking up through the gaps. *There.* He spotted a dark figure jumping between them. David took aim, and fired, all while still in motion himself. He missed the mark but hit close enough to make the shooter dodge and lose his footing; he took a rough tumble down between the boxes.

That was good enough. When David questioned this guy, he'd have to ask him where he learned to shoot and dodge like that.

David charged in for the attack, gun pointed in the hope his attacker would give himself up easy. "Stay down!" he shouted, as the other guy picked himself up and rose to his feet.

They faced each other. The shooter was dressed in head-to-toe black combat gear, with a black beanie pulled down over his head, and a black scarf on the lower part of his face. The only part of his face showing was the eyes, like a Hollywood-style assassin.

David guessed it was the same guy who'd tailed him from Tijuana.

They were about the same size: not tall. Possibly, David had a slight height and weight advantage. He was stocky while this guy was slimmer. That was good news for David.

"Don't move," David said, aiming his gun, but of course the guy moved.

He moved lightning fast and caught David off guard. One roundhouse kick, and David's gun went clattering uselessly to the ground.

He still had his knife, so he yanked it free and angled the blade down. He was good with his knife; he'd had quite the reputation back in his old unit.

He lunged in for close quarters combat and attacked the other man with full force. He hoped the fight would be over quickly, because he was experienced, yet David was in for more surprises when his attacks were met, blocked, and returned.

It all happened so fast. David barely had time to register they were equal in speed, strength, and skill before he lost his knife; his opponent twisted David's wrist painfully and took it away, while also delivering a sharp knee blow to David's gut, winding him.

Then David had to block attacks from his own knife, a bitter pill to swallow. He managed to deflect the blows and knock the knife from his opponent's hand, only to receive a swift punch to the face, sending him staggering backward from the force.

David tasted the bitter tang of blood on his lower lip. He glared at his opponent. "Who are you?" David demanded. "What do you want?"

No answer. His assailant in black stood there observing him.

David was pissed and charged forward to attack. His opponent stepped into motion, curling his arms with fists clenched in a classic running pose as he kicked one foot up. David assumed he was about to run forward and meet him in combat but, instead, got a surprise boot under his chin as his opponent flipped upside down and kicked him in the face with enough force to send David flying.

It hurt. David grunted as his back hit the ground and he skidded to a stop in the dirt. He was dazed from the blow, but he recovered quickly, as he usually did these days. When he rolled over onto his front, he saw his opponent standing in the same spot a few feet away, not moving, merely observing him.

David decided to try something else.

"So, you got moves," he taunted, wiping blood away from his mouth with the back of his hand. "I got moves, too, pal."

The man didn't answer but quietly observed. It got under David's skin so much that he decided to play dirty.

He fisted the ground and grabbed big clods of dirt. When he rose to begin the fight anew, he threw those dirt clods and aimed at the man's face.

Enough dust went in his eyes that he became distracted, and

David could get a good punch in his solar plexus.

"Oof!" The other man huffed.

David found it satisfying to hear the wind knocked out of his opponent.

The fight continued, evenly matched, as they traded blows and grappled across the ground. At some point, the other man's hat fell off. He had a head full of glossy dark curls, and David felt instant hair envy.

When they got into a stalemate hold facing each other, David's eyes locked with the other man's above his black mask. His eyes were dark brown with a curious silver glint to them.

For a strange moment, David felt he recognised him.

It would make more sense if this assassin was someone he knew, someone from the Agency sent to finish him off. But, no, this was someone else. All of David's senses were lighting up in a new and different way, and still the recognition was soul deep.

I know you.

The fight drained out of him as every bone in his body recognised the person in front of him. With the recognition came a strong sense of relief.

I found you.

But David didn't even know the guy.

It didn't make sense.

The other man had paused as well, staring back at David and searching his eyes with an indecipherable look.

Whatever was going on here, David still needed answers. He swept his foot out, knocking his opponent off balance. David slammed him onto his back and used his body weight to trap him there, though the man wasn't fighting now. David leaned over him and yanked the face covering down.

Yes, it was the same man who'd tailed him in Tijuana. The

cute one. This confirmed he was a stranger; David didn't know him.

"Who are you?" David demanded. "¿Quién eres?" he added in Spanish, because he didn't know if this guy spoke any English.

The man grunted again. "Take your knee off my fuckin' balls, mate," he replied, in an unmistakably British accent.

"Your...? Oh," David said, totally caught off guard. He adjusted his knee, shifting his weight off the other man's nuts.

That was a mistake, of course. As soon as David shifted, the other man used his feet to flip David upside down and overhead. David sailed through the air and landed heavily on his back with a grunt.

He rolled over, ready to make a dash to grab the other man... but he wasn't running away. David watched him limp to his feet, adjust his crotch, then stand there catching his breath like this had merely been a friendly workout.

The sense of urgency and danger had faded.

David rose to his feet too and watched him carefully. This time they stood there facing each other, roughed up and winded, but neither making a move to fight again.

David wasn't sure what was going on. "Who are you?" he asked.

The other man smirked. That smug smile again, like this was nothing but fun and games.

"Me?" he replied. "I'm just like you, sunshine."

Chapter Four

Two months ago
London, England

Sonny queued up at his favourite independent coffee shop and waited his turn to order. It was 10:00 AM. He'd already had his first coffee of the morning back home; now he was ready for the second.

Since he was headed to the office, he'd taken a detour from South Kensington Tube in a bid to get himself a fancy coffee as a treat. A big brand coffee shop was two doors down, but Sonny didn't want any of that malarkey. He wanted a coffee with some wallop behind it, and this shop was owned by Iranians.

Sonny had never spoken to them beyond ordering his coffee. He didn't know or recognise any of them, but had heard them speaking Farsi behind the counter. It would be so easy to reply in Farsi, strike up a conversation. But he didn't. He kept schtum and ordered his coffee in English to blend in. Easier that way. He didn't need a spotlight on him or to make new friends, not this close to the office anyway. He was supposed to be high stealth, incognito, under the radar. Billy-no-mates.

Sonny ordered one double espresso, and one iced latte with a double shot. The iced coffee was because he was a gay cliche and proud of it. Once Sonny got his coffees to go, he left the store and walked down the street double fisting his caffeine. If he mixed cold and warm caffeine, he could almost feel the hit…for about ten seconds. Then it vanished, because nothing had an effect on him anymore.

Small sacrifices to pay for special enhancements.

Sonny cut up Cromwell Place, a quieter side street, and came out onto Cromwell Road. The iconic Natural History Museum loomed over the lawns directly ahead, partially obscured by tall trees. On his left, the first building on the street corner was the French Consulate. Sonny turned right, passing terraced Edwardian buildings. At the end of this block was the Consulate of Venezuela, and before it an unmarked building.

The office.

Sonny walked up its front steps. He juggled his coffee cups to press the button, then removed his sunglasses and raised his face to the camera for facial recognition. After that, he was buzzed in.

"Awright, Kev," Sonny said to the security guard on desk duty, a middle-aged and amiable White chap.

"Awright, Sonny," he replied casually. "Got your coffee, I see."

"Too right," Sonny said. He was a regular face around here, so he didn't need an escort. He walked across the thick carpeted floor and headed to the stairs. All these old buildings had stairs, but the offices were only one floor up.

Sonny tossed his empty espresso cup into the cup recycle bin as he passed and slurped his iced coffee enroute to the briefing suite.

The door was unmarked. Most things were around here, being a hush-hush business. They always met for briefings in the same one though.

Sonny knocked before entering. When he poked his head inside, he spotted Guv standing over by the window. Guv, AKA Vincent Haywood, AKA Lieutenant General Haywood of the British Army, was a distinguished and good-looking Black man in his fifties. Tall, slim, often quiet until it was necessary to speak, he was a palpable presence in any room.

"Guv," Sonny greeted, entering the room. As he looked about, he realised it was empty. "Er…did I get the wrong day? Where is everyone?"

Guv turned around, glancing pointedly at the clock on the wall. "No, this is the right day. Shepherd is joining us shortly."

Blimey. Shepherd? This was important, then. He approached the table and pulled out a chair.

"Don't even think of putting that drink on my table, Sonny," Guv said. As usual, his tone indicated he was not to be trifled with.

Sonny clutched his cup and looked around for a coaster. The table was bereft. "Where…?" he asked.

"I don't care where," Guv replied, "as long as it isn't on my table."

"Right. Um…" Sonny looked around for ideas. Nothing came to mind, so he was left with no choice but to set the cup in his lap, between his thighs and nestled up against his crotch.

On a warm day, the cool drink sitting there wasn't an unpleasant sensation, but the only drawback would be damp balls by the end of this meeting.

Good job he had worn black jeans today.

Guv sat at the head of the table, as usual. His movements when sitting down were a little stiff, because one of his legs was a titanium prosthetic from the knee down—one of the reasons Guv had made the move from active field duty over to British Intelligence.

They waited, and within moments, Shepherd, AKA Valerie Jones from MI6, entered the room. Shepherd was a blonde White woman in her late forties, usually wearing a crisply pressed pantsuit, and always with a salon-fresh blowout. Sonny had often joked that she kept a secret hair stylist on-site somewhere.

Shepherd and Guv coordinated this secret little division between them.

"Sonny," she greeted, "thanks for coming in on your downtime."

"My pleasure, ma'am," Sonny quipped, as if he had a choice.

Shepherd handed out paper files, which of course meant this was off the books and top secret. Standard procedure, then.

"For your eyes only, gentlemen," she said. "This is strictly a need-to-know basis."

Sonny opened the brief. Inside, the first page was stamped TOP SECRET in big letters, which always made him want to laugh, along with the usual disclaimers typed out manually from a typewriter. Sonny breezed past all that and looked at the mission itself. What he saw was a collected file on one man: former US Marine, last known employment in private security. The collected photos were from past ID's like Marine Corps and the DMV, and included some candids and hospital patient logs.

Handsome guy, Sonny thought idly. Tan skin, short brown hair, a strong jawline. Sonny wasn't too sure of the guy's ethnicity until he clocked the name.

"The file is Sergeant David Luis Cortez," Shepherd said. "US Marines scout sniper." She sat down at the opposite end of the table to Guv. "Peak physical health while on duty," she went on. "Loyal. Follows orders. Impressive stats. Fifty-two confirmed kills, one of which being a one-and-a-half-mile sniper shot from a thirty-storey window."

Sonny felt equally annoyed and impressed to hear that. *He* was the trick shot in this division, and he didn't need another hotshot coming for his wig.

"Served in Afghanistan, Sudan, and South America, as well as several black ops missions. Honourable discharge, moved onto private security and diplomatic detail," Shepherd went on. "Assigned to US diplomat Philip Sherman, thwarted an assassination attempt, but fell victim to poisoning from thallium sulphate."

Sonny leafed through the hospital files. These medical records were official, along with a copy of the death certificate.

Sonny guessed what had happened before Shepherd confirmed it: they had another resurrected government experiment on their hands. Sonny should know; he was one himself.

"His condition in civilian hospital deteriorated," Shepherd explained. "Through an Army connection, Cortez was recommended for special medical trials, codenamed Trial X. His first round of tests proved successful, when not many subjects pass that stage..." She glanced up pointedly. "As we well know."

Sonny kept quiet and lifted his cup to take a sip. The slurp was noisy in the quiet room.

Guv gave Sonny a warning look. Sonny stopped slurping and smirked. He'd made his point. He was a special case who'd survived testing and was worth his weight in gold. He got away with murder on a daily basis.

"So," Shepherd continued, "the CIA faked Cortez's death, and moved him to one of their black sites for further testing. Cortez was renamed Specimen X."

Sonny turned the page and saw copies of top secret CIA medical files, including a colour photo of the poor bastard inside a tank filled with bubbly blue liquid. He was naked except for an oxygen mask over his face and various cables attached to his limbs. The photo cut off below the waist. Sonny, being a thirsty bitch, immediately zeroed in on the man's toned abs and pecs, and biceps to die for.

Was it uncouth to lust over him in that condition? Probably. Did Sonny care? Not really.

In the photo the man's eyes were closed. His hair had grown longer than the short army cut, and he also had a beard now. He'd be hot shit, if not for the fact he was stuck inside a human-sized test tube.

"Was it Wallace's team?" Guv asked Shepherd, referencing a top CIA operative.

"We don't know for sure," Shepherd replied. "My mole was tight lipped about the department. But we do know they were working with their own version of Sample A-X, which is why I've brought this to the front of our queue. It's amazing we got as much intel as is, considering their operation was all shut down and relocated after his escape."

Escape? Sonny perked up at that. Excellent! He loved drama.

He flicked through more of the file, speed-reading reports detailing the subject's general disorientation after the procedure, then his violent outbursts toward medical staff... But Sonny never trusted a doctor's word on patients. Who wouldn't get pissed off after being poked and prodded then shoved in a tank? Sonny could sympathise.

There were some printouts of shots taken from a black-and-white security feed showing the naked (and *ripped)* subject overpowering several doctors and guards in the lab in order to break down the door and escape.

Sonny felt vicariously proud of the guy.

He probably shouldn't have smirked over it, because Guv and Shepherd noticed. "I'm glad you think this is amusing, Sonny," Shepherd said haughtily, "because you're the one who's going to track him down."

"Yes, ma'am," Sonny said. He'd figured as much. What tickled his curiosity was what their department wanted with the poor fella once they caught up to him.

"He has family in San Diego, and in Mexico City," Shepherd informed him. "You'll start there. Track him down. Your team can back you up."

"Yes, ma'am," Sonny said, agreeing to the task. "And after I track the poor sod down...?"

Shepherd glanced at Guv, and the two of them shared a silent look. They did that a lot, having a conversation with their eyes alone.

Guv nodded imperceptibly.

Shepherd nodded back, then looked directly at Sonny. "Suss him out," she instructed. "If he can be of any use to us, bring him into the fold. We have that Mexico op fast approaching; he could be an asset on that."

Sonny nodded. "And if he's not...?"

"If he's unstable or unwilling, you have orders to terminate," Shepherd said. "The Circus are willing to bring on another asset to the team and give him full immunity from the Americans if they come looking, but only under the assumption that he's a viable working asset for us."

"Yes, ma'am," Sonny replied.

"He's been off radar and on the run for roughly seventeen weeks," Guv pointed out. "My guess is he'll be ready to come in and play ball for a good enough deal, or he'll be a nervous wreck and no use to anybody."

Sonny agreed with that estimate. He nodded.

"The file can't leave this office," Shepherd told them. "You can have the rest of the day here to plan your strategy; then Sonny flies out to Mexico with the team tonight. You'll have the extra time ahead of your scheduled op to track him down."

"My shorts are already packed," Sonny quipped.

Shepherd ignored him. "At the back of the file are copies of Cortez's old DMV photo, plus a digital sketch of him with a beard so you can make a positive identification. Memorise them."

"Smashing," Sonny said. He found the printouts and had a look. The DMV photo showed a clean-shaven Cortez. The digital version had the beard. Sonny rather liked the beard. *Hello, daddy.*

"Unless you have any questions," Shepherd said, "I'll leave you gents to strategize."

"Thank you, ma'am," Guv said, signalling the end of the meeting.

Shepherd got up and left the room.

Sonny and Guv both remained seated, going back through the file in more detail. Sonny slurped his coffee until it was gone. There was no bin in the office, so he'd have to go dispose of the cup in the hall.

"Just nipping to the bogs, Guv," he announced, pushing his chair out.

"Thank you for sharing that," Guv replied without looking up from the file.

Sonny smiled. He enjoyed winding people up; it was his

favourite pastime.

He went out into the quiet hallway and sauntered to the water cooler and the recycle bin there. Sonny peered in, but before dropping his empty latte cup inside he realised the remaining ice would make a mess inside the bin. Shepherd would have his guts for garters.

Sonny made a detour to the bathroom, which was much fancier than any semi-public bathroom had a right to be: fresh flowers in a vase, marble sink, gold-plated taps, matching fancy-pants handwash and hand lotion, even a scented candle. Sonny's home wasn't this well-furnished.

He opened his cup inside the sink to toss the excess ice away and rinse it out.

Then the door to the bathroom swung open dramatically and Sonny yelped in surprise. "Ah!"

It was Shepherd, and she'd caught him red-handed.

Surprisingly, she didn't mention the cup. She came in and closed the door behind her, then walked past Sonny to check the two stalls to make sure they were empty.

Hello, hello. Something told him he was about to get extra intel. He hoped it was juicy.

"About Cortez," Shepherd said, coming to stand in front of him. She was around five foot two in height but with the additional three inches from her high heels today, she was nose to nose with Sonny.

"Yes, ma'am?" he replied.

"It's not in his file," Shepherd said quietly, "but I have it on good authority that his sister, speaking at his funeral, made references to him being a gay man."

"Oh, right?" Sonny was mildly curious, though truthfully, he was more interested in how the CIA had staged a fake funeral. He was assuming it was a closed casket to dupe friends and family.

"Off the record," Shepherd told him, "I want you to use every tool in your belt to bring in this asset."

Sonny struggled to keep a straight face. "You mean my natural charm?" he quipped.

"Use everything at your disposal," Shepherd said, as if she were discussing the weather. "Find out what he wants, and then use that to bring him in and buy his loyalty. We could have a real opportunity here if there's two of you on a team."

Sonny liked his team as it was and felt reluctant to go changing that dynamic. "We don't know if he's worth flipping yet, ma'am," he said.

"Your discretion," she said. "If he's useless, get rid of him. I don't want the Americans or anyone else finding him and twisting him into their own asset. But if he's compos mentis, I want him. Are we clear, Sonny?"

"Crystal, ma'am."

Chapter Five

Present
Mexico

"What do you mean, you're like me?" David asked. "Explain."

"How's about a time out?" the other man said, making the universal T shape with his hands. "Let's have a chinwag."

David was thrown by his British accent. Cockney London was his best guess, but he had only heard that accent in movies so couldn't be sure.

Before he could respond, the man leapt up onto one of the containers, and he did so by jumping between crates to propel himself upward. This was some wild parkour, as far as David was concerned. He did not have skills like that.

He tensed automatically, because he thought the guy would make a break for it or start the fight again. But he didn't. Once he got to the top of the box, he sat down and dangled his legs over the side.

"C'mon, sunshine!" he called down. "Truce while we talk?"

David was intrigued.

He couldn't do that fancy parkour, but he could climb. Using the hinges and handles of the container, David used his best rock-climbing technique to the top of the container.

"Nice of you to join me," the other man quipped. "Take a seat."

"Are you going to tell me who you are?" David asked dubiously.

"Sure," he replied.

"What's your name?" David asked.

This made the other man smirk. Seemed like he found this all amusing.

"Call me Sonny," he said. "Everyone does."

David wasn't sure if that was Sunni or Sunny like the weather, or... like a son?

"Okay, Sonny," David replied as he sat down at a safe distance. "I take it you know who I am?"

"That I do, sunshine." Sonny grinned. "Bet you weren't expecting me, eh? You were expecting the Americans?"

David nodded. "So, who do you work for, and what do you want?" He had a hunch but wanted to hear Sonny say it.

Sonny tilted his head, like he was considering. "Let's keep things simple, shall we? I represent British Intelligence. They're interested in you."

David had suspected something like this. He tensed once more. "Well, I'm not going back into a lab; that's for damn sure."

"Don't blame you, mate," Sonny said. "Been there, done that. Life of a lab rat ain't fun, eh?"

"Wait, back up," David said. "You...? That's what you meant?

They experimented on you too?"

"I didn't get shoved into a tank like you did," Sonny said, "but, yeah, basically the same. You got poisoned, right? So did I. Almost popped me clogs, innit? As it 'appens, my cousin works in a department with advanced medicine. All very hush hush. I became their new test subject." He smiled wryly. "Lucky ol' me."

David took this in. For the first time in months, he seemed to be a step closer to getting some answers.

"Okay," he said cautiously. "So why did you try to kill me if you're planning to take me in?"

Sonny smirked. "What's the matter, love? Can't handle a bit of action?"

"I beat you, didn't I?" David retorted.

Sonny tilted his head like he disagreed with that statement. "We're on a pause, that's all."

It was a veiled threat. David wasn't stupid; he knew to stay on his guard.

"We both paused," he replied, remembering that bizarre moment of recognition. He knew Sonny had felt something too.

"And then you threw dirt in my eye," Sonny said with a chuckle. "Fuckin' hilarious, that was."

David returned a small yet cautious smile. He could see that Sonny was naturally quite charming, but David didn't trust him fully.

"So what now?" he asked.

"Well, here's your options," Sonny said, his tone light. "Option one, I kill you. Although," he added conversationally, "wouldn't be my first choice. Just so ya know."

"Noted," David said.

"Option two," Sonny went on, "I leave you alone, and someone else kills you. Par for the course, you being on the run from the Intelligence Community. Option three...and this is the option my boss wants me to sell you, mind. You come work for us, and we keep the others off your back."

That, David hadn't expected.

"Is that code for being in a lab?" he asked.

"Nah. Field work," Sonny said. "They want you to join *my* team." He raised his eyebrows at David, as if to say this was an appealing offer.

"Say I believe you," David replied. "What's the catch?"

"That's when I'd suggest a fourth option," Sonny said. "You kill yourself. Only way to guarantee nobody can use you in their shady experiments ever again. Well, I say that, but we both came back from the brink of death, eh?" He laughed wryly. "They'd probably resurrect you again. Incineration!" He held up one finger like a eureka moment. "Probably the only way to keep your body to yourself and their grubby mitts off."

"Hmm, incineration doesn't sound appealing," David quipped. He looked out at the dark depot around them and sighed quietly. "Tell me more about option three? Do they experiment on you?"

"Eh." Sonny leaned back on his hands, kicking his booted feet up and down. He seemed to have a very unserious attitude about all this, but David guessed some of it was a front. "You do a little lab time. They check your vitals, jab you with needles and take some blood. I'm on a medical leash."

"Meaning?"

Sonny pursed his lips. He gazed out at the night sky, instead of looking at David. "They have me on a complex set-up that needs regular replenishment. An injection every seventy-two hours. Without it, I'll slip into a coma and die. Or so they say. That's their fail-safe to keep me tethered."

David was surprised by his candidness. He was horrified to think of the same fate befalling him.

"But," Sonny added, tone lighter again, "the leash is long. I get to fuck around more than find out, innit?"

David was more confused than ever. "What is it that you do exactly?"

Sonny grinned. "Ever seen *The X-Files*?"

"Once or twice," David said.

"Bit like that," Sonny said. "Go investigate weird stuff. Contain it. Follow orders. Bit of wet work. Be a good little soldier."

"You were army?" David asked.

"SAS, mate." Sonny smiled smugly. "Most of the team is. Not sure how we'd feel about letting in someone who wasn't."

"I was gunnery sergeant in the US Marines," David replied.

"Yeah, I read your file," Sonny said. "If you wanted to join the SAS, you'd lose any rank you had and start at the bottom, where we all did, as a trooper. And I made it up to corporal, so I'd outrank you."

David felt his hackles rise but forced himself to appear outwardly calm. "But your team isn't the SAS now, is it?" he asked.

"Yes and no," Sonny replied. "Anyway, it's all moot, because my team already has a Sergeant. You'd still have to start at the bottom, sunshine."

"I can work with that," David said.

Sonny raised his eyebrows in challenge. "Sure about that? Not gonna be a grumpy-chops about it?"

"You know," David said calmly but with feeling, "you're kind of an ass."

This only seemed to amuse Sonny. "And the sooner you realise that, sunshine, the better. Is option four looking more appealing now? Kill yourself instead of work with me?"

He said it in jest, and it smoothed David's hackles back down. This guy was a joker. He was probably saying shit to feel David out. He'd been on his own so long he'd forgotten what it was like to banter, but he understood now. David had talked shit with his old unit, and he missed that.

This felt like the same type of banter but with a British twist he wasn't used to yet.

But David could adapt.

"What about an option five?" he said on a whim. "We both go on the run. With your inside intel, it would be easier to dodge the authorities."

Sonny smacked his lips together. "Ah, can't, mate. After seventy-two hours, I'd be sick as a dog. Need those injections they ration out."

"There has to be a workaround," David said, thinking out loud. From the way Sonny glanced at him, he guessed he was onto something. "But you're already working on that, right?" he asked. If he were in Sonny's position, that's what he would do: look for a way out, a bolthole.

Sonny smiled, though it was less smug this time. "Maybe. Maybe."

"I certainly don't want to deal with anything like that in my system," David went on. "Can I refuse it?"

Sonny shrugged casually. "You can, but they'd probably find a way to slip the formula into you. That's kinda their thing. Spy shit. Their bread an' butter, innit?"

David nodded. He'd assumed as much. He was starting to form a crazy idea. "Maybe there's a way to study it if they do it to me," he said. "Find out more about it. Like, are we talking a regular need for methadone like an addiction? Or would it be more of a one-time antidote?"

"Good questions, mate," Sonny said, nodding slowly. He didn't elaborate, which probably meant he didn't want to divulge anything yet. He was being cautious.

David couldn't blame him.

"I have a hundred questions," David said, "but for now, I say we make a deal between us. Whatever happens, the two of us can help each other."

"How's that?" Sonny asked, looking at David with mild amusement.

"If you're right," David said, "and they want me to do what you're doing? They'll put the same drug into me. We can use that opportunity to collect our own data. That'll help us reverse engineer the formula. I'll help you get the antidote. You keep me alive. Win-win."

Sonny tilted his head in consideration. "Not a bad idea. Glad I didn't kill you now, sunshine."

David allowed a half smile. "I'm glad too," he said wryly. "Besides, I still want to know what it was they pumped into me in the first place. Have you got answers for that?"

And why do I feel like I know you from somewhere, David thought but didn't dare say out loud.

"Wanna know all the sordid details, eh?" Sonny said. "Well, that CIA department is a little different to ours, but they're all working off of similar asteroid samples. The sample was lab engineered into a formula the Intelligence Community calls Compound A-X, or some call it Sample A-X."

"Okay," David said dubiously. "Sorry I asked. So, what is it? Minerals?" He didn't know a lot about asteroids. They were rocks from space?

Sonny chuckled. "Minerals, sure. And some long-dead alien DNA."

"Back up," David said. "Alien *what?*"

"Alien DNA," Sonny repeated, probably noting the look of horror on David's face. "That's right, sunshine. You and I are walking alien experiments. Bet you didn't have that on your bingo card."

"Well, damn," David murmured.

Chapter Six

David needed a moment. Several moments, actually.

And Sonny said he was hungry, so they migrated over to the food truck and queued up for tacos with the Mexican truck drivers.

It was one of the more surreal nights of David's life; that was for sure.

Sonny ordered loaded tacos for them both, spoke in perfect Spanish with no detectable accent, and paid the vendor in cash.

David stared at him as he handed over one of the tacos.

"Here," Sonny said, then noticed David staring. "What?"

"Are you Mexican?" David asked.

"No, mate." Sonny raised his taco to take a bite, casually strolling away from the food truck.

David walked beside him to keep up. "Spanish, then?" he asked.

Sonny chuckled as he ate. "Keep guessing," he mumbled,

busy eating the taco. "Mm, this is good, innit?"

David shook his head.

Surreal.

He ate his own taco, and they walked side by side into the lit-up lot. When they were far enough away from the truck drivers or anyone overhearing, David spoke up.

"Not sure I believe the alien thing," he said.

Sonny shrugged. "Believe what you want, sunshine. But we been finding test sites all over, all of 'em experimenting with similar strains of this asteroid DNA. All making their own compounds for human testing. Every government wants their own super-humans, right?"

That would make perfect sense if this were a science fiction movie. But this was real life.

"You're only telling me this to blow smoke up my ass," he said.

They meandered over to David's pickup, still where he'd left it. He leaned against the tailgate, for moral support. David's world was fast turning upside down. Whether the story about aliens was true or not, other agencies were out to get him and that was a fact. His life was on the line.

"What does alien even mean?" he asked. "Like, foreign DNA? What does it look like when it's alive?"

Sonny was busy munching his taco. "Like little green men?" he said flippantly. "We don't know what they look like, sunshine. Whatever the DNA was once upon a time, it's long dead now. As in, millions of years dead. That's how long the asteroid travelled in space or whatever. The quacks grew samples on their own in the lab, but the samples just get to a gooey phase before popping their clogs."

"Their what now?" David asked.

"Their clogs. Dyin'." Sonny finished his taco and balled up the paper. He licked his fingers like he didn't have a care in the world.

Meanwhile David's brain went blue screen. If the CIA had really pumped him full of some weird alien DNA, he was going to be so pissed.

Sonny licked another finger, glancing at David. "Look, mate," he said, "if you want to have a gander at the lab, I can take you there. It's back in England, which is where we work from."

"You work in the lab?" David asked.

"No, I told ya," Sonny replied, "I do field work. My cousin and the doc work in the lab. I pop in now and then. It's near the office."

David was reeling from all this. He didn't want to believe Sonny, but...he was starting to get a sinking feeling this was the missing piece to the puzzle. Ever since he'd busted out of that medical facility and gone on the run, David had noticed changes in himself. He could run faster, jump higher, see better, go for longer periods without rest. He was more agile and didn't get stiff. Little things like that. He was hungry more often, but he also felt stronger.

He'd assumed it was steroids; whatever they'd put in him to cure him from the poisoning. David had been waiting for the effects to wear off.

He felt naïve now.

"Man," he said, mind racing. "But it sounds too far out there to be true."

"Let me ask you something, then," Sonny said. "Have you noticed if your eyes are a different colour?"

"My eyes?" David shook his head. He hadn't really looked. "I don't think so."

"What about weird dreams?" Sonny asked. "Any odd dreams

about… Let's call it a big scary bugger?"

"A what? No," David said. "The only dreams I have are about the lab, if you must know."

"No dreams about monsters?" Sonny said with a note of surprise. "Huh."

"Why?" David asked him, then realised why. "Wait, are you saying you have dreams about what the alien looks like?"

This sounded absurd even to his ears, but he had to ask.

"Yeah," Sonny said breezily. "I saw mine in the mirror, too. Just a flash. I s'pose you could call it a vision."

David was equal parts enthralled and horrified to hear this. "Well, what did it look like?"

"I told ya, didn't I?" Sonny said. "Big scary bugger. Like this." He raised his hands up like claws and growled in the least scary way possible. "Grr! Anyway, I call her Scary Spice."

David blinked at him. He was starting to believe Sonny was only messing around. David's theory about steroids still seemed more plausible than aliens.

At David's blank stare, Sonny put his hands down and began to chuckle. "If the wind changes, mate, your face will get stuck like that."

David felt annoyed at him again. "Quick question," he asked. "Are you always like this?"

"Like what?" Sonny quipped. "Witty and hilarious?"

David scoffed. "Keep telling yourself that."

"I will," Sonny said, leaning back against the pickup. "I'll add it to my daily mantra."

The little back and forth they kept falling into was distracting David from the more serious matter at hand.

"Why do you call it Scary Spice?" he asked. This wasn't the serious matter, but it was the first question that popped into his head.

"The Spice Girls," Sonny explained.

"I know who the Spice Girls are," David said, exasperated. "Why are you calling your nightmare a Spice Girl?"

"Cause it's scary," Sonny said with a laugh. "She's scary."

"She?" David said. "You know it's a she?"

"No, I don't know." Sonny shrugged. "I thought, well, if she's anything like me, she'll turn into a right mean bitch when she's cross, so I gave her a name. Like an alter ego, or a dragsona."

David's ears perked up. This sounded promising.

Sonny glanced at him, one eyebrow raising. "Is this the part where you realise that I'm a raging homosexual?" he asked dryly.

David had suspected, but it was nice to hear it confirmed.

"Is raging your Brit slang for flaming?" he asked, unable to stop his own smile.

"Raging. Flaming." Sonny chuckled. "Both of those at once."

David chuckled too.

It was the first proper laugh they'd shared together, and something changed. Maybe it was only David who felt it, but he got a clear visual of what daily life could be like working with Sonny, and it seemed a much brighter prospect than living alone.

Especially when he had this... *unique condition* to deal with; alien DNA, or experimental steroids. *Jury was out on which condition was the real one.*

"What you gonna call yours, then?" Sonny asked him.

"My what?"

"Your nightmare alien friend."

David frowned. "I haven't dreamt about an alien," he said. *And I don't want to, either, thanks very much.*

Sonny hummed thoughtfully. "Did they stick you into any machines in the lab? Like a big MRI scanner?"

David thought back, but he wasn't fully conscious for much of the lab time. What he recalled most was the gurney and the tank. "I can't say for sure, but I don't remember anything like a scanner."

Sonny nodded. "Okay, so maybe they didn't get to that stage with you. Because you escaped, right? You interrupted them. Or maybe they never had the idea to use a particle accelerator on a test subject. So, hear me out. We've both had the same or a similar compound of alien DNA injected into us, and I've been in a particle accelerator. You haven't been in the accelerator, and you're saying you haven't dreamed of, or seen, your version of it yet. That's probably the reason. You were a bit behind me in the experiments, that's all."

"I sincerely hope you aren't suggesting I get into some particle machine?" David said warily.

"No, no." Sonny chuckled, shaking his head. "I'm just saying, innit? Your one's probably not revved up yet. Maybe it's more dormant or something, and that's why you haven't seen a dream or seen your eyes change. I'm not a doctor; this is purely my guess."

"Do your eyes change?" David asked, somewhat dubious.

"Sometimes," Sonny said.

"Get outta here," David drawled. He didn't want to believe all this. It was probably nonsense to lure David in. Create a bogeyman to put him off his game.

"Anyway," Sonny said cheerily, "back to the matter at hand. If and when your beastly guest wakes up, what are you going to name it?"

"Okay, I'll play along," David said. "If this was all real like you say it is, why would I want to name a monster that's supposedly inside me, but so far hasn't made itself known? That seems like inviting trouble to me."

"No, it's putting you on friendlier terms with your new lodger," Sonny retorted. "Give it a name, and you'll feel much better. Now, what would you call it?"

David sighed. His head wasn't in this game. "I don't know."

"May I make a suggestion?" Sonny asked.

"No," David replied, but Sonny kept talking anyway.

"Posh Spice," he said.

"Shut up, man," David told him.

"Sporty, then."

"I'm not calling it a damn Spice Girl name," David said. "If it even exists anyway."

"Well, please yourself," Sonny said. "Right. This is where we part ways." He pushed himself off the pickup.

"Wait, I have more questions," David said. He hadn't even finished his taco.

"Trust me," Sonny said, "the more you ask, the more questions you'll have, and we don't have all night. All you need to decide is which option you're picking."

"Wait, what?" David said. "I thought we made a deal? I'll work with you. Option three."

"And maybe that's where we end up," Sonny said. "But me being such a stand-up fella, I'm giving you twenty-four hours to think it over. If you leave, I won't come after you." He looked at David pointedly. "Nicest thing I could do for ya given the situation, innit?"

"Okay," David said, dubious. "And…if I don't leave?"

"If you still want in"—Sonny shrugged—"be back at that sorry little trailer of yours tomorrow night. I'll swing by to pick you up. You can get on the payroll and start right away."

That was what David wanted; he felt it in his bones, but his common sense told him to exercise a bit of caution.

"Start by doing what exactly?" he asked.

"Working with me, innit?" Sonny said.

"Doing...?" David prompted.

Sonny smirked. "I gotta go see a man about a dog."

"Right," David drawled. Obviously, he wouldn't be getting a more in-depth answer right now. "But would you call it, like, a typical working day?"

"We don't have anything *typical* in our line of work," Sonny replied, "but, yeah, you could call it a milk run, if you like."

"Okay," David said. "Okay."

"Awright, then," Sonny said.

"Wait, I left my gun over there," David said, gesturing to the furthest lot where they'd had that fight.

"Don't worry, sunshine. I'll go clean up," Sonny replied. "You sort yourself out, and be on your merry way, whichever way that is. Me, I'm heading back to my hotel to put me feet up and eat my body weight in those tasty li'l churros with the cinnamon sugar. See you...maybe never again?" He smirked as he turned around, then walked away.

This was it, then?

David watched him go, walking out of the light and melting into darkness. A strange sensation tugged in his chest, an urge to go running after the other man.

The fact remained, David didn't know Sonny, and he couldn't trust him. No fool would trust a man he'd just met, especially not an assassin who'd tried to shoot him.

And yet...

And yet, David really wanted to trust him.

Chapter Seven

Sonny got his churros, an entire tray full of them. No half measures taken. All these street vendors and late-night shops with their array of tasty food were too tempting. Sonny popped the churros onto the passenger seat of his rental and surreptitiously snacked on them as he drove back in the direction of Tijuana.

He had some time to kill, and he wasn't sleepy, so he decided to go bother the team. Rafe had been texting to ask where he was anyway.

Driving in Mexico was *slightly* more peaceful at night with less cars on the road. Surveillance and assassination? No problem. Easy-peasy. Driving in Mexico? Jesus. After a few weeks of it, Sonny was almost at his wit's end. He was thankful for the quieter roads out here in the middle of nowheresville, it gave him time to wind down. He switched on the radio and listened to some Mexican soap opera being played out on the airwaves. *The Archers* this was not; the drama was at eleven the entire time.

Sonny eventually switched it off again for some peace, but that left him alone with his own thoughts. The further away he drove from David, AKA *the target*, the less sure of everything Sonny felt. He began to doubt himself and his decision to let David make a clean getaway, because if Shepherd ever found out she'd have Sonny's head on a pike.

Then there was the new little problem of feeling a strange pull toward David. Sonny didn't want to examine his feelings too closely lest he discover the root of the issue was him *missing* David already. Because that would be bloody bonkers, not to mention scary on every conceivable level.

"Shit," he muttered to himself and switched the soap opera back on.

Thinking too much only ever led to headaches.

Sonny kept driving, heading for the team's post on the outskirts of the city. They were staying in a holiday villa picked out by their local agent on the ground. Easier to transport their cache of weapons and equipment here than in some hotel with too many nosy tourists.

By the time Sonny got there, it was the middle of the night, and things weren't dead quiet, but they were relatively calm. A couple of the local mercs hired in were guarding the gate, and Sonny had to flash his ID card to get through. He also handed out one of the paper bags of churros, which went over well. Guards always wanted snacks.

Finally, he parked, grabbed the remaining churros, and headed inside the villa.

Sonny expected to see the whole team there, like he'd left them nineteen hours ago. But Rafe, Mac, Esteban and most of the local mercs were gone. Only Naz, their comms tech, was here, ensconced on the couch in front of the TV, a bowl of chips in his lap and a pot of guac to the side. He looked way too comfortable, and Sonny couldn't wait to annoy him.

"Oi, oi," he announced loudly upon entering the room, making Naz startle. "What's all this then?"

"Sonny!" Naz hurriedly set aside his chips and grabbed his nearby laptop. "Guv wanted to speak to you…!"

"Hold up, hold up," Sonny replied. "Before you do anything, feast your eyes on these." He presented the tray of leftover churros.

Naz's eyes went wide behind his tinted glasses. "Churros? Have you got any…?"

"Little pots of sauce?" Sonny pointed to the tray. "Indeed I do, my good fella." He approached the couch and made as if to hand the tray over, but when Naz reached for it, Sonny whisked it out of his grasp. "Only if you don't call the gaffer."

Naz groaned. "Sonny, you know that man makes me nervous! He said you had to call him back."

"And I will," Sonny replied. He handed the churros to Naz, then checked his watch. "They're seven hours ahead in London, mate. It'll be arse o' clock in the morning right now."

"Guv never sleeps! You know that!" Naz clutched the tray of churros and began eating, still babbling away. "He'll be on my case if you don't call him back."

"Relax, big man," Sonny told him. Naz was a large guy, a bit overweight, and always full of nerves. "I told you I'll give him a bell later." He plopped down on the other side of the couch, putting his booted feet up on the coffee table. "So where is everyone?"

"We had a lead on that lab," Naz explained, mouth full of churros. "They went to check it out. I'm tracking their progress here but they're in silent mode."

That meant no banter.

Sonny grinned at Naz. "Looks like it's you and me, then."

"What are you doing here anyway?" Naz asked him. "Did you make contact? Guv wanted to know if you made contact."

"I wish you'd both keep your hair on," Sonny admonished. Although, Guv's head was smooth and hairless. "I'm cooking, innit? Sit tight, mate."

Naz responded by muttering in Arabic, which meant he was getting annoyed.

Sonny smirked. Mission accomplished.

Twenty minutes passed. Naz demolished the churros, then began worrying again about calling Guv back. "Can you please call him?" Naz begged. "I don't want to get in trouble. It's all right for you—you're indispensable. I'm just the tech guy, I can get fired and sent to prison. It's unfair, that's what it is. You're such a pain in the arse, Sonny. Will you call him back?"

"All right, Nazeem!" Sonny relented. "I'll call him!"

"Alhamdulillah!" Naz said in relief. "Thank God." He opened his phone to contacts, then handed it over. "I suppose you conveniently left your phone somewhere else?"

"I can't do a bloody stakeout with you lot blowing up my smartphone, can I?" Sonny replied. He took the phone and pressed call on Guv's name.

At least this was only voice and not video call.

Sonny checked the time. It would be around seven AM in London. Guv answered after one ring.

"Yes?" his smooth voice answered.

"Guv, it's Sonny," Sonny said, injecting cheer into his voice. "Naz said you wanted me?"

"Sonny," Guv said, his tone clipped, which was pretty normal whenever he addressed Sonny during an op. "You weren't answering your phone."

"Stakeout, Guv," Sonny said. *Also, I didn't want to answer my phone.*

"Did you make contact?" Guv asked.

Naz was watching Sonny intently, probably to see how he was going to wriggle out of this one.

"Yes, Guv," Sonny replied. Despite having rehearsed this in his head, Sonny found himself floundering over what to say. What came out was "Everything's in hand."

Naz made a face at him as if to say *what does that even mean?*

Luckily, Guv didn't ask for the details; he was more concerned about the time frame. "This is taking too long," he informed Sonny. "You've got another forty-eight hours to bring him in. That deadline is non-negotiable, Sonny."

"No problem, Guv," Sonny replied. "I'll have a resolution for you in twenty-four."

"See that you do," Guv said. "And Sonny?"

"Yes, Guv?"

"Answer your bloody phone," Guv ordered, then ended the call.

Sonny shrugged and handed Naz his phone back.

"I heard that," Naz said. "I agree—answer your bloody phone when we call you."

Sonny mock saluted. "Yes, sir!"

Naz shook his head. "This job will make me grey. Look, I've already got grey hairs here!" He pointed to the side of his head, at his dark curly hair, and to the middle of his beard.

Sonny had to laugh. "You're forty-one, you plonker! With natural black hair! Of course you'll have some grey coming in."

"It's this bloody job!" Naz insisted. "You wait. You'll be next. Your hair will turn grey too."

Sonny shrugged. "If I live that long." And, he thought, if the alien DNA inside him allowed it. Maybe he'd never go grey, or maybe he'd get killed in the field tomorrow and never get to find out. Grey hairs were the least of his problems in the grand scheme of things.

"I think grey looks nice," Sonny mused. "Distinguished."

"You wouldn't say that if you had it," Naz replied.

Sonny rolled his eyes. "You give yourself grey hairs, Naz. Getting upset over every small thing. Shut up and let's watch one of those telenovelas."

He needed distracting from daydreaming about David and his slick fighting moves. Nope, couldn't go daydreaming about all that. Dangerous. Absolutely no daydreaming.

Chapter Eight

David really did consider leaving town that night, as originally planned. The only person he could trust was himself; everyone else was a liability.

He sat at the truck depot for a couple of hours thinking it through, but when the opportunity to drive a truck out of there came along, David found himself turning it down. He walked away, took his pickup and drove all the way back to his trailer.

This was crazy…but his entire life had been crazy since waking up in that lab. He still wasn't buying the alien thing, but he knew enough that whatever the CIA had injected him with, they wanted it back. That meant David had to keep himself out of their hands, or his life wouldn't be his anymore.

What was he going to do, stay on the run for the rest of his days? With no funds? It was lonely, and stressful. Six months of this life had already worn him down. David wanted companionship—he wanted to be in a team again. He wanted his dignity back.

He was curious about Sonny's offer. Curious enough to stay behind and find out a little more.

The sun was rising, and David managed to doze a little. As he lay on his narrow and familiar cot, he began to dream.

Dreams weren't a nice thing of late. The nightmares had been with him ever since the lab. Of course, he had nightmares about being back in that lab; shackled to a gurney while being injected by doctors in white lab coats who ignored his screams, their faces impassive. They only saw him as a lab rat, not a human being.

He also dreamed of the narrow tank, trapped in the bubbling water. Even with a mask over his face for air he had nightmares about suffocating, drowning. His screams inside the tank made no noise, only bubbles.

Through the tank's glass front, David saw the familiar faces peering in at him in his dreams: The US Army Colonel with the greying moustache whose name tag said Col. Blake. And the other man who bore no name tag or insignia, but always wore a dark suit and tie like he was dressed for a funeral. Agency was David's guess. David didn't know his name, but he'd committed the man's face to memory, and it often resurfaced in his dreams.

And that wasn't all. Those were the regular nightmares; the events David *knew* had happened. Since breaking free from the lab, his anxiety nightmares had been peppered with other dreams.

Strange stuff.

David had assumed whatever they'd pumped him full of had given him those dreams. They were hard to describe, more of a *feeling* than seeing anything specific. Darkness, total blackout, sometimes with tiny pinpricks of light in the distance like stars, but not always. With the darkness was a vivid feeling of being crushed in a tight space, like a dark weight was bearing down on him from all sides, and he was powerless against it.

This part of the dream brought with it an intense feeling of claustrophobia.

At first, he'd assumed it was from being stuck in the tank, and David had dismissed it as something conjured from his own fraught imagination. But if Sonny's wild story was to be believed, this could be connected to the alien DNA he'd been given.

Usually, the nightmare about feeling trapped was brief, almost forgotten upon waking. That morning as David woke from the nightmare, he realised that this could be what Sonny had meant—his dormant alien parasite.

No.

David didn't want to believe it.

Another and simpler explanation could be the power of suggestion; Sonny had given David the ideas, put them in his head, and now David was dreaming about weird creatures.

Except...David had been having that claustrophobic dream for months, before he'd met Sonny.

David didn't have all the answers, but the jury was still out on aliens. He didn't want to think on it any longer. He closed his eyes again and fell back asleep.

He dreamed, and the next time he awoke he remembered a different dream, a new dream. He'd been fighting, probably dreaming about the fight with Sonny still fresh in his mind. David hadn't had to fight like that for a while. Now all his senses had stirred, and this dream was less of a nightmare and more of a kick-ass dream where he was sparring with an equal.

David lay awake on his cot, staring up at the cracked ceiling. He replayed that part of the dream, what he could remember, over and over in his head so he didn't forget it. The fight had been *fun*. David liked Sonny.

There it was.

His choice was clear in the light of day. David had to stick around and see where this went. At the very least, he could potentially get the Agency off his ass by signing up with another. He could be part of a team again, have some meaning to his life.

And do his own digging into whatever the hell this DNA was, and learn if it was possible to undo it.

Decision made, David got up and made himself breakfast. He cleaned up and packed another bag—a bigger bag this time, taking more clothes, and his spare gun and knife. He still had hours to kill.

When it got hot in the afternoon, David had a siesta. When he woke, he made some food, finishing off his supplies. He went to speak with one of the neighbours, a Mexican guy who had two teenage sons. They spoke Nahuatl, and David was fluent. He explained he'd be leaving later tonight on a long trip. He offered his trailer to them, saying he'd leave the key in the door. They accepted the offer. Their trailer was too small for that many boys. David shook the father's hand, then went back to his trailer.

One way or another, at least his trailer wouldn't go to waste.

Evening came, bringing some relief from the hot sun as it set. David sat on his porch and drank a beer, gazing at the shrubs, trees, and other trailers in the distance and *thinking*.

So many thoughts swirled around in his mind, but what he kept coming back to was Sonny giving his so-called alien a funny name. David turned the idea over and over, going through names he could give his own nightmare.

It wasn't that he suddenly believed he had an alien inside him, nor did he particularly feel the need to give it a nickname. No, this was about assimilation. David wasn't stupid. If he wanted to get in with a group, he had to speak their language.

The language here was banter.

Sonny had laid out the terms loud and clear. It wasn't about whether the alien part was true or not, but about David fitting in with Sonny and his team. If David wanted to stay in the running, then he had to play ball.

So, he wracked his brains for a fun name to call his so-called alien. Setting aside the fact that he hadn't seen any proof and also had no idea what an alien would look like, David knew he'd have to pick something from pop culture in order to sync with Sonny. He fell back on what he knew, digging into his often-suppressed fun side. He went through singers and actors he liked. Not only did he need to hook Sonny with his choice, but he also had to like it himself because he may get stuck with this nickname down the line.

And, David considered, it couldn't hurt to dilute the fear of his potential nightmare. Naming the scary monster under the bed made a lot of sense for survival purposes because it took its power away.

He needed something funny, then, a name that would bring him some comfort. A beloved Latino character from films sprang to mind. David knew instantly this was it. He'd found the perfect name that would elicit the right reaction.

Now all he had to do was tell Sonny.

*

Sonny got back to his hotel in the early hours to get some kip. The team had a solid lead on the location of the illegal lab using Compound A-X, and the plan was to hit it that night. Sonny told them to sit tight until he was ready.

He awoke late afternoon, after dreaming about sparring with David in the truck yard. *Nice dream too. Made a change from creepy nightmares*. He showered and dressed, putting on black boots, black combat trousers, a black undershirt.

Then he began the task of strapping on all his weapons; gun holsters, and knife holsters, both visible and concealed. Then Sonny checked his weapons. Knives were inspected, then slotted into place all over his person. He checked his handguns, loaded them, and slotted them into their holsters. Sonny had a gun on his outer thigh, and one under his arm. He had to wear a long jacket to conceal it all.

Mexico was too hot for all this nonsense. Sonny hoped the next op was somewhere cold.

Lastly, Sonny collected his rifle case, and checked out of the hotel. He went to his car and let his rifle ride shotgun. Sonny drove out into the rural area where David's trailer park was located. He drove slowly, not in a rush. It was still light outside. He would have to wait for the cover of darkness.

He already knew where to park, having scoped out this spot previously when spying on David. Sonny parked the car, took his rifle case, and stepped into the warm evening air. Farewell, car air-con; now he had to trek around on foot.

Sonny walked.

Mostly dust and a few trees out this way, he'd already picked his sniper spot. He walked for nearly a mile, listening for anyone who might stumble into his path. All was quiet, the only noise coming from the trailer park nine hundred yards away, with a few young kids playing kickball in the dirt. As it was dark now, they used the lights from nearby trailers to see. Sonny could hear their exuberant cheers in the distance.

His sniper's nest was a great little spot. Remnants of an old fence, probably from a farm, were situated near a large tree. Sonny took off his jacket and climbed up there. The tree provided ample cover. Once he was nestled in its branches, he assembled his rifle in quick practised movements.

Then he found a sturdy branch to balance on and looked through the scope. He focused in on the trailer park, the kids playing ball. Moving the scope, Sonny found David's trailer.

As Sonny had expected, the lights were on, and David was moving about inside. Through the windows, with no curtains on them, Sonny could see David from the waist up. He had on a moss green T-shirt. Sonny had a clear shot to take him out.

Keeping his target in his crosshairs, Sonny moved his finger to the trigger.

It was better this way, he told himself. He was sparing the poor chap from getting trapped in a gilded cage, the same cage Sonny was trapped in. He was doing David a favour.

Sonny watched him, his finger hovering over the trigger. He watched David milling about, totally unaware, and he hesitated.

It was a shame...but this was a kindness, he reasoned.

In his crosshairs, David was pinning something to the far window of the trailer. Sonny couldn't see what until David turned around and pinned another to the window facing his direction. A scrap of paper with thick black letters drawn neatly.

I have a name for it...

Sonny was confused for a moment, until he realised what David meant. He'd picked a nickname for his alien? Sonny watched and waited. No other notes followed. David went out onto his porch to casually sip a beer. He had on green camo trousers and brown boots, combat ready but appearing at ease. He was waiting for Sonny to respond, like he knew he was being watched.

"Hm," Sonny grunted to himself. *Clever.* He took his finger off the trigger and checked the time on his watch.

Well, he couldn't hang around all night. They had a lab to check out. Sonny needed to decide right now: kill David, or bring him in. Sonny looked back through his scope, zeroing in on David. He was still acting casual, like he had all the time in the world.

Sonny wanted to know what nickname he'd picked. Was it another Spice Girl? Was it someone else?

"Bloody hell," Sonny muttered, as he packed his rifle away again. He climbed down from the tree, put on the jacket, and jogged back to his car. Then he sped around to the trailer park and drove right in there, honking at the stupid kids to get out of his way.

Sonny drove up to David's trailer, cut the engine, and got out. "Right," he announced, standing beside his open door. "Let's hear it, then."

David responded with a smile. A smirk, really. He calmly stepped down from his trailer and walked over to Sonny.

Standing opposite each other, David paused for dramatic effect until Sonny was nearly bursting to hear his answer.

David cleared his throat softly. "Gomez," he said.

Sonny raised an eyebrow. "Gomez?"

"Gomez Addams. You know...?" David raised one hand and snapped his fingers twice.

Sonny's mouth popped open with a gay gasp of delight. "That Gomez!" he exclaimed, as images of the dashing Latino filled his head. "Now that is a galaxy brain name!"

David grinned. "Yeah, I thought so."

"Gomez Addams!" Sonny chuckled. "Hey, I could..." He abruptly cut himself off before he suggested switching his alien's nickname to Morticia Addams.

Christ, Sonny, calm down.

"Er, right," Sonny said, changing the subject. "So, I take it you want to…?"

David nodded. "I'm in. Bag's packed."

"All right." Sonny exhaled. David had won this round. "You better hop in, then. I'm late to see this man about a dog."

"Bueno," David said, looking suitably smug.

Sonny leaned into his car and moved his rifle off the passenger seat to the back. David went inside his trailer to fetch his bag.

So. They were really doing this.

Well, Sonny reasoned, he could always kill David later. Accidents on ops happened all the time.

He removed his coat, sat down in his driver's seat, and pulled the door shut. He exhaled again as he watched David exit the trailer and toss his keys to a neighbour standing nearby. In fact, a few of the neighbours were all watching David's departure with interest.

David opened the passenger door, ducking his head in briefly to check it was safe to get in.

"C'mon, sunshine," Sonny prompted him. "Got quite a drive ahead."

David got into the car and closed the door after him.

Sonny started the engine and slowly reversed out of the trailer park, allowing David a full view of his trailer and neighbours out the front window as they drove away.

"You realise you can't come back here, right?" Sonny said.

"I know," David replied quietly.

"Good." Sonny managed to get them out of the park without incident, despite several of those kids running alongside the car to see who was inside. He turned the car around and pointed it in the direction they needed. "Off we go, then."

Chapter Nine

David still had hundreds of burning questions, but he kept quiet when the phone on the car dash holder lit up with a call.

They'd only been driving for a few minutes, but Sonny pulled the car over to answer it. David looked at the screen and saw the contact was labelled *Rafe.*

"Wotcha," Sonny said, addressing the person on the phone. "Am I coming to you?"

"Are you ready, then?" a man's voice replied, a British accent like Sonny's but in a deeper tone.

"Yeah, literally right now," Sonny said.

"Awright. I'll send you a pin," the man replied. "We'll hold off until you get here."

"Right," Sonny said. The call ended, and he waited for a pin location to arrive, then used the map app.

David wondered how he got such good cell service here.

"Aw, what?" Sonny muttered, sounding annoyed. "It's

fuckin' miles away."

"Where are we going?" David asked him.

"A spot right outside Mexicali," Sonny replied. "Over a two-hour drive."

"The Federal Highway is the quickest route but it has tolls," David warned him. "And the only ID I have is a fake ID, seeing as I'm supposed to be legally dead, so there's that little issue too."

"Never you mind about ID, sunshine," Sonny told him. "We can whiz through checkpoints." He tapped the screen, selecting the route with the highway. "Two hours and twenty-six minutes. Guess we better get a wriggle on." He tapped start on the screen, then restarted the car.

"Turn right," announced the computerised voice.

"Yes, hang on a second, love," Sonny muttered, busy swinging the car back onto the road.

David smiled. "She wants you to turn right."

"She needs to learn to enact a little fuckin' patience," Sonny said, his tone a mix of ticked off and amused.

David was still getting used to his way of speaking, his sheer Britishness. It was new to him and very interesting. "Can I ask you something?" he asked, once they were driving along the road again.

"Knock yourself out, son," Sonny replied.

"Are you from London?" David asked.

Sonny chuckled, bright and surprised. "Of all the questions to ask," he mused.

"Are you?" David pressed.

"I am," Sonny said.

"And we're gonna go to London?" David asked. "When this job is over?"

"Bloody hope so," Sonny muttered. "We been out here six

weeks already, and it's hotter than Satan's armpit."

"Welcome to Mexico," David said. He gazed out at the dark road lit up by the car's headlights.

Sonny was quiet for a moment, then mentioned, "Food's tasty though. I'll give you that."

David smiled. "Sure is."

"Right," Sonny said. "Seeing as we got a couple hours, we may as well find you a call sign. A nickname to use."

"Okay," David replied. "Well, my old unit called me Sarge."

"You can't have that, you plank," Sonny said. "Would mess up the chain of command. I've already told you we have a sergeant. You'll need another call sign. Preferably one syllable. Luckily for you, I have several suggestions."

David harrumphed with amusement. "I can't wait to hear those," he quipped. "What's your call sign?"

"Sonny."

"I thought that was your name?"

"It is," Sonny said with a chuckle.

"So what's your actual name?" David asked.

"Aha," Sonny replied. "Wouldn't you like to know, sunshine. Hey, we could call you that. Sunshine."

"No," David said firmly. "I thought you said only one sylla-ble?"

"Well, exceptions happen," Sonny said. "Like me."

"I bet," David murmured. "Okay. Er... Hombre?"

"No," Sonny said.

"Tio?" David suggested, but Sonny shook his head. "Ma-chete?" he quipped.

"One fuckin' syllable, mate," Sonny said. "And use English. We don't need to announce who you are to everyone."

"Fair," David said. He stared out the window, even though it was dark. He couldn't come up with another cool nickname on the spot like this. "Well, shit, I don't know."

"We'll think of something, couple of smart brains like ours," Sonny said wryly. "It's a long drive."

"Who came up with yours?" David asked him.

"My teacher at school takes credit for that," Sonny said. "If any of us misbehaved, he'd be all like, now listen 'ere, sonny Jim!"

David wasn't sure if he was telling the truth, but picturing Sonny as a naughty schoolboy certainly didn't seem out of the realm of possibility.

"So," he said dubiously, "your work call sign is your childhood nickname?"

"Yep," Sonny said. He glanced over at David briefly. "What? You don't like it?"

"Er," David said, caught off guard. "No, it's...it suits you. I'm just wondering how it's covert."

"Listen, this is for everyday use," Sonny explained. "If we're going dark on an op, we use secure call signs like alpha this and alpha that. But the rest of the time, to all the lads at work, we use nicknames."

David thought about it, then realised he may be an odd man out. "None of you are on the run or legally dead like me?"

"No," Sonny said. "We live and work mostly out of London where, besides our resident northern lass, we all grew up."

"So, I'll be the only fugitive?"

"Yeah, if you put it like that." Sonny chuckled. "Cheer up, mate. You chose to come in on this. You could've been halfway to Cuba by now."

"I do want in on it," David replied. "But, it's a lot to get my head around."

"Well, put a pin in it," Sonny told him. "We have an op to do first. We'll call you 'fresh meat' for now." He chuckled as if he'd made a funny joke.

"And what is the op?" David asked.

"Told ya," Sonny said cryptically. "We have to see a man about a dog."

*

They drove down the federal highway and had to stop at two toll booths.

David was nervous when the guards shone their flashlights at the car and asked them to roll the windows down. He'd been on the run for months and had specifically avoided situations like this.

"Nice and easy, sunshine," Sonny told him smoothly. "Let me 'andle this."

David watched him speak to the guards in Spanish, flash them some ID card in a black wallet, and even slip them some pesos as a bribe. It was all done super-fast and casual, like Sonny had done this a hundred times and had no fear of them.

David noticed that Sonny asked the guards about seeing a blue Kia-Rio pass through here. He asked that at both toll booths, except the colour of the Kia changed from blue to green at the second booth.

After they'd driven away from the second toll station, David asked Sonny, "Why are you looking for a Kia?"

"I'm not," Sonny replied. "Just throwing them off the scent an' all that."

David nodded. Misdirection.

"What's the ID you showed them?" he asked.

Sonny had slipped it back into his pocket, and David was curious.

"Here." Sonny fished it out and handed the slim wallet over to David to look.

David opened it, surprised to see a simple ID card with a DMV-style photo of Sonny's face, along with the name Nate Smith and "UK national." At the top of the card was a blue Earth logo and the word INTERPOL.

"You're Interpol?" David asked in surprised. "Nate Smith?"

Sonny chuckled. "It's a cover, sunshine. And so's the Interpol bit. Tilt the card thirty degrees."

"Huh?"

"Tilt the card," Sonny instructed.

Curious, David examined the ID card again, and tilted it to the side. He noticed a subtle holographic effect when he tilted it, and now the card read PRISM instead of Interpol.

"Prism?" he said. "What's that?"

"Your new employer," Sonny said, "if it all works out. Consider tonight your audition."

"Right," David said, still examining the card. "What does it stand for?"

"Paranormal Recon, Intel, and Special Measures," Sonny recited.

"Well, I hope the pay's good," David quipped.

Sonny laughed. "Don't get your hopes up, son. But it's better than a kick in the teeth."

A two-hour drive should've felt long, but they got to Mexicali in no time. They were on the outskirts of the city, all wide roads and imposingly large warehouses here. A high-rise freeway ran above them, and Sonny parked the car underneath the street bridge.

Up ahead, also under the bridge, was a stationary grey van that looked like it had seen better days.

"Blimey," Sonny murmured, killing the engine. "See, this is what the rental company fobs us off with."

"What? The van?" David asked.

"Yeah," Sonny said. "You can see why I prefer driving this cushy number." He undid his seat belt and grabbed his phone off the dash. "C'mon, then, Fresh Meat," he said. He popped the trunk. "Time to gear up."

David followed him out of the car and to the back. Sonny was transferring what looked like a rifle bag from the back seat to the trunk.

"Want your gun back?" Sonny asked, opening another bag and producing the handgun David had lost the night before.

David had brought his spare, but he liked that Sig. It was a classic. "Thanks," he said, taking it. "Did you get my…?"

Sonny produced the knife, flicking it around in his hand to show off before offering it, handle out, to David.

"Thanks," David said. He glanced around on the street, dark and quiet in the shadow of the underpass, but not entirely deserted of people. "We're doing this out on the street?"

"Yeah. Chop, chop," Sonny said. He was already loaded up with guns and knives and he picked out a shorter jacket from the trunk, black with soft leather, to put on.

David was still in a T-shirt.

"What are we walking into?" he asked.

"Well, first we'll walk into that van and meet the lads," Sonny explained. "Then they'll give us the lowdown. Here." From the mess of the trunk, he pulled out a shoulder holster, and a black tac vest with reinforced front and back. "Pick your poison," Sonny told him, holding one in each hand.

If David wasn't sure what he was getting himself into, he'd rather have the protection. He chose the tac vest and put it on.

Once he'd loaded his guns, clips, and extra knife into the vest, David grabbed the ball cap from his bag. He put it on backwards.

"Yeah, that's right," Sonny quipped, watching him. "Fashion comes first, innit?"

David smiled and looked pointedly at Sonny's hair. "I bet you're in the hair salon every other week with a cut like that."

Sonny tittered. "You're not wrong," he said, and shut the trunk. He led the way over to the van and knocked on its back door. "¡*Hola*! Pizza delivery," he said.

The door opened outward to show a good-looking Black man with close-cropped hair and neatly cut stubble. He seemed surprised to see David there.

"Awright, Rafe," Sonny greeted. "Got some fresh meat with me."

"Yeah, thanks for the heads-up," the man, Rafe, replied deadpan. "You better come in."

Sonny entered the van, and David followed him in. Rafe shut the door.

Inside, David got a quick introduction to the team, which consisted of three, including Rafe. All were sitting on built-in benches, dressed for stealth infiltration in black tactical gear, except the big guy with the beard and the laptop, who was probably the tech.

It all felt familiar to David, despite not knowing the three new people.

"Lads," Sonny announced, "this is Fresh Meat." He gestured at David. "Fresh Meat, these are the lads. Rafe," he said, pointing to the Black guy. "He's CO."

"Correct," Rafe said. He had a military bearing that David recognised, so this was probably the team sergeant that Sonny had mentioned.

"That's Mac," Sonny went on, pointing to the only woman present. "TEMS officer and long-range cover." She was lean, with watchful eyes. White, with strawberry blonde hair tied back off her lightly freckled face, she nodded at David but didn't say anything yet.

"And this is Naz," Sonny went on, pointing to the final member of the team. "Tech. Comms. Snacks." He was a large, bearded, Middle Eastern-looking guy with tinted glasses and wavy dark hair. He was not dressed for combat at all. He was wearing a fashionable tracksuit and sneakers, with a gold chain around his neck.

"Fresh Meat?" Naz questioned, looking at Sonny.

"We're working on a name," Sonny said. "Tonight, it's Fresh Meat."

Naz shook his head, some mild exasperation showing.

David caught Mac, the woman, looking at him with a small smile. "Talked you into joining, did he?" she said.

"Yeah, he talks a lot," Naz added. "If you think he'll shut up, you're wrong. It's nonstop yap all day, every day."

"Every day," Mac confirmed.

"Oi, excuse me?" Sonny said sharply.

David noticed smirks and smiles among the team. They were a close-knit group, and British. Very British. It was different and familiar to David all at once, but he had a good feeling about this team.

"Okay, pipe down," Rafe said, his tone commanding silence from the team. "Naz, brief Sonny and...Fresh Meat."

Naz tilted his laptop to show them a street map. "This warehouse is where the lab is," he explained.

"Security?" Sonny asked.

"Couple of armed guards," Rafe answered. "I did a drone fly-by while we were waiting for you. Thermal imaging shows minimal security, maybe six or seven bodies total."

"Piece of piss, then," Sonny said. "Where's ol' Esteban and his boys?"

"They're waiting down the street on standby," Rafe replied. "Guv said he doesn't want them seeing the lab unless we need backup."

"Right," Sonny said.

David eased back and watched their exchange. It was clear that the two men had a history from serving together.

"They have one main entry point," Rafe continued, pointing at the screen showing the thermal images of the building. "Reinforced steel door, locked up tighter than a bank vault. There's a window exit on the roof, but it doesn't look to be in use, and we could cover it with a sniper. Mac? You take the high ground."

Mac nodded without saying anything. She seemed focused on the mission.

"That leaves the two of us to infiltrate, with—" Sonny looked at David with a smirk. "—Fresh Meat makes three."

Chapter Ten

Naz handed out the comms; earpieces and a wireless bracelet for their wrists. The bracelets were a simple band of black, housing both a mic and a tracker. Naz gave David a quick rundown of the comms but they were standard and David had experience.

Rafe set a black helmet onto his head with NVGs attached to the top. He noticed David watching him and smiled. "Yeah, I protect my head in this game," he said.

David looked between him and the others. Mac would be using a sniper scope. Sonny had no helmet or NVGs in sight. David could see well in the dark, but he hadn't realised how well until this moment.

"Testing," Naz said, his voice in their earpieces. "Line two is secure."

"Copy," the team murmured one by one.

"Copy," David said. He was starting to feel the pre-mission buzz set in.

They exited the van together, leaving Naz there. Mac peeled away first, with a rifle bag over her shoulder. She jogged across the street and around the other side of the building, melting away in the darkness.

Sonny held his wrist up and said softly, "Let me know when you're in position."

"Nearly there," Mac's voice answered.

While they waited, Sonny and Rafe got their guns ready. Sonny had a Sig handgun, a newer model than David's. Rafe had one Sig plus a semi-automatic assault rifle in black. He also had a backpack of considerable weight that David was willing to bet contained explosives. That was some heavy firepower for only a dozen targets.

Still, this was an illegal lab in Mexico. The targets inside were likely armed to the teeth.

"I'm in position," Mac informed them. "Covering the roof."

"Copy that," Rafe said. "Let's go." He motioned for Sonny and David to follow.

They crossed the dark street, walking quickly but aiming for casual. A few yards down the street, a scooter drove by noisily with some exuberant *whoops*. Young men heading out to a bar, probably.

At the building corner, they ducked in on its shadowy side.

"The only external security cameras we detected are over the front door," Rafe explained.

"Well, that makes things easy," Sonny said, and stepped out into the glow from the lone streetlight. "I'll get us in. Wait here for my signal."

"How are you getting through that door?" David asked him.

Sonny threw a smirk over his shoulder. "I'm gonna knock."

He strutted away down the street. David stared after him in part disbelief and part admiration. When he glanced at Rafe, he said, "He goes in first because he heals quickest." He paused, then asked, "You probably do, too, right?"

David was unsure how to answer that. "I haven't exactly done a field test," he admitted.

"Well, no time like the present, bruv," Rafe replied with a chuckle.

David peered around the corner, watching Sonny saunter up to the front door. He was laid back and acting casual as he pressed a buzzer and waved at the security camera. "Buenas noches!" Sonny declared, his voice carrying down the quiet street. "¿Qué tal? What's up?"

David wasn't sure how this would go down, but somebody must have answered the door, probably through an intercom, as Sonny began conversing quickly in informal Spanish. He babbled something about coming to pick up a dog, having cash, and affecting an air of obliviousness.

The ruse worked surprisingly quickly, and the heavy door opened. Likely, they didn't want their whereabouts advertised to the whole neighbourhood.

David watched Sonny pretend to get his wallet from his pocket before pushing his way inside. David expected gunshots, shouts, but heard only silence.

Then Sonny's voice was in his ear. "You're clear for entry," he said softly over comms.

"That's our cue," Rafe said and took off at a jog.

David followed, easily catching up as he jogged beside Rafe. They arrived at the door, which Sonny was holding open for them. David noticed the two dead Mexicans on the floor first. They were lying with their heads at odd angles, which suggested Sonny had snapped their necks as easily as cracking open a can of beer.

It gave David pause. He hadn't been in a combat situation for nearly two years. Rafe pushed past him and stepped over the dead bodies to take up position with his gun aimed, NVGs flipped down over his eyes.

Sonny pulled David inside, shut the door quietly and drew his gun. He signalled with his hand in the direction he wanted to take. Rafe nodded. David snapped out of his shock and fell into formation with the two men.

The warehouse was big inside, but full of junk. The light wasn't great, which meant plenty of shadows for bogeys to lie in wait and ambush them.

Sonny led the way, David in second and Rafe on their six.

Now his head was in the game, David fell back on his training and swept the area with them as one. In many ways this was as familiar to him as slipping on a pair of old shoes: it fit.

They didn't come across anyone yet, and Mac reported no movement from the roof, which meant Sonny's entry ruse had bought them some time. They were able to clear the first floor quickly. All the junk and old car parts were a cover; when they came upon another reinforced door on the southwest side, it was clear that this was pay dirt.

Above the door, next to a lamp, was a basic security camera. Sonny nodded to Rafe, and David watched Rafe point a black re-mote control at it—some sort of scrambler.

Then he and Sonny crowded in by the door. David followed.

Rafe had another cool gadget to use: a flatscreen tablet, the size of a large cell phone. He held it up against the door, and a thermal image presented itself. Two bodies directly ahead, in sitting positions. Another three bodies off to the side, near several smaller thermal blobs.

David realised those must be animals, and his heart sank a little. He mentally prepared himself for what he was about to burst in on.

Sonny and Rafe were having a silent conversation with hand gestures only. Sonny gestured at the door. Rafe put aside his tablet and his gun. Next, he unhooked a long black instrument from his belt, and attached it to the lock on the door.

Sonny switched position, ready to go in first. He gestured with one hand for David to get behind him.

David said nothing and moved to stand behind Sonny. His breathing was steady yet a little elevated from the adrenaline.

In no time at all, Rafe's gadget had unlocked the door. With a nod from Sonny, Rafe pulled at the door to swing it wide open.

Sonny stepped inside, swift and fluid. Before the occupants even realised they had intruders, Sonny had shot the two seated men with a direct bullseye to their heads. Then he swung right, gun pointed. David followed his lead.

This was a lab set-up, albeit a grimy back-door lab bathed in an eerie red glow, like a photographic dark room.

The gunshots had alerted the three remaining men, all dressed in simple shorts and T-shirts, that they were under attack. One of them dived for cover, the other two drew guns. Animals in cages shrieked: chimpanzees, dogs, rodents. David observed them—caged; not an immediate threat—and kept his focus on the human targets.

He and Sonny had to duck and dodge fire from the two with guns, the bullets going wide and hitting everything except them. These guys weren't military trained.

They returned fire immediately, and their aim was better. The two went down and the brief firefight was over.

The third man, the one who'd ducked for cover, was trying to crawl away on the floor. Sonny chased after him, so David followed. As they passed by one of the larger cages, the primate occupant inside flung itself at the bars and roared, its maw opening to an unnatural degree, teeth huge.

"Jesus!" David exclaimed, caught off guard. He brought his gun up, but the creature was caged. It had just given him a start.

Sonny hadn't broken stride, and he caught up to the fleeing man. Sonny stood over him with his gun aimed. "Who's your broker?" he asked in English.

"Por favor!" the man cried, seemingly pathetic.

"¿Quién es?" Sonny demanded.

David turned to them in time to see the Mexican break into a smug grin. "Chinga tu madre," he replied, telling Sonny to get fucked, basically. Then his mouth filled with fang-like teeth, and he roared, lurching upward like a Hollywood Dracula from his coffin.

David couldn't believe his eyes, and he froze. In the back of his mind he panicked that *this* was what awaited him, some weird mutation with fucked-up teeth.

Sonny shot the Mexican point blank in the forehead, a double tap, and he crashed back down to the floor.

David approached cautiously, staring down at the corpse. The mouth hung open in death, and David watched the sharp fangs slowly retract back into the gums.

"What the fuck?" he murmured.

"You get used to it," Sonny murmured back, unfazed. He was still pointing his gun at the corpse. "Sometimes," he added, gesturing with the gun nozzle, "they get back up."

"What? How?" David asked. "Is this...? Are they...?"

Sonny glanced at him and smirked. "Like us?" he finished. "No. Different breed, innit? The two long front teeth? The black eyes? They're the giveaway. These guys deal in vampire genes."

Thank goodness, David thought, the relief forefront in his mind. He looked down at the corpse and its weird teeth, then back up at Sonny as the words sank in. "Wait, what?" he said. "Vampires?"

"Yep," Sonny said. "We're not the only freaks around here, sunshine."

*

That dead Mexican with the teeth did *not* get back up.

David was relieved about that. He was also confused. "I thought vampires were, like, undead?" he asked.

"They won't be full vampires yet," Rafe explained. He took out a pocket torch and flicked it on, shining a bright column of blue light onto the corpse. "This is UV light. If they were full vampires, they'd flame up with this shining on them."

David watched the light on the dead guy's forehead, and only the smallest puff of smoke sizzled off the skin. He could hardly believe his eyes.

"Fledgling," Rafe said, turning off the torch again. "And a human to start with. They inject the vampire genes, but it degrades their bodies after a while. It doesn't stick."

"Aha! Let there be light," Sonny called out. He'd wandered away to find the light switch, blinding them all with the overhead lights as they flickered on one by one.

Several lab mice exploded as soon as the light touched them. Luckily they were in glass tanks, so the mess was contained.

"Gross," Rafe commented. He lifted up his NVGs. "You just blew up some mice, bruv."

"Ah, whoops," Sonny said, as he came sauntering back. "Unstable li'l buggers, eh?"

"Please don't tell me the bigger animals will blow up?" David questioned.

"It's possible," Rafe answered. "Look. If they blow up, they're dusty." He pointed to the nearest mice cages, where the aftermath of the exploded mess was more soot than blood. "The more vampire they are, the more dust there is. These mice were maybe fifty-fifty."

David peered in, and he saw that Rafe was correct. Even now, mere moments after the fact, the dust was starting to evaporate on the air.

"Well, damn," David murmured. "Vampire mice? Why?"

Sonny burst out laughing, doubling over in his amusement.

Rafe was the one to answer. "Ignore him," he said. "This lab was probably testing out the batch of vampire genes they had. Hence the lab rats."

"Oh," David said, realising the obvious now. "Yeah, of course. Duh."

Sonny was still laughing, and he wiped a tear away. "All right, enough sightseeing. Let's get on with it."

"Get on with what, exactly?" David asked.

"You stand guard, Fresh Meat," Sonny told him. "We'll clean up."

Chapter Eleven

Cleaning up, it transpired, meant exterminating anything alive, taking samples, and setting the building with explosives to blow.

Mac had joined them from the roof, and the three agents got to work. Their practised and methodical actions suggested they'd done this numerous times.

David was on sentry duty while they worked. He became a little distracted watching them. Sonny and Rafe went around the cages to euthanise the animals; they each had a handgun that fired special bullets, and several of the test subjects burst into dust upon impact.

"Is all this really necessary?" David asked.

"You really want a vampire chimpanzee running around town?" Sonny replied.

David watched one of the chimps with too many teeth snarling at Sonny, hissing. "I suppose not," he conceded.

"There's too many subjects infected with vampire genes," Rafe explained. "We don't have the resources to contain and ship all of them securely, and they'd likely explode or burn in the sunlight anyway."

"I get it," David replied. He still felt weird about it though.

Mac was going around the lab tables, collecting samples and carefully slotting them into a bag; vials of liquid, petri dishes, swabs. She also snipped off the index finger from the dead Mexican who'd been part vampire and put it into a sealed plastic bag.

"Wherever they got their batch from," she said, "it wasn't very good. His body is already decomposing."

David looked down at the body, the skin looking saggy and discoloured. "Why does it do that?" he asked.

"The vampire genes are like a parasite," Mac replied, glancing up at him. "When introduced to a living human, anyway. Often the body can't sustain the parasitic blood cells without a fresh supply of blood. The host may not even be aware that their body is dying until it's too late. We've seen cases like this a lot recently."

"Why would they take the risk?" David asked.

"They probably don't know what they're getting themselves into." Mac closed her bag and got to her feet. "Humans like this are the gofers for the full vampires. They're usually the ones behind operations like this. The brokers."

"Yeah, that's why we shouldn't hang about," Sonny called out. "Chop, chop, lads."

"Wait," David said, "you mean there's more vampires around?"

"Very likely," Sonny replied.

"Don't worry," Mac mentioned quietly. "They usually keep their distance from their grunt workers." She smiled at David, then walked away to investigate more of the lab.

Rafe had crouched down to unpack his bag and handed out explosive charges between himself and Sonny. "Sooner we outta here, the better," he mentioned.

"Boys, you missed one," Mac called out. "A dog."

"Well, get rid of it," Sonny called back.

"It's tiny," Mac replied. "Also, I don't think it's infected yet."

"You mean it's a dog, dog?" Rafe asked. He rose to his feet, cradling bricks of semtex and wires in one arm. "I'll shine my torch on it."

David watched him go, while Sonny was busy setting his charges down.

"Oi," Rafe's voice called out. "I think it's a dog, dog or, failing that, the vampire genes took so well, we can't tell."

"Fuck's sake," Sonny muttered. "Just shoot it!" he called back.

"I'm not shooting a dog," Rafe replied.

"Me neither," Mac added.

David watched Sonny's reaction. The other man put his explosives down with a mild sigh and drew his gun. He walked through the lab, past the wall of cages at the back. David didn't particularly want to see this, but he followed anyway.

"Fuck me," Sonny said, "it is tiny."

David rounded the corner to get a clear view and saw the team standing beside the only occupied cage in this end of the lab. The dog in question was a small Xolo, probably a toy or miniature breed, around fourteen inches by David's guess. Looked young too, not much older than puppy age.

"Is it a Chihuahua?" Rafe asked.

"I don't know," Mac replied. "It doesn't have any hair."

"Yeah, don't look like no Chihuahua to me," Sonny said.

"It's a Xolo," David said, as all three of them turned to look at him. "Xoloitzcuintle," he explained. "This breed's hairless. Perro pelón Mexicano in Spanish." Inside the cage, the mottled brown dog lifted its head with interest, perking its large ears at David. He felt an instant bond with the canine, a camaraderie. "This is Mexico's dog right here," he said. "My abuelito had one to help with his arthritis. They'll cuddle up to you and keep you warm."

"That's all very nice," Sonny said dryly, "but we still have to shoot it."

"I'm out," David said. "My people believe these dogs ward off evil spirits."

"Why's that?" Mac asked. "I can't look it up; our phones are still in dark mode."

"Yes, do tell," Sonny said sarcastically, lowering the gun to his side.

"Xolo's are named after Xolotl," David explained. "Aztec god with a man's body and a dog's head. He's the soul guide for the dead."

Mac and Rafe made noises of interest and exchanged a look. "Maybe they were keeping it as a sort of talisman?" Mac said. "Superstitions."

"I'm definitely not shooting it," David said. "I don't want that bad luck on me."

"I sure as shit don't," Rafe muttered.

"Oh, for cryin' out loud," Sonny said, raising his gun. He pointed it at the dog, whose head cocked as it looked back at Sonny. A small whine escaped, and Sonny didn't pull the trigger.

The moment was tense, but finally Sonny lowered his gun with a sigh.

"All right, fine," he grumbled. "Fresh Meat, you're in charge of the dog. You can take it outside and send it on its way."

"Are we absolutely sure it isn't a vampire dog?" Rafe asked.

Sonny shrugged elaborately. "Do you see any teeth?"

"We could take it back with us?" Mac suggested. "Test at the lab."

"Oh, yes!" Sonny said. "I can imagine how well that will go down with the gaffer! This thing's probably got rabies an' all."

"Looks healthy at my reckoning," Mac told him.

"Guys!" Naz's voice said in their earpieces. "Two Jeeps full of unknowns are headed to your location. Do you want our guys to engage?"

"Shit," Sonny said. "No, tell them to sit tight," he instructed. "We'll handle it."

"Time to go," Rafe muttered and hurried away. Mac followed him.

"Fresh Meat," Sonny said to David. "Sort the dog." He hurried after Rafe.

David holstered his gun and unlocked the cage. He couldn't see a dog leash anywhere, and the dog didn't have a collar on anyway. "Vamos," he said, clicking his fingers to get the dog interested enough to come out.

The little Xolo got up and stretched its legs like it had all the time in the world, then hopped out of the cage. David observed the dog's body and ascertained this was a female.

"Vamos, señorita," he said, but the dog didn't move until he did. When David jogged back to the main lab to find the others, the dog trotted along beside him.

"The Jeeps have pulled into the street," Naz informed them all over comms. "They'll be at your door in seconds."

"Tell our lads to form a wide perimeter," Rafe said into his comm. "We'll draw the hostiles into the building and exit via the roof."

"Copy that," Naz said.

"All set?" Rafe asked Sonny.

"All set," Sonny replied. "Get to the roof now." He jogged off toward the door.

"Where are you going?" David called after him.

"I'm gonna let the bastards in!" Sonny called back.

"Come on," Mac said, touching David's arm. "It's this way."

"Doesn't he need help?" David asked.

"He'll be fine," she said.

"Yeah, and you got this package now." Rafe pointed down at the dog beside David, who was looking up at him expectantly.

"Yeah, okay," he agreed. "Vamos, señorita," he told her and followed Mac up the metal walkway to the next level. The dog obediently followed. Rafe was right behind them.

Mac led the way to the lab's top level, which was full of storage. The windows on that level were large hinged windows, easy to slip through and step out onto a flat roof. The night air out here wasn't much cooler than the warm lab had been.

"Fire exit is on the northeast corner," Mac informed them.

"Aren't we waiting for Sonny?" David asked.

"He'll follow," Rafe assured him. "C'mon, we gotta climb down before the charges blow."

They hurried across the roof. Down below in the street, gunfire started up and echoed off the other buildings. *Rat-at-at-at, rat-at-at-at.* They had to keep moving. David glanced down at the Xolo, still there, sticking close to David's side, her little paws a blur as she trotted speedily.

When they got to the fire escape, he was relieved to see it had steps that a small dog could navigate.

"Are the charges going to collapse the building?" David asked.

"No, shouldn't affect the structure," Rafe replied. "The charge is controlled, but the blast may still come out from windows."

David nodded. They had to get clear, and fast.

Mac went down first, encouraging the Xolo to follow her. David went next, with Rafe on their six. All efforts to be quiet now gone, their boots clattered on the metal fire escape as they ran down.

Gunfire was still going on round the other side of the building. They were lucky to not be in the middle of it.

"Human mercs?" David guessed, glancing back at Rafe.

"Yeah, most likely!" Rafe replied, as he followed right behind him.

As they were getting to the last set of stairs, the battered van came peeling around the corner.

"There's Naz," Rafe said. "Go on, I'll cover you!"

They reached ground and made a run for the van as it braked hard to stop. Rafe ran backwards, gun trained on the building. They didn't have any bogeys on their tail, which was a small miracle.

David kept checking on the dog, but she broke into a run quite easily and kept pace with him, her big ears perked up like she was enjoying the exercise.

Mac raised her wrist and spoke to her receiver. "We're clear!"

The next second, a loud explosion sounded inside the building. David paused to glance back. The lower level had held the charges, and orange flashes burned at the windows followed by thick smoke.

Where was Sonny?

"Come on!" Mac said to him, opening the van's door. "Get in!"

"But...?" David said.

"He'll let us know where he is," Rafe said, pushing David to the van. "Let's go."

David got in. Mac and the little Xolo followed. Rafe shut the door on them and went around to the front.

Sirens blared in the distance, signalling the emergency services were on their way. They'd have to haul ass.

The van lurched away, with Naz driving.

"Sonny, talk to me," Rafe's voice said in their earpieces. "We're all in the van."

David held his breath, listening.

That beat of silence before Sonny replied felt very long.

"Swing southwest," Sonny said. "I'll drop in."

David caught Mac rolling her eyes fondly. "He's on the rooftops," she explained.

There were no windows to see anything, but David remembered how easily Sonny had jumped on top of those box cars the other night. It wouldn't be out of the realms of possibility for Sonny to get from roof to roof.

"Did you jump the roof earlier?" David asked her.

"I used a zipline," she replied. "Angle was good. Sonny can jump a lot further than me, so he doesn't need those."

David nodded. He had so many questions, but now wasn't the time.

The van sped down the street, away from the burning building and scattered gunfire. They stopped at the next warehouse block, and David got the fright of his life when the van's back door was yanked open. He raised his gun, and so did Mac. The Xolo barked.

"Oi, it's me!" Sonny said, raising his open hands at them.

"You scared me shitless," Mac told him, lowering her gun.

David lowered his, and he shushed the Xolo gently. He didn't attempt to touch her while she was riled up.

"You brought a dog?" Naz exclaimed, twisting around in his seat to goggle at them.

"You did mention you wanted a dog," Mac said, smirking.

"Yeah, but not a potential *vampire* familiar!" Naz replied, his voice hitching to a high note.

"She's not a vampire," she replied.

Sonny came into the van and shut the door. "Right, lads," he announced. "Esteban and his lads have cleaned up outside the building and they're heading to their fallback spot. Lab's all blown, job done, and the local fuzz are on the way, so I suggest we all vámonos."

"Where's our fallback spot?" David asked.

"We did our job, Fresh Meat," Sonny said. "There's no new leads to follow, so now we can head home."

"London?" David guessed.

"That's right, my son." Sonny smirked at him. "London."

Chapter Twelve

They drove to Mexicali MXL airport, near the US border.

David was pleased to get out of the van when the whole team exited together and stretched their legs. The little Xolo got out too and did a cute stretch with her front legs.

"Aw," Mac commented, watching her. "Big stretch."

Rafe and Naz came to join them, and everyone picked up a bag of gear from the van while they stripped off body armour and put away the biggest guns.

David wondered if all their weapons would be an issue for customs. He followed the team's lead.

The airport was active but not huge. The single runway was lit up by ground lights, with one commercial aircraft taking off at the far end. Another commercial plane was on the second apron, currently refuelling.

They were right on the airfield, having parked outside one of the airport's buildings. That's how small it was.

David spotted military aircraft in a nearby hangar and figured this airport doubled as a port for military operations.

Soon enough, an officer dressed in Mexican military uniform came to see them. Sonny stepped up to speak for the group, flashing his ID card and handing over a folded piece of paper. He spoke fluent Spanish to the officer, and David listened in as he said they were here for a private charter.

The officer took the paper and read it, his dark eyes flicking up to regard the group. He looked down, noticing the Xolo sitting quietly next to David.

"El perro?" he questioned, assuming the dog was male.

"Perra," David corrected him, which only earned him an unimpressed glare from the officer.

Sonny also sent David a sardonic look, then reached in his pocket for a wad of cash. "This is coming out of your first wage slip, Fresh Meat," he said in English. He leafed through several notes in a casual manner, letting the officer see them.

David smiled, glancing down at the Xolo as she watched the proceedings. Bribes always helped grease the wheels, and one generous wad of cash later, the Xolo was granted passage.

As they walked over the tarmac on foot to their light aircraft, Naz grumbled in English about them taking the dog across borders, reeling off a laundry list of health issues it could bring.

"Pipe down," Sonny told him. "I can always send you home on a commercial flight, Naz. Remember what it's like as a bearded Muslim flying commercial?"

"You can't do that!" Naz said, instantly worried. "You're really mean, you know that, Sonny?"

Sonny snickered.

David watched the exchange with interest. Mac, who was walking alongside him, mentioned quietly, "Naz has OCD. He tends to worry."

David nodded. "To be fair to him," he replied, "an unquarantined pet is a legitimate concern."

"She looks healthy to me," Mac said. "My parents were veterinarians. I don't see any warning signs, and we'll be taking her straight to HQ with us so she won't come into contact with other animals until we've done some blood work."

"The doc likes dogs," Rafe added in a sarcastic note.

"Yeah, and she'll let me use the lab," Mac said.

"But she'll be okay?" David asked. "You're not...gonna do weird tests?"

"Standard blood work," Mac assured him. "Same as any stray animal would get in a veterinary clinic. If she gets the all clear, we can see about rehoming her."

"Oh, I see," David said. "Bueno."

Their plane was taxied out onto the smaller runway, stopping outside a hangar. It was a small jet, sleek, new, and finished in metallic grey tones. David had never been on a private jet before.

Naz got on first, walking up the steps and squeezing his large frame through the little door. David watched Naz's progress through the windows; he was so tall he had to duck to walk to his seat. He went all the way to the back of the plane.

"After you," Mac said, gesturing to David.

He boarded next, carrying his bag. He glanced at the cockpit with two pilot seats on his left, then walked inside the plane to find a seat. He didn't need to duck as much as Naz, but he had to duck some. There were five passenger seats total; two singles on either side of the plane, each with its own generous window, and a three-seater at the back which Naz was currently sprawled out upon.

David chose a single seat.

As he looked around the interior, he thought it looked like a cross between a limo and a nice car. The seats were cream-coloured leather, smooth as butter, and the interior was bright and clean. It really did feel like sitting in an elongated car.

The Xolo boarded next, with Mac right behind her. David watched the Xolo trot around the cabin, eagerly sniffing the leather seats.

Mac came to sit beside David, on the other single seat. Sonny and Rafe boarded next.

David wondered how they would all fit, before he realised the pair were getting into the cockpit together.

"You're flying the plane?" David asked in surprise.

"Yep," Sonny replied, twisting around in his seat to grin at him. "Why? Do you want a go?"

Naz, seated behind David, uttered a quick string of Arabic.

David recognised a few of the words, recalling the thirty-six hours he'd spent escorting an Iraqi nuclear engineer out of a tight spot in North Africa; he'd heard a similar prayer uttered a few times to relieve anxiety. David didn't have to look at Naz to know the guy was nervous as hell. Was he simply a nervous flyer, or were Sonny and Rafe new to this?

"He's teasing," Mac said. "Can we go home, please?"

"Right you are, Mac," Sonny said. He and Rafe put on headsets and began performing control checks with ease.

It appeared they knew what they were doing, at least. David was relieved to see that.

Mac perched on the edge of her seat and opened a bag. She rooted around looking for things, then produced a collapsible, plastic cereal bowl. "Will one of you grab some water?" she asked.

Miniature water bottles were stashed by each seat. David grabbed one and opened it. He realised what Mac was doing when she put the bowl on the floor, so he poured water in.

The Xolo came over to sniff it, then lapped at the water gratefully.

"Poor little thing," Mac commented. "I might have some beef jerky in my other bag, but that's a bit salty for dogs."

"How long's the flight?" David asked.

"Too long!" Naz piped up.

"That's a point," Mac said. She got up from her seat and went to the cockpit to talk with Sonny and Rafe. The conversation was brief, and when she came back, she said, "We'll make a stop in Miami. I'll give Manny a bell and ask him to fetch some dog food."

"If you feed that dog," Naz piped up again, "it's going to shit on the plane."

"I'll get some doggy bags, then," Mac replied, unfazed.

Naz grumbled in Arabic.

"Who's Manny?" David asked, watching Mac get out her cell phone.

"One of our contacts in Florida," she said, as she typed out a text. "Do you want anything for the flight? It'll be nine-ish hours from Miami to London."

"Maybe some food?" David said.

"We'll get food," Mac said. "Any allergies?"

"No, I'm good," David replied. "I'll eat anything."

She smiled. "I like an easy customer," she said, then pointedly glanced around at Naz.

"What are you looking at me for?" he said, wound up already. "You know I have food allergies! I can't help it! I have a delicate digestive system!"

Mac only smiled and went back to her texting. David could see that this team clearly enjoyed winding each other up.

"Next stop, Miami," Rafe called from the front.

*

The small plane was quieter than David had expected. Obviously, it was a new model, its engine a gentle hum as they flew over the Gulf of Mexico. Had it not been the middle of the night, David would've had a clear view of the sea below. He saw the distant lights of ships and boats, including one large cruise ship lit up like a Christmas tree.

To their right, they passed Guatemala and Cuba, while on their left they passed Louisiana, Alabama, then straight onto Miami, Florida.

Miami was two hours ahead of Mexico, so daybreak was setting in. David got to watch the first rays of the sunrise from his window seat.

"This is your captain speaking," Sonny's voice spoke over the cabin intercom, which was unnecessary because the plane was so small, but funny because he was putting on a smooth, Midwestern American accent. "We are now approaching Miami, Florida. Strap in."

Mac smiled and shook her head. David smiled too. Naz began muttering in Arabic again, praying. The dog had curled up on the floor beside Mac's chair and gone to sleep and remained unbothered.

David watched from the window as they approached land, flying over so much green: the Everglades National Park and only one visible highway through the whole space.

Their destination was the Miami Homestead General Aviation Airport, a small airport between Miami and Homestead. David spotted two runways, with a third runway for ultralight planes.

Their plane banked around to get in line with the runway, and they came in with a smooth landing. David glanced round at Naz to see his reaction, and the poor guy was gripping his seat white-knuckled the entire time. Mac was far more relaxed, and clapped her hands in relaxed applause as they touched down.

"Nicely done, lads," she said.

David had to admit, he was impressed. He could fly certain choppers, but he hadn't tackled planes yet. He wouldn't mind giving it a go some day.

The plane taxied around to a hangar, lit up on the dark grey tarmac. The skyline showed a warm orange in the sunrise. Looked like it would be a hot day in Florida.

Outside on the tarmac, a couple of engineers were ready to top up the plane's fuel and do safety checks, Along with someone else waiting outside for them.

"Oi, oi!" Sonny called through the glass. "Manny's here!"

David looked out the window to see a middle-aged White guy with greying hair, slightly overweight, and dressed like most White dudes in Florida would dress: in loose chinos and a colourful print shirt. He had some bags with him, like he'd been shopping.

The team exited the plane. The little Xolo stretched and turned around in her spot but didn't make moves to get up.

"Better if she stays in here," Mac said. "We're wheels up in thirty."

David nodded.

Outside, he stretched his legs and watched the team interact with this Manny guy. Sonny and Rafe seemed overly familiar with him, slinging arms around his shoulders and asking him how he was.

Manny seemed uncomfortable, like he was nervous.

"Hope you've been keeping out of trouble, my son," Sonny told him.

"What trouble can I get into when you summon me in the

middle of the night?" Manny protested. He was American, that much was clear.

"Did you get the dog food?" Mac asked.

"Yeah, it's all in there." Manny pointed at the bags. "Am I getting reimbursed for this? I had to drive all over the place looking for a store that sold dog supplies at this hour."

"Send the bill to the usual," Rafe said.

"Bills take time," Manny complained. "Why can't you give me some cash now?"

"You can have my pesos," Sonny said, digging in his pocket. "Lads, give him your pesos."

"What am I gonna do with pesos?" Manny protested.

"You can take them, and shut the fuck up," Sonny said casually, offering a wodge of notes to the man. "Do you want the cash or not?"

Manny made a face, like he was torn. Then he made a grab for the cash. "I'll take it," he said urgently. "You know, next time you can use American dollars."

"It'll be our highest priority," Sonny said sarcastically.

David smiled. He figured Manny was some associate of theirs, and the team spent a lot of time busting his balls.

Mac crouched on the ground to root through the bags, inspecting the dog supplies. "Hey," she said, getting David's attention. "Want to try putting these on her?" She held up an adjustable collar and leash.

"Me?" David said with surprise.

"It was your bright idea to bring it along," Sonny piped up. He, Rafe, and Naz were opening bags of takeout to eat—burgers and fries. They smelled delicious.

"Chop, chop," Sonny told him.

David didn't argue. He was the prospect so he would get all

the tasks they didn't want to do. He took the leash and collar and went back aboard the plane.

He knew the saying went that it was best to let sleeping dogs lie, but they had less than thirty minutes on the tarmac, and this would be the only chance for her to do whatever business she needed to do.

"Hey, niña," David murmured, not wanting to startle her. He spoke in Spanish to her, talking softly. He hoped she would cooperate.

Though she did stir when David carefully slipped the collar around her neck, she only regarded him with watchful eyes. The fact she seemed tame made him think she hadn't been a stray after all, and he wondered what her story was.

"Buena, niña," he said, securing the collar but not too tight. He clipped the leash on. "Estupendo. Great."

That had gone surprisingly well.

David got up and gently encouraged her to come with him, which she did. He stepped back out onto the tarmac and smiled smugly when Sonny and the others looked shocked.

"Blimey," Rafe said. "Nice one, mate."

"Oh, well done!" Mac smiled happily. "Bring her over here. I've got a bowl of food ready."

David walked the Xolo over there, and once she noticed the food in a doggy dish, she fell upon it and ate with enthusiasm.

"She must've been so hungry, poor thing," Mac said, still crouched on the ground.

Naz, in between bites of burger, asked, "What if she'd bitten you? You could've gotten rabies."

"I think she's domesticated," David said. "She's fine with the collar." He was still holding the leash, as he didn't want her to go running off if an aircraft startled her.

"Yeah, yeah," Sonny said, taking out a wrapped burger and handing it to David. "Get that down ya. And," he added, addressing the team, "if anyone needs to piss, you'll have to do it in the next twenty minutes. Manny will show you where the bogs are. Won't you, son?"

"Oh, sure!" Manny said sarcastically. "I've got nothing but time! I don't have a bed to get back to or anything."

David detected a little Brooklyn in Manny's accent there. Manny reminded him of the actor, Elliott Gould.

"I think I need a number two," Naz said, which made the team groan en masse.

"We ain't got time for you to take a dump, Nazeem," Sonny told him.

"You said twenty minutes!" Naz replied. "I can go now and have enough time!"

"Oh, for Christ's...Manny?" Sonny gestured at the older man. "Take Naz to the shitter and time him."

David noticed both Mac and Rafe smiling at these proceedings. He smiled too and unwrapped his burger to take a bite. It was tasty.

Manny left with Naz, and the rest of them stood around munching their food in the early morning sun.

The two engineers finished the refuel and gave the thumbs up before they left. "Radio the control tower for your take-off slot," an engineer said.

"Right you are!" Sonny called back. "Cheers, mate."

Mac was still crouched on the ground, feeding the Xolo and putting down a water bowl. She ate a few fries but no burger. "I think you're right, Fresh Meat," she mentioned. "She does seem domesticated."

"Question," David said. "When will I have a name besides

Fresh Meat? Or can you call me David for now?"

"Don't get ahead of yourself, sunshine," Sonny said. He finished up his burger and scrunched the wrapper in his hands. "Right. I'm gonna go yell at Naz to shit faster. You two," he gestured at Rafe and Mac, "watch the newbies." He pointed at David and the dog. "We need a name for the dog an' all."

"Ooh, let's name the dog," Mac said with a grin.

"I was calling her niña," David suggested. "For girl."

"Pick something British!" Sonny instructed (in his accent: Bri'ish).

"How about Nina?" Mac said. "She looks like a Nina."

"You can't call a dog Nina!" Sonny waved a hand at them before walking away. "You're 'opeless, you lot."

"Ignore him," Mac said, glancing at David. Then she smiled down at the Xolo. "Nina."

Chapter Thirteen

Sonny walked across the tarmac toward the building. He didn't go straight in to find Naz and Manny; he had a call to make first.

He took out his phone and went to lurk around the side of the building. With the time difference, it would be nearly eight in the morning.

Sonny called him, and Guv answered after three rings.

"Yes?" Guv said.

"Guv, it's Sonny. On our merry way home as we speak. Job is a wrap."

"Good," Guv said. "And the package?"

"On board," Sonny confirmed. "You were right. He was eager to flip."

"Good," Guv repeated. "Keep me up to speed after you land. You may inform the rest of the team they've earned a short rest period. I'll be in touch."

"Er, right," Sonny said. He was confused. "Sorry, er, where am I dropping the new recruit after we land?"

"The package is in your charge, Sonny," Guv said. "Roll out the red carpet. Shepherd's orders."

"Er, oh," Sonny said. "Right."

"And keep me in the loop," Guv said, then ended the call.

Sonny immediately selected Shepherd's contact, then called her next. He was starting to think there had been a breakdown of communication somewhere.

She answered on the second ring. "This better be important, I'm busy," she said, her tone ice cold. Sonny pictured her either getting her hair done by stylists or sitting at the head of a MI6 conference table, busting balls and intimidating the stuffy old men of British Intelligence. Maybe both things were happening at once. They were in Sonny's mind, anyway.

"Sorry, ma'am," Sonny said. "Wanted to be clear on something…" He purposefully trailed off to annoy her.

"Go on," she said.

"You have your new recruit," Sonny said. "So, after we get in, what am I doing with him? Drop him off at HQ, or…?"

"No, no," Shepherd said. "That's too much shop at once, especially for someone who's come in from the cold. Ease him in with a softly, softly approach. Just a couple of days or so."

"Okay," Sonny said. "And where am I easing him in?" He couldn't help making the pun.

"I don't care, Sonny," Shepherd bit out. "Use some initiative, would you? Book him a hotel room. Take him to your place. Make him feel welcome. Roll out the red carpet."

"Yes, ma'am," Sonny said. "Quick question. If I was to use a hotel, can I pop it on expenses? And what about food? Wining and dining an' the like. Travel don't come cheap neither. Maybe you can slip me a tidy bonus for all these extra expenses?"

"Don't push it, Sonny," she said firmly.

"One bonus would be easier than all these receipts I'm going to claim on expenses," Sonny told her. He smirked because they were on the phone and she couldn't see him.

There was a beat of silence, and then he heard Shepherd exhale softly.

"All right," she agreed. "I'll send you one sum to your account today for all your expenses. Anything over that, you can pay for yourself."

Sonny raised his fist in a silent gesture of victory. "Thank you, ma'am," he said. "Much obliged."

"He's in your charge, Sonny," Shepherd said. "If you lose him, or if anything goes wrong, I'll be holding *you* accountable."

"Understood, ma'am," he replied. "There shouldn't be any problems."

"There better not be," she said, and ended the call.

*

The team took turns to dog sit Nina and visit the toilets before take-off. In those thirty minutes they were on the tarmac, Nina managed a small pee on the ground, but nothing else. Mac said she probably hadn't eaten enough to poop yet.

"She'll poop after all that food you gave her," Naz said to Mac.

"She seems house-trained," Mac replied. "She's so polite. Look at her."

Nina sat there quietly, staring up at Naz with her big ears pricked.

"I suppose she is cute," Naz said, then turned away to board the plane.

"I knew you'd crack!" Mac called after him.

"She could still have rabies!" Naz called back, disappearing inside the jet.

"He's not wrong," Sonny said. "Right, everyone back on. Chop, chop!"

They trooped back on board. Manny had long gone, and the only person to wave them off was one of the ground crew in a high-vis vest, signalling which way to take off.

David sat back in his original seat, with a good view out the window in the morning sunlight.

Sonny and Rafe were in the pilot's chairs, performing checks. Naz murmured urgently in Arabic at the back of the plane. Mac settled into her seat, and this time Nina jumped onto her lap and curled up.

"Aw, look!" Mac said softly. "I'm taking a photo."

"You still don't know if that dog is clean," Naz said. "She could have fleas."

"Oh, hush up, Naz," Mac said gently. "She doesn't even have hair. I'm sure she doesn't have fleas."

David chuckled. "If she did, we'd know by now."

The plane powered along the runway and took off smoothly. David removed his hat and gazed out the window. Port side, Biscayne Bay and the city of Miami twinkled below them in the sunlight.

They flew over the small island of Grand Bahama, home of Freeport and Pelican Point. Great Abaco curled around it. Then it was out over the North Atlantic Ocean. David saw fishing vessels and more cruise ships down below, then nothing but blue glittering waters as far as the eye could see.

They hadn't been in the air all that long, barely making a dent into their long flight. Mac leaned back in her seat and closed her eyes. David heard soft rumbly snores behind him, signalling Naz had fallen asleep.

David was still wide awake, probably from all the adrenaline.

Rafe pushed his seat back along the floor runner and climbed out of the co-pilot chair. He made his way into the cabin. David thought he wanted something from Mac or Naz, but Rafe approached David's seat first.

"Switch," he said. "Go see the captain."

"Is everything okay?" David asked.

"Yeah." Rafe smiled tiredly. "I just need to sleep."

"Oh. Sure." David grabbed his hat and got out of his chair. He set his hat back on his head and moved his way up front.

Out of the front windows the view was all blue sky and fluffy white clouds.

"Awright, sunshine," Sonny said softly. "Pull up a pew."

David didn't want to knock into anything, so he performed a visual check of the space first. The last thing he wanted to do was step on anything important or flip a switch he shouldn't be flipping. Luckily, the footwells were spacious, given the plane's long nose, and all the important things were up front on the dash or situated on the gear box.

Carefully, he slid into the chair. "How does it go forward?" he asked, looking around for a lever.

"Right there," Sonny replied. He reached out to point at the lower part of the chair.

David found it and shimmied his seat forward. He stretched out his legs into the footwell below the dash and sat back to have a good look around.

"Ever flown one?" Sonny asked, giving him a sidelong smirk.

"No," David replied. "Only choppers."

"Love a good chopper," Sonny said in amusement. "But I think these jets are the easiest to fly."

"Whose is it?" David asked. "Your agency's?"

"Not exactly." Sonny chuckled. "It's a civilian aircraft. Belongs to some rich geezer our boss has on speed dial. So don't break nothin', and don't get used to it because usually we're all suffering through economy travel with the rest of the riff-raff."

David smiled. "Are there many flights on the job?"

"A fair bit," Sonny said. "It's usually Europe, nice and quick flights."

"Yeah, this is a long flight," David mused.

"That's why you're up here," Sonny said. "Let the regular humans get their kip. Meanwhile, I'll show you how to fly this bird."

"Great." David was eager to learn. He'd been eyeing the radar screen right in front of him with interest.

Sonny went through the whole dashboard with him one instrument at a time. He talked quieter than his normal level, which showed he did care about his team getting some shut-eye.

David listened attentively. They covered the radar, altitude, fuel, comms, wings and flaps. Sonny chuckled deviously when he said the word "flaps," like a schoolboy who'd only recently discovered what swears were. David asked questions when he had them. It did seem relatively easy to grasp; the dash wasn't even that big. This jet was single engine, and some new form of hybrid.

Sonny explained the mileage they could do if they cruised slowly at two hundred and eighty miles per hour, or they could do less miles if they accelerated to three hundred and fifty miles per hour. To conserve fuel, they had to maintain a steady speed, flying at around thirty thousand feet.

He tested David on what he'd learned, and he passed, so he let David take over flying. He made a quick joke about David touching his joystick, which caught David off guard and made him snicker.

They spoke quietly, the cockpit becoming a close and intimate environment with just the two of them. The rest of the team were silent, most likely asleep. David's heart hammered in his chest as he took over the control stick and kept the plane steady, but it was an exciting feeling. He watched the levels on the instruments in front of him and listened to Sonny's instructions.

The sky was calm, making it an easy cruise. Still, David was proud of himself.

"Nicely done, sunshine," Sonny murmured, watching closely. "Keep 'er steady. Now, we're about to pass a hot air current, so…"

They both reached for the same instrument at the same time, their fingers brushing for the briefest moment. Sonny's skin was warm.

David moved his hand away, letting Sonny take over the flying. They passed through the air current with some mild turbulence, and then it was back to smooth sailing.

"Sorry," David said.

"No, you're fine," Sonny told him, flashing David a sidelong smile. "You're doing just fine."

Chapter Fourteen

The strong winds over the Atlantic required focused and skillful piloting, and Sonny had to guide David through it. There wasn't much chance to chat during all of that. David hoped there would be time for questions and answers once they landed.

The sun set over the water hours into their flight, turning the sky and sea beautiful shades of orange and gold.

Behind them in the cabin, the rest of the team were fast asleep. So was Nina the Xolo. David had thought he'd become sleepy, especially after all that adrenalin from an Op, but he wasn't feeling drowsy yet. Maybe the adrenaline was still in him, or maybe his endurance was part of his...new DNA.

It was true he hadn't needed as much sleep since the lab, but he'd put that down to anxiety.

Sonny, too, was wide awake. If he'd been awake as long as David, they were both approaching twenty-four hours.

They still had hours to go, and as they maintained their

course northeast, they flew into darker skies. In the far distance on their right, the twinkling lights of coastal towns in Portugal and Spain spread out into the water like so many stars.

They had reached Europe.

"Am I landing this bird?" David asked Sonny.

"I can wake Rafe up if you want?" he replied.

David didn't want to bow out so easily. "No, I'm good," he said. "I was just asking."

"I'll do most of it," Sonny said. "You do as I say, and we'll be golden."

"You're the captain," David told him.

They flew on, guiding the plane amid strong winds. A few scattered shipping vessels were visible down below, as were some lights across the distant coastlines of Ireland to their left, and France to their right. The blackness up ahead was now interspersed by lights, signalling land.

As they aimed for it, David asked, "Which part do we fly over first? I'm curious."

"Southwest," Sonny said. "Penzance will be below us in a minute. As in *The Pirates of Penzance*."

"I've heard of it," David said. He wished it was brighter so he could see England below.

Sonny had the headset on, and sporadically replied to the air traffic control communication. "Copy, Control Tower. Destination is Luton," Sonny said.

"I thought we were going to London?" David asked him.

"We are," Sonny replied. "Luton is north of London. Small airport there. Calmer than the big one."

David nodded. He noticed they'd been using smaller airports throughout this trip. Probably easier with a private jet stuffed with firearms and an illegal, such as himself.

They flew over Britain, city lights twinkling all around them in the dark.

"There's London now," Sonny pointed out. "Should be able to see some landmarks."

As they were cruising steady, David took a moment to gaze out the windows. He did indeed spot some landmarks on the Thames River: Tower Bridge (the one that opened up) and the big wheel called the London Eye. David was excited to see a new city as he had never been this side of Europe before.

Within minutes, they left the city of London behind them and flew north to Luton Airport.

The hours of calm flying were over. Now they had to land the plane, David's heart rate picked up. Sonny's voice was calm as he took the joystick and guided David on which controls to check; altitude, lights, flaps, and then wheels. He knew Sonny was doing most of the work, and he appreciated the lesson in flying.

The lights of the runway were laid out ahead of them in the dark. Sonny spoke calmly but rapidly to the control tower. David watched him carefully guide the plane in as winds outside buffeted them. They descended quickly and landed with a gentle bump on the short runway.

"Yes!" David exclaimed.

"Look, you drive her over there," Sonny told David, pointing at the window.

Up ahead, David saw signallers on the tarmac.

"Aim for them, but don't run 'em over," he said.

David chuckled. "I'll try not to."

While he was doing that, Sonny spoke first to the control tower, confirming their landing, and then he pressed the intercom for the cabin. "This is your captain speaking," he said brightly in his regular accent. "We have now arrived in London, England, where the local time is nearly eight o' clock, meaning that we missed *EastEnders*."

Behind them, David heard chuckles from Mac and Rafe.

Naz let out a groggy groan. "Are we there?" he asked. "I slept through the landing? Alhamdulillah!"

"Because it was such a smooth landing!" Sonny called out. "Next time I'll make it bumpy." He glanced at David with a wink.

"No!" Naz wailed. "Don't you dare!"

"We could prescribe you something for the flight?" Mac asked Naz.

"No, I don't want to take drugs for a flight!" Naz protested. "That's your answer to everything!"

"Here we go," Rafe said, sounding tired.

Sonny ignored the team bickering, looking out the window to make sure David was steering the plane where they needed.

David was doing okay, in his opinion, but he didn't mind being supervised. It had been a while since he'd flown anything, and this was his first time flying and parking a plane.

When they got to their designated parking spot, Sonny told him, "Well done." They went through end of flight checks and opened the door for the team to exit.

"I need the toilet!" Naz announced dramatically.

Both David and Sonny glanced around to see him bustle through the door first, and outside on the tarmac he began to jog to the nearest building.

"Can someone please go make sure he doesn't get lost?" Sonny said.

Rafe yawned. "I'll go." He exited the plane at a more leisurely pace.

"Is Naz new to field work?" David asked Sonny.

Sonny laughed. "Not quite. He's been with us about eighteen months now. But he wasn't trained for it."

"What was he trained for?" David asked.

"Nothing." Sonny removed his headset and set it on the dash. "He's a computer hacker who got caught and would've been sent down for a long stint in prison, but our Guv saw potential in him."

David nodded. "I get it now. He seems kind of nervous."

"Yeah, he's a big ball of anxiety," Sonny said.

"Can someone take Nina outside?" Mac called from the cabin. "She needs to spend a penny."

Sonny twisted round to look at her. "Can't you do it?"

She looked at him pointedly. "We better do your thing. You're due in four hours."

"Oh, right." Sonny glanced at David. "Take the dog, Fresh Meat. We'll be out in a second."

David had questions, but he kept quiet. He moved his chair back so he could get out of the cockpit, crouching in the cabin as he reached out a hand so Mac could pass the leash to him.

"Come on, Nina," he said to the Xolo. "Let's go."

Leading her with the leash, they exited the plane. It was good to be out in fresh air again. As he stood on the tarmac, waiting for Nina, he looked around at the small apron they were on. Given its size and the other private jets situated here, David guessed this section was for private charters. There appeared to be more airport off to the south, and dark roads beyond chain link fences. All was quiet, considering.

The sky was dark but still had some inky blue in it from the last of summer daylight. The stars were out in full force.

Nina spent ages sniffing around before choosing a spot to squat and pee, and during that time David was approached by someone who wasn't ground crew. She was a gorgeous, slim Black woman, maybe thirty or younger, in smart business attire and heeled shoes. Her hair was braided neatly and drawn back in an up-do. In her arms, she carried a manilla envelope, with a small tablet on top.

She glanced down at the tablet before looking David in the eyes and smiling. "Are you Cortez?" she asked, her accent crisp British.

David was wary. He'd been caught here on foreign soil, with nobody else around. She could've been sent by anyone. David did a quick assessment of her and noted things like the clothes she wore (designer), the height of her spiked heels (high), and her long nail tips (French manicure), and he trusted his gut instinct that this woman wasn't here to harm him.

"Yes," he replied.

"Compliments of PRISM," she said, offering out the manila package to him.

David held Nina's leash in one hand and accepted the envelope in the other. "What is it?" he asked her.

"Welcome pack. Standard issue." She smiled and held up her tablet to take a photo of his face, temporarily blinding him with the flash. "Welcome to London," she said, then casually walked off.

David blinked and was still seeing spots when Sonny joined him on the tarmac.

"Wassat?" he asked.

"Er, a welcome pack," David said. "Someone gave it to me."

"Someone? Who?" Sonny asked. He had a hand on the back of his right hip, rubbing himself through his clothes. David assumed he had a cramp from sitting.

"She didn't give me a name," David replied. "Black woman. Thirty? Nice-looking. Braided hair."

"Oh, probably Dinah," Sonny said. "Aide for the bosses." He got his phone out but glanced at David before unlocking the screen. "Go get your stuff. We'll be gone soon."

"Okay," David said. He looked down at Nina, who had finished peeing but looked like she might do more. "You wanna hold this?" He offered the leash to Sonny.

"Suppose I'll have to," Sonny said, and took it.

He seemed engrossed in his phone, so David left him to it. He boarded the plane again and went to fetch his bag.

Mac was still in there, packing up some medical supplies. David saw a needle being disposed of in a small plastic tub for sharp items.

The injection.

David put two and two together; Sonny had been rubbing at his lower back, right above his hip. He must have had an injection there.

Mac noticed him looking, but she didn't say anything.

David said nothing. Forefront on his mind was the fear of having to rely on injections himself. If Sonny was to be believed, this was the method his agency used to keep him in line.

Now he was even more cautious of what was inside that welcome pack. What if there was a sharp item in there, ready to prick him?

David decided to look. He took out his knife and sliced the top of the envelope open. He peered inside, finding the contents innocuous enough: a new phone, a paper leaflet, and a plastic card inside a thin wallet.

David took out the card first to examine it. Oyster. It wasn't a credit card, that was for sure.

"That's for public transport in and around London," Mac said, watching him. "Buses. The Tube."

"Oh, okay." David put it back. Sounded useful.

The phone was sure to have tracking on it, David assumed. He'd go through it later.

"What!" Sonny shouted outside. "Are you 'avin' a laugh?"

"Oh, what now?" Mac murmured. She gathered her bags together and exited the plane.

David threw the envelope inside his bag, put away his knife, and followed her out.

Sonny was still staring at his phone screen, standing while Nina the dog sat next to him. Nina hadn't done anything offensive, not to David's eyes, so whatever had offended Sonny was on his phone.

"What's up?" Mac asked. She took the leash from Sonny, taking charge of Nina again.

"Nothing," Sonny grumbled. He locked his phone and shoved it in his pocket. "Stingy bastards."

"Grindr?" Mac quipped, which earned a sardonic smile from Sonny.

"I fuckin' wish it was Grindr," he replied. "Right!" He clapped his hands together. "I'm going for a slash. You two stay put. We're supposed to hand over this plane and nobody's fuckin' 'ere yet. Bloody typical."

He turned and stomped off toward the nearest building. David shared a look with Mac.

"Yes, waiting around for things is most of what our job entails," she said, smiling.

David shrugged. "I'm used to that," he said. "What happens after the plane is returned?"

"We've all got a couple of rest days, I believe," she replied. "Did they give you a phone in that pack?"

"Er, yeah," David said.

"I'll give you my number," Mac said, getting out her phone. "If you need anything or want to see Nina, feel free to call me."

David opened his bag and took the phone out. It looked new, but it wasn't boxed. He swiped the screen to check. The phone was loaded with apps and showed a full battery. Clearly, it had been set up and curated for him.

David opened the contacts and saw that one contact had already been added: Guv. That would be their boss, he assumed.

"Which model did you get?" Mac asked, glancing at the phone. "Oh, they're all right, that one. I wish I'd stuck with it instead of switching."

She was making small talk, David noticed. Trying to put him at ease, perhaps.

He made a new contact for her, and they exchanged numbers.

"I'll put your name in as Mac, then?" David asked, a gentle probe.

She smiled at him. "It's Lindsay. Lindsay McTaggert. The Mac part is a general nickname for anyone Scottish."

"Oh, you're Scottish?" David asked. That would explain her fair complexion.

"Yes, but we moved when I was little. Grew up a wee bit lower down in North Yorkshire."

"I don't know where that is," David replied. "But it sounds very nice."

This made Mac chuckle. "It is nice. Listen, I'll take Nina. I can pop her into the lab, have some tests done. But my guess is she's in the clear. Seems healthy to me."

"What's gonna happen to her?" David asked.

"If she's a normal dog?" Mac shrugged. "Find a nice home for her? I'd like a dog, but I'm not really home enough to justify getting one."

And David didn't have a home here, so he couldn't offer.

"I think she was someone's pet in Mexico," he said. "Is there any way we could find out?"

"I'll look into it," Mac said. "Or tech support can look into it. If anyone posted about her online, they'll find it."

"Thanks, Mac," David told her. "Lindsay," he added. "I really appreciate you taking care of her."

"Not at all, she's been good as gold," Mac said.

Their conversation was interrupted by some ground crew arriving, along with a harried White man in a suit and glasses, carrying a briefcase with him. He looked like a lawyer type.

"Ah, this is our sign-off," Mac murmured to David. "He works for the plane's owner. Once the handover is done, we can be on our way home."

Chapter Fifteen

The last thirty minutes spent in the airport was a rush of activity: signing the plane over, getting all their luggage off, trips to the toilet while also dog-sitting Nina.

Once all that was done, they were free to go home, as Mac had said.

David wasn't sure where home was for him, exactly. He guessed maybe a hotel. The problem was, he didn't have funds. He'd handed over his pesos to Manny in Miami, and that was all David had because he was legally deceased and without a bank account.

They all walked down a dark footpath toward the car lot. A large passenger plane took off overhead, engines roaring, and David gazed up at it absently.

"Want a lift home, Naz?" Mac offered to him. "Be quicker than the train."

"Are you bringing the dog?" Naz asked dubiously.

"Yes," Mac said.

"I'll take the train," Naz said.

Both Sonny and Rafe laughed.

"Bloody 'ell, bruv," Rafe said. "It's only a little dog."

"And you hate public transport," Sonny added. "All those well-worn seats and rando's talking, nobody wearing a mask, not to mention the pee stains, the puke stains…"

"Ah! Shut up!" Naz huffed. "Fine! You can drive me home."

"I'm so honoured," Mac said sarcastically.

"Well, keep the dog on another seat," Naz said.

They reached the lot, and he and Mac headed off to the left to find her car, taking Nina the dog with them. The goodbyes among the team were brief: head nods, a quick "Ta-ra!"

"Did I drive?" Rafe said to Sonny, looking around. "It's been so long, I can't even remember where I parked."

"You drove, and it's over there," Sonny said, pointing right.

"I'm bloody hungry," Rafe said.

"An' me," Sonny replied. "Grub?"

Rafe nodded. "Grub."

Sonny smiled at David. "Hungry, Fresh Meat?"

David nodded. "I could eat."

They found Rafe's car, a black Range Rover, and got in. David elected to sit in the back, letting Sonny sit up front with his team-mate. Rafe drove them out of the car lot, and after a minor drama to find the correct ticket, the barrier lifted, and they drove away.

It was 9:00 PM, dark, with only the road and sporadic vehicle lights to look at. Nothing scenic.

Rafe put the radio on, the station playing golden oldies from the '80s as they drove along a motorway. David gazed out the window, feeling a sense of excitement and something else.

Something like relief.

He hadn't expected that, especially given that a new agency was now asserting its dominance over him, but... He did feel relieved. He wanted to stop running and he hoped he'd found a way to do that now.

*

The drive took around an hour, so it was ten at night when they all got out of the car.

Rafe had parked in a small car park with scant light; David was willing to bet it was for staff, given its size and location, boxed in by dinky red brick buildings boasting multiple air-conditioning units.

They exited the car park and walked out onto the street between two of the buildings. David saw he had been correct, and they'd parked behind an Indian restaurant.

Out on the street, it was all concrete road, more brick buildings, and a few cars driving past in the dark. It felt like a ghost town: no vibrancy, no street vendors, not even any pedestrians.

"I'm so hungry," Rafe announced, rubbing his hands with glee. He led the way to the Indian restaurant. Its windows had red drapes drawn across so David couldn't see in, but the lights were on inside.

The sign above the door read in golden letters: HANGRI-LA. David looked at the space in front of the H and saw the faint outline of a letter S. When he glanced round at Sonny, the other man was smirking.

"Yeah, the *S* fell off," he said. "Hangry is funny, though. That's why ol' Rizwan didn't bother to get it fixed."

David smiled back. "Hope the menu is better than the sign."

"Don't you worry about the food, sunshine," Sonny replied.

"You're in for a treat."

Inside, the restaurant was the opposite of the dull street: Hangri-La was warm, colourful, vibrant, filled with enticing smells from cooked food, and plenty of happy customers seated at the tables. The chatter was smothered by lively Indian music playing on hidden speakers.

A South Asian man in a pressed shirt and slacks, and neatly combed hair, spotted them immediately. He looked to be around forty or so.

"Ah! Sonny! Rafe! My best customers!" he exclaimed and made a beeline for them. "I ain't seen you for weeks! I thought you had abandoned me, innit?"

He sounded even more London than Rafe and Sonny put together.

"Don't be silly, bruv," Rafe responded, as the two men enthusiastically shook hands and patted each other on the arms like old friends. "This is our favourite spot. You know that. We'll always be back."

"Too right, mate," Sonny said, shaking the man's hand next. "We came straight down as soon as we could. We missed ya."

"Excellent! Glad to hear it, lads," Riz replied, grinning. He noticed David and offered out his hand. "And who is this dashing gent?"

David automatically took Riz's hand but stopped short of saying his name. When he glanced up, he saw a brief look of panic pass between Sonny and Rafe, like they remembered they hadn't given David a proper name to use yet.

David smiled wryly. "A pleasure," he said politely, shaking the man's hand.

"Oh, an American!" Riz said in delight. "Excellent! What's your name?"

"Dash," Sonny said, obviously taking the inspiration from what Riz had used. "This is Dash."

"Well, that's a fitting name!" Riz exclaimed joyfully. He patted David's hand before relinquishing it, and David wondered if he was being flirted with.

"Yes, isn't it," Rafe said flatly. He sent Sonny a curious look.

Sonny rubbed a hand over his stubble and avoided eye contact. From David's point of view, it was an amusingly awkward moment.

"Table for three?" Riz asked, either not noticing the odd moment or choosing not to comment on it. "Or is Naz coming?"

"Nah, not tonight, mate," Sonny told him. "Only us three amigos, but we'll eat for four."

"I have a special table!" Riz said. "Follow me."

*

David hadn't expected the restaurant to be so spacious, given its low ceilings and small rooms. He wondered if the building used to be residential and had been converted into a restaurant years ago.

They were shown to a cosy back room set with one generous dining table, and they had the whole space to themselves. It was closer to the kitchen, judging from the amazing smells wafting by.

Before they'd even taken a seat, Sonny asked Riz to bring them drinks, starters, and side dishes.

"Bring it all in, mate," he said. "Give our American a taste of everything."

"Coming right up!" Riz announced, a big grin on his face.

Rafe sat down, and David followed his lead. They picked up menus from the table.

Sonny remained standing. "Order whatever you want, lads.

It's on me tonight. Just gonna nip round to the cashpoint, innit?"

"Riz takes cards, bruv," Rafe said.

Sonny shrugged. "Everyone likes cash, bruv. Besides, I need some currency on me." He exited the room.

Rafe shook his head and opened his menu.

David did the same. As he perused the items, he mentioned quietly, "I think I prefer Dash to Fresh Meat."

Rafe chuckled. "If you ask me nicely, I might tell you what I used to call Sonny when he first joined my squadron."

David lowered his menu. This he had to hear. "Oh, please," he said, barely hiding a chuckle. "I would love to hear that."

Rafe smiled too. He looked around, to check the coast was clear, then he leaned in close and murmured, "Scallywag."

"Seriously?" David asked.

Rafe nodded. "Got right on his tits, it did."

David filed this piece of intel away for later use. "Noted. Thanks."

"Li'l streak of piss," Rafe went on. "Came swaggering in fresh out of school. That were eleven years ago. Time flies."

"You've known each other eleven years?" David asked.

Rafe nodded. "I'm ten years older than Sonny," he said. "Oldest member of the team. I made some noises about retirement, now they're bringing you on. Looks like my wish may come true. Funny." He exhaled softly. "Now I'm feeling nostalgic."

David hadn't expected all of this to come tumbling out. Maybe it was the jet lag talking.

Since they were alone, with nobody listening in, David asked, "How do SAS guys go from that to doing what you do now?"

"It's special ops, innit?" Rafe said. "But if you're talking about the unusual op we just did, that's all down to Toff, Sonny's cousin. She got us on board. I'm sure you'll meet her soon. I agreed to come on with Sonny because the pay was better, and the risks were supposed to be less hazardous than regular duties."

David wasn't entirely sure what to make of that confession. Going off their last mission, which was his only experience of the job so far, it certainly felt hazardous enough.

*

The food, David was pleased to discover, was quite delicious. The waiters, a pair of younger men in long black shirts with gold bands down the front, presented plate after plate and tray after tray of starters and main courses. The smells were amazing. David tried multiple dishes, and though he had an appetite, he was unsure they'd be able to finish everything that kept arriving to their table.

Rafe ate a couple of starter dishes, then his choice of curry with naan. He ate like a regular person.

Sonny ate a lot. Which was a relief to witness, because since breaking free of the lab David had noticed his own appetite increase. Sometimes he couldn't even keep up with his appetite; he had to eat at regular intervals, or the hunger consumed him. As the team hadn't eaten anything since Miami over ten hours ago, they were all hungry. Sonny ate for three men, easily. David could see why Rizwan said they were his best customers.

"How's the food, Dash?" Sonny asked, smirking at him across the table.

"Yeah, love it," David replied. "I could eat here every day."

Sonny laughed. "That's the spirit, son."

They had plenty of beer to wash it all down—new brands to David. The flavoured yoghurt smoothies were called lassi. Perfect to wash down the spicy curries.

"Is this Indian food?" David asked.

"Some of it, yeah," Sonny replied. "Rizwan and the boys are Pakistani."

David nodded. "I'm coming back here, for sure."

"Too right," Sonny said. They shared a smile across the table.

"There you go," Rafe mumbled, "replacing me already. Not even out the door yet."

Both Sonny and David looked at him. Rafe picked up his beer bottle and took a long drink.

"What was that, Raffers?" Sonny asked him casually.

"I see what's going on," Rafe said. He set down his bottle and went to pick up his fork. His grasp was sloppy.

David realised he was probably drunk on top of the jet lag. He shot Sonny a look of concern, but Sonny didn't seem worried.

"What's wrong?" he asked Rafe. "Apart from you sagging into your curry?"

"I can't keep up," Rafe said. "Too old."

Yeah, he was drunk.

"Oh, you're in one of those moods," Sonny said to Rafe. "Is this a good or bad time to mention that you missed a visit from the princess earlier?"

"Di?" Rafe perked up. "Where?"

"She did a fly-by," Sonny replied. "Welcome wagon for Fresh Meat, I mean, Dash."

"Oh, she's gone?" Rafe sagged down again. "She's out of my league anyway."

"Don't say that, mate," Sonny said. "I've seen Dinah giving you the eye. You should cheer up; she's probably watching us now."

"No, she ain't," Rafe said. "And she'd be watching you, not me."

"She watches all of us," Sonny said. "Go on. Do a sexy dance for her."

"No," Rafe said.

"Want me to do one for you?" Sonny offered.

David felt like he was at a tennis match watching the two of them go back and forth, and things were starting to heat up. Sexy dancing? David would like to see it.

"Rafe, shall I do it?" Sonny prompted.

"No," Rafe sighed. "The curtains are drawn, you plum. Nobody's seeing anyone's dance moves."

"Nah, it shows up on thermal imaging," Sonny retorted. "She'd be watching and thinking, who is this sexy fella with the slick moves, innit? Go on, Raffers. Give her a dance."

Rafe snorted. "Yeah, no." He sat back in his chair and looked around, like he was contemplating leaving. "Got another bird to see anyway," he said, moving up from his chair. He took the tablecloth with him, not seeming to realise.

Sonny and David both shot forward to grab the cloth, pulling it back before Rafe caused a mess.

"Don't take the bloody table with you," Sonny told him.

Rafe stood still, blinking slowly.

David looked at Sonny pointedly. "He's drunk," he mouthed.

Sonny nodded. He took his cell phone out. "Let me call you a cab, bruv. Put your head down for a few hours, you'll feel right as rain."

"No, no," Rafe said, swaying on his feet. "I'm fine. Gonna go...hit the town. See my bird."

"Uh-huh, right," Sonny said, not sounding convinced. He wiped his mouth with the napkin, then rose from the table. "Keep an eye on him," he told David. "I'll be back in a jiffy."

David nodded.

Rafe was starting to slump, like he might fall asleep on his feet. At least he wasn't going anywhere.

Sonny exited the room, and David saw Riz meet him through the open doorway. "Riz, mate," Sonny said in hushed tones. "Can you bag the rest to go? I gotta get the old man home."

"Yeah, sure," Riz replied. He signalled to his wait staff, and they trooped in to collect the dishes.

In no time at all, their food had been boxed up inside two large paper bags, and placed on the table. David didn't have any cash on him and assumed Sonny had paid already because nobody asked them for payment.

Riz came back in to inform David that Sonny had the car out front. "You take him," Riz said, indicating Rafe. "I'll take these." He picked up the bags of food.

"Great," David murmured. He'd done his fair share of walking drunk friends home in the past, but it was different with someone he didn't know well.

David cautiously put his hands on Rafe to steer him toward the door. "This way," he said gently but firmly.

"Are we going?" Rafe asked, perking up. "Paint the town red!"

"Yeah," David agreed to get him out the door. "That's right."

Outside in the street, Sonny had brought the car right up to the restaurant's front door. He got out of the driver's side and opened the passenger door.

"Pour him in," he instructed David.

While David struggled to fold a drunk Rafe into the passenger side, Sonny stood there with Riz watching, and they both giggled. Rafe was like an octopus, arms everywhere, all floppy limbed and hard to wrangle. David managed to get him in and buckled the seat belt on.

"Nicely done," Sonny said.

David stood back on the curb and had to bite his lip against cussing.

"That was fucking funny," Riz commented. He handed the bags of food to Sonny. "Always a pleasure, lads. Come back soon, right?"

"We certainly will, my son," Sonny told him. He took the bags and placed them on the back seat. "'Ere, Dash," he said to David. "Go guard the food. Don't let them spill."

David went around and got into the back. He shut the door after him and buckled his seat belt. Rafe appeared to be asleep already.

"What now?" he asked, as Sonny got into the driver's seat.

"Now, we go drop off Sleeping Beauty," Sonny replied. "Oi, bruv," he said, shaking the man's shoulder to rouse him. "Where do you want dropping off? Wife? Mum? Or sister?"

"Ex-wife," Rafe corrected.

"My apologies, but you're not divorced yet," Sonny replied. "Is that who you want to see? Wife and kids?"

"No," Rafe groaned. "No, take me to Sharice."

"Who the fuck's Sharice?" Sonny asked.

"Was seein' her," Rafe murmured. "Mmm, Sharice." His eyes closed and he had a big smile on his face, like he was remembering. "The tits on 'er, Sonny. You should see 'em."

"Yeah, not my cuppa tea, mate," Sonny replied. "I'm sure they're lovely tits though."

The whole thing was a lot funnier now that Sonny had to deal with Rafe, so David chuckled to himself.

"I love her," Rafe declared. "Gonna marry her next."

"You're still married," Sonny muttered and started the car. "I'm taking you to your sister, Casanova."

"No, I want Sharice," Rafe protested.

"Tough cheese, mate," Sonny replied. "I'm sure this Sharice bird don't want you turning up sloshed on her doorstep at midnight anyway. Sleep it off, and you can go see her tomorrow." He put the car in gear, checked the road, and drove away.

Chapter Sixteen

Sonny drove them through London. David saw grey buildings, a few statues, and more trees than he'd expected to see. Still not many people around.

David didn't know which part of London they were in, as the focus was on getting Rafe to his sister's front door in one piece. Sonny parked the car on a residential street, in front of a town-house nestled in a row of terraced houses. Most of the windows were dark, and David was aware that plenty of people would be sleeping peacefully inside those houses.

Rafe, on the other hand, had decided to wake up and start talking loudly. He kept talking about going to Seven Veils, which David guessed was a strip joint. He and Sonny had a job on their hands walking Rafe up the front steps to the door, where it was opened by a tall, curvy Black woman in her thirties, her long hair tied up neatly in a colourful satin scarf like she was ready for bed. She had a furious expression on her pretty face.

"Awright, Chloe, love," Sonny greeted her. "Special delivery."

"The fuck did you do to him, Sonny?" she demanded.

"Me?" Sonny's voice went up in pitch at the accusation. "'Scuse me. I'm only bringing him home safe and sound."

"After binge drinking, no doubt," Chloe accused, taking over from them and hustling Rafe through the door.

"We had a curry!" Sonny protested. "He literally had *two* beers. I didn't know he'd turned into a lightweight, did I?"

She gave Sonny a hard look, then glanced at David. Likely trying to get the new guy's opinion.

"That's what happened, ma'am," David said politely. "We brought him straight here after our meal."

Her face changed instantly, morphing from pissed off into a bright smile. "Ooh, are you American?" she asked, her brown eyes twinkling.

"Yes, ma'am," David replied. "We're very sorry for disturbing your evening."

"Oh, not at all," Chloe said, leaning on the door jamb to grin at David. Behind her, Rafe stumbled into the coat stand then apologised to it. Chloe ignored him. "Would you like to come in for a cuppa?" she asked David. "I'll put the kettle on."

"That's very kind of you, ma'am," David replied, his eyes flicking over to Sonny who had the most shocked expression on his face. David savoured the moment.

"Come on in," Chloe said to David, and stood aside for him. Behind her, Rafe tripped over some shoes in the hallway and fell down...in slow motion.

Chloe continued to ignore him.

"Erm, excuse me, love," Sonny interjected. "Your esteemed brother has gone arse over tit. Perhaps you'd best look after him before you go batting your eyelash extensions at my new apprentice."

Chloe fixed Sonny with an unimpressed look. "Oh, fuck off, Sonny," she said.

"Apprentice?" David said in protest.

"Can someone help me up?" Rafe said from the floor.

"Mum?" a child's voice called from upstairs.

Chloe whipped round to call out, "Go back to bed!"

The ruckus caused lights to switch on in the houses left and right of them. An old White lady in a pale nightgown, closely resembling a Victorian ghost, stuck her curler-laden head out of an upstairs window. "Oi!" she shouted down at them. "Pipe down! Typical of you lot, comin' over 'ere, an' makin' all that racket! I been here fifty-two years!"

"Oh, piss off, Karen!" Chloe shouted up at her.

"Yeah, piss off, Karen!" Sonny shouted in agreement. "Aren't you late for the Titanic?"

"Disgraceful! I'm calling the police!" the old lady wailed, outraged.

"We are the bloody police!" Sonny yelled back.

"Are we?" David asked him.

"No." Sonny shook his head, grinning. "C'mon. We better go."

"Park my car?" Rafe called out.

"I'm taking your car hostage, mate," Sonny replied, jogging down the steps.

"Hey, Mr America," Chloe said before David turned away. "Come back for that tea, yeah?" She smiled at him.

He smiled back. She was cute. "I certainly will, ma'am."

She closed the door, and David jogged down to the car. Sonny was waiting, having watched the exchange.

"What's with all this ma'am shit?" he demanded.

David shrugged and opened the passenger door up front. "Are we going, or waiting for the cops to show up?"

"Good point," Sonny said.

They both got into the car, now smelling pleasantly of curry, and buckled their seat belts.

"Is this a regular occurrence?" David asked, as Sonny started the car.

"What? Rafe being a lightweight?" he replied, hitting the gas. He peeled out of the quiet street, driving away from the scene at top speed.

"All of it," David clarified. "I take it you're well acquainted with both the sister and the neighbour?"

Sonny laughed, a loud guffaw. "Yeah, you could say that."

"Not your biggest fans, huh?" David commented.

"Yeah, you could say that," Sonny repeated. "Chloe certainly liked you. All that yes, ma'am, no, ma'am. She was about ready to drop her knickers on the doorstep."

David smiled and shook his head. "I was being polite."

"Well, it worked," Sonny said, peeling around a sharp bend. "Shame she was barking up the wrong tree."

"What do you mean?" David asked.

"Well, you know," Sonny said. "You're gay, right?"

David raised an eyebrow. "I'm bi. So, no, she isn't barking up the wrong tree."

"Oh," Sonny said, a note of surprise in his voice.

David waited for him to say more, but Sonny went uncharacteristically quiet.

Curious, David asked, "Intuition, or intel?"

"Come again?" Sonny asked.

"Intuition, or intel?" David repeated. "What made you think I'm gay, not bi?"

"Oh, well... I guess both," Sonny replied. "But the gaffer told me that your sister spoke at your funeral and said you were gay. Or..." He frowned in thought. "Maybe I misheard. She cornered me in the bogs, and I was unprepared."

David frowned too. First, he was surprised to hear that about his sister. Why the hell would she bring that up at his funeral? She'd always made out that she didn't want to know about his queerness, so they had rarely talked about it. He really had to die for her to be able to say it out loud? Jesus.

And, since he'd let everyone assume he was dead for their own safety, he couldn't go back and correct her mistake.

Second, what was Sonny talking about? He needed some answers.

First things first.

"Bogs are bathrooms, correct?" David asked.

"That's right," Sonny said. "You're catching on quick, sunshine."

David smiled wryly. "And gaffer is your boss?"

"One of them," Sonny said. "That's who I call ma'am."

"Sounds like mom, the way you say it," David told him.

"I'll try not to think of that the next time I see her," Sonny said. "She'd be a right scary mum."

"So, back to what she asked you in the bathroom," David said. "She told you I was gay?"

"Yeah," Sonny said. "I told you this already, didn't I? They instructed me to lure you in. Obviously, they asked me, being the most charming member of the team." He said it in a jokey, self-deprecating way.

David's lips involuntarily pulled into a smile. It was on the tip of his tongue to tell Sonny his charms worked plenty fine.

"Wait a minute," Sonny said, frowning in thought. "I wonder

if she told Mac the same thing. Did Mac flirt with you?"

"Mac?" David thought about it. "I don't think so? At least, I'm not aware of any flirting. We talked about the dog. She told me her first name."

"Huh. Okay," Sonny said. Then he went quiet again.

If he was feeling put out or a little jealous, it stroked David's ego. He didn't know everything that was going on, but if he had to pick a handler, he would pick Sonny.

After a while, he decided to make light of the situation. "Honestly," he said, "out of everyone tonight, I think Rizwan was flirting with me the most."

Sonny chuckled. "Yeah, he flirts with new customers. Enjoy the attention while it lasts."

"I will," David replied. He looked out the windows, seeing more dark London streets pass them by, the street lights blurring into orange.

"Where are we going?" he asked after a few minutes. It suddenly occurred to him he had no idea.

"Finsbury Park," Sonny replied. "My place. Prepare to be swept off your feet by the alluring smell of unwashed socks and the old pizza boxes of my swanky bachelor pad."

"Then I shall make the appropriate preparations for being swept," David quipped, and they shared a chuckle.

David appreciated a good sense of humour, and he and Sonny seemed to click.

*

Sonny drove. It was nearing two AM, and the streets were quiet. Much quieter than David had expected London to be. They passed a couple of red night buses, their windows lit up golden, and David craned his head to look at them. The passengers on board were a mix of ages, from older people sitting quietly to younger people listening to music on headphones.

Buses aside, there wasn't a whole lot else to see that night. David suspected Sonny was taking back streets and keeping off the main roads, or out of the city centre. He hoped he'd get some time to do sightseeing tomorrow.

"I know plenty about Rafe now," David mentioned. "Divorced, has kids. I've even met his sister."

"Well, they're separated, not divorced," Sonny corrected. He stared straight ahead, driving fast. "It's been ages though. They should really get on with a divorce or get back together."

"Point being," David replied, "I know all this about Rafe, and I also know things about Mac. I still don't know much about you. Well…" David smirked. "Apart from what Rafe told me before he got drunk."

Sonny glanced at him but didn't act too surprised. "Oh, yeah? Something embarrassing, no doubt?"

"I don't know." David's smile grew. "He said it used to annoy you. But maybe I'll save this nugget for later. When you're not expecting it."

"Great, I love surprises," Sonny said, dry sarcasm in his voice.

"Okay, I can't wait that long," David said. "Apparently, your old nickname was scallywag?"

Sonny chuckled. "Ah, yes. I remember that. He used to call me a lot of things back then, but scallywag was the most affectionate."

"What was the least affectionate?" David asked.

Sonny tittered again. "All the major swears in one sentence," he said.

He sensed they were getting close to home when Sonny

slowed the car, cruising a quiet residential street for a spot to park. The street lights were dim and orange, not a lot of light, but David gazed out the window at the rows of tightly knit terraced houses. Some were red brick, and some were painted in colours: cream, grey, mint green. All of them had white detail around classic sash windows.

They looked old, and while moderate size, David could tell they were expensive.

Sonny parked the car on a street named Chatterley Road. It immediately put racy movies and bodice-ripper books into David's mind, and he voiced the thought. "Like Lady Chatterley," he said.

Sonny tittered. "Yeah, that's partly why I picked this road. The name."

David smiled as they both got out of the car. They opened the back and grabbed their bags, plus the food from Hangri-La. David waited for Sonny to lead the way, and he pointed to a red brick house on the end of the terrace.

"That's the one," he said, walking ahead. "Of course," he added, twisting round to smirk at David, "when discussing Lady Chatterley, one cannot neglect to mention the lover in the equation. The gardener."

"I thought he was a gamekeeper?" David replied.

"Whatever," Sonny said. "The geezer tending to her ladyship's needs. Now, the question is, which one was the best lover? National treasure Sean Bean? Or newcomers like Richard Madden and Jack O'Connell?"

David considered. "I think I only saw one. The actor from *Bodyguard*."

"That's Richard Madden," Sonny said. "You haven't seen the Sean Bean one, then?"

"I've only seen *National Treasure*," David said.

"Yes, he's a national treasure," Sonny replied, bending down to nudge a tiny wrought iron gate open. He could've easily stepped over it.

"No, I mean," David said, following Sonny through the tiny gate, "Sean Bean is in *National Treasure*. That movie with Nicolas Cage?"

"Oh." Sonny chuckled. "You're right. I forgot." He walked up to the front door, which was painted black and had a big, brass door knocker.

While Sonny was taking out a key for the door, David looked around at the front yard, and another yard over the low red brick wall beside them. Sonny's neighbour, presumably. Both front yards were well kept, boasting shrubs, flowerbeds, and neat paving.

Surprisingly, at least to David, Sonny's yard was the prettiest with numerous blooming flowers in the beds, and a few scattered plants in ceramic pots.

"Didn't know you had a green thumb," David commented, gesturing at the yard when Sonny looked at him.

"Oh. Yeah, those are my grounds, though currently without a groundskeeper or any sort of keeper because the chap I usually get round has fucked off," he said.

"Vacation?" David asked.

"No, prison," Sonny said. "Fraud or something," he added, and opened his door. "Welcome to my humble abode." He flicked the light switch on and led the way into the narrow hall. The first thing he did was see to the softly beeping security alarm on the wall, punching in a code and setting his thumb onto a digital scanner.

Hi-tech, David noted.

He entered the hallway after Sonny. He knew he wasn't one

to talk, having recently stayed in a dinky trailer, but this house was small. Everything felt narrow to him, like the builders had been short on space. The hall was narrow, barely enough room for his elbows, and the staircase directly ahead was narrow. Yet, it had been made well. The ceilings were high; painted white with detailed filigree at the edges and around the light fixtures. The finishings gave it an air of grandeur, despite the size.

Sonny set his bags down onto a narrow wooden sideboard. "Shoes off," he instructed, toeing off his own boots in the hallway. "I know that's weird to you Americans, but it's shoes off in this country."

"I'm also Mexican," David corrected him. "I'm used to shoes off." He did the same, setting down his bags then taking off his boots. Under the coat hooks was a shoe stand, and they set their boots on there. David noticed the multiple sets of slide slippers in various sizes, assuming that some were for guests. He was used to that in Mexico; spare slippers had to be available for guests.

What he did find curious was the slim laundry hamper right next to the shoe rack.

"I told you get ready for socks, didn't I?" Sonny joked. "Dirty socks in 'ere." He pointed at the hamper. "Clean socks from this pile here. Help yourself." He took out two neatly rolled up pairs of black socks and tossed one to David. "First thing they taught us in SAS; always look after your feet."

David couldn't argue with that. "Thanks," he said.

They swapped out their socks for clean ones, depositing the dirties into the hamper. Sonny closed the lid quickly, because the smell wasn't pleasant.

"Guess I'm doing laundry tomorrow," he quipped.

They slipped some slides onto their feet and took the food bags into the kitchen.

David hung up his hat and ran a hand through his hair. He was excited to see Sonny's home and looked around for clues to his personal life; photos on the fridge, letters on sideboards, knick-knacks, anything.

Unfortunately for him, there were no personal touches visible. No photos, hardly anything on the walls or mantles. Nothing on the fridge door bar a couple of takeout menus. The only letters David spotted on the kitchen table weren't addressed to a name, only addressed to the occupier.

The most personal thing David had seen was the sock hamper in the hall. It made him think that this residence wasn't Sonny's only one, or perhaps he kept his personal effects in storage under lock and key. It would fit his personality type to be squirrelly and secretive.

"Any family nearby?" David asked him.

"Nope," Sonny said casually. He shrugged off his jacket and draped it over the back of a chair at the small kitchen table.

This was the first time David had seen him without a jacket in the light. His arms were the same tan colour as his face, with dark curly hair on the forearms. David watched as Sonny unpacked the food parcels on the table, inspecting each one.

"Where are your family?" he asked.

"Mostly East." Sonny got a blob of curry on his finger and stuck it in his mouth to lick it clean.

"East, like Middle East?" David guessed. He knew Sonny meant East London; he was simply trying to probe the guy for more information. He was curious. David had a hunch Sonny's ethnicity was Middle Eastern, or somewhere around there.

Sonny smirked. "East London. You peckish?"

"I could eat," David said.

Sonny fetched clean plates from the cupboard, and they

shared some curry, rice, and naans between them, with plenty of leftovers to be put into the fridge for tomorrow. Which was good, because when David looked inside the fridge, it was empty save for one small bottle of tomato ketchup, and a six-pack of beer bottles.

David's favourite. It seemed a fortuitous sign.

"Can I take a beer?" he asked.

"Knock yourself out, sunshine," Sonny replied. "Bottle opener is by the sink."

"Thanks." David helped himself to a beer and opened it. The first swig was refreshing and reminded him of home.

"You wanna bring it through?" Sonny asked.

David grabbed his plate and beer and followed Sonny to the room at the front of the house. He'd thought it would be a dining room, but it was more of a den.

Sonny turned on some side lamps for mood lighting. David saw a big L-shaped couch strewn with cushions, pillows, and comforters. It looked like a well-used nest.

A single recliner sat nearby, also facing the large flat-screen TV. David opted for the chair.

"Awright, sunshine," Sonny told him. "Get ready for your crash course in British culture and slang." He flopped onto the couch, balancing his curry in one hand and grabbing the TV remote with the other.

"What crash course?" David asked.

Sonny grinned. "*EastEnders.*"

Chapter Seventeen

David found he did not care for *EastEnders*. He was confused by the accents, and with so much talking it was hard to keep up.

Sonny seemed to be enjoying it, given the number of times he chuckled at the drama on-screen.

Having finished eating, they placed their empty plates onto the coffee table. David hadn't spotted any other signs of takeout food, despite Sonny's joke from before about empty pizza boxes. In fact, the place was very clean and tidy.

It was fast approaching three. David was starting to lag now, full of warm food and in front of a TV. His eyelids drooped.

Sonny had already nestled into the couch with a pillow and comforter, his legs stretched out on the L part. David guessed that he did some sleeping on there. Surely there were beds upstairs? If David slept in this chair, he'd get a crick in his neck.

The *EastEnders* marathon was still going strong, so David

decided to call it a night. "Think I'll hit the hay," he said.

"Go for gold, mate," Sonny mumbled. He sounded sleepy himself. "Up the stairs. Last door on the right. Bed's made."

"Thanks," David replied. "Er, good night."

"Night," Sonny said. He didn't move from his nest on the couch, so David got up and left the room quietly.

He found his bag out in the hall and took it upstairs with him. It was easy enough to find the light switches, and David took the opportunity to look around Sonny's home some more.

The floorboards creaked, so he couldn't do too much snooping, but he did a little. He could get away with a little. The two rooms at the front of the house, above the lounge, didn't yield interesting results: one small room empty, save for empty laundry baskets and a bare clothes airer. The second room, larger, also empty but with fitted closets.

There could be interesting stuff hidden away in those closets, but David didn't want to advertise his snooping yet.

He continued down the hallway, finding one generous bathroom with a shower and toilet inside, and one bedroom next to it.

David knew there was a smaller toilet downstairs, but this was the only bedroom.

The only bed.

It was a double, and the sheets looked clean. In fact, it looked unslept in. The nightstand boasted one lamp but had nothing else on it. Only the chest of drawers across the room gave any hint that the bedroom was occupied; hair products and combs were on the top, with a small mirror on a stand. David quietly opened the drawers, finding regular socks, underwear shorts, and cotton T-shirts inside.

This was certainly Sonny's bedroom.

Confused, David left the bedroom. He set his bag outside the bathroom door and walked back downstairs.

Sonny hadn't moved from the couch. He looked up when David stood in the open doorway. "What's wrong?" he asked. "Lost your toothbrush?"

"Er," David said, uncertain. "That's your bedroom?"

"I don't sleep in the bed," Sonny said, turning his eyes back to the TV. "Sheets are clean. Make yourself at home."

David's hunch about him sleeping on the couch was correct, then.

"But..." he started, unsure what to say. "Are you...? I mean, will you be comfortable?"

"I won't do any sleeping in a bed, mate, trust me," Sonny told him. He didn't make any jokes. It was a rare moment of honesty about a very personal subject.

David understood. His first time getting home from serving, he'd stared holes in his own ceiling for a long time. Sleeping in a bed could be hard with PTSD. Sometimes falling asleep on the couch was easier, so he wasn't about to give another soldier a tough time about it.

"Okay," he said quietly. "Well, thanks."

"No worries, mate."

He left Sonny watching TV and headed back upstairs.

David used the bathroom, brushed his teeth, looking at himself in the mirror above the sink as he contemplated trimming his beard. Maybe tomorrow.

He undressed in the bedroom. It wasn't as hot here as Mexico or San Diego, so he didn't strip all the way off. He kept his shorts on and slid into bed between the crisp, cool sheets.

The bed linen was clean but David smelled Sonny faintly on them. He'd detected trace scents of Sonny in this house, but that smell was more pronounced in the bed, so he must've at least laid on it at some point.

David kept the nightstand lamp on while he settled on his back and gazed up at the ceiling. Here he was, he thought, in Sonny's bed, without the man himself. This was certainly not how David had envisioned things starting off.

Still, maybe it was better this way, slowly easing into...whatever this relationship was. Working or otherwise. Flirty, with a question mark hanging over them.

David was fine. He had an active imagination to keep him occupied, and the scent of Sonny enveloping him was tantalising. He switched off the light, then reached a hand down to cup himself through his shorts.

*

Sonny had recently dozed off and was in that sweet space of falling through dreams before reaching deep sleep. In those dreams, he wasn't himself anymore; he was something else, something enormous with strong limbs and long fingers. Sonny felt so large and strong.

He knew it was a fleeting glimpse at the alien thing inside him, the thing that shared his DNA structure.

Often, the alien cried out with an ear-piercing shriek, like letting loose an emotional roar that would wake Sonny with a start. The alien was frustrated; he knew that much. Sometimes it made a curious chittering noise, raspy and dry, like insects or small animals would make to signal to each other. It often called out but never got an answer.

Sonny didn't know for sure; he could only guess. It's possible the dreams were purely his own overactive imagination. He'd never spoken about them, except to David.

Now the other man was here, sleeping in the same house,

Sonny felt his inner monster shift around, searching for David. The chittering rasp grew louder, more urgent. Sonny saw through its eyes as the beast moved, elongated legs making the sprint easy, covering ground faster than humanly possible. It tore around the dream, searching for its mate.

Sonny wasn't sure what happened next. His monster had found David's monster, or perhaps he was reliving a memory of the two of them together.

They *knew* each other. No, more than that...

The two giant aliens collided violently, holding onto each other as they spun around in some other-worldly, celestial dance.

Oh, God, this was an alien sex dream, wasn't it?

Sonny didn't realise at first, because the creatures were so large and alien-looking, but they were definitely mating. And, most shockingly, he felt what his alien was feeling: a wondrous, rising pleasure like a star exploding.

The dream abruptly ended as the orgasm rocked through him, and Sonny awoke on the couch. He was disoriented, the dream still on the edge of his vision as his human body was in the grips of a very real orgasm.

Sonny gasped silently, drawing in breath as the pleasure crested and washed over him. He bit his lip against a moan, muffling his cry, but the TV was still playing, masking any sound.

As the orgasm subsided, he lay there wondering what the hell had just happened.

Chapter Eighteen

David slept well.

He must've been in a deep sleep, and he had absolutely no dreams whatsoever until right before he woke. Blissful darkness and rest gave way to a single dream: David saw a clear image of Sonny in the distance, standing in a posture that suggested his hackles were up. Sonny was facing away from him, so he was pissed at someone else.

The image was gone as quickly as it had appeared. David opened his eyes, blinking against sleep. He realised he heard voices downstairs, and they were why he'd woken.

David sat up, alert in an instant. He silently got out of bed and crept to the door. He pulled it ajar to listen.

Two voices. Sonny, and a woman, conversing in another language. Given the way their voices echoed slightly, David guessed they were in the kitchen. Sonny sounded annoyed, but the conversation didn't seem to be an emergency.

Curious, David pulled on his pants and headed downstairs bare chested. He wanted to get there before the conversation stopped. He couldn't place the language they were speaking. To his ear, it sounded like Arabic, but different—a similar pattern and cadence.

Sonny was arguing back and forth with the woman, whoever she was.

Downstairs in the entryway, David spotted a pair of brown, heeled boots—women's boots. Whoever she was, she'd been comfortable enough to remove her shoes and take a pair of guest slippers. A girlfriend? But hadn't Sonny said he was gay? An ex, then, or a friend?

David realised as he reached the bottom of the stairs that he probably should've put a T-shirt on. Too late now. He approached the kitchen. Through the open doorway, the first thing he saw was Sonny; still dressed in yesterday's clothes, looking rumpled from his sleep on the couch. He bore an annoyed expression and was using one hand to gesture as he spoke the vibrant language.

David watched him curiously. In his gut, he knew this was Sonny's ethnicity on display. Something about it clicked, and the fact that the newcomer was in Sonny's home this early suggested a level of familiarity between them.

Sonny finally noticed David standing there, glancing round at him and then staring at his bare chest for a moment too long.

David hoped Sonny liked what he saw.

"Sorry, mate," Sonny said in English. "Did we wake you?"

David shrugged. "It's fine," he replied, entering the kitchen. Now he could see around the corner, he looked at the other person. It was a woman. She was busy unpacking plastic containers onto the kitchen table, and she seemed very comfortable there.

She looked good. A catch for sure. She was maybe around

Sonny's age, maybe a bit older. Hard for David to gauge, as he was distracted by her looks. She was slim, brown skinned, with long dark hair, and she was dressed casually in a fitted jacket, designer jeans, and a pair of guest slippers on her petite feet.

As soon as she met David's eyes she broke into a charming smile. "Hi!" she greeted, striding forward with her right hand out. "Dr Farah Ahmadi! So pleased to finally meet you!"

"Hi," David replied, shaking her hand. "David...er, oh..." He'd messed up the code names already. He quickly glanced at Sonny, who was now leaning on the breakfast counter with a re-signed expression.

"She knows your name, Dash. It's fine," Sonny told him. "This is Toff."

"Okay," David said, looking back at the woman in front of him. "Sorry, I thought you said doctor...?"

"Dr Farah Ahmadi," she repeated. "Salam!"

"Oh. Salam," David replied, as recognition pinged in his mind. "Wait, Toff? You're Sonny's cousin?"

"I am!" She smiled.

Sonny rolled his eyes. "Nobody's my fucking cousin at nine in the bloody morning," he grumbled in English.

"Zer nazan! Hush up," Farah said to Sonny. She waved a hand at him in a dismissive little gesture. "You need some caf-feine."

Sonny muttered something in the other language. His tone sounded irritated.

David was dying to know what the language was.

"So, Dr Ahmadi?" he said, sidling up to her. "Love the name. Where's it from?"

She grinned at him. "Iran."

David smiled back, triumphant. "Iran? Wow." He looked at

Sonny, who was again rolling his eyes heavenward. "You're Iranian?"

Farah, busy unpacking coffee packets and pots, pulled a face at Sonny. "You didn't tell him?"

Sonny pursed his lips. With the sleep-rumpled appearance and dark frown, he looked cute when he was annoyed.

David decided to annoy him further.

"Oh, Sonny won't even tell me his real name," he informed Farah.

"Well, he's funny about his name," Farah said, spilling the tea instantly. "But he should tell people where he's from. *Tsk*."

"I'm from London!" Sonny burst out.

"But we're Iranian!" Farah insisted. "Be proud of that."

"Right, that's it," Sonny replied. "It's too early for all this bollocks. Fuck off home."

"No, you fuck off," Farah replied calmly, her cut-glass accent different to Sonny's. She sounded more upper class, a world away from her cousin's accent. "I'll make coffee, and we will eat brunch together," Farah said, firmly. "I thought you liked brunch? You're gay, aren't you?"

"Oh, my God," Sonny muttered, turning on his heel and leaving the kitchen.

David tried very hard not to laugh. He did grin though. "Hey, I love brunch."

"You're gay, too, right?" Farah asked him cheerily.

"I'm bi," David replied.

"Oh, really?" Farah paused what she was doing and looked at him. "So, attraction to two genders?"

"That's right," David replied.

"Which genders are you attracted to?" she asked.

That was a specific question, one that most people never thought to ask. David wondered what type of doctor she was.

"Men and women," David replied, and quirked a smile at her. He figured he'd throw her a bone. She was cute.

Farah nodded, looking into his eyes. "That is very interesting." A smile bloomed across her attractive face.

This was getting flirty and David was acutely aware of that. She was a good-looking woman, fiery, and intelligent. Clearly, hot genes ran in the family.

Before the moment could develop, Sonny reappeared in the doorway with an annoyed expression. "Dash!" he barked. "Go upstairs and put some bloody clothes on."

The jealousy was palpable, and it stroked David's ego, but he withdrew to keep the peace.

"Actually," he said, walking up to Sonny so they were face to face, "I would like a shower first, if that's at all possible?"

"Yeah, go have a cold one," Sonny replied. "Towels are in the bathroom. Help yourself."

David smiled. "Okay. Thanks." He glanced back at Farah one last time before exiting the kitchen and walking away.

"And don't forget to get dressed this time!" Sonny called after him.

*

David undressed and stepped into the shower, planning to stroke off. But when he reached for the shower hose, he noticed something unexpected.

Next to the chrome showerhead, with matching chrome hose and wall mounted unit, was a second hose and showerhead clipped to the wall. This head was...

Well.

It was a chrome penis.

David stared at it in surprise for a long moment before he

reached for that one out of curiosity. Upon closer inspection he saw holes in the cockhead. It was a douche.

A fancy one.

David felt the weight of it in his hand, his fingers gripping the weighty shaft. He was only mildly curious. He didn't plan to use another man's douche; not without asking first. David had never been in a house with such an overt display of a gay lifestyle. He was, admittedly, a little jealous, and at the same time he was overjoyed to see the chrome cock on display.

He put it back in its wall mount, his mind now filled with images of Sonny using the douche himself. Or maybe his house guests used the douche, but David had a gut feeling that it was Sonny's. He'd been picking up on some bottom energy for a while now.

David started the shower using the regular showerhead. The chrome cock kept catching his eye, and as he stood under the pleasantly warm spray of water his mind drifted again to Sonny, picturing him in the shower.

His morning wood became increasingly hard to ignore. David also considered the fact that, if he dealt with the issue head on, so to speak, he wouldn't be distracted or horny when he went back downstairs to speak to Sonny and his hot cousin.

The solution was simple.

David took himself in hand and, as the water beat over him, he began to jerk himself off. It had been a while since he'd had sex, and it was starting to gnaw at him. God, he hoped he could get laid soon.

As his climax crested, his thoughts drifted to Sonny again. David thought about him and let the pleasure take him over.

*

Sonny was downstairs, listening to his cousin banging on and on in Farsi. She was berating him for not telling her that they were back, even though he'd only been back five minutes.

As usual, Farah was work focused, eager to start interviewing David and making notes, getting him to the lab...

She had no idea how cagey David was about labs, given his experience with the Americans. Sonny's instructions had been to lure the bastard in, not scare him off with doctors in white coats on day one.

Farah didn't get it. She'd never been a lab experiment. She couldn't know what it was like.

Sonny was thinking all of this, and Farah was still talking. He was this close to frog-marching her out the door. He didn't want to deal with this all before he'd properly woken up. Now she was here, talking a million miles an hour, and laying on an Iranian brunch that he hadn't asked for. When he tried to get a word in, she steamrolled over him.

Sonny rubbed his temples with his fingertips. He felt hot. His temples were damp with sweat.

How strange.

He rarely got sweaty now, so this was an unusual occurrence. Sonny glanced at the thermostat on the kitchen wall. It hadn't been touched, and the room's temperature was cool, just how he liked it. So why did he feel hot? He pulled at his shirt collar as his breaths started to come in ragged. Was he sick? Hungover? Something else?

Farah kept rabbiting on while serving up homemade Dolmeh, fresh dates, and baslogh snacks, using Sonny's plates without asking and rearranging his kitchen cupboards while she worked.

Sonny felt so hot. Also...horny. What the hell?

"Are you all right?" Farah asked, looking at him curiously.

Sonny didn't want to be analysed, not this early in the morning. "I'll be back in a second," he said, making a run for the downstairs toilet.

Farah tsked. "You ate too much curry at Rizwan's again, didn't you?"

Sonny ignored her and shut himself in the bathroom. He turned on the little light over the mirror and looked at his reflection.

He *was* sweaty. It was beading all around his forehead. And his pupils were huge. His breathing was coming in hard.

Had he been drugged?

Sonny gripped the porcelain sink in both hands as he tried to figure out what was happening. Could he get through it, or did he need the lab? He'd rather avoid the lab if he could.

Then, before he had time to make any sort of decision, the most amazing feeling washed over him. A familiar feeling: a powerful orgasm. It came out of nowhere and knocked into him like a great wave.

Sonny had to steady himself by putting a hand on the wall. He gasped through it, trying his best not to cry out at the pleasure shaking his body to its core. The ghost of it lingered in his crotch, while the explosion set off in his brain.

A moment later it subsided, taking all the strange symptoms with it. Sonny was still breathing hard, but he felt back to normal.

Well, whatever was normal for post-orgasm. Sated and happy.

What on earth was that all about? This had never happened before.

Wait...

Sonny remembered that the same thing had happened last

night, while he'd been asleep. He'd almost forgotten. Why were spontaneous orgasms ripping through him with no warning?

What the hell was going on?

Chapter Nineteen

After David's shower, he towelled dry and helped himself to some of the products on display around the bathroom sink. He'd brought his own antiperspirant, but he felt like using Sonny's spray to see if the other man would notice.

David looked at himself in the mirror above the sink. His hair was long and scraggly, as was his beard. He wouldn't mind getting a cut to tidy himself up a bit. For now, he combed his wet hair back. He'd put a ball cap on it anyway.

Finished, he opened the bathroom door. With a towel secured around his waist, David paused on the landing to listen in on the conversation from downstairs, but Sonny and his cousin were speaking in Persian.

Well, Farah was doing most of the talking, from what David could hear.

David smirked, mildly amused by their dynamic, then he returned to Sonny's bedroom to dress.

He opened his bag to pick out some clean clothes and found the package he'd been handed by PRISM yesterday. He'd forgotten about it.

First things first; he pulled on a clean pair of shorts, and a white T-shirt. Then he quickly made the bed, because that was the polite thing to do as a guest. He tucked in the corners nice and tight in a forty-five-degree angle, like he'd learned in the marines. Tough habit to break.

David pulled on clean socks, and a comfortable pair of jeans. Sonny had mentioned a rest day, so David didn't need combat fatigues today.

Now he turned his attention to the welcome pack. He figured he had a few more moments to himself, and he wanted to look at the phone. He opened the packet up and tipped the contents out onto the bed: the phone, the Oyster card, and the paper leaflet.

David put the Oyster card into his jeans pocket. It would be useful to get around, since he didn't have a car here.

He realised he hadn't read the paper leaflet yet. David picked that up next, opening it. Inside was typewritten text, a short list of do's and don'ts. One section was innocuous and expected, such as: *Find enclosed your complimentary new phone and Oyster card; both can be used right away. Any questions or further expenses please refer to Sonny or another member of the team. You answer to Guv, contact in phone; please only call in an emergency; otherwise wait to be contacted. You will be issued a bank account and your wages upon coming into the office after your rest period.*

That part was what David had expected and aligned with what Sonny and Mac had told him. The promise of a salary and a bank account was what David was really interested in; the first steps to regaining a legal identity again.

That was all fine. Better than fine.

The other section gave David pause. His eyes skimmed over the most ridiculous sentences he'd ever read: *Do not talk to anyone outside of team members. Do not discuss your work. No cavorting with civilians. No engaging in sexual activities or the exchange of bodily fluids.*

David brought the leaflet closer to his face and read the sentences again. Yes, it really said, *"No engaging in sexual activities."*

David pulled a face.

Why? Was it a safety thing?

He would ask Sonny about this. David folded the leaflet and stuck it in his back pocket.

Before he went downstairs again, he wanted to check his escape routes. David opened the phone and went straight to Maps. He checked his location and was pleasantly surprised to discover there were multiple Tube and bus stops all within walking distance. The nearest Tube station was called Arsenal, like the soccer club.

David wasted a minute checking that area onscreen. Highbury, within walking distance, was home to Arsenal Stadium. David wouldn't mind checking that out. He enjoyed soccer games.

He zoomed out again on the map to look at the surrounding area. Finsbury Park, north of London city centre. David spotted several interesting sights he wouldn't mind seeing in person. He wondered if there would be time to be a tourist.

Sightseeing would have to wait. David quickly memorised the route from his location, Chatterley Road, to Arsenal Tube station, so he would remember which way to walk without looking at the app. He had no idea what Sonny planned to do today, so he had to assume he was on his own if he wanted to walk around.

David pocketed his phone and headed downstairs. His damp hair was starting to fall in his eyes, so he paused in the entryway by the front door to grab his hat from the coat hooks. He smoothed back his hair and slipped the ball cap on backwards like he preferred.

The conversation in the kitchen was still going down.

David turned in that direction, then stopped and paused to shove his feet into the slides he'd borrowed last night. He walked to the kitchen and cautiously entered.

Farah was sitting at the table in front of her brunch spread. She was talking more than she was eating. Sonny was engrossed with his phone and had donned an oversized black hoodie that looked very cozy.

"Hi!" Farah turned to David with a bright smile. "Come! Eat!"

Before David could speak, the sound of a noisy scooter disrupted the quiet street outside. It sounded like it was stopping nearby. Sonny rose from the table and swept out of the kitchen, sidestepping around David.

The doorbell rang.

"Who's that?" Farah asked in English.

David shrugged. He half turned to watch Sonny down the hallway as he opened the door and greeted the driver of the scooter.

It was clearly a delivery of some kind; the driver didn't even remove his helmet, and he handed over a paper bag.

"Thanks for the tip!" the driver said, voice muffled through his helmet.

"Welcome, mate," Sonny replied. He took the bag and shut the door. Outside, the scooter revved up again and left.

"What's that?" David asked as Sonny approached him.

"Breakfast," Sonny said, delving a hand inside the bag. He pulled out a plastic cup filled with milky brown liquid, ice, and boba pearls.

David recognised the drink. It appeared Sonny had ordered multiple bubble teas.

"Want one?" Sonny asked, smiling.

It was the first time he'd smiled that morning. David smiled back.

"Sure. Thanks."

"You can have taro, or the dirty milk tea," Sonny said.

"What's taro?" David asked.

"It's this purple one." Sonny juggled the cup and bag, allowing David to peer in and see a tall plastic cup with lavender-coloured liquid inside.

"But what does it taste like?" David asked him.

"Sweet," Sonny said.

David remembered his comment that night in the truck yard about eating his body weight in churros. Clearly, Sonny had a sweet tooth.

"The milk one has caffeine?" David asked.

"Yes."

"I'll try that one," David said.

Sonny handed him the first cup, then picked out a thick straw and handed that over.

"Thanks," David told him.

"You're welcome, sunshine," Sonny replied.

"Who was that?" Farah called from the kitchen.

David caught Sonny rolling his eyes.

"Nobody," Sonny replied. He re-entered the kitchen and went straight to the fridge. David followed, curiously watching Sonny unpack two cups into the fridge before closing it and taking his bag over to the counter.

Sonny unpacked the remaining cup, a tall lavender drink, and a packet of some Asian candies.

Farah, still sitting at the table amongst her homemade food, also watched him. "Really, Sonny?" she said flatly. "You've ordered in? I literally brought brunch to you, and you order in."

"I'm sorry, I thought I was in my own house?" Sonny quipped. He busied himself opening his candy packet and emptying the contents into a bowl. He stabbed a big straw into his drink cup.

David was picking up on some tension between the cousins. It was giving sibling energy for sure.

"Can we at least sit at the table?" Farah directed to Sonny.

"You can do what you like," Sonny replied, picking up his cup and plate like he intended to go.

David wasn't a fan of the tension in the room, so he decided to make a distraction.

"Before you do that," he said, "can I ask a question?" He set his cup on the table, then reached in his back pocket for the leaflet.

"Ask and you shall receive," Sonny quipped.

David opened the leaflet. "So, this was in my, uh, welcome pack? It says, quote, no sex allowed." He glanced up to watch Sonny's and Farah's reactions. "What's up with that?"

Sonny blinked, then immediately turned to his cousin and gestured with his ridiculous lavender-coloured drink to her, as if to say, you take this one.

Farah nodded. "Yes, correct," she said, all businesslike. "We cannot risk any impregnation with civilians, as any offspring would carry your alien-infused DNA. And in the case where impregnation is not possible, you must still refrain from passing bodily fluid to civilians, as there's a high chance your semen is corrosive and that can obviously damage their skin. A health hazard."

"Wait, what?" David said. "Corrosive? Health hazard?"

"Yes," Farah replied. "As in, merely touching your fluids could burn your partners."

David was gagged. He'd had no idea. "Um," he said, reeling. "But...what about condoms?"

Sonny snorted quietly, like he was trying not to laugh.

Farah shook her head. "We simply can't risk semen samples falling into civilian hands, or those of competitive agencies. Semen or blood samples containing alien DNA would go for huge amounts on the black market and could have devastating results."

"Oh," David repeated.

"And," Farah continued, "there is no guarantee condoms would work, given the corrosive element to your semen. It can burn straight through a condom."

David couldn't believe this. His chances of getting laid were looking less likely by the minute. "Hold up," he said. "How would you even know this?"

Sonny stuck his straw into his mouth and slurped his drink, waiting for his cousin to answer.

Farah cleared her throat. "Sonny is our only test subject so far, but given you went through a similar procedure with Compound A-X and Sonny confirmed you have enhanced strength and speed like him, it seems fair to presume you would have similar side effects. Of course, we won't know for sure until we get you in the lab..."

Sonny stopped slurping and made a nuh-uh noise in his throat. "Hang about, love," he said. "We have some rest days to use up before you go work mode on us."

"Sorry, sorry!" Farah held up her hands. "I'm just saying. The only way to know for certain is to run some tests in the lab."

David had more questions now than he'd had five minutes ago. His head was reeling. "I don't feel like rushing into a lab," he said, feeling uneasy. "And even when I get there, I'm certainly not in a hurry to provide *samples*."

"I completely understand," Farah replied. "But this is why they're telling you to not go around offering samples for free to the public."

Sonny snorted and laughed. "Hah! Like those free tasters at the entrance in the supermarket? Free sample, sir?" He waved his bowl of candies around like it was the samples he was offering. "Free samples!"

His jovial attitude helped put David at ease, and he fought against a smile.

"That's where your mind goes, huh?" David quipped.

"Seems like it'd be better than Grindr," Sonny quipped back. "Who wants a free sample, lads? Form an orderly queue out back."

They both chuckled.

Farah remained quiet and when David glanced at her, he saw she was staring at them with an unamused expression.

"Joke about it all you want," she scolded, "but make sure you stick to the rules. That applies to both of you."

"Yes, we will," Sonny replied. "Get off our case, woman."

"Since we're on the subject," David said, "can I ask some more questions?"

Farah gestured to the seat opposite her. "Fire away."

"God, if you're gonna talk shop," Sonny complained, "I'm going back to the couch." He swept out of the room, leaving David alone with Farah.

David suspected the talk of all this alien stuff made Sonny uneasy, but David had questions. He sat down across from Farah and tried to get his thoughts in order.

After a long moment, he drew in a breath and asked, "What is Compound A-X? What am I living with here?"

"I'll explain what we know," Farah told him.

Chapter Twenty

Six years ago
London

Dr Farah Ahmadi was a busy woman, and a happy one. She was thirty-six years old.

She got up early every day at six, showered, dressed in smart clothes, then went downstairs to make her kids their lunches and prep breakfast.

By seven, she went back upstairs to draw the curtains and wake them for school. Bahar, eight years old, the eldest, had an artistic streak, from painting pictures to decorating her school bag. And Farid, six years old, was a quietly studious boy who currently loved anything to do with dinosaurs.

"Time for school," Farah said, clapping her hands. "Get dressed, wash your faces, and come down for breakfast."

"Maman?" Bahar called after her. "Are you taking us to

school?"

"No, I have an early lecture today, Bahar Joon," Farah replied. "Nana will take you to school."

She turned away before she could see Bahar's disappointed little face. Farah couldn't be everywhere at once.

She set breakfast on the kitchen table. Traditional Iranian breakfast adapted to kids born and raised in London: toast corners (using whichever store-bought bread both children would deign to eat that week), feta cheese cubes, fried eggs with seasoning, slices of fresh fruit in individual bowls, walnuts, fresh herbs, tea, and fruit juices.

They always ate breakfast together, but with one empty chair at the table that morning.

"Where's Daddy?" Farid asked with such a child's innocence that it nearly broke Farah's heart.

He's probably with his mistress, Farah thought but didn't say. She made herself smile at her son. "Daddy is working early today."

"Daddy does that a lot," Farid said blithely.

Farah didn't say anything. She was running out of excuses for her husband. Either they'd have to patch things up soon or talk about separating officially. It wasn't fair to the kids otherwise.

Thankfully, her mother, Mahnaz, entered the front door using her key. A welcome distraction.

"Nana is here," Farah told the kids. "Go help her with her coat and slippers. She'll take you to school after breakfast."

"Could we come to work with you?" Farid asked her.

Farah chuckled. "Maybe in a few years, dear."

She loved her kids. They were so smart; they would do great things. Being a single parent would be challenging, Farah thought, but she wasn't afraid of taking on a challenge.

*

Farah was an anthropology lecturer at LSE, the London School of Economics and Political Science in Westminster.

Every day she walked up the street from her house to Victoria Station, took the Tube north to Oxford Circus, then changed for the Central Line, getting off at Holborn. She'd walk down the main street, past restaurants and pubs, passing the Shaw Cafe and LSE Law School on her left before turning into Portugal Street and walking to LSE campus.

Nearby were the Royal Courts of Justice; Temple Church, built by the Knights Templar in 1185; King's College London; and a little further afield were Royal Opera House and the London Transport Museum.

Farah walked by all these incredible sights every day. She went to her building and straight into the lecture hall. She was always early for her lectures so she could prepare with the tech, and she had a prompt start for 9:00 AM. Some students were already seated and waiting for her, also prompt. She liked that.

The tech, Stuart, got her started with the laptop connection for her slideshow, and they made quiet small talk while waiting for students filing into the hall to find their seats.

"Want a coffee?" Stuart asked her.

He was a good-looking young man. White, with light brown wavy hair and three-day-old stubble. Farah had allowed a little flirtation here and there, especially since her ratbag husband had picked another woman over her. Stuart was probably ten years her junior, but did that matter for a little harmless fun?

"I wouldn't say no to a cup of tea," she replied, smiling at him.

"I'll bring you a tea." Stuart grinned. He moved to leave, then turned back to her. "Oh, also, there's a guest sitting in on your lecture. Said she's from a museum."

Farah smiled, but she wished Stuart would've gotten more details. Which museum? How exciting! Hopefully she'd find out after the lecture.

"Thanks," she said, and checked her watch: 8:59 AM. Time to start. Farah set her mic on her jacket lapel and greeted the hall. "Good morning, everyone," she said. "This lecture is titled "Ancient Parasites," and today we'll be looking at parasites, host behaviour, and how they have infected and affected humans throughout our entire evolutionary history."

*

It wasn't the first time Farah had given her Ancient Parasites lecture. It was usually a popular one; students loved parasites. But today was the first time she was approached afterwards with a unique offer.

"Dr Ahmadi?" A petite East Asian woman with shoulder-length black hair offered Farah a business card. "I'm Dr Mi-Seon Lee. I work at the Natural History Museum."

Farah's soul lit up at those words. The Natural History Museum over in South Kensington was a renowned institute for the study and preservation of the natural world. Farah had been trying for years to get her foot in the door there.

Farah took Dr Lee's card and beamed a smile. "How do you do?"

"I'll get straight to the point," Lee said. She spoke with an accent, suggesting she hadn't grown up with English as a first language. "My boss has given me freedom to choose an anthropology consultant. I've read your work on cross-cultural behaviour and parasitic infections. You have insight. I'd like to show you what I'm working on, get your opinion."

"Can I simply say yes right away?" Farah said with a chuckle. "I've dreamed of working for the Natural History Museum in any capacity, plus my young son would be thrilled. Just set a date, and I'm there."

Lee smiled faintly, the barest curving of her lips. "Tonight?" she asked.

"Tonight?" Farah was surprised. That soon?

"The museum closes to the public at six," Lee said. "I can give you the private tour, including behind the scenes."

Farah was stunned. She nodded. Her mother could give the kids dinner, even if she had to beg and plead.

This was the opportunity of a lifetime; Farah knew it.

*

Lee took Farah on a quick museum tour after hours. The lights were still on, a couple of security staff by the main entrance, but all the crowds had vanished. Farah was inside the Natural History Museum getting special treatment, and she was overjoyed.

A tour of every space would've taken hours, at least four, so this tour was shorter. Farah had been to the museum numerous times anyway, so she knew the main exhibits by heart: the blue whale skeleton and the animal taxidermy rooms, the statue of Charles Darwin in the main hall watching over them all, the high ceilings of the museum's interior right down to its mosaic floors.

Lee breezed past most of those and started in the newer sections of the museum. In the space exhibit, past the large glowing installation of the moon, was a selection of asteroid rocks on display.

Some of the sections were aimed at kids, informing them about the asteroid that killed the dinosaurs, which were on display in the next room, Farid's favourite room.

Lee showed Farah to one interesting rock on display, behind plate glass.

"This is a replica of the largest found fragment from a deep space asteroid that entered our atmosphere in 2017," Lee explained. "This fragment landed in the north of England."

"Where's the original?" Farah asked. The display said this was the asteroid.

"In our lab," Lee replied. "It has been the basis for our work." She led Farah out into the hall, walking toward the Zoology Studio.

They were at the back end of the museum now; when they came out into the gallery, Farah glanced down at the ground floor below them to see glass frontage showing the night sky and museum grounds beyond, and a fire-exit door with one security guard in attendance.

When she looked up, she was astonished to see several floors of lit office and lab rooms above them. "Tons of space here," she commented.

Lee nodded. She led Farah into an illuminated hallway that showed off some of the museum's famous "Spirit Collection" for visitors: mammals, reptiles, and various fish species preserved in jars of alcohol. Hence the name, Spirit Collection.

"I hope there's time to look at the collection," Farah said, itching to get into those sealed archival rooms behind the plate glass.

Lee showed her to a service elevator, swiping her ID card for access. "This part of the collection is not open to the public," she said.

They got into the elevator, its glass panels allowing Farah to see illuminated jars of animal specimens on either side. The jars appeared to glow in many different shades, from nearly clear and off-white to stained yellow or pale green. The different colours indicated varying stages of decomposition and renewed alcohol preserve; some of these specimens were over two hundred years old.

"Magnificent," she said.

The elevator took them down, slowly whirring.

Farah watched the walls as they descended, passing jars upon jars of specimens. The lower they went, the more bizarre the specimens became. Angler fish with mighty jaws gave way to human skulls with sharp canine teeth, like a vampire. Larger jars boasted deformed human babies with webbed legs, like little mermaids.

Farah looked at Lee in question, and Lee nodded.

"Welcome to PRISM," she said, as the elevator stopped. "We deal in all things weird and wonderful."

The door opened out into a generously spaced, high-tech laboratory. Right away, Farah spotted the asteroid. The real one. It was whole on one side; the other side having been cut into and quarried for samples. She walked around the asteroid to get a closer look at the open core.

A curious, blue-tinted mineral was visible inside. It appeared to catch the light and sparkle as she stared at it.

"What mineral is that?" Farah asked.

"That," Lee replied, "is my life's work. We have named it Project A-X."

She led Farah to one of the benches, where two techs were working on blue samples in Petri dishes, like culture samples. The blue substance they had grown was gooey, moving very subtly.

"Fascinating," Farah murmured. "This came from the asteroid?"

"Yes," Lee said. "After many tests, we've confirmed it is DNA of a lifeform unknown to us. Long dead. We've managed to revive the largest samples, but it isn't very stable."

"Lifeform?" Farah said. "So, it's alien DNA?"

"That is correct."

This was an anthropologist's dream. Farah had been waiting for an opportunity to make her mark all her academic career, but never in her wildest dreams had she imagined she'd be asked to consult on something this big.

And, she couldn't wait to see the look on her husband's face when he found out.

She smiled at Lee and said, "When can I start?"

Chapter Twenty-One

Five years ago
Special Air Service Garrison and HQ, Herefordshire

Sonny woke up at six sharp along with all the other lads in the barracks. Just another Wednesday. He was twenty-four years old.

They went outside for their morning jog around the yard in the bitter cold of February to get the blood pumping. Then it was straight into the showers, get dressed into combat fatigues, and go to the mess hall for breakfast.

"Oi, budge up," Rafe said, coming to sit on the bench next to Sonny. "Think we'll get deployed later," he murmured amidst the noise of the mess hall.

"Oh, yeah?" Sonny replied, midway through his boring bowl of oatmeal. "Heard something juicy?"

Rafael "Rafe" Campbell was their staff sergeant, so he often knew things ahead of the troops.

"Hostages on an airfield," Rafe replied. "They're currently pinned down by Special Branch, but if their hotshot negotiator can't make a deal for the hostages, we'll be up to bat next. This would be a good opportunity to show off for the promotions board, corporal."

Sonny smirked. Rafe only called him by rank when he was being serious.

"Aren't I always a show-off?" he quipped.

"I mean it, bruv," Rafe said. "If there's an op today, I want you to lead it. I've already spoken with 'arris and he agrees. You put yourself out there and impress the brass. You've got what it takes."

Sonny liked the praise, especially coming from Rafe. He felt shy, though, so he made a joke to cover for it.

"I do enjoy putting myself out there," he said, making Rafe smile and roll his eyes.

They finished breakfast and went to gear up. Every day was spent practicing special tactics and manoeuvres, unless they were deployed. Until that call came, they would carry on as if it was any normal day training.

Today it was back into the dark warehouse with stud walls set up, exercising infiltration manoeuvres with guns and flash-bangs. Sonny led one of the infiltration teams but unfortunately, he had Clarke on his team, and Clarke was a fucking dickhead who didn't listen to orders so it made things difficult.

After their last assault run of the morning, Rafe called a halt and proceeded to chew Clarke out in front of the lads. Sonny had to suppress a smile. Clarke was on his last chance; that much was obvious.

They broke for lunch and had barely taken the first bite when Major Harris ordered the squadron into the meeting room.

Sonny hurriedly stuffed half a sandwich in his mouth.

"Told ya," Rafe said.

They filed into the meeting room and took a seat, facing the situation board.

"Listen up," Major Harris said. "At 0400 hours this morning, unidentified terrorists infiltrated a private airfield outside Ledbury." Harris indicated the map on the board. "As most of you know, that's not far from here. Police on scene have counted six males in masks. We'll be calling them X-Rays from here on out. They broke into one private plane and tried to steal its cargo shipment as it was unloading but were interrupted by on-site security. A shootout began, no loss of life so far, but they have taken four hostages." Harris indicated the mugshot printouts of civilians on the board; two men, two women. "Two pilots and an air steward, and one airstrip signaller. These are confirmed civilians, and Special Branch have been attempting to negotiate with the terrorists for the last several hours, to no avail. So, now it's our turn."

Murmurs broke out around the room, some of the lads itching for action.

"Settle down," Harris called out. "We're having a small-scale model built of the building where the terrorists are pinned down. We are a last measure, but if there's any danger to the hostages, any confirmed killing of civilians, we will be going in hard. Two teams." Harris looked Sonny's way and nodded. "Sonny, I want you to head the assault team. Rafe will lead the second team."

"Yes, sir," Sonny replied, all but bursting with pride. He couldn't wait to tell his gran about this when he called her.

*

The plans were made.

Since they were less than a half hour's drive down the

road, they did their prep before setting off. The model of the building had been made from paper and cardboard, set on a table to give them a bird's eye view. They all gathered around and agreed on infiltration tactics. Sonny would lead his team in as first assault and create the distraction, while Rafe led his team in from the back.

They would only be called up as a last resort, so there was a high probability they'd go all the way there, wait for ages, and not get used. That was a best-case scenario for the hostages, if they could be negotiated to safety peacefully.

Even with that in mind, they had to go in prepared for action. The squadron geared up, dressing in standard black tactical uniform with no insignia. They wore minimal body armour for better ease of movement, only a black bulletproof vest and black helmets for protection. They had full gas masks strapped to the front of their vests, ready to put on at a moment's notice.

When they were ready, they piled into the van, boots stomping in unison across the ground.

"Let's go, let's go!" Rafe shouted. "Let's go, lads. We're on!"

The van doors slammed shut, and they joked among themselves as they drove down the country roads. The joking faded away gradually as they fell silent, each of them settling into the zone. They had to focus.

Sonny was quiet too. He had a lot riding on this op. If they got the green light, he wanted to impress. Promotions meant more money, and he wanted to buy things for Gran. Nice things. A new oven. Maybe a new telly. She'd like that.

He wanted her to be proud of him.

The journey to the airfield was quick. They arrived mid-afternoon, but the sky was dark. Looked like rain clouds rolling in.

"Major Harris?" A man in pressed trousers and a shirt and

tie, with a bulletproof vest over the top, approached the squadron. Special Branch—they always wore suits. "We've cleared an office for you. Right this way."

Inside the office, they grouped together and loaded their weapons. Rafe's team were ground assault; they had an assortment of door charges to blow open an exit point with flash-bang grenades and firearms. Sonny's team were aerial assault; they'd be infiltrating via the roof and windows, so they had batons for breaking glass, smoke canisters, flash-bangs, and firearms strapped to their backs and legs.

Harris went through their infiltration orders once again, then they split up to go wait in their separate locations. Rafe took his team to south side of the building. Sonny led his team to the roof, where they waited inside a service stairwell on the top floor.

Now it was a waiting game.

An hour slipped by and then another. They were told over comms that negotiations were breaking down. The terrorists wanted a plane with fuel to take them out of there and planned to take some hostages with them, along with the fifty-kilogram case they'd robbed from the plane that Special Branch suspected was cocaine.

"Sounds more like useless drug runners than terrorists," Clarke muttered.

Of course, Clarke was on Sonny's team.

Another hour, then they heard shots fired inside the building. If they received confirmed death of hostages, this would be their cue.

"Get ready, lads," Sonny said. He pulled on his gas mask, securing it into place. The other boys did the same.

They waited, tense and ready. It was their job to be a coiled spring in situations like these, even if it turned out to be a false alarm.

"Okay, we're going in," Harris informed them over comms. "Sonny, make your entry now."

"Yes sir," Sonny replied.

This was it.

They opened the service door and poured out, guns trained at all angles in case they came across an X-Ray. They moved quickly as a unit, booted feet silent on the rooftop. Once they made it to the north side, they worked together with one on watch while three set up the abseiling lines. They'd done these moves a thousand times, and got the rigs set up fast.

Mike stayed on the roof while the rest of them abseiled down the front of the building, stopping short of the windows on the floor where the X-Rays had holed up.

Sonny watched his teammates, checking the other two were in position before they made entry. "Now!" he ordered. They whipped out batons to smash glass and tossed in the flash-bangs and smoke canisters.

"Smoke deployed!" Sonny reported. "Flash-bangs deployed! Going in now! Go, go, go!"

The three of them crashed through the broken windows, dropping to the floor with guns trained. One X-Ray was in sight, coughing from the smoke. He had a gun in hand. Finch had been through the window first and shouted at the X-Ray to get down on the ground. When he didn't comply, Finch shot him. It was all done in less than three seconds.

The other X-Rays must've moved into another room. Sonny stood at the closed door and waited for Finch and Clarke to get behind him, slapping his shoulder to signal they were ready. Mike joined them at the rear, and they moved in as one, sweeping each room for hostages.

When they finally came upon the hostages, they were in the Air Traffic Control Room, along with two of the five remaining X-Rays.

"Get down on the ground!" Sonny shouted; his order echoed by the other men as they shouted for everyone to get down. "Get down on the ground! Get down!"

The hostages complied. They were terrified civilians, and one injured hostage was already sprawled out on the floor. One of the X-Rays complied, lying flat on the floor, but the other one rose up with a gun aimed at Clarke. Sonny shot the X-Ray first, saving Clarke's bacon.

Sonny heard shouts from below them; Rafe's team taking down the last two X-Rays.

"Get the hostages out!" Sonny ordered. "Cuff the X-Ray! Take him outside!"

They led everyone outside, away from the smoke. The injured hostage had to be carried; he had a gunshot wound to the shoulder but would survive.

The mission was a success; they had contained the terrorists and rescued the hostages without sustaining any losses on their end.

Sonny's team had taken out two X-Rays and arrested a third. Rafe's team had shot and injured the remaining two, one of whom was still living and would be arrested after medical attention.

Major Harris was pleased. A swift and simple, "Good job, lads," in passing was the sign he was tickled pink.

The X-Rays and hostages were all handed over to Special Branch, who would detain and question everyone before determining if they were to be released or charged with drug smuggling. Even the hostages were treated with suspicion, in case the terrorists had had inside help.

Sonny and the rest of the squadron disarmed, emptying cartridges from their guns before handing all equipment over to the police for the enquiry that would follow. Every bullet had to be accounted for. Sonny placed his rifle into the evidence bag, along with the loose cartridge.

Once they were free, some of the lads smoked a cigarette out on the tarmac. Sonny didn't smoke, but he stood with his team to join in the banter. As he was listening to Rafe recount their entry, Sonny noticed Harris lurking a ways off and motioning to Sonny to come talk to him.

Sonny casually peeled away from the group and approached Harris. "Sir?" he said.

"Went well today, Corporal," Harris said.

"Yes, sir."

"You've always stood out in any group I put you in," Harris went on.

Sonny almost made a quip but kept his lips buttoned. Harris didn't talk a lot, and when he did, it meant he had something interesting to say. Sonny didn't want to blow it by being a cheeky git.

"There's a unique opportunity on the horizon," Harris said. "I need a good sniper for some black ops. These are highly classified missions for the British Government, either working alone or on a two-man team. Your staff sergeant is already on board, so potentially you could do these jobs together. You'll still be on the squadron, but away on assignment for a few days now and then. There's extra pay in it."

Sonny glanced beyond Harris's shoulder to where the boys were standing and noticed that Rafe was looking his way. Rafe made a motion with his eyes to Harris, nodding his head as if to say this is it, take it.

Sonny smiled and faced Harris. "Sounds good, sir. Sign me

up."

*

Two years later
Paris, France

Sonny returned to the surveillance apartment with the sandwiches and coffee, as per his CO's instructions.

It was just the two of them on this op; a tidy little trip that had so far been mostly surveillance. He was twenty-six years old.

"Dinner is served," Sonny said sarcastically, setting down the sandwiches. The food here in Paris wasn't great, and Rafe had been complaining about it all week.

"Gimme that coffee," Rafe said, twisting round in his seat. He was monitoring the target's various buildings within the vicinity, headphones on. He took a grateful sip of coffee and sighed with pleasure. "How can they fuck up food so bad, but the coffee tastes like heaven?"

Sonny smiled. "Ain't you half French?" he asked, knowing full well he was.

"Yeah, French," Rafe replied testily. "*Not* Parisian. Paris is my least favourite place on earth. Can't get a decent fucking sandwich anywhere. Even half the restaurants here are fucking crap."

His CO's frustration made Sonny chuckle. Rafe in a grumpy mood was always funny. "Don't worry, mate," he consoled him. "We'll be back home soon, with crap British food."

"I'll take crap British food over crap French food any day," Rafe replied. "As soon as you shoot Nemiroff, we can fuck off 'ome."

He was referring to the target; a sleazy Russian oligarch that British Intelligence had deemed too dangerous to live due to his habit of bribing politicians and funding European terror organisations. So far, no charges or convictions had stuck to the man; he was too slippery.

So, assassination it was.

Sonny shrugged. "Can't shoot him if he ain't here, can I? Where the fuck is he?"

"Intel reckons tonight," Rafe said. "So much for knowing all his movements."

"Yeah," Sonny agreed. He didn't like it when targets did something unpredictable; it usually made his job harder. "They still reckon he's going to his suite?"

"Yep," Rafe said. "We'll find out soon."

"All right. I'll head out in a minute, then." Sonny sat down to eat his crap ham sandwich. Rafe ate his, too, but complained after every bite.

At least the coffee was top notch.

Afterward, Sonny took his backpack of gear, and his rifle, disguised in a guitar case, and headed off.

He'd already scoped out a sniper's nest for Nemiroff's suite, with a clear view of the large windows. Nemiroff had a big ego, and his penthouse suite had huge windows with only floaty, sheer curtains. It would be an easy shot.

Sonny entered the apartment building opposite Nemiroff's building and took the stairs to the top floor. This building was going through renovations, which meant that the top three floors were currently empty of tenants, and the top floor itself was still covered in plastic sheeting, waiting for new windows to be put in.

As far as sniper's nests went, it was ideal.

Sonny set up shop there. He rolled out a padded mat and crouched on it while he set up his rifle. He'd already calculated the distance and wind from this position, having been in this nest for the past three nights. It wasn't as windy tonight. That would affect his shot. Sonny adjusted his rifle. He laid out on the mat and peered through the scope for final checks.

Now all he had to do was wait.

*

Five hours later, when Sonny's limbs had gone stiff from the cold, he finally got the word from Rafe: Nemiroff was en route to his location.

"About chuffing time," he murmured. He flexed his hands to warm his fingers, then got into position on his stomach, peering through the rifle scope.

Maids and assistants switched on the lights in Nemiroff's suite across the way, illuminating all the rooms.

Perfect.

Within thirty minutes, the man himself appeared; a White, middle-aged man in a suit and gold cufflinks, thinning salt and pepper hair— a positive ID.

"Target in sight," Sonny whispered. "Not a clean shot." There were assistants and hangers-on flitting around Nemiroff; talking to him, pouring him a drink. A mix of men and women, including one young woman in a red dress and fur stole.

"Wait for a clean shot," Rafe's voice said through his earpiece.

They'd been waiting for days, but Sonny knew this hit was important to the brass.

"Copy," he murmured. He tracked the target using his scope. Nemiroff moved from one room to the next, heading to the seated area. This would get tricky; Nemiroff picked a chair on the far side of the room, facing the window (no doubt to get that view of the Eiffel Tower) but this left space for the other people to get in Sonny's way.

Unless one of them moved, this wouldn't be a clean shot.

"Anything?" Rafe asked.

Sonny exhaled calmly. "Not a clean shot. One potential casualty."

Rafe went quiet, probably relaying that information to the brass back in London. "Negative," he replied. "Clean shot required."

Fuck's sake.

He waited, keeping Nemiroff in his crosshairs. The wind picked up outside, Sonny felt the draft. He adjusted his rifle.

Finally, *finally*, a clear path was presented as the people blocking his shot stepped aside. They were opening a bottle of champagne, smiling, laughing over the spilled bubbles. Nemiroff was grinning like a Cheshire cat.

"Green," Sonny murmured.

"Take it, take it, take it," Rafe replied.

Sonny exhaled softly, and slowly pulled the trigger. The bullet shot out, punching through the glass window and hitting Nemiroff square in his forehead. He sagged into the chair while his comrades looked around in surprise, the split second before they pieced together what had happened.

Sonny released the shell and prepared to load a second bullet for a double tap. In that same split second, he realised someone was approaching him; a dark shadow across the room. Sonny gripped his rifle and rolled aside. A bullet skimmed the floor where he'd just been, lodging into the padded mat.

This was a problem.

Sonny spun round, aiming his rifle and loading his bullet in one practised move. This would not be pretty. He fired at his assailant, hitting him square in the chest. The force of the bullet knocked him backward, and he didn't get up again.

"I'm made," Sonny said, getting to his feet. He had to get out of here and fast.

"Nemiroff is down," Rafe informed him. "Get out of there, bruv."

"I'm trying." Sonny pulled his backpack over his shoulder and gripped the rifle to his chest. He had to leave the guitar case and the dead body. "Who the fuck knew I was here?" he demanded, taking one brief glance at the body as he ran past; White male, athletic build, street clothes, balaclava over his face. Probably ex-military in disguise; could be anyone.

"Get out to the street," Rafe replied. "I'll extract you. ETA ten minutes."

"Copy," Sonny said, running to the stairs.

As he burst through the door, another man attacked him, lunging at Sonny with a knife. Sonny dodged the lunge, but the blade nicked his ribs, slicing through clothes. A surface scratch; a close call, nothing more.

Sonny used his rifle as a shield, blocking the second knife thrust, and pushing the man back. This one wasn't wearing a balaclava, and he had visible tattoos snaking up his pale neck.

Someone else took a shot at them as they grappled.

"Fuck's sake," Sonny gritted out. He spun his sparring partner around, so his back took the bullets. The man shouted and convulsed as he was shot three times. Sonny pushed him over the stair rail, along with his rifle. Man and rifle both tumbled down the shaft. Sonny drew his handgun and fired back at the shooter one floor below.

This op had turned into a right royal shitshow.

Sonny was trapped on the stairs in a shootout. Whoever the shooter was, he was trained, and a good shot. Sonny retreated back up the stairs. If he couldn't get down, then he'd lure the bastard out.

Sonny went back into the penthouse suite, using the plastic sheeting hanging from the ceiling for cover. He shrugged out of his backpack, gripping it tight in one hand. He held his gun in the other. His adrenaline was pumping but he forced his breaths to remain even, calm. Slip into the zone and get the job done.

When the shooter followed him into the suite, Sonny waited for him to come within range, then attacked. He lunged in, swinging the backpack into his outstretched gun hand to throw him off balance. A shot rang out, but it went wide. Sonny had already raised his gun and shot the other man at close quarters, right in the chest.

He went down.

Sonny stood over him as he died. Another White guy, probably ex-military judging by his shooting skills. Sonny didn't recognise him. As the man clutched at his bleeding wound, Sonny noticed a tattoo on the back of his hand; a simple black circle with a dot in its centre. A gang sign? Sonny didn't recognise it.

He had to go. His position was compromised.

Sonny picked up his bag and returned to the stairwell. He kept his gun raised as he made his way down the stairs. At the bottom, he retrieved his rifle. Nobody else had tried to kill him yet. He'd made it.

Using his bag to partially conceal the rifle, he exited onto the street and walked briskly around the block. Even though it was night there were still pedestrians about, and carrying a rifle like this wasn't ideal. Sonny heard sirens in the distance, probably heading straight for Nemiroff's building.

Rafe came skidding around the corner in their hire car. Sonny was relieved to see him. He knew he could count on Rafe.

He got into the car, and Rafe drove him away from the scene.

They should've been home free, but Sonny noticed a queasy feeling come over him. He started to sweat, and his limbs felt stiff.

"Are you okay?" Rafe asked him.

Sonny shook his head. "Something's wrong," he said through gritted teeth. The nick on his ribs stung. Not like a normal cut; it burned.

"Shit," Sonny said. "Mate, I think I've been poisoned."

Chapter Twenty-Two

Meanwhile, at the PRISM lab

Human trials were not going so great.

In the two years she had been working on Project A-X with Dr Lee, the lab team had made a breakthrough with the asteroid samples. Thanks to her insight on parasites, Farah had advised Lee about allowing the alien sample to have enough host tissue to live on while in liquid form. Combined with Dr Lee's groundbreaking work in stem cells and cloning, they had managed to create a formula stable enough to sustain the glowing blue matter.

They called the formula Compound A-X, and it was considered a huge breakthrough in the testing.

Farah was thirty-eight and now divorced. She was single, while her ex-husband was remarried. It was vital that she do well, that she prove herself. Unfortunately, so far, all her work on

Project A-X had to remain confidential. She told her friends and family that she was consulting with the Natural History Museum, and that was partly true, but her real employers were PRISM, a division of British Intelligence.

If the lab team were to produce something incredible—repair tissue or cure the common cold—then there could be a chance Farah would be invited to government conferences and awarded for her work. Until then, she had to keep quiet. Keep the secret. And yet, they hadn't made any new breakthroughs that were worth gathering a conference for.

Farah was concerned that Compound A-X would be a non-starter. She'd had grand ideas about how it would be the next big thing for modern medicine; all the stem cell research had been so promising, even Dr Lee said that the compound stabilised the stem cells during fertilisation procedures.

Yet, so far, their only successes had been cloning several guinea pigs, and a couple of dogs. When it came to the human trials, Compound A-X refused to co-operate with the humans. The only cell growth and adhesion that was a success was on the burn victims. Cell repair for skin damage was a minor success, but only with a small percentage of subjects. In many cases, the alien DNA expanded too rapidly for the host to absorb and exposing them to further treatment would result in a complete breakdown of their red and white blood cells.

In short, they hadn't gotten anywhere in months.

"What if we take it back to formula?" Dr Zheng suggested. He was Lee's junior assistant on the project.

Dr Lee looked tired at the suggestion, but she didn't refute it.

Farah stayed silent herself, drumming her pencil on the table in thought. There had to be some better way to administer the formula. Their tried and tested method was a series of intramuscular injections, but this didn't have a great success rate.

"We need to do *something*," Zheng said, talking out loud. "The boss wants answers."

"These things take time," Lee replied, her Korean accent more pronounced because she was frustrated. "This is not a microwave meal ready in three minutes."

Farah looked up. "Microwave?" she said, looking at Lee. "What if that's something we can replicate?"

Zheng looked confused. "Microwave a human?"

"No," Lee said, eyes widening as the same thought occurred to her. "But the next best thing. A particle accelerator."

"Do we have one?" Zheng asked.

"No," Lee said. "But we can borrow one."

The machine arrived two days later, shipped down from Liverpool. It resembled a small MRI scanner in appearance, and it was on loan from a cancer research institute. They were borrowing it with the stipulation that they would share their research on cancerous cells and mutations.

Dr Lee had plenty of tumours from organ donors to work on, as well as other skin diseases and infections the lab kept in Petri dishes.

The team got to work, repeating all their previous trials introducing Compound A-X to infected human cells, setting the samples into the particle accelerator (also called a cyclotron) for designated times, then recording the findings.

The experiment was positive, which Farah was relieved about. The compound reacted to human cells and tissue after being in the cyclotron, with varying results. Under the microscope, Compound A-X's cells were very active and adhered to the human cells in every sample.

The problem was Compound A-X only made positive

adhesions to healthy human cells. Any trace of illness or disease made the alien samples withdraw entirely. Trying to get it to play ball was like trying to control liquid mercury.

"It's only interested in healthy subjects," Lee mused one day.

"But we're supposed to be curing illnesses," Zheng said with a sigh.

"There must be a workaround," Farah said. "Maybe instead of human trials for illness, we could focus on a different cross section of subjects instead? Subjects without illness, but with some disability?"

Lee and Zheng nodded. "I've studied bone growth for babies born without limbs," Lee mentioned. "And for veterans, with reattachment of severed limbs. I'd be very interested in tendon repair trials."

"So, babies, or veterans?" Zheng asked, sliding his chair over to his PC and cracking his knuckles.

The British Government gave them test subjects as and when needed from local hospitals. Most of the subjects were seriously ill or ill enough that signing off on a new experimental drug trial and signing the NDA was something they'd agree to all too readily. Sadly, as the human trials hadn't been much success, Compound A-X usually made no difference to their condition, and they died during or after the trial had ended.

Hopefully the cyclotron breakthrough would change that.

"Veterans," Lee said. It was her call. "Any age."

Zheng tapped his keyboard, entering requirements to the system. "Okay, what have we got..." He adjusted his glasses, leaning into the screen. "Got a couple of potentials. Soldier with lower leg loss from an explosion, at St. Thomas's hospital. Oh, this is interesting; soldier with strychnine poisoning at Chelsea and Westminster. Got dropped off by air ambulance yesterday."

"The poison subject," Lee said. "How bad is it?"

Zheng clicked on the file. "They've administered a muscle relaxant for the cramping," he read out. "Patient arrived with typical symptoms; respiratory failure, minor seizures, responding to treatment but vitals weakening. You'll like this part, Doc," Zheng added. "It says, 'due to the classified nature of his op, his next of kin are not informed. The British Government already has authority over his medical decisions.' You know what that means—they don't want anyone to know how he got poisoned."

"Probably Secret Service," Lee said. "He sounds useful. Request access."

"Special Air Service," Zheng replied. "I'll send the request now."

Farah got a sinking feeling in the pit of her stomach. She rose from her chair and went to stand behind Zheng, leaning in to read his screen. When she saw Sonny's legal name on the patient file, she felt the blood drain from her face.

"That's my cousin," she uttered.

*

Farah made the call to their boss while Lee and Zheng packed a medical bag. Her hands shook, her breaths shallow. Her cousin was lying sick in hospital, and the Army hadn't informed his family. *Her* family.

When Guv answered the phone, Farah quickly explained the situation. She wanted a fast-tracked approval since Sonny was in a bad way. They usually got their test subject approvals within forty-eight hours, but she was worried he wouldn't have that long.

Guv asked her to hold for a moment, probably checking the files on his laptop. Farah waited, tapping her foot from nerves. Lee and Zheng were rushing around the lab collecting what they needed; syringes, dressings, blood-taking kits, and blue vials of Compound A-X fresh from the particle accelerator.

"Dr Ahmadi?" Guv said, coming back on the line. "I'll approve the test subject. I'd go ASAP if I were you."

"Thank you," Farah breathed. "We will leave now."

"If his CO presents an obstruction, have him call me," Guv said, "but keep all intel confidential. And do not inform any other family members. Are we clear?"

"I understand," Farah replied. She ended the call, feeling shaky but determined. This needed to work. Her mother and aunt loved Sonny, even if he wasn't the most congenial of relatives at times. Farah had to do something to save him.

"We're ready," Lee told her.

Farah nodded. The hospital was less than fifteen minutes' drive away. "Let's go."

*

Sonny had quite a high pain threshold compared to most people he knew, but the last two days had been on a whole other level of pain.

The blade he'd been grazed with had poison on it. Strychnine. Not enough to kill him right away, but enough to slowly break him down. The thing about strychnine was it wrecked the muscles and the body, while the mind stayed lucid. Sonny knew exactly what was happening to him and felt every excruciating muscle cramp and spasm. A mere touch to his skin was extremely painful for him and set off more muscle contractions.

The various doctors and nurses in France and now in London had injected him all over with a muscle relaxant, and he'd screamed in pain from the heightened stimulation of needles jabbing into him. Now he was on a breathing machine, because his lungs didn't want to do their work anymore. He gasped into the mask over his face, eyes half shut because the light hurt. They'd darkened his room, but any stimulation was still too much to bear.

Through it all, Rafe had been by his side, looking on with a grim expression.

"You'll pull through this, mate," he said, for the hundredth time that day.

Sonny swallowed. His throat was dry. "Don't tell me gran," he rasped out. "Don't tell 'er how I died."

He knew it was coming, and it wouldn't be long now. He was twenty-six years old, and eight of those years he'd been a soldier. It'd been a good run.

"You can't die on me, you plum," Rafe said, voice breaking. "I wish we'd never taken that op. Fucking France."

Sonny closed his eyes again. "Not...your fault," he managed. "We'll blame...Paris."

This earned a little chuckle from Rafe.

Sonny didn't blame him; he only blamed himself for getting nicked with a dodgy knife.

"Did...the brass...say who?" he asked. Who had known he was there to assassinate Nemiroff?

"Nothing yet, mate," Rafe said. "They said counterintelligence is looking into it."

Sonny might have rolled his eyes if the movement wasn't so painful.

"Great," he wheezed.

He'd be long dead by the time they had any clue. Bloody useless.

The door to his room opened, light from the hallway streaming in. Sonny winced against the brightness.

"Oi, who are you?" Rafe demanded.

"I'm his cousin," said a familiar voice. "And we are all doctors."

Sonny opened his eyes a little. "Farah?" he wheezed.

"I must ask you to step outside," Farah told Rafe. "We need to begin treatment right away."

"What treatment?" Rafe replied.

"This comes from the top," Farah told him, handing over a white card. "You can call Lieutenant General Haywood on this number. Now, please exit the room."

Rafe looked pained, and he glanced at Sonny for his approval.

Sonny nodded once. "I'll be fine," he rasped. What were they going to do anyway, pump him full of some Vitamin C? He was a lost cause, and they all knew it.

Rafe reluctantly left the room.

The two East Asian doctors Sonny didn't recognise got to work opening their bags and snapping on plastic gloves.

"Bit late," Sonny rasped. "Last...legs." It was getting harder to talk.

"This is a little experimental," Farah said gently, standing beside Sonny's bed. She extended her hand to clasp his, but one of the other doctors warned her not to.

"Any muscle stimulation will hurt him," the woman said in accented English.

"I forgot." Farah stood back. "Sorry."

Sonny watched her closely. "Since when did...you work for...Bri'ish gov?"

"I might ask you the same thing," she replied.

Sonny huffed a breath; it came out raspy. "Same...employer..." Since he'd signed up as a teenager, he wanted to say. He couldn't manage it. The SAS were the spearhead of the British

Government doing whatever was needed: assist the police, or go bump somebody off. It was all for the government.

What had his relatives thought he was doing all these years? Polishing boots?

And when had Farah started to work for top brass? Seemed like the two of them had more in common than Sonny had realised.

"We're ready," the woman doctor said, brandishing a big needle full of a curious blue liquid.

Great, Sonny thought. More pain.

Farah muttered a quick prayer in Farsi while Sonny braced himself.

Using the cannula on his hand, the woman doctor inserted the needle and slowly injected it. The slight movement on his hand caused him pain, and Sonny felt the liquid whooshing up his hand and into his arm.

Incredibly, his arm stopped hurting.

It felt almost too good to be true, after fifty hours of painful muscle contractions.

From his arm the feeling spread out, first into his chest then his other arm, and down his legs. This was more effective than the relaxant the previous doctors had used.

Sonny exhaled a long sigh as the pain dissipated.

"It's working?" the male doctor whispered, like this was a surprise.

Farah uttered praise for God in Farsi. Sonny did roll his eyes this time.

"I want blood samples," the woman doctor said. "Then continue introducing the compound."

As they spoke and worked around him, Sonny drifted off into a peaceful sleep.

*

When he woke, he was ravenous.

Rafe was sitting next to his bed, no one else in the room. "You're awake? Oh, thank fuck," Rafe said, sitting bolt upright. "I thought you was a goner, bruv."

Sonny blinked his eyes and looked around. The room was still dark and gloomy, but his eyes didn't hurt anymore.

In fact, he felt pretty good, considering.

"Mate, can you draw the curtains and get me some food?" he asked. It was then he realised he wasn't wearing an oxygen mask, nor was he hooked up to anything other than a basic heart monitor with a clip on his finger.

The cannula was still in his hand, but currently empty.

"Course, bruv," Rafe replied. "You sit tight, I'll sort you out."

"Am I okay?" Sonny asked. "I thought I was about to pop me clogs."

"Yeah." Rafe got that pained look on his face again. "We all did, you lucky bugger. Then your cousin came in with those doctors and cured you."

"That's a stroke of luck, then, eh?" Sonny said. "Suppose I better put her back on my Christmas card list."

Rafe got him some food, and Sonny wolfed it down. It was only basic hospital food but to him it tasted like manna from heaven.

A doctor breezed by and informed them that Sonny's vitals looked good, and his transfer was set for that afternoon.

"What transfer?" Sonny asked him. "I thought I was given all clear?"

The doctor shrugged. "Your treatment wasn't done by us, so I can't tell you much, I'm afraid."

"Well, that's great, innit?" Sonny grumbled. After the doctor left, he said to Rafe, "I can just discharge myself."

Rafe looked at him but didn't say anything.

"What's that look for?" Sonny demanded. He wanted to get out of the bed, get a curry, and go the fuck home.

"I don't know, it's all a bit cloak and dagger, mate," Rafe explained. "They wouldn't even tell me the full story. All I know is, top brass approved some testing on you, and they want to keep you under observation for a bit."

Sonny groaned. "I wanna go 'ome."

"It's probably only a few more days or something," Rafe replied. "Better this than dead, right?"

"Jury's out," Sonny quipped.

That afternoon, patient transport came to collect him. After much griping, Sonny was allowed to sit in a wheelchair in lieu of being wheeled out in the hospital bed. He was given a dressing gown to put over his backless nightie, and warm slippers for his feet.

"I feel like I'm being carted off to a fucking old people's home," Sonny joked, as the paramedic wheeled him away. "I'm pretty sure I can walk."

Rafe walked alongside them. "Pipe down and enjoy it while it lasts," he said.

"You wouldn't be saying that if it was your bollocks flapping free in the breeze," Sonny replied.

Rafe chuckled. "Sounds nice. Give them an airing."

They kept up the banter until they got downstairs to the ambulance. Then Sonny waved goodbye to Rafe and was secured in the back of the ambulance for transport.

Probably best Rafe went home, Sonny thought. It'd been four days since their Op was officially over, and his wife and kids would be wondering where he was.

The journey in the ambulance was short, barely ten minutes. He had no idea where they were taking him, but he felt the vehicle tilt as it went down a ramp.

When the back of the ambulance opened and he saw people again, it was inside some gloomy car park, with Farah and that tiny East Asian doctor waiting for him.

"Salaam alaykum!" Farah called out in greeting, a wide grin on her face.

Christ, she's going to fuss over me now.

Still, he bit his tongue against sarcastic replies. By all accounts, Farah and her colleagues had saved his life. Time for some humble pie.

They took him to a shabby little service elevator, where they went down a couple of levels.

"Where are we?" Sonny asked. They had to be in Zone One still, because the drive from the hospital hadn't taken long at all. He assumed it was some private facility, but nobody was forthcoming about an answer.

"This is Dr Lee's research space," Farah said, gesturing to the petite, female doctor. "It's very classified."

"Uh-huh," Sonny said. "I know how to keep my mouth shut, love," he told his cousin while eyeing Dr Lee, whose face gave away nothing.

"Once we get into the lab," Farah continued, "you can get settled in and we'll run some checks."

"I want food and proper clothes," Sonny replied. "Otherwise, the temptation to moon you all will be too much, I'm afraid."

"Don't you dare," Farah scolded, ever the mum.

Dr Lee's lips curved in the barest of smiles. Hopefully that indicated she had a sense of humour.

"And make sure it's decent food," Sonny added. "I could

murder a curry.”

“Here.” Dr Lee tapped her phone, then turned the screen round to Sonny. “Choose what you want. I’ll have it picked up.”

The screen was showing one of the local food delivery apps.

Sonny took the phone gratefully. “Now we’re talking.” He selected the restaurant, then picked several curries, naans, sides, and a can of soda before offering the phone back.

While he’d been choosing food, they had reached their floor and wheeled him along a narrow white corridor to a bare bones white room with one narrow bed, a tiny water closet, and a large mirror on the far wall which was obviously an observation window.

Sonny directed a look at his cousin. “You’re all gonna watch me have a wank, are you?”

Farah was bad at lying. Her face had too many tells, and to Sonny it was clear she didn’t know what to say. She’d always been a bit of a pearl clutcher.

Dr Lee, on the other hand, appeared unconcerned. “Your food will be brought to you. Clothes as well. May we collect blood samples now?”

“Yeah, awright,” Sonny replied, resigned.

He wanted to ask if he could call his gran, since he didn’t have his phone on him. Maybe Rafe had it. She wouldn’t have been aware that he’d had a near death experience, and Sonny wouldn’t tell her either; he simply wanted to hear her voice.

But he didn’t want to show his cards to the doctors too soon. Hopefully he’d be out of here in a day or two and could go home on leave for a bit. Give Gran a huge cuddle.

But in the back of his mind, he was starting to get a sinking feeling about this. That observation window was the first red flag.

Chapter Twenty-Three

Over the next few days, Sonny was kept under observation in that room, only occasionally escorted out to visit the main lab.

He'd joked that the two East Asian doctors, nicknamed Doc and Zee, should strap him into an upright gurney and wheel him around like Hannibal Lecter. Zee had laughed. He had a sense of humour. Dr Lee had looked contemplative, which only made Sonny regret putting the idea into her head.

They took blood samples from him nearly every day—urine samples too. Sonny had never peed into so many cups in his life. The docs gave him courses of injections, put him on drip feeds from pouches of blue liquid, without saying exactly what it was, and sometimes they made him take a CT scan.

They *said* it was a CT scan, but the machine looked different to what they normally did.

So far, the docs said he was in the clear healthwise. No more poison in his system, no more muscle contractions or seizures.

They gave him clothes, and all the food he wanted—he was very hungry, abnormally so. They gave him a phone to use, but Sonny assumed it was tapped. He called his gran anyway; he couldn't wait any longer.

It wasn't like his identity was a secret. The docs all knew who he was, and Farah probably would've told them anyway.

Gran asked when he was coming home, like she always did. Sonny reluctantly told her that he was working, but he'd get home to visit as soon as he could. She knew he was in the SAS, and that he couldn't tell her or anyone exactly what he did.

Sonny worried about her being at home alone, but she insisted she could manage. She hadn't wanted to move house after Granddad had died a year before; all her memories were there.

Sonny called Rafe, chatted with him. They commiserated with each other's woes; Sonny being cooped up with doctors, and Rafe being in the doghouse with his wife.

"She wants me to change jobs," Rafe complained. "So I'd be at home more. I've tried explaining that if I take another job now, it'll mean being out the same number of hours as I'm already doing, plus the time I'd waste waiting during rush hour. She doesn't believe me. I'm damned if I do, damned if I don't."

"Buy 'er a bunch of flowers," Sonny told him. Marriage sounded like stress.

"I don't think flowers will cut it, bruv," Rafe replied. "It's gonna take something drastic. But I don't wanna start all over again. It took me all that time to get to staff sergeant, and now special projects. Fifteen fucking years, bruv."

"And you deserve it, Sarge," Sonny told him. "Stick to your guns. She'll come around."

"Hope so," Rafe said. "I'm sick of the moaning."

Sonny grinned but didn't say anything. Rafe did his fair share of moaning too. He hoped the pair could sort it out.

After the call was finished, Zee came to collect Sonny and take him for a CT scan.

"Another one?" Sonny complained. He got up and slipped the foam flip-flops onto his feet, then shuffled along the ceramic floor. The sports casual look they had him in was not his cup of tea.

"You're responding so well to treatments," Zee told him. "All vitals are perfect."

"That's me," Sonny quipped. "Walking perfection."

He was getting bored of all this. Going from one lab to another, running on a treadmill while hooked up to the heart monitor. Surely, he could go home soon.

Zee took him to the room where the CT scanner was. Sonny laid on the gurney and waited while the circular machine buzzed around his head. It reminded him of being a kid and watching his gran in the hair salon getting her hair dried by a noisy machine.

At least this scanner was quiet. Usually Sonny felt nothing; he'd been feeling fine for several days now. Normal.

Better than normal.

As the machine turned around his head, Sonny heard a high-pitched noise. It started off faint, growing louder until it became a painful shriek in his ear.

"Argh!" he shouted, reaching out to push the machine away on reflex. "Turn it off!"

The noise abruptly ceased, replaced by a crunch of expensive equipment falling onto the tile floor.

Sonny sat up and realised that he'd managed to shove the entire machine onto the floor, effectively breaking it.

"Shit," he murmured. "Er, sorry?"

Dr Zheng stood back, staring at the mess on the floor, then glancing up at the security camera.

"They're not gonna bill me for that, are they?" Sonny asked, only half joking. "I already have a credit card without any credit left."

"Um?" Zee said, seemingly unsure. "It was an accident?"

"Well, yeah, of course it was an accident," Sonny said. "The sound was hurting my ear, and I just..." He waved his hand to mimic the motion. "I didn't mean to throw the thing on the floor."

"I'm sure someone will pick up the bill," Zee said, sending another pointed glance to the security camera. "Maybe we better call it a day for now. You get some rest back in your room."

"I've had enough rest," Sonny grumbled, but he liked Zee so he didn't argue too much. He let Zee lead him back to his room, where the door was shut and locked.

Sonny sighed. He really hoped he wouldn't get in trouble for breaking stuff. On a whim, he strolled up to the mirror and tapped his knuckle on the surface.

"I'm sorry about the scanner!" he called out to whoever was watching in there. "I can't take full blame; there was a weird noise, and it hurt my ear. If you use faulty equipment, this is what happens."

No answer, as usual.

Well, he'd said his piece. Sonny turned around and went to the water closet, shutting the door behind him.

It was more of a cupboard; like the bathrooms on airplanes. Tiny, cramped. Barely enough room for a bog and a sink, with one mirrored cabinet above.

Sonny bent down to splash cold water on his face. He was annoyed, frustrated. He felt fine, and he wanted out of here. He'd never liked being cooped up.

He raised his head to meet his own eyes in the mirror. He needed a haircut. He was two weeks overdue. They'd given him a beard trimmer, but he needed to visit a salon to have his hair cut. Sonny had a vision of himself looking like Tom Hanks at the end of *Castaway*: long hair, long beard, withered away. He refused to be shut away that long.

His eyes in the mirror flashed, a silver glint in the pupils.

Oh, God, what now? Was he getting sick, or was the bulb in the light fixture flickering?

Sonny leaned in to see, watching his eyes. Yes, there. A silver shimmer in the irises. What was it? He watched his eyes shimmer, then his black pupils shifted form, narrowing down to slits.

Inexplicably, Sonny saw another face in the mirror; a large, blue-tinted face with several eyes, and long pointed teeth in a gaping mouth coming toward him like they were about to bite his head off.

He yelled out in fright and jerked backward, knocking the door and stud wall divide of the water closet clean away like it was mere paper.

What was happening? Was he seeing things now?

In a panic, Sonny tried the handle of the door to his room. Still locked. He wanted answers, so he decided to go get them himself. He braced himself and pushed his shoulder into the door, expecting to meet resistance but instead found himself bursting out of the door easily, lock broken and door swinging back on its hinges. Sonny stumbled out into the wall of the corridor with his momentum, leaving a faint imprint where his shoulder met plaster.

Sonny stared at the mess he'd made. Either this place was made of flimsy paper, or he was *strong*.

An alarm rang out overhead. Sonny first assumed it was a

fire alarm, then realised it must be for him. Quickly, he jogged down the hallway and headed to the lab. He had to find his cousin.

Doctors and techs in lab coats scurried out of his way in alarm. No security yet. At the door to the lab, Sonny was met with a coded lock. He didn't know the code, so instead he yelled up at the camera, "Farah! Are you there? Oi!"

The door opened, and when Sonny walked through, he saw his cousin there, along with Dr Lee who was holding a tranquiliser gun pointed straight at him.

"Sonny, calm down," Farah said, hands outstretched to placate him like he was some wild animal.

It was insulting.

"What the bloody hell did you do to me?" he demanded, taking one step forward.

Lee shot him with a dart, hitting him square in the chest. Sonny let out a grunt, but the pain was minimal. So was the effect of whatever she'd stuck him with. Sonny yanked the dart free and held it in his hand, ready to use it as a weapon if need be.

The look on Lee's face was priceless.

"Yeah, you want some of this?" Sonny taunted. "The fucking nerve of you lot!"

"That's enough," said a new voice, laced with steel and brimming with authority.

Sonny whirled around, seeing a man he didn't recognise but knew instantly was army: a slim, older Black man, standing with his hands casually held behind his back.

"Put the dart down, Corporal," he said. "And come into my office."

Sonny remained in a defensive stance. "Why should I?"

"Because," the man said calmly, "I've been authorised to make you a very generous offer for your continued cooperation.

Now, come with me."

*

Two weeks later
Special Intelligence Service Headquarters, Vauxhall

Valerie Jones was in her fifth-floor office with a waterfront view of the river Thames. She had another busy day ahead of her with not enough hours to do all the work needed.

Sat at her desk, she was drafting dual sternly worded emails. The first to her mole, overseas in the US spying for her, and the second to the Home Secretary.

The intercom on her desk buzzed. "Your eleven o'clock is here, ma'am," said her secretary.

Valerie had been looking forward to this meeting. She pressed the intercom to reply. "Send him in, Sharon." Valerie rapidly finished her drafts and saved them before Haywood entered the room.

"Lieutenant General," Valerie greeted as she closed her laptop shut. "Do sit down."

"Ma'am," the lieutenant replied. He walked steadily to the chair. Valerie knew he had a prosthetic leg. Haywood moved the chair out a smidge, then sat.

He had a paper file in hand and set it onto the edge of Valerie's desk. She was dying to read the report, but she kept her poker face.

"So," she started, sitting back in her chair. "Have you got good news for me?"

Haywood had a rather good poker face himself. The man was unflappable, rarely gave anything away.

In answer, he inclined his head a fraction. "It's early days, ma'am, but I do believe Asset A is a viable option."

"Good," Valerie said. That's what she liked to hear, especially after the complete cock-up Haywood's department had made of Asset V, the rogue vampire. "Give me a run down," she said.

Haywood picked up the file and offered it out to her. "Asset A is in week three of treatments," he said. "After being introduced to Compound A-X and responding positively, treatment was accelerated...with promising results."

Valerie flipped through the paper file. Handwritten reports of the medical trial, along with photographs of the subject himself, plus photos of the damage he had wrecked, albeit accidentally, on lab equipment and his own room.

Enhanced strength and senses, the report said. All things Valerie was extremely interested in when it came to British assets.

"And his temperament?" she inquired.

Haywood hesitated a short moment, which Valerie read as him trying to spin things positively.

"He has requested leave," Haywood replied.

Valerie nodded. Three weeks of being cooped up in hospital? She'd be climbing the walls too.

"So far, I've managed to stall him with half-truths and promises of a substantial bonus," Haywood continued. "Dr Lee is working on countermeasures to keep him in line."

"Yes," Valerie said, letting her frustration show in her clipped tone. "We don't want another runaway asset after pouring in valuable resources."

"No, ma'am," Haywood replied, voice even, no trace of emotion.

Valerie set the file down, page open on a lab photo of the subject running a treadmill; he was shirtless and wired to a heart monitor. A good-looking young man, she thought. That could prove to be useful for intelligence work. Some of Valerie's best agents were handsome.

"Tell me about the countermeasures," she said, looking up at Haywood. "And I'm not a scientist, so give me the layman's summary."

"Yes, ma'am," Haywood said. "In short, Dr Lee and her team used a particle accelerator to bolster Compound A-X in the subject. It worked a little too well on him, so now they're taking backward steps to...counteract it. This has involved a type of chemotherapy."

"Is it working?" Valerie asked.

Haywood hesitated again, adjusting his glasses for a pause. "Possibly," he said. "From what the doctors ascertain, Compound A-X remains in the subject, but retreats into a more dormant state when exposed to certain radiation. We told Corporal...we told the subject that the treatment was an attempt to remove the alien DNA. He doesn't know the results yet."

Valerie understood. It was only a matter of time before the test subject realised that he wasn't going back to normal; that normal wasn't an option anymore.

"Dr Lee is working on a prototype for a chemical tether," Haywood went on.

"And, again, in layman's terms?"

"A safeguard," Haywood explained. "Dr Ahmadi came up with the idea of introducing a dormant yet lethal agent to the subject's immune system, similar to a flu jab but the next level up. The working theory is that without a regular dose of special antibiotics administered by us, the subject will become seriously ill and unable to function within a matter of hours. Two, maybe three days tops."

"My word," Valerie exclaimed. "That sounds handy. There

are one or two field agents I wouldn't mind trying that out on. The ones that go AWOL far too often."

Haywood inclined his head in a nod. "If it all pans out, ma'am, Asset A would only be able to go AWOL for a couple of days before having to check in. We would be in full control of his functions."

"I can work with that," Valerie said confidently. "Send me his full file, and I'll run this up the flagpole. An enhanced soldier should be a much easier sell than a bloody vampire."

"Yes, ma'am."

"And," she added, "get me the file of his CO. The one he was on special projects with. A familiar face may help to ground our asset. Then I can pitch an enhanced team for assignments, ready to go."

"A good idea, ma'am," Haywood said. "I'll send the files right away."

*

Sonny was still stuck in his room—a new reinforced one—at the lab. He had a flatscreen TV now to make him less bored, they said. But he was still a prisoner here.

Apparently, he had a chance of being let out soon. At least, that's what Haywood had promised, if Sonny was willing to play ball. (Hard to play ball when he didn't know what the game was.) He was the one being played; he knew that for a fact.

He stared up at the ceiling, feeling queasy after a new round of injections. Doc and Farah said it was for getting the alien DNA out of him, but Sonny wasn't sure he believed them. He'd stopped having the visions and the freak outs when he was awake, but he kept having dreams.

Nightmares.

He woke up sweating and gasping for air. The dreams were so real, so vivid; the recurring one was that he was in a dark void with no air to breathe. He struggled but his limbs (long, huge limbs) couldn't move, and he felt he was wading through soup.

Sometimes he'd glimpse points of light in the dark void around him, but not always. Was it space, or underwater? It felt suffocating, whatever it was. And, then there was the noise. A chittering, growing louder until it pierced his ears. It took several nightmares for Sonny to realise that the raspy chittering noise came from *him*.

That sound chilled him to his bones.

Scary shit.

For the hundredth time that day, he mentally ran through his options. Stay, and let them keep experimenting on him, with the hope that he'd be released and get his life back soon. Work for Haywood, with a pay rise and chance of a private care home option for Gran, when she needed it. Sonny couldn't afford private care on his own.

Alternatively, he could break out and make a run for it, take his chances while at the same time leaving his gran to fend for herself, and leaving Rafe to face the consequences for his desertion.

Haywood had made it clear that Rafe was in this mess too. If Sonny ran, Rafe would face a criminal trial and possibly prison time, leaving his family without their primary provider. Sonny couldn't do that to them. Rafe was like a brother to him.

One thing was for sure, this whole thing was a shitshow, and he blamed his cousin, Farah, for all of it.

So, without dropping innocent people like Rafe in it, Sonny made the tentative decision to stick it out and play the long game.

From the sound of things, Haywood wanted him to continue doing special projects, AKA black ops, which Sonny would agree to if only to get the hell out of this lab. Going dark on ops was always the perfect opportunity to afford himself a little freedom, do some digging of his own, and find a way to get out of this cross-DNA mess they'd put him in.

And, he thought with some glee, a chance to start plotting some payback of his own. Once Sonny was finished with this shady department, they were all going to wish they'd never laid eyes on him.

Chapter Twenty-Four

Present Day
London

After hearing all of that, David stared down at the knots of wood on the kitchen table. He found it difficult to look Farah in the eye now, knowing she was one of the doctors in charge of human experiments.

It put him on edge, made his skin crawl.

A long silence of several moments followed before Farah broke it by asking, "Do you have any questions?"

David had several. The more he knew about all this alien stuff, the more questions he had. But the question now burning in his mind was how could she so willingly experiment on Sonny like that?

It reminded him of something that Jaime, from his old unit, had said a while back. He'd said that civilians really had no idea what it was like for the military; first the Armed Forces chewed them up and spat them out, and then civilians treated veterans as disposable. They couldn't win. It was a lose-lose situation whatever they did.

Thankfully for David, Farah's phone chimed and drew her attention. She answered the call. "Yes?" she said in English. "No, I'm at Sonny's. Oh, really?" Her tone changed, indicating surprise, and she rose from the table. "No, it's fine, I can leave right now. I have the car. Okay, see you shortly." She ended the call and slipped her phone back into her jacket. "So something came up," she said to David.

He watched her as she strode across the kitchen to grab her purse. "Uh, sure," he said, admittedly relieved.

"Tell Sonny to eat all this," she added, waving her hand at the remaining food spread out all over the counters. "We'll have to catch up later. Maybe dinner?" Before David could answer, she answered for him.

"Oh, shit," she said. "I have the kids. Okay, not tonight. Tomorrow? I'll call Sonny!" She waved a hand as she strode off, leaving David sitting in the kitchen. She didn't pause to say goodbye to Sonny, only to put her boots back on in the hallway before she hightailed it out the front door.

She was quite the whirlwind.

He remained seated at the table for a couple of minutes, gathering his thoughts. He was on edge, though, so he got up and began tidying the kitchen for something to do. He took the used dishes to the sink. He scraped uneaten food off plates and back into their containers and put them into the fridge.

Inside the fridge, of course, were the remaining couple of boba drinks Sonny had ordered; standing tall and colourful amid the cluster of takeout boxes and plastic containers.

David smiled wryly. Now he thought he understood a little better why Sonny was pushing back against his cousin, rejecting her food so blatantly. David closed the fridge, and slowly made his way down the hall. The door to the front lounge was closed, so maybe Sonny wasn't aware Farah had left.

David hesitated a moment, then knocked softly.

"Yeah," Sonny called from inside.

David twisted the handle and opened the door.

Sonny was sitting on the couch, back in his comforter nest with his feet up. He'd finished his drink, the cup empty save for a few pearls at the bottom. The TV was on, playing a lively episode of what looked like *Drag Race*.

"Has she gone?" Sonny asked, looking up at David.

David nodded. "She has."

"Good," Sonny said, turning back to the TV. "Peace at last."

"Yeah." David smiled. "Mind if I join you?" he asked.

"Pull up a pew, mate," Sonny replied easily.

David was grateful he was still welcome. He decided to perch on the far edge of the couch so he was closer.

"Mochi?" Sonny asked, picking up the candy box and waving it in David's general direction.

"I'm good, thanks," David said. "Is this *Drag Race*?"

"The UK one," Sonny replied. He set down the candy box and picked up the remote, muting the TV. "So," he said without elaborating.

"Yeah," David drawled.

There was a beat of silence, like Sonny was waiting for him to speak. David was still struggling to put his thoughts into words.

"She told you what you needed to know then?" Sonny asked.

David considered that. He nodded slowly. "Yeah, I guess she did."

"Great!" Sonny said breezily. "Less questions for me."

David shook his head with a smile. Sonny's dry sense of humour did help to lighten the mood.

"I may have some questions for you," he said at length. "As far as I understand it, you and I are the only two people in our...er...unique position."

"That we know of," Sonny replied.

"Yeah," David said. "So you and I are really the only two people who know what we're going through. You see, before, I thought I was going insane or something. But now I find out it was all real."

"Well, I'm sure there's plenty of time to get into all that," Sonny said, seemingly hinting that he'd rather delay the conversation than start now.

David was beginning to understand that Sonny wasn't keen on the topic. He'd rather make light of it with a joke than talk about something else. David supposed he couldn't blame him.

"So, what do you want to do today?" Sonny asked.

David took the change of subject in stride. "You know, I'd really like to visit a barber," he said. "Just a trim."

"Oh, yeah?" Sonny chuckled. "Okay. Yeah, we can do that. There's a couple up the road."

"Great," David replied. "I haven't had a proper haircut in months."

"All right." Sonny flung his comforter aside and got up from the couch. He offered the remote control to David. "Lemme go freshen up, and we can head off."

"Sure," David said. "Do you want me to pause *Drag Race*?"

"Nah, I've seen this one," Sonny replied. "Watch whatever you like. I won't be long."

"Okay," David said.

Sonny took his empty cup and his candy box and left the

room. David settled more into the couch, trying to ignore the inviting, warm-smelling nest Sonny had vacated on the other side. He pointed the remote at the TV and pressed the home button to see what news options there were. He wanted to check out the regional news to see what it was like here, something he often did when he was new to a country. It appeared Sonny had live TV options as well as streaming, so David chose *Sky News* and watched that for a few minutes.

British news was different to American, Mexican, or Arab news stations, David found. Maybe it was a slow news day today, but none of the headlines would've made the top ten in America.

He switched over to BBC news for comparison, and it was more or less the same stories. The British news jingles were super serious, comparatively, and none of the anchors were dolled up the same way American or Mexican anchors were. It was no *Telemundo*, that was for sure.

Sonny didn't take all that long with his shower, and David was still getting acquainted with British news when he came downstairs smelling clean and fresh. He'd dressed in different clothes, still mostly black: black skinny jeans, a dark burgundy shirt with an open button collar, and a fitted, black leather jacket. His hair was freshly blow-dried and styled in an effortless way that made David envious.

"How'd you do your hair so quick?" he asked.

Sonny smirked. "Bish, bash, bosh, innit?" he replied, which made no sense to David. "'Ere, did Toff say where she was goin'?"

It took David a moment to decipher the question, due to Sonny's British accent, which seemed thicker with certain words.

"Er, no," he replied. "But my guess is something to do with work."

"Hm." Sonny took his phone out to check the screen but

made a face to suggest he hadn't been informed. "Well, no news is good news. Shall we depart?"

"Yeah," David agreed.

While David went to grab his jacket, Sonny went to the kitchen to grab the two remaining bubble drinks. David was tying his boots when Sonny strode up to him and handed them to him.

"Hold these," he instructed.

David took the drinks while Sonny bent down to pull his boots on. He also picked out a pair of clean balled-up socks from the shoe rack and stuffed them into his pocket.

"How often do you change your socks?" David quipped.

Sonny smirked. "If you're gonna get your hair done, I'm nipping in for a pedi, innit?"

"A what? A pedicure?" David asked.

"You have to take care of your feet," Sonny replied, somewhat defensive.

"I agree," David said to placate him. Wearing boots in combat would do a number on anyone's feet. On impulse, and mostly to see how Sonny would react, David asked, "Will there be time for me to get one too?"

Sonny's eyebrows flicked up in surprise as he glanced at David. "Oh. Yeah, sure," he said easily. "You want extra socks?"

David was so amused by all this, he couldn't keep the smile off his face. "I think I'm good," he said. "Thanks."

He was starting to see that Naz wasn't the only member of the team with OCD quirks.

Sonny set his security alarm, then strutted out the door.

"What about Rafe's car?" David asked.

Sonny already had a straw from one cup stuck in his mouth to slurp, and he hummed in realisation before releasing the straw. "Oh, bollocks," he muttered and had to go back inside the house.

He thrust both cups at David to hold again. "Where did I put the keys?" he asked, talking to himself as he searched the entryway, feeling the pockets of the jacket he'd worn last night. The security alarm beeped until he reset it.

David was mostly sure by now that Sonny's laissez-faire attitude to general things was simply his nature and not an act like he'd first suspected. Then there were the OCD tendencies with clean socks. It was oddly endearing.

All of this simple domesticity was also very nice for David, after several months of being completely alone and on the run.

Sonny found the keys, swinging them on his finger as he strode past David and out the door.

"I hope you have your house key," David asked him.

"Yes," Sonny replied, though he patted his pocket to be sure. "Ha, ha!" he laughed. "Just pull the door shut, mate."

"I don't actually have a hand free," David pointed out.

"I'm sure you can figure it out, bright lad like you," Sonny quipped.

"Guess I can't argue with that logic," David said, juggling the two cups Sonny was determined to bring, so he could pull the door closed. He checked it had shut properly, then followed Sonny down the garden path.

Sonny was standing at the miniature gate, holding it open for David to pass.

"After you, sunshine," he quipped.

David was secretly starting to enjoy that nickname. In the back of his mind, he thought that this what living with a partner must feel like—the pet names, the banter. He found he liked it.

"Thanks," he replied, offering the drink cups back to Sonny. "Are you really gonna drink both?" he asked.

"Yes. Why, do you want one?"

"No, I'm good," David said.

Sonny held both boba cups and used his foot to kick the gate closed after them. Then he resumed slurping the entirety of one cup at an alarming rate.

David watched him as they walked side by side down the quiet street.

"What?" Sonny asked, glancing at him.

"Why are you so thirsty?" David asked out of curiosity.

Sonny broke into a dirty chuckle. "Said the bishop to the priest," he quipped. "I'm not parched, mate. Simply put, I'm a glutton."

David laughed. Sonny was a dork, and David liked that.

"You'll have a piss the size of a racehorse when you're done with those," he pointed out.

"Oh, I don't doubt it," Sonny replied. "Now, where did I park the car?"

Chapter Twenty-Five

They found the car without too much issue, and Sonny drove them a few streets through the neighbourhood before stopping quite abruptly on a corner when he spotted a free parking space.

"Get in, you beauty!" Sonny announced in delight, yanking up the handbrake and cutting the engine.

"I think I got whiplash," David quipped.

"This is a free spot!" Sonny replied. "Gotta grab 'em when you can, innit? Said the bishop…"

"Okay," David said, as they unbuckled and got out of the car. "I mean, innit?" he added for Sonny's benefit. He'd said it to be annoying, and the reaction he got from Sonny was not disappointing.

"Don't you get smart with me, sunshine," Sonny replied, voice going up in volume as he leaned over the top of the car to point at David. "You can wind your neck right back."

David smirked. He waited a beat before asking, "Did you neglect to add the 'innit' on the end of that sentence?"

"Fuck off," Sonny said, fighting a smile. He slammed the door shut and walked around the front of the car. David did the same, and they met at the hood. Sonny held up the car keys to lock the car with a beep and led the way around the corner onto a high street with a few stores and pedestrians. David was surprised to see not as many cars as he'd expected, but he didn't think they were anywhere near central London yet.

"See that place?" Sonny pointed across the street to a storefront that said "Lee's Nails."

David nodded. "The nail salon?"

"The nails," Sonny confirmed. "I will be in there. Come find me after you're done. Look both ways before crossing the street. I will not be held responsible for death by car."

David quirked one eyebrow and glanced left and right at the quiet little street with hardly any cars at all. "I think I can manage," he said dryly.

"See that you do," Sonny said. He spun on the spot and gestured to the store right behind them: a barbershop. Across the window the red and white letters read, "The Ali Barber." "And this!" Sonny told him. "Is where you will be getting dolled up."

David chuckled. He couldn't hold it in, but that was what he liked about Sonny; he made it okay to laugh about things that some men got hung up over. David felt at ease with Sonny.

They approached the barbershop together, and David saw through the glass window that it was almost certainly a West Asian barbershop. The barbers and the customers were all dark haired, full bearded, and brown skinned.

"C'mon, then," Sonny said, striding forward and opening the door. "Mohawk and goatee, right?"

David smiled. "No, just a trim."

"Shave it all off, right," Sonny quipped.

David was starting to regret this decision, especially when one of the barbers came up to them and started speaking in a language David didn't understand. It wasn't Arabic, and it wasn't Persian either. It was something else. Of course, Sonny responded perfectly in the other language. His brilliant linguistic skills were starting to annoy David.

As the barber spoke swiftly with Sonny, all David could do was watch and try to ascertain what they were saying from their numerous hand gestures.

It also gave David an opportunity to watch Sonny interact with another man, and with the language barrier, David focused more on their tone of voice, their body language, and hand gestures. The two clearly knew each other, but probably not overly well. The banter was brief but friendly, and Sonny was clearly joking around.

He handed cash over, presumably to pay for the haircut, and then the exchange was finished.

"Right!" Sonny clapped one hand onto David's shoulder in a parting gesture. "Kemal will sort you out, mate. All shaved off! See ya later."

And with that parting quip, he was out the door.

David watched him go, then he looked back at Kemal the barber with a small degree of apprehension. "Er, not shaved off," he said in English. "Just a trim. Please."

"Yes, come," Kemal replied in English, gesturing for David to take a chair. "Sit. Sit."

Oh, well, David thought as he sat in the barber's chair. At least his hair grew quick. He removed the hat from his head and clutched it tightly in his hands.

Kemal threw a black gown around David's shoulders, covering his body. David half expected Kemal to turn on the clippers and buzz all his hair off right away, but Kemal surprised him by taking a moment to examine David's hair, standing behind him and running his fingers through the long strands.

"Very split," he said in heavily accented English. "Split ends."

"Oh, yeah, probably," David replied. "I haven't cut it in a while."

Kemal nodded. David watched him in the mirror, the way his thick black eyebrows bunched as he frowned in thought. He was taking this seriously. Behind him on the wall, David noticed a framed picture showing a red flag with a white crescent moon and star. Turkish, then.

Kemal produced a comb and brushed David's hair back off his face and, with expert fingers, began shaping the hair into some semblance of a style.

"Like this?" Kemal said. "Long here."

David was relieved that Kemal seemed to know what he was doing. "Yeah, great," he replied.

Kemal nodded, letting the hair fall back. "And beard?"

"Keep the beard," David told him. He'd grown attached to it these last months.

"We make tidy," Kemal replied. Then he grabbed a water bottle and got to work, spraying David's hair down before he began cutting.

Kemal was very efficient. He cut, dried, and styled David's hair and beard in no time. A lot of the bad split ends landed on the floor where they belonged. When Kemal was done, David liked the cut he'd been given; thick and long on top, styled back with some height, and shorter at the sides and back. Along with the general trimming of his beard so his lips were visible at long last, he looked more sharp, less scruffy. Younger too.

Kemal dusted off the hairs, squirted some powerful cologne onto David's neck, then whipped the gown away. David smiled at himself in the mirror. Cinderella was ready to go to the ball.

"That's what I'm talking about," David said. "Thanks, man."

"You come back," Kemal said, handing David his business card while also touching him on his shoulder in a friendly manner. "Good price for you."

David liked the hospitality. It reminded him of Mexico.

"I'll come back, for sure," he said. "Thanks again."

He left the barbershop, swishing his head side to side in the breeze to get a feel for the new cut. He couldn't wait to show Sonny. David didn't put his hat back on, only shoved it into his back pocket and set off across the street for the nail salon.

*

Sonny was enjoying a nice hand massage, sitting opposite Minh as she chatted in Vietnamese about her family. She had two young kids in school and a chef husband who worked in a fancy West End restaurant.

Sonny was learning Vietnamese to speak to her and the other ladies in the salon. He'd had a few weeks practising with Minh since finding this place.

Unfortunately, their catch-up got interrupted by Sonny's phone vibrating in his pocket. "Sorry, Minh," he said, "I have to check that."

She rubbed a small towel over his hands to remove the moisturiser so he could get his phone out.

Sonny checked the screen and sighed inwardly.

Shepherd.

He accepted the call and put the phone to his ear. "Yes,

ma'am?" he answered.

"Since you're alone, I thought it would be a good time for you to bring me up to speed," Shepherd's voice bore into Sonny's ear.

She knew he was alone. Sonny almost looked around the salon to see if she was sitting at another nail station to spy on him, but then he spotted the security camera up in the corner.

Of course, she was watching, she always was.

"Yes, ma'am," Sonny repeated. He held his phone in one hand and offered the free one back to Minh to continue the massage. Maybe it would help alleviate his stress levels.

A beat of silence followed, then Shepherd said, "Well? How's it going with your charge?"

"Er, good, I think, ma'am," Sonny replied. He felt a bit put on the spot, especially having to talk in front of Minh.

"Good, you think?" Shepherd repeated, sounding very unimpressed.

"Er, yeah," Sonny said, schooling his expression so he didn't wince. Why was she annoyed with him already?

"And have you rolled out every red carpet at your disposal?" Shepherd asked him.

"Er, yes," Sonny replied. "All the carpets, ma'am."

Minh caught his eye and smiled.

She only knew that Sonny had a boss he called ma'am, and she could relate to interfering bosses.

Sonny smiled back, but inside he was panicking. He didn't really understand what Shepherd wanted him to do. This was only day one, what had she expected by now? He and David were just getting to know each other.

"What are your plans for the rest of the day?" Shepherd asked.

"Er," Sonny said, because he hadn't planned anything yet. "I don't know. See what he wants to do, I suppose."

He heard Shepherd sigh lightly on the line. He winced slightly.

"Well, that's great, Sonny," she said sarcastically. "I can see you've put a lot of thought into this."

"I thought I'd play it by ear, ma'am," Sonny replied, making it up on the fly. "Did you want to make any suggestions?" he added cheekily.

"Yes," Shepherd bit out. "Make sure he is your number one priority," she said. "I know you have downtime, but that's no excuse to slack off. No going down the pub with Rafe or anyone else. Got it?"

"Yes, ma'am," Sonny said. "Got it."

"I expect your undivided attention on our new guest," Shepherd said, at the same moment David strolled in through the salon door looking ever so handsome with his new haircut and causing several of the women to stare openly.

Sonny stared as well. David spotted him and smiled brightly.

"Ooh, very nice," Minh muttered quietly in English.

"Sonny?" Shepherd barked in his ear.

"Er, yes, ma'am," Sonny replied. "Undivided attention. Shouldn't be a problem."

*

David had never had a professional pedicure done before now. It felt okay. Weird, but okay. Besides his haircut earlier, this was probably the most prolonged skin contact David had had in months.

Since escaping the lab.

He was a little tense with someone sitting by his bare feet and touching them, but he forced himself to remain still and calm.

It helped having Sonny next to him, laid back and chatting to both the South East Asian women doing the pedicures. It also helped that the women were cute and smiley.

David didn't understand a word they were saying, but he got the impression that all three of them were talking about him.

In an effort to turn the conversation back to English, David asked Sonny, "How many languages do you speak, exactly?"

Sonny smirked. "A few."

"So, spill," David said. "Modesty doesn't become you."

Sonny tittered. (An amused little laugh that David was fast becoming fond of.)

"Come on," David prompted. "I know you're dying to show off."

"Seventeen," Sonny said.

David was gagged. "What? Get out of here."

"Nineteen if you count the two I'm learning but not totally fluent in yet," Sonny added.

"Get out of here," David repeated. "Nobody's fluent in that many languages."

Sonny side-eyed him with a proud smirk.

David smiled and shook his head. "Jesus. How?"

"I'm a cunning linguist," Sonny said, then broke into a dirty chuckle.

"I don't doubt it," David said. "But seventeen? I don't believe you."

One of the women spoke, not in English. Their conversation picked up when Sonny replied in their language, excluding David. It appeared she was asking Sonny a question, glancing at David as she did so.

When Sonny answered, her facial expression changed to surprise, then settled on an unimpressed look that she tossed in

David's direction.

The other woman looked up with a similar disdainful expression.

"Okay, what are you talking about?" David asked Sonny. "My ears are burning."

"Oh, they figured out you're American, mate," Sonny said with glee. "They're Vietnamese."

"Oh," David said. The looks made sense now.

"Don't worry, mate," Sonny said. "Nobody likes the British much, either."

"I'm Mexican, too," David reminded him. Then he switched to Nahuatl to prove the point. "¿Tināhuatlahtoa?"

Sonny looked at him with a blank expression, answering David's question, 'Do you speak Nahuatl?'. He didn't speak it.

David smirked. "There's a new language for you," he said in English.

The corner of Sonny's mouth tilted up in a smile, like he was enjoying this. "Challenge accepted, sunshine."

Chapter Twenty-Six

After their pedicures were done and David's feet were the softest and most moisturised they'd ever been, they both donned their footwear again (with clean socks for Sonny) and left the salon.

"I feel like I should be wearing flip-flops after that," David commented. "Pity to put our feet back into boots."

"Flip-flops?" Sonny scoffed. "Not 'appening."

They approached the parked car on the street, and Sonny's facial expression morphed into alarm. "What!" he declared, striding forth to rip a ticket from the front windshield. "What the bloody hell?"

"Got a ticket?" David drawled. Sonny had been so proud of that parking spot earlier.

Sonny read the ticket and pulled a face. "Yes. Well, correction. Rafe has a ticket. It's his car." He opened the driver's door and tossed the ticket over the seat like discarded confetti.

"Won't he get mad?" David asked, amused. He opened the passenger door but didn't get in yet.

"If you keep mum, he won't know it was me," Sonny replied. He got out his phone and scrolled his contacts, leaning against the open car door.

David watched him make a call, presumably to Rafe, but when no one answered Sonny shrugged and put his phone back in his pocket.

"Probably sleeping it off," Sonny said. "All right, so." He drummed his hands on the roof of the car. "What do you wanna do? Tourist things?"

"I... yeah, actually," David said. "I feel like I haven't seen anything that proves I'm actually in London yet."

Sonny laughed. "Prove? Okay. What would prove it, then? Big Ben? Tower Bridge?"

I love his accent. Tah Bridge, indeed.

"Yeah. Those sound good."

"Sorted." Sonny slid down into the driver's seat and shut his door.

David did the same and buckled in. "You don't mind doing tourist stuff?" he asked.

"As long as I can get a coffee and a sandwich," Sonny said, starting the car. "If you ask nicely, I'll even take photos for you."

David chuckled wryly. "Thanks." He didn't really have anyone else to share the photos with. "It's not like I can post them to social media if I'm legally dead, right?"

"Best not, sunshine," Sonny replied. He shoved the gearstick into gear and took off down the street at breakneck speed. When he screeched to a halt at a traffic light, he added, "We do have a team notice board in the tech room. You can put a photo up there."

David was surprised to hear that. Sounded like their setup

operated under friendlier terms than what David had woken up to back in the US.

"I guess a photo or two would be cool," David said.

*

Sonny drove them south, avoiding the city centre and traffic by taking the long way round through quieter and more residential streets with beautiful old houses and leafy green trees lining the sidewalks.

David saw a few pedestrians and people waiting at bus stops. He noted their clothes and how differently they dressed from Americans or Mexicans. Every country had their own styles, every city, but London seemed like the most eclectic mix yet.

Sonny had the radio playing while David gazed out of the window, soaking it all in. The residential areas faded away as they drove into wider streets with bigger buildings, old and varied in architecture; some beautifully crafted, some plain and utilitarian. Government buildings, David guessed. The trees planted along the streets were bigger too, their green treetops obscuring the city around them, muffling the soft hum of traffic.

Considering how big it was, London wasn't as noisy as David had thought it would be. It had a reserved elegance about it.

The red phone booths were particularly quaint.

As Sonny drove down a wide street, tall buildings on their right, he nodded to the left-hand side. "There you are, sunshine. Tourist traps over there."

David looked, and beyond the trees and sidewalk, he saw a riverbank: the River Thames. He couldn't see the water yet, but he saw tops of boats and one large ship sailing past, the London Eye wheel visible behind it.

He was excited. It had been a long time since he'd been able to relax enough to enjoy being in a new place.

Sonny turned right, taking them into the narrow driveway of a plain, cream-colored building. David dragged his gaze away from the landmarks of the river and ran a quick visual analysis of the building. No signs, nobody outside. Two other cars parked in the tiny gravel car lot out front, protected by a low wall from the street. David's gut told him this was a government building. He hoped Sonny wasn't trying to ambush him with something.

"Right, hop out," Sonny instructed, killing the engine. They got out of the car. Sonny locked it, then twirled the keys on his finger. "Stay right here," he told David, walking around the hood. He was headed for the front door of the building.

David was in no hurry to follow, so he waited.

When Sonny came back within a couple of short minutes, David guessed he had dropped the keys off inside so they could leave the car.

"What's that place?" he asked.

"Like a diplomat's concierge," Sonny replied. "I'm leaving the car here because Rafe lives south. I'm not taking it back to North London again."

"Right," David said. "Are you really a diplomat, or only enjoying their amenities?"

Sonny grinned and raised a finger to his lips. "Shush."

David smiled back. He mimed zipping his lips.

"This way then," Sonny said, leading the way out.

David walked alongside him, and once they were out in the leafy green street on foot, he marvelled at how peaceful it felt here. The river ran along their left, and David was dying to see it up close.

They crossed the street at some traffic lights, now the same side as the river so David could walk right up to the low wall and look down. He was surprised to see a whole dock right below them, with dozens of ferries and tourist boats of varying sizes coming in or leaving with a boatload of passengers.

Good to see he wasn't the only tourist here.

When he looked out at the river itself, he got another surprise: they were close to a flyover bridge, with Big Ben and the Houses of Parliament right on top of them. David hadn't realised they were so close. He instinctively reached for his phone, itching to christen it with some photos.

"Happy?" Sonny asked. "Here, I'll take your picture."

David handed him his phone. Sonny went a few paces back then held it up to take his picture. David felt a touch awkward at first, self-conscious in front of Sonny. That was, until Sonny called out, "Cheer up, misery guts!"

David laughed, and Sonny caught it on camera. (Those photos ended up being pretty great.)

They walked a little further, Sonny leading the way up some stone steps from the embankment to the bridge. Immediately they were surrounded by the bustle of a busy street, with hundreds of pedestrians, tourists, cyclists and cars vying for space. A tourist trap stall selling T-shirts and other knick-knacks caught David's eye while Sonny rolled his.

"I suppose you want a T-shirt an' all?" he teased.

"I mean, I could use clothes," David replied. "But it's not a big deal."

"No, you may as well," Sonny insisted. "Which one do you want?"

Of course, David didn't have his own money yet. He was looking forward to when that happened. In the meantime, he picked a white shirt that had the word LONDON emblazoned over the chest, and a matching blue baseball hat. Sonny paid in cash, and the vendor bagged the items in a brown paper bag.

Sonny handed the bag to David. "There you go," he teased. "And if you behave yourself, you'll get a lollipop later."

David caught his eye and tried to determine if lollipop was a euphemism, or if Sonny was joking.

"Thanks," he said. "I might take some photos." He handed the bag back to Sonny, only to annoy him.

"I hope you're not one of those weirdos who's obsessed with the royal family," Sonny answered. "I am not going down to Buckingham Palace."

David laughed. "No, I'm not into them. My mom was the family weirdo about British royalty. She loved them, especially Meghan."

"Even I like Meghan," Sonny replied. "You'd have to be a right misery guts to dislike her." He stood there waiting while David held up his phone, snapping photos of Big Ben looming over them. The architecture was incredible. David walked a few paces away for better angles, and he took a lot of photos. He figured, why not?

When he turned back, he noticed the wall Sonny was leaning on was actually the base of a statue. David snapped a candid of Sonny while he was gazing off at something on the street.

David returned, glancing up at the bronze statue of a warrior woman on a horse-drawn chariot. "Who's that?" he asked.

"Hm?" Sonny glanced up, craning his neck. "Oh. Boudica."

David drew a blank. "Do I have to google her?"

"Queen Boudica," Sonny elaborated. "Led the Iceni uprising against the Romans."

Well, that sounded cool.

"Okay, I am gonna google her later," David said. "She sounds dope."

"Probably find you a documentary or two to watch as well," Sonny offered. "After I've caught up with *EastEnders*, of course."

"Of course, can't miss *EastEnders*," David quipped, smiling. "And I'll take you up on that. I love a good documentary."

"Great. Rager all set, then," Sonny quipped. "Documentaries, and in bed by nine."

David wasn't sure if that last part was a Freudian slip, but he decided to call Sonny out on it. "Oh? Is that an offer?"

David had the pleasure of seeing Sonny flounder for a moment. And was that a blush tinting his cheeks?

"You already have the bed," he retorted.

Yeah, but you aren't in it yet.

*

They left the bustle of the bridge and headed back down to the riverside dock. David still wanted to see Tower Bridge, the one that lifted for big ships. Sonny suggested they take a boat and led the way down to the ticket office.

"I can pay you back for all these things when they choose to pay me," David told him.

"It's fine, mate," Sonny replied. "I wrangled a bonus for our expenses. Not as much of a bonus as I'd like, mind you, but still a bonus."

David recalled Sonny yelling at his phone right after they'd landed, and now he thought he knew why. He smiled and shook his head.

"You're a hustler. I like that."

"Yeah, see if you like the boat I hustled for us," Sonny replied.

David had assumed they were getting onto a ferry full of tourists, but he was wrong. Their dock was for a smaller, more streamlined boat with less passengers. It had an open-air top deck, and an enclosed lower deck with all glass windows where staff were serving a champagne lunch. Luxury tourism indeed.

"Did you upgrade for the food?" David teased him.

Sonny laughed. "Honestly? Yeah."

The boat ride was pleasant and smooth sailing. For a river this big, the water was calm. Probably because it was a nice day.

On the lower deck, they opted for coffee instead of champagne. Then David watched Sonny inhale several slim-cut sandwiches with the crusts cut off, one after the other. There were other nibbles on offer, like cakes and biscuits. Sonny scolded David for using the word *biscuit* and told him that they were scones. The pair of them quibbled over this point for a few minutes.

When they headed up top, with the wind blowing gently in their hair, David was able to get a good view of the river and all the buildings on each side of it. He took photos of everything.

The boat travelled slowly east along the river, heading toward Tower Bridge in the distance with its iconic blue metalwork. There were numerous boats in the river with them, from tiny tugboats to huge trash barges, and a tall sailboat with white sails further down.

While David was busy gazing around, snapping photos, Sonny had his phone out and had been quietly engrossed with it for a few minutes. Then he started speaking, apparently to himself. "Cualli teotlac," he said, which was "good afternoon" in Nahuatl. "Nechpactia nimitzixmati," which was "nice to meet you".

He barely hesitated and got the pronunciation almost entirely correct the first time. David stared at him. "Nimitzixmati," he said, correcting him slightly. "Are you reading the words?"

"Yeah, I like to sound it out myself first," Sonny replied. He tilted his phone at David, showing him a list of Nahuatl phrases on the screen. "Interesting language. No gendering, so that's always helpful."

"Er, yeah," David said, surprised. "I didn't expect you to start speaking it right away, you know."

Sonny shrugged. "I need something to do while you're drooling over bridges."

David chuckled and shook his head. "I just... Man, how are you even doing it? This is gonna be your twentieth language? Who even speaks that many?"

Sonny fought a smile. "I'm the linguistics expert. It's kinda my job."

"What do you mean, *the* linguistics expert?" David asked. "For the team?"

"Yeah, and the department," Sonny said. "I was before too. When I was in the service.

"But obviously you're good at it," David said. Yeah, he was jealous. He was an Aries, competitive in nature.

"Well, yeah," Sonny replied, "that's what helped me get into a specialist position. Languages have always been my thing. I'd read books for fun as a kid, learn the languages."

"Right," David drawled. (He was so annoyed.)

"Also..." Sonny looked around, making sure there wasn't anyone too close to eavesdrop. "It helps to have your skillset amplified by the you-know-what."

"The what?" David asked, as Sonny raised his eyebrows at David in a 'you oughta know' gesture. "Oh," David said. "The... thing." He frowned. The alien DNA. "Wait, what? It helps you learn language?"

Sonny nodded. "It accelerates your skills, your learning. Haven't you noticed?"

David frowned hard in thought. Accelerated learning? This was the first he'd known about it. "I don't know," he said honestly.

"I spent all those months laying low. I didn't have a lot of time to kick back and read books or whatever."

"Okay, well, you can read books here," Sonny replied. He leaned back casually on the railing, holding his phone precariously in one hand. David was worried he'd lose his grip and drop his phone into the water below.

"How will I know if I'm...accelerated?" David asked.

"This is what they'd want to check in the *l-a-b*," Sonny said quietly, spelling it out. "Maybe a reading test or two. Then check your progress. They still do it with me sometimes. It's a piece of cake."

"Hm," David said.

Sonny's lab was starting to sound less awful than the one David had been trapped in, but it was still a lab.

"Maybe I can test myself," David mused out loud.

"Sure, why not?" Sonny said. "You can put it to the gaffer anyway."

David nodded, lost in his thoughts as he gazed across the river. It sucked; as soon as he started to forget about all that stuff, aliens and government testing, reality came crashing back down around him. The impending threat of going into the lab, however friendly on the surface, was making him anxious.

Sonny fell quiet again. He slid a little closer on the railing, leaning into David. "Haven't you noticed any changes?" he asked. "Physicality? Speed?"

"You said that before," David replied. "I guess so? I felt...better, maybe? I don't... I don't know." He shrugged. "Maybe I didn't want to examine it too closely."

"Look, I get it," Sonny said. "It's a lot to take in, but extra skills will help you out in the field. I know for a fact you're fast, and strong. You'd have to be to keep pace with me, let alone knock me on my arse."

David smirked, remembering their fight in that truck stop. "I think you let me knock you down. You paused."

Sonny chuckled. "Yeah, you threw me, I'll admit. I had this weird feeling that I knew you."

"You did?" David looked at him in surprise. "I thought that too. As soon as we were up close, I got this crazy feeling that I knew you."

"Well, that's interesting," Sonny said, then went quiet.

David was quiet too, thinking. He gazed down at the water below them.

"Wanna know my theory?" Sonny said.

"What theory?" David asked him.

"My theory on why we both felt deja vu, or whatever?" Sonny said.

Now David was curious. "Yeah, let's hear it."

Sonny twisted around on the rails again, facing out to the river. He knocked his shoulder into David's, a flirty gesture. "I think," he said softly, "our two scary guests knew each other. Wherever they're from and however long ago, they knew each other back then."

Oh, David thought, as his gut flipped in excitement. Yes, that was the most obvious conclusion, and yet David hadn't even thought of it till now.

Of course, the aliens knew each other.

"Perhaps," Sonny added cheekily, "they were even husband and wife."

David looked at him in surprise. "Now, why did you have to go putting that in my head?" he quipped.

Sonny laughed, whether because he was nervous and trying to cover it up, or because he was genuinely amused, David wasn't sure.

"You'd be the wife," David told him.

Sonny stopped laughing and raised both hands. "Obviously?" he said, so unexpectedly serious that it made David laugh.

They were so busy larking around that they hadn't noticed a middle-aged lesbian couple approach and ask if one of them would mind taking their photo together. They had Canadian accents. David obliged, and after the photo was taken, one of them mentioned they were visiting London for their ten-year anniversary.

Then the other one asked how long David and Sonny had been a couple.

David wasn't sure how to answer that, especially when Sonny's reaction was laughter promptly followed by dropping his phone over the side of the boat.

"Oh, fuck me," he said, watching it tumble into the water.

"I knew that would happen," David told him.

"She's always dropping her phone and smashing the screen," one of the ladies said, thumbing her partner. "I take it he's the clumsy one?" she added, motioning to Sonny.

"Sure looks that way," David said wryly.

Chapter Twenty-Seven

As pleasant as it was chatting to the Canadian lesbians, David really wanted to talk to Sonny alone.

The boat docked for more passengers on Embankment Pier, within sight of Cleopatra's Needle, a tall Egyptian obelisk guarded by stone sphinxes. Sonny motioned to David that this was their stop. It was a little further down from Westminster, where they'd hopped on an hour ago.

Tourists congregated on the embankment exit in the afternoon sunshine. David followed Sonny through them all, up stone steps and down a side street.

"Where are we headed?" David asked him.

"Hopefully toward food," Sonny replied.

David smiled. Of course.

They walked for less than ten minutes, cutting down side streets away from busy traffic. David looked around, admiring the architecture that he wasn't used to seeing. When they came out into a busy square, it was alongside several restaurants and big stores all bunched in together. Some had columns outside, so David guessed they hadn't always been restaurants. Sonny bypassed all those and headed straight to a Greek food truck on the corner.

David expected him to start speaking Greek to the dark-haired man inside the truck, but Sonny surprised him by ordering the food in English.

"Dash, what d'ya want?" Sonny asked.

"Whatever you recommend," David replied.

Sonny ordered falafel and halloumi hot wraps, which he paid for, then handed one to David. They stood under a small tree to unwrap them and begin eating. He bit into it and nodded with approval. It reminded him of eating a burrito.

"Mm," he said.

"Nice, right?" Sonny said, mouth full.

"Don't you speak Greek?" David asked him.

Sonny nodded, busy eating his food.

"But you didn't say it to show off?" David prodded.

Sonny chuckled. He finished his mouthful before speaking. "I'm supposed to keep a low profile, innit?"

"Could've fooled me," David said.

Sonny raised one black eyebrow in response, then wiped his mouth and stubble with the napkin, balling up the wrappers. He'd demolished his food so fast.

"You could pass as Greek though," David mused. "Right?"

"Yeah, probably," Sonny replied. He tossed the wrappers into the tiny trash can beside the truck. "Coffee?"

"I wouldn't mind a soda," David said.

Sonny nodded and went back to the food truck queue. David calmly finished his wrap, and when Sonny came back cradling drinks, he handed a soda to David.

"Thanks," David said, and watched in disbelief as Sonny attempted to open his own soda bottle while juggling a hot cup of coffee. "Can I...?" He reached for the coffee, offering to hold it.

Sonny smirked, finally opening his soda with a pop. "Thanks. This twat was tight."

David felt his mouth tilt into a smile automatically. "Why does everything feel like a euphemism with you?"

"Welcome to England," Sonny said and tilted his head for a huge gulp of soda.

"You want this back?" David offered the coffee.

Sonny took it with his free hand, and their fingers brushed. He didn't show any outward sign, but he had to have noticed.

David watched him gulp the coffee, holding the soda bottle in his other hand. "You sure like treats," David commented.

Sonny chuckled. "Pot, kettle, mate. I saw you munching your arse off walking around in Mexico. All those tacos? The fresh OJ? Damn, you made me hungry. Good taste though. Those tacos, fuckin' yum, innit?"

David smiled. "Innit?"

"Shut up," Sonny said, smiling. "C'mon, you cheeky twat. I'll introduce you to Nelson."

"Nelson?" David said. "Who's that?"

*

Nelson, it turned out, was actually the statue of Admiral Nelson upon Nelson's Column guarded by four bronze lions at the base. They'd been a stone's throw away in Trafalgar Square.

"Oh, that Nelson," David quipped.

Sonny held his soda bottle for him while David snapped some photos. As they wandered through the square, amid tourists and local Londoners, David noticed a small dog on a leash. A terrier, he thought, a hairy one. The owner was busy chatting to someone else and didn't notice their dog growling quietly at David.

David gazed back at the dog in surprise. He hadn't expected the dogs here to be wary of him. They had been in Mexico, but they had been mostly stray dogs, wary of people.

Or, that's what he had assumed. Now, as he felt his hackles rise, he stared back at the dog in bewilderment and annoyance. The dog backed away, quit growling and let out a scared whine as it hid behind its owner's legs.

It all happened so fast; David didn't even realise he'd been that close to throwing hands with a dog. He turned away, ashamed. Two things popped into his mind at the same time. First, that the dog *knew*. Somehow it knew he wasn't human, and if this dog knew, then maybe all those other dogs in Mexico had known, and maybe that's why they'd been wary of him.

And, secondly, he thought of Nina the dog.

David looked at his phone screen, checking the time. It was nearing three. Hadn't Mac said she'd let him know about Nina first thing? He toggled through to his contacts and selected Mac's name.

Sonny noticed him making the call. "What's up?" he asked.

"Gonna check in on Nina," David said, listening to the line ring.

After four rings, Mac picked up. "Hello?" she said.

"Hey, it's me," David said. "I was wondering how Nina was?"

"Oh, yeah, fine," Mac replied. She sounded distracted. "Sorry, I meant to text. I'm just walking her now, and she's going number two. Can we catch up later?"

"Sure," David agreed. "Sorry. Didn't mean to interrupt."

"No, it's no problem," she replied. "How are you? Everything all right?"

"Uh, yeah, all good," David said. "Having a walk around."

"Sonny with you?" Mac asked.

"Yeah, he's here."

"Okay, great," Mac said. "Let me call you back when I have a hand free, okay? Talk soon."

"Sure, 'bye." David ended the call.

Why did he have an odd feeling? Mac had sounded off. Maybe she'd only been caught in a bad moment of having to pick up a dog turd and it was nothing.

Still, David couldn't shake the sense that something was off.

"How's the bloody dog, then?" Sonny asked, making it clear he didn't really care. Jealous, perhaps?

"Going number two," David reported. "Mac's picking it up."

Sonny burst out laughing and doubled over. Soda and coffee spilled onto the ground with the action.

"You're easily amused," David drawled. In truth he enjoyed making Sonny laugh. "I only called because I'd been expecting to hear back from her about Nina."

"Sounds like she's fine," Sonny said, straightening up again.

"Do dogs like you?" David asked him. He hadn't mentioned the growling terrier yet.

"Not usually," Sonny replied and winked. "They know I'm a cat person."

*

They walked through the square, which was relatively small for such a famous landmark. Sonny led David to a grand building at the top of the square, with big stone steps and columns out front: the National Gallery.

David hadn't expressed an interest in seeing art right now. He'd rather stay outside and look at landmarks. But soon, Sonny's intentions became clear. He led David toward the coat check area and motioned for David to put his phone into the paper bag containing his souvenir items.

David did so, leaving the phone on, and it got checked in. Sonny then led him back out of the main entrance, stuffing a note of money into the donation box on the way.

"Phone's bugged?" David asked, when they were back out in the square.

Sonny nodded. "Let's go someplace quieter."

It occurred to David that Sonny dropping his phone into the Thames hadn't been an accident after all. David felt all the hairs on the back of his neck sit up. He knew something exciting was about to happen.

He followed Sonny's lead, walking beside him up Wardour Street. The traffic wasn't busy, yet it felt noisier here. The street was narrow; scaffold was set up on one building with workmen drilling something, and the noise echoed all around.

There were buildings on each side of them, but not as tall as the ones in the US. David spotted a Mexican restaurant, or that's what the neon sign claimed. Next to it, a boutique designer store. Next to that, a wall with sprawled graffiti and hastily pasted up posters for nightclubs. London was very eclectic.

And after a five minute walk, they turned a corner and were greeted by a crossroads of pedestrian streets and ornate buildings, and strings of red paper lanterns strung between them—a side entrance to Chinatown.

This was what David was more interested in seeing: a riot of color, good smells filtering out of the restaurants, and spoken languages that weren't English. It reminded him of being back in

Mexico, and he instantly felt happy here.

"C'mon," Sonny told him. "There's a bubble tea place up here."

"Because you haven't had enough of those today?" David quipped.

He followed Sonny through Chinatown, content to gaze around for now. He had a feeling that Sonny was taking him to a quiet spot where they could talk, and David didn't mind waiting for that.

On all sides were Chinese and Asian restaurants, markets, souvenir stores, and vendors walking between them carrying new stock, from freshly baked goods to sealed boxes. Among the bustle and noise, and strings of red paper lanterns overhead, David saw it was easy to slip through unnoticed. That's why Sonny had chosen Chinatown.

Up a narrow side street, Sonny ducked inside a hole-in-the-wall place serving bubble tea. He ordered two, speaking a language David had to assume was Cantonese, but he was no expert.

The dark-haired, petite East Asian woman behind the counter responded in the same language, took his money, then began making the drinks.

"Wait for them, would you?" Sonny asked David. "I'll be back in a second."

"Okay," David replied. He waited on the drinks while Sonny exited the tiny space. While he was gone, David watched the drinks being made. One pink, one lavender.

He smiled wryly. Sonny and his pastel drinks.

By the time the drinks were ready and she slid the cups across the counter, Sonny reappeared in the doorway. He motioned for David to come with him. David took both cups, thanked the woman in English, and followed Sonny.

They didn't go far, only to the very next doorway, guarded by an older East Asian woman wearing a leopard print dress, and a fashionable black leather jacket. She was tiny, under five foot for sure, but she guarded that doorway with a steely authority.

David knew in his gut what kind of place this was.

She looked at David with a smirk and murmured something in Cantonese. Sonny tittered and glanced around at David. "Soo says you're handsome. Don't let it go to your head."

David smiled. "Thanks."

The woman, Soo, stood aside and gestured for them to go in. "Number three," she said in heavily accented English.

Sonny went in first, leading the way up a narrow set of steps. David, carrying the drinks, followed. He noted the peeling paint on the walls, the red-tinted lightbulb in the ceiling illuminating the small space.

After walking up one flight of stairs, they had another flight to go. David almost asked Sonny where they were going and what would await them; he had a small worry Sonny had booked them in with working girls.

But, when they got to the top floor and into the tiny room, David saw with relief that it was empty.

This was certainly a brothel. And this was a seedy bedroom (despite the bedsheets looking clean), but at least it was empty.

David entered the room. Sonny shut and locked the door after him.

"Which one do you want?" he asked, gesturing at the drinks David held.

"I really don't mind," David told him. Boba was the last thing on his mind right now.

Sonny took the lavender cup and walked over to the bed.

David watched him stand beside the bed, pause, take a loud

sip of the drink, and then shift awkwardly from foot to foot.

"So, er," Sonny said, then trailed off and didn't elaborate.

"What's going on?" David asked. He'd thought Sonny had brought him here for the obvious, but now he was wondering if he'd misread the situation.

"Er," Sonny said, looking everywhere but at David. "Well, you know, er…" He gestured with his cup at the bed. "If you want?"

"If I want…?" David repeated. "Wait," he said, a grin forming on his face. "Is this you making a move?"

Sonny shrugged. All of his usual bravado had evaporated.

"Oh, my God, it is," David said. "Why did you pick a brothel? Here I was expecting *Lady Chatterley's Lover*."

This earned him a surprised laugh from Sonny. "What, bonking in the fucking garden?" he quipped.

David gestured at the room with his free hand. "You picked a brothel instead?"

"It's more private!" Sonny exclaimed. "Hotels have security cameras. I know for a fact there's no cameras in here."

"Oh," David said. That was a fair point, he supposed.

"Christ," Sonny muttered, sitting down on the edge of the bed. He placed the drink onto the nightstand, which, David couldn't help noticing, boasted a generous bowl of condoms and one-time use packets of lube.

Sonny didn't say anything.

David picked up on his sudden nervousness and decided to cut him some slack. He placed his cup on a sideboard and went over to the bed to sit down beside Sonny. Not too close that it was crowding him, but close enough to be friendly.

"So," he said, aiming for levity. "You come here often?"

Sonny smiled wryly. His eyes were downcast, still not looking at David face on.

"What's going on?" David asked him.

Sonny shrugged. "I'm not great at this. I usually rely on Grindr."

So, he was nervous, David realised. This was the first time he'd seen Sonny without that swaggering exterior, and it struck him how important it was that he was allowing David to see him like this.

"Want me to text you?" David quipped. "Oh, you don't have your phone."

His joke got another smile out of Sonny, so that was something.

They sat side by side in quiet for a long moment. It occurred to David that they may not have much time.

"They don't know where we are right now?" he asked.

"Well, they do," Sonny said, shifting on the bed. "I have trackers in me. They know where I am, but they won't come looking for a while."

"Trackers, plural?" David asked, shocked.

"One in each limb, one in my torso, one in my head," Sonny said. "If I really want to go off grid, I'd have to block their signal, and that's a pain in the arse."

"Jesus," David murmured.

"They reasoned if I lose a limb they'd want to find it before it gets sold on the black market," Sonny explained. He let out a wry laugh. "Check my arse for a stamp, it says property of HM Government."

David smiled wryly. "I have got some questions," he said. "I know you don't like the questions, but..."

"It's fine. Knock yourself out," Sonny replied. "We should have a while before they get their knickers in a twist about not being able to listen in. Kinky buggers."

"Can I ask," David started, "about… that whole sleeping with civilians part?"

"Mm?"

"Do you?" David asked.

"I have done," Sonny replied, shrugging. "I do, sometimes."

"But technically you're not allowed to?" David asked.

"No, not really, but they're more concerned about…" Sonny trailed off and lifted his gaze to the ceiling as he thought about his words. "How shall I put this? So, as long as you don't leave samples of yourself in civilian hands, you'd be okay," he said. "Don't make any deposits, basically."

"Don't ejaculate?" David clarified. "That doesn't sound fun for me."

Sonny shrugged.

David sighed tiredly. "This is kind of bullshit, actually."

"How long has it been?" Sonny asked.

"Months," David said. "Feels longer. I almost got together with someone in Tijuana, but then I heard a sound outside the window that spooked me. Ruined the mood."

Sonny nodded, his eyes shifting away again. "Look, er… I'm not very good at talking about this kind of stuff, but if you want me to take the edge off…?"

"Are you offering because you want to?" David asked him. "Or because your superiors want you to?"

Sonny pursed his lips for a moment, eyes drifting around the room before they settled back on David with a steely glint. There was the Sonny he recognised.

"I can make my own decisions, love," he said testily. "The order was to kill you or bring you in. They let me decide which. You're here because of me."

The hairs on David's neck stood to attention. That threat of danger was still present between them, and it probably shouldn't have been arousing but David couldn't help that it was.

"So, you decided to bring me in?" David probed. "Why?"

"Why, what?" Sonny's eyes flashed with something: anger, irritation? The probing was starting to rile him; that much was obvious. "You ticked the boxes for a viable working asset. Simple as that."

Just what every man wanted to hear, David thought wryly.

"Okay," he drawled. "And, gonna go out on a limb here, perhaps also because you liked me a little bit?" He nudged his elbow against Sonny's, a small prod to soften the words.

He wasn't sure how Sonny would react, given the look in his eyes. David half expected this to end with Sonny's fist in his face, but then Sonny smiled and shook his head.

"All right. Maybe a little bit."

"See?" David replied, sensing victory. "Now we're getting somewhere."

"Yes, fine, Wordsworth, but we don't have all day," Sonny said tersely. "Do you want your dick sucked, or not?"

David chuckled in surprise. "Such a way with words."

"Look, I'm gay. I'm not a poet," Sonny said. He shrugged out of his jacket and pulled his shirt off over his head, exposing brown abs and a defined chest covered in curly black hair. "Are you in or out?"

The gauntlet had been set. David accepted the challenge, quickly removing his own clothes.

"In."

Chapter Twenty-Eight

David hadn't gone into this tryst thinking that sex with Sonny would be all soft words and romance. He was a specialist soldier, and David knew their type. He was one himself, and they tended to like it rough. It had been in the back of David's mind to expect it, and yet when they got into bed together, he was surprised by how rough Sonny liked it. Less like lovemaking, more like naked wrestling.

Even when David was on top, Sonny clamped his hands around David's throat for some awesome breath play. The sex was rough, thrilling, and a little violent. They did everything short of full penetration, focusing on frotting and hand jobs in their haste to get off.

Sonny wanted David to slap his face. Some men liked that, even civilians. David didn't mind (and, honestly, Sonny needed a good slap). He enjoyed the noises Sonny made when he did it, the soft grunts when David hit him hard across the face. He thought it would leave a mark on Sonny's skin but there was none.

Indeed, no bruises left on either of their bodies by the time they were done, despite all the bites and scratches—evidence that David was healing quicker than he'd realised. He tried not to think about it too hard, the same way he tried to ignore the way Sonny's dark eyes changed sometimes. A silver glint, a narrowing of the pupils. Something alien. Something scary. Easier to turn him around and not look him in the eyes at all. Focus on the sex, not the elephant (or alien) in the room.

And he'd really needed the sex. Nothing beat a passionate fucking, and over an hour later, David was finally sated. They lay side by side in the messed-up bed together, staring up at the ceiling.

"So, what's your skillset?" Sonny asked, picking up some conversation David had long since forgotten.

"Huh?" David panted. "In bed?"

Sonny chuckled. "No, you plum. When you were in special ops. What did you do?"

"Oh. Well, sniper, of course," David replied. "Engineer. Explosives. Infiltration."

"Okay," Sonny said thoughtfully. David almost heard the gears turning in Sonny's head. Then he snickered. "Yes, you could say your skill for infiltration translates to the bed as well."

David smiled. Back to the quips. The mood was certainly lighter now.

"You know, for someone who never stops talking, I expected you to say a whole lot more during sex."

"No, no, no. Nobody wants to hear Brits talk during sex," Sonny retorted.

"I would," David replied. "I'll get you talking more next time."

"Oh, fuck off." Sonny laughed. He shifted over onto his side, facing David and hooking a bare leg over one of his. "I'll leave that to you. The American accent sounds better. In fact, you should speak in Spanish."

"Bueno," David said. He made a mental note to speak more in Spanish next time. And judging by the way Sonny was flirting more with him post-coitally, David had high hopes there would be a next time.

"Can I ask you something?" he said, trailing his hand along Sonny's shoulders. "Why did you want to come to this, uh, fine establishment?"

Sonny shrugged under David's hands. "For a bit of privacy. I joke about the brass listening in but, honestly, knowing that they are puts me right off my game."

David nodded. That, he could totally understand.

"Who listens? Anyone you know?"

"Di for sure," Sonny said. "That's Dinah, who you already met. We call her Princess Di. But there will be others, other agents. It's not the end of the world, or anything. Just sometimes I don't want to give them every single detail of my life."

"I get that," David replied. "Well, this was nice. Maybe next time it could be a hotel."

Sonny smiled wryly. "No. Hotels have cameras, remember?"

David smiled back. "I forgot. So, what are they gonna do with these sheets after we're gone?"

"Sell 'em to the highest bidder," Sonny quipped. "Nah, Soo has everything thrown in the wash. She's good like that. I slip her a few extra bob to keep her sweet."

"Does she know she's handling government property?" David quipped back.

Sonny laughed. "No, or she probably *would* sell them." He

wriggled out from David's hold and sat up. "C'mon, then, hot rod." Sonny patted his hand on David's thigh. "We better go."

"Hot rod." David shook his head with a smile. "I like that better than Fresh Meat."

"Think I'll call you big meat from now on," Sonny joked, making David laugh again.

For two short guys, David possessed the thicker cock. Sonny certainly seemed to appreciate it.

They got out of the bed and dressed on separate sides.

"Hey," David said to him, pulling on his clothes. "Did you mean to leave that chrome douche in your shower for me to see?"

Sonny snickered. "No, I completely forgot he was there until I got in the shower this morning, saw him, and thought, 'oh, fuck'."

"Him?" David asked. "Does he have a name?"

"I usually name anything shaped as a cock after Tory prime ministers," Sonny explained. "Because they will shaft you the most." He shimmied into his tight jeans and did up the fly. "But we've had so many of them lately, I can't even remember what that one's name is."

David wasn't sure if he was kidding or not. Hopefully he was. "Great mental image. Thanks, Sonny," he drawled.

Sonny tittered again. "Wait a mo'," he added, tilting his head at David. "Did you rub one out this morning?"

"Yeah, in the shower," David replied a little guiltily. "Why?"

"Hm," Sonny said thoughtfully. "And last night?"

"Er, yes, last night also." David wondered why Sonny was going down this line of questioning. "Why?"

"Oh, nothing," Sonny said, waving him off.

Obviously, it was something, but David let it go for now.

"We better get a move on," Sonny said, hustling David along.

They finished dressing, preparing to leave the room. Sonny grabbed the two bubble drinks, condensation dripping down their sides.

Some of his dark curls were askew. David reached out when Sonny approached, aiming to fix his hair. He hadn't expected Sonny to lean back and avoid the touch. A reflex.

"Whoa, easy," David said calmly. "Your hair is a bit..."

"Oh." Sonny's face remained blank, but the tops of his cheeks pinked.

David was growing fond of that blush. He slowly reached out again, telegraphing his movements, and fixed the errant curls on Sonny's head. Next time, he'd remember not to startle him.

Sonny didn't speak, but he did offer one of the drinks to David. David smiled and took it.

There wasn't anything left to say for now. They'd had sex, they had an understanding, and for the time being they would be working together, and that probably meant more sex in their immediate future.

David was more than okay with that.

*

Even though it was the weekend, Valerie Jones was working from home.

She'd had a long conference call with the deputy head of MI5, and later she was attending the Belgian ambassador's supper with the intention to rub her elbows with numerous persons of interest.

She barely had enough time in between the two to shower and change. While she was standing in her bedroom, half dressed, musing between a dress or a suit for dinner, her laptop began chiming with alerts.

"Fuck," she muttered, putting down the clothes. She walked

barefoot to her dresser to check the laptop.

She had two messages. Both encrypted on the secure channel, which meant they were from her special projects agents. Valerie sat with her laptop on the side of her bed and opened the messages with her decryption key.

One was from Dinah, stating that Sonny's phone had stopped transmitting audio thirty-five minutes ago, and now Cortez's phone had gone muffled.

The second message was from one of Valerie's Chinatown moles, confirming eyes on Sonny plus one male entering a store. He'd sent the pin, and Valerie cross-checked the locations. Cortez's phone was stationary, in Trafalgar Square. Sonny's phone was stationary slap bang on the Thames, while his internal trackers were all showing up in the same pin drop that her Chinatown mole had sent. Valerie clicked on the pin to zoom in on the location. It was a knocking shop.

She frowned.

Two queer men walk into a brothel in Chinatown. It sounded like the start of a joke, but she didn't have the punchline yet.

"What is he up to?" Valerie muttered. She wasn't too concerned yet, merely curious. Sonny had a tendency to drop off the radar, but he usually resurfaced shortly after.

She replied to her agents to standby and keep her posted. The more pressing matter she had to attend to tonight was supper with the Belgian ambassador, and Valerie refused to be late. She would keep one eye on this situation and check in with Sonny if she had any reason to suspect he was going off the rails with the new asset, but hopefully he would behave himself.

For now, she would observe.

*

"I have something else to ask you," David said quietly. "Can you teach me to fight like you?"

They were walking through a long, stately room inside the National Gallery, with enormous classical art paintings hanging on the walls. They only had a few minutes before closing and were making the most of it.

Sonny nodded. He'd had to ditch his drinks before entering the gallery and now had his thumbs hooked into the front pockets of his jeans.

"I hated you in the moment," David went on, "but I particularly liked that move where you kicked upward while turning upside down. Like something out of *Mortal Kombat.*"

Sonny broke into a grin. "Yeah, that's a good one, innit? Gave you a good wallop."

"Where the hell did you even learn that?" David asked. His mind flitted back to their earlier session in bed, flipping each other over and grappling on the mattress.

Talk about sexy MMA.

David was in danger of getting a woody in the gallery, so he had to clear his mind fast.

"All in good time, mate," Sonny said vaguely. He stopped in front of a huge painting of two medieval guys and tilted his head to look at it. "This one's my favourite. "The Ambassadors," innit? See the skull?"

David looked and saw an unusual shape in the foreground. When he stepped to the side, he saw the shape of a skull shift into place before his eyes. An optical trick.

It was eerie and reminded him of the way Sonny's eyes had changed in bed. David didn't mention it, was still trying to wrap his head around having seen it, and wondered if his eyes would ever do the same.

Chapter Twenty-Nine

Sonny had dreaded David asking him to hit the town that evening. He'd recently come home from several weeks away, and one day out in Central London was quite enough for now. (Wow, he was getting old. He was twenty-nine pushing forty.)

Luckily for him, David seemed more than agreeable to Sonny's suggestion of going home to eat leftover curry and watch a documentary on Boudica.

Thank fuck.

As a compromise, he made sure to take David on a more scenic route home, hopping on and off the red double-decker buses and sitting up top for a good view. He'd noticed David seemed to enjoy looking at the buildings, the people. He was busy being a tourist, not paying attention to the streets or his surroundings.

Sonny wasn't sure if this change was temporary, because David had been alert back in Mexico, alert enough to give Sonny the runaround anyway. Maybe he was simply exhausted from months on the run, ready to exchange his freedom for a leash.

It gave Sonny pause, made him wonder if he'd ever make it as a fugitive himself. If David was ready to come in from the cold after a few short months, how long would Sonny last? The question hung over him, as it had done for a long while now. If, and that was a big if, he was ever able to break away from PRISM, could he last out there by himself?

Or, as David had suggested, not alone, but together?

The possibilities swirled around in Sonny's mind, providing anxieties and happy fantasies of escape all rolled into one. The prospect of breaking away was scary. The cocoon of security, the leash around his neck, however tight, was a comfort, a safety net. Better the devil you know, or so he'd been telling himself for the past three years.

Lately, that devil had become increasingly harder to live with. Sonny hadn't voiced the feeling with anyone but David, but he felt caged.

And if Rafe was seriously considering retirement? Well, fuck. One less ally for Sonny. What would he do without Rafe? His best friend, who'd always looked out for him? They'd been working together in the same unit, joined at the hip, practically married, since Sonny was eighteen. He was nearly thirty now.

But Rafe was ten years older, forty. He'd said lately that physical work was getting harder. His knees weren't the same, and he was losing speed. Maybe they could transition him to office work, and he could be in Sonny's ear instead of beside him in the field.

In a way, Sonny would be relieved for Rafe to get out safely. Many of their old SAS unit hadn't been so lucky; injuries and early retirement for the ones who were fortunate enough to survive, except those who later succumbed to suicide.

Chewed up and spat out. Soldiers couldn't win.

"There's a lot of statues," David commented, drawing Sonny out of his dark thoughts. "Who's this one?"

"Hm?" Sonny glanced across at him. David was in the window seat and gestured down at the street below.

They'd not long gone past the Sherlock Holmes Museum up Park Road. The statue David gestured at was in the centre of a small roundabout. Quite a famous one.

"That's Saint George," Sonny said. In his head he was calculating their route home. They'd have to get off this bus soon and get another one headed northeast to Finsbury Park.

"Why's he fighting a fish?" David asked.

"Hah!" Sonny burst out laughing. A fish! Americans were hilarious. "That's a dragon, you plum. Saint George and the dragon."

Their bus moved on from the statue. David craned his head to watch it recede from vision.

"Huh," he said. "Looks like a fish."

Sonny laughed and wiped a tear away. He pressed the bell to request a stop. "We'll get off at the next stop."

David hummed amiably; then he asked, "So is there a documentary about Saint George?"

"Lots," Sonny replied. "He was also Roman era but born in modern day Turkey."

"Saint George is Turkish?" David drawled.

"No, Greek," Sonny said. He glanced at David to see a mild expression of disbelief. "It's true! He was a Roman guard." He laughed. "You can learn all about it later."

"So where's the dragon come in?" David asked.

"I can't remember exactly," Sonny said. "From what I recall, Saint George was the real historical figure, and the dragon myth popped up later. I think the dragon is symbolic of whichever

Roman Emperor it was that was persecuting people at the time."

"Okay, that makes more sense," David said sagely.

"Not a believer in dragons?" Sonny teased. "Haven't you seen those big Komodo bastards?"

This earned him an amused laugh. David's eyes crinkled up with mirth. "Those are some big bastards," he agreed in his American drawl. "Like in that James Bond movie."

"Yeah." Sonny chuckled. "The one where Daniel Craig was flirting with Javier Bardem."

"I remember that part vividly," David said. "I think I was around nineteen? I remember watching it at the time, like, okay, there's no doubt in my mind that I'm into guys."

Sonny nodded in agreement. "Too right."

Despite all his worries, Sonny conceded that it was nice to be able to relax and natter with his new companion.

They clicked.

*

They got home while it was still light. Sonny parked David in front of the TV in the lounge with a plate of reheated curry from the night before.

"Here you are," Sonny told him, flicking through the streaming options with the remote. "I'm gonna queue up all the documentaries you could ever want."

"Are you watching too?" David asked.

"Yeah, after I've had a shower," Sonny said. "You can watch Boudica first, then Saint George." He set the first program to play.

"You watch documentaries a lot?" David asked him.

"Good to fall asleep to," Sonny replied. It was the truth. Late at night, he liked quiet and calm programs droning on about ancient history. Perfect aid for insomnia.

He left David downstairs with the TV playing.

Sonny did want a shower, but he also had something to test out. First, he went to his bedroom, where David had been sleeping, and opened the dresser drawer. He kept a few spare burner phones in there, and he took one out along with its charger to plug it in. He did not switch it on yet, but wanted one to be ready if he needed it later.

Next, he went to the spare room across the hall, where he kept his more secure items. Inside the cupboard was his small safe. Sonny opened it with a thumb impression and a code, then took out his laptop. He hadn't been here for a couple of weeks, so the laptop needed charging as well. Sonny plugged it in, setting it on the floor because the room was bereft of furniture. He crouched beside it and opened a secure line to Shepherd.

If he didn't check in, with his phone kaput, she would only start breathing down his neck, so he sent her an update. He wrote: *The fish is on the hook.*

Short and sweet. So, hopefully, she'd get off his case now.

He closed the laptop. Now he intended to shower and test his theory about David.

*

The documentary about Queen Boudica and the Romans was interesting. David was invested.

When it was almost over, David heard footsteps stomping down the stairs. Sonny appeared in the doorway fresh from his shower, wearing a white bathrobe, his black hair wet and in his eyes. He'd rushed down here for something, David could tell.

"Did you feel anything?" Sonny asked, looking at him.

"Feel what?" David asked, perplexed.

"Something unusual?" Sonny asked. His eyes flicked up and

down David's body, assessing him.

David had been enjoying that curry, eating while he watched the TV. He wasn't aware of anything out of the ordinary happening.

"I don't think so?" he replied. "Why? Is everything okay?"

Sonny had a peculiar look on his face. Bewilderment. Irritation, too, perhaps.

"Oh," he said. "No, not to worry. Must just be me."

Now David was curious. "Why? What happened?"

"Nothing, nothing. I gotta dry my hair." Sonny turned away, heading back upstairs, footsteps thumping.

David would've followed him, but he didn't want to crowd the man in his own home.

Odd. But he decided if it was important enough, Sonny would bring it up himself later.

*

S onny's hunch hadn't paid off.

One hand shandy in the shower, all well and good, but when he'd raced downstairs to check on David's status, the other man was unaffected.

It didn't make any sense.

Was David doing something different when he masturbated? Sonny had seen him naked now, had seen his cock up close and personal, and it all looked and worked like he'd expected it to.

No, it had to be related to Sonny's earlier theory. The alien DNA in David was more dormant than Sonny's was. David's eyes didn't shift at all, Sonny had checked. Whatever was inside him was at least partially dormant, which likely explained why David wasn't having weird nightmares, nor picking up on Sonny's experiment.

It felt frustrating.

Sonny wondered if he should mention it. *Hey, by the way, you can't masturbate without giving me an orgasm!* How would David react to that? Would he stop masturbating to be polite? Would he be cross about it?

Or, Sonny's hindbrain provided, was this something they should experiment with together? Masturbate in bed and see who could make the other have a hands-free orgasm?

Except it wasn't that simple, because the reason behind all this was likely due to Sonny's other theory. That their alien guests had some connection. It was the most obvious conclusion, and Sonny's senses seemed to be more attuned to whatever was happening. Maybe David would catch up, maybe not.

But either way, every conversation always came back around to aliens, and that was awkward. More awkward than talking about sex on its own. Sonny was thrown. He'd need to gather more data before he mentioned this to David, just to be sure.

Stalling. Sonny's go-to tactic.

He hoped he hadn't bitten off more than he could chew with all this.

Sonny shelved the thoughts for now.

He dried his hair, styled it, and dressed in comfortable, casual clothes. An evening in front of the TV beckoned. First, he checked the laptop for a reply from Shepherd. Nothing yet.

No news was good news, in Sonny's opinion. He closed the laptop and left it on charge.

When he went downstairs, he fetched himself some dinner, and more for David. They watched a documentary about Saint George together. David certainly seemed more invested in the documentary than he had been in *EastEnders*.

After they'd finished what was on their plates, David offered to clear up and took them to the kitchen.

Sonny wasn't going to argue. David was staying here rent-free after all.

As Sonny wrapped himself in blankets and stretched out in his favourite part of the couch, he watched the TV with half-open eyes, listening to the soft sounds of David washing plates in the kitchen. He could fall asleep like this, easily. The energetic sex that afternoon had helped.

Sonny's lizard brain thought about the opportunity for sex on tap, having David nearby. It would certainly be a perk. While the more grounded part of Sonny's brain felt reluctant to share his space so readily with a stranger. But realistically, he expected Shepherd's office to offer David his own residence soon. That would be easier.

Sonny liked David just fine, but he also liked his own space.

He was half nodding off to sleep when David reappeared in the doorway to ask if he could take a shower. Sonny woke up enough to tell him yes, it was fine. David left. Sonny almost dozed off again, then woke up wondering if David would be giving himself a handjob in the shower.

Sonny half hoped he wouldn't, because he'd had his own shower and he didn't want to get all sweaty again from a surprise orgasm.

Curiously, the two times he'd had those unexpected orgasms, he hadn't ejaculated. His dick hadn't had a chance to get all the way hard before the feeling hit him. No, the orgasms were different. Internal, in his head. And like nothing he'd ever felt before.

The other half of Sonny wanted to experience that feeling again. He was sure he would. Some kind of channel was open between them. That much he knew for sure. And even if it appeared to be a one-way street for the moment, Sonny felt in his gut that this was only the beginning.

*

Sonny waited, listening. He heard David taking his shower upstairs, heard the water going, but so far hadn't felt anything.

When the water shut off and he heard David's footsteps walking around upstairs, Sonny knew the window had passed. He concluded that David had only washed himself and hadn't diverted his attentions to his cock.

Sated from their Chinatown session earlier?

Sonny relaxed back into his nest. He'd have to wait until the next time to gather more data on this little conundrum.

It was getting dark outside. The street lights came on, shining through the blinds. Sonny got up, casting his blankets aside, to draw the curtains shut, then he dived back into his nest.

He should probably check on Rafe, but he'd left the burner phone charging upstairs, and he couldn't be bothered to get up again.

Days off were supposed to be relaxing.

Upstairs, the hairdryer turned on. That meant David was attempting to style his hair. Sonny smirked to himself. He pictured David standing naked in the bathroom, or with a towel around his waist. David had a great body. He was short, like Sonny, but stocky. Athletic and tan. He also had a tattoo on his hip, a black swirling design. *Sexy place to put a tattoo.*

He was so busy daydreaming, when David's phone began ringing he jumped. David had left the phone in the souvenir bag, next to the coffee table.

Sonny knew it would likely be only one of two people calling David. He scrambled out of his nest to pick up the phone.

When Sonny saw the screen, he winced to see Guv's name.

So much for a peaceful evening.

Sonny accepted the call. "Hello, Guv," he said. "Our new recruit is in the shower."

"It was you I wanted," Guv replied evenly. "You weren't answering your phone."

"Ah, yes," Sonny replied. "Sorry, Guv, it had an accident."

"You have a burner, I take it?"

"Yes, Guv."

"Good. Now, I know you're on a rest day..."

Here comes the but, Sonny thought.

"But," Guv said, "we have a lead. The ferret got himself arrested in Soho, and I want you to go pick him up. Night watch will coordinate. Take the new guy. Show him the ropes. Have you got a codename for him yet?"

"Yes, Guv, we do," Sonny replied. "It's Dash."

"All right," Guv said. "I'll have a van sent to pickup location four."

"Yes, Guv," Sonny said. "On our way."

Guv ended the call, and Sonny sighed lightly.

Oh, well, he thought. At least "Merritt the ferret" was a relatively soft target. Another milk run.

"Oi, Dash?" he called out, walking out into the hall. "Change of plan. We'll have to get dressed for business."

Chapter Thirty

David was half dressed when Sonny announced they had a job to go to. Sonny came bounding up the stairs, and David met him out on the landing, shirtless, wearing lounge pants only.

"A job?" he asked. "What kind of job?"

"A lead off of the Mexico one," Sonny replied, brushing past him and going into the bedroom.

David tensed. "So, more vampires?" He followed Sonny into the room, watching him open the wall closet.

"Hopefully not tonight," Sonny replied. "We're going to interview a known associate. Human." He pulled out a selection of black clothes. "Still, best be prepared."

David only had a limited selection of clothes in the bag he'd brought from Mexico, and most of them were in earthy shades of green and brown, not black. Luckily, Sonny had a closet like Batman's, with multiple black outfits at the ready. He handed over black fatigues, and a couple of black jackets with a biker vibe to them. They were similar in size and length for pants. David was broader in the shoulder than Sonny was, so he had to try on a couple of different jackets to find a good fit.

"You have a lot of jackets," David commented, trying on yet another one. This one had some good pockets.

"That's an old one of Rafe's," Sonny said.

That's why it fit better across his shoulders, David thought. He was still bare-chested under the jacket.

"What shirt should I wear?" he quipped. "My London one?"

"Don't you fucking dare," Sonny said, smiling. "Pick something dark. We may be doing surveillance later, for all I know. So much for time off."

"Awesome," David said with a hint of sarcasm. "We'll get paid, right?"

"Yes, it's always paid," Sonny confirmed. He gathered his own selected clothes in his arms. "Get dressed and come meet me in the room down the hall."

David nodded. Sonny left the bedroom, and David got changed. He put on black underwear and black socks, the black tactical pants, and the darkest T-shirt he had, in forest green. Before putting on the jacket, he secured a knife holster to his belt, then slotted the knife in.

David had one handgun, the same one he'd used in Mexico on that crazy op, but he was out of ammo. He didn't have a holster either. He held the gun in his hand and picked up a brown baseball cap from his pile of clothes. Then he walked out into the hall, listening for Sonny.

David heard faint sounds from the second room, the one above the lounge. He had a feeling he was about to find out what Sonny kept in there. David kept his footfalls silent, and slowly approached the open door to peer in.

Sonny was in the centre of the room, now dressed in all black: tactical pants that hugged his thighs and ass, and a thermal long-sleeved top. He was in the middle of securing a tac belt around his waist.

"Wotcha," he greeted, glancing at David. "You gonna wear the boots you got downstairs?"

"Yeah," David replied. He stepped inside the room, noting the black jacket Sonny had chosen was currently draped over an empty laundry basket. David also noted that Sonny didn't have any guns on his person yet. "Hey," he said, gesturing to the gun he held. "I'm out of ammo."

"No worries, mate," Sonny told him. "Let's sort you out." He finished buckling his belt and walked over to the closet.

David watched him open a concealed panel and pressed his thumb to an invisible scanner. The closet mechanism whirred softly, front panels sliding away to reveal a fully stocked weapons cache complete with backlighting.

David whistled quietly. "Nice. I feel like Bond meeting Q for his new gadgets."

Sonny chuckled. "I have called it my Q closet before. Q meets Clueless. Q-less." He pulled up a rack of handguns. "You should probably swap that one you got for one of these. Keep a clean trail, innit?"

"Sure." David handed the gun over, and in return got a brand-new, matte black SIG Saur in a leather holster, and extra clips. David checked the sight on the pistol, and the clip inside, before he removed his jacket so he could put on the holster. "I can keep my knife, right?" he asked.

"You can keep that," Sonny confirmed, securing his own gun under his arm. "Do you want any more?" He pressed a button to automatically switch gun rack for knife rack. "These are some of my knives," he said, introducing them.

David let his gaze roam over them all. Beautifully displayed in holders, backlit so the light caught the shiny blades. From combat to special skill, there were bayonets, bowies, a variety of karambits, drop knives, push daggers, and short throwing knives.

"That's a lot of knives," David said, absently wondering how often Sonny cleaned and polished them all, and how bloody they got in his work.

"I said *some* of my knives," Sonny pointed out. "If you're good, maybe I'll show you the others one day."

"I'll look forward to it," David replied, as he pictured Sonny on a red velvet chair by a fireplace, polishing knife after knife. "Now I know what to get you for Christmas," he quipped.

Sonny tittered. David was starting to recognise that chuckle as the one that escaped when Sonny's guard was down.

It was a boost to his ego, knowing that Sonny liked his dorky jokes.

They were pushed for time, so they had to get down to business. Sonny let David choose, and he went with what he knew best, opting for a medium combat knife and holster he would strap to his ankle, and a couple of push knives. He had plenty of pockets for concealment.

Sonny chose multiple knives. He slotted them into concealed spots on his person with speed and efficiency, something he clearly did on a regular basis. The combat knives tucked into his belt, and two on his ankles. The push daggers and throwing knives went into his jacket.

David watched him and got momentarily distracted. Now he knew what Sonny looked like naked (the shape and curves of his lithe body, all that tan skin with dark hair on his chest and legs) it was easy to get distracted. His hindbrain wanted to know when they'd have more sex. David had to keep it to the back of his mind for now. Mission first.

Sonny produced a couple of black cotton bands in thin material. "You can keep this around your neck or in your pocket," he advised. "It's small enough to tuck inside a jacket or shirt."

"Okay." David took the material offered. "Oh, is this a face covering?"

"Always useful," Sonny said. He pulled the scarf over his head and shuffled it into place around his neck. "Now, have you got your phone?"

David copied him, pulling his own scarf into place and tucking it inside his jacket collar. "Yeah, in my pocket. Question: hat or no hat?" He held up the baseball cap.

"Put it on, let me see."

David set the ball cap on his head, facing front. If things got more serious, he'd turn it backwards, like he'd grown used to wearing in the marines.

"That'll work, actually," Sonny said. "It keeps your face obscured from any security feeds."

"Where are we going?" David asked.

"Back to central," Sonny replied. "I'll tell you on the way."

*

They tied their boots on, set the alarm, and left Sonny's house. David followed him as he led the way, walking casually down the darkened street and carrying a black gym bag. They were bathed in the glow of orange-tinted streetlights. Visibility was high, but in contrast, all the shadowy street corners were very dark. Ambushes could easily occur.

David was on medium alert, having slipped into work mode. He took his cues from Sonny's casual gait. Clearly, they were moving away from Sonny's home to a secondary location. Probably ante up from there, so it wasn't high alert yet.

They walked for several minutes. These residential streets and back streets didn't see a lot of footfall at this time of night, but plenty of traffic rolled past them, mostly cars but a few trucks and vans too.

When they came to a crossroad with an old inn-style bar on one corner—Brits called them pubs—Sonny gestured to a black van approaching them from the south.

"That's us," he said, leading the way across the road.

"Is everything with you guys black?" David asked, making Sonny titter.

The van pulled up at a layby, under a street lamp. David could barely see the driver through the tinted windshield, and whoever it was, they were short.

When the driver got out and came around to meet them on the sidewalk, David saw they were a petite, pale white person of ambiguous gender, wearing worn jeans and a hooded top, square glasses, several ear piercings, and a fashionable crop of electric-blue-dyed hair. They had a tattoo behind their right ear.

"Awright," they said casually and handed the van keys over to Sonny, along with a glasses case.

"Awright, mate," Sonny replied. "Oh, this is Dash. Dash, meet Kip."

"All right," Kip greeted, nonchalant.

"Hey," David replied.

"Who's in the hot seat tonight?" Sonny asked them.

Kip adjusted their glasses. "Mother," they said. "Earpieces and receivers in the case. See you later." They turned to walk down the street, leaving them the van.

"Dash, hop in," Sonny said, walking around to the driver's

side.

David opened the passenger door and climbed inside. A quick glance behind him, and he saw this van was set up with a cage in the back. Prisoner transport, but off the books, clearly. Currently empty, it smelled faintly of disinfectant, not a comforting smell under the circumstances.

When Sonny closed his door, the overhead light went off. "Right," he announced, opening the glasses case first. Inside was a set of earpieces in tan instead of the usual pale pink, and matching wristbands housing one receiver each.

The colour, David noted, was close to Sonny's skin tone. Made to go unnoticed.

Sonny picked out one set of earpiece and receiver and handed them to David. The colour was a shade darker than David's tan skin, but it would work.

"Another member of your team?" David asked, meaning Kip.

"Kip? Yeah, tech department," Sonny replied. "Same department as Naz, but they always do the nightshift. And Mother's supervising."

"What, your mother?" David asked.

"No, just Mother. Codename." Sonny inserted the earpiece into his right ear. He pulled the wristband on over his left wrist then held it close to his mouth. "Testing, one, two, one, two," he said, injecting some cheer into his voice. "Did you miss me?"

David inserted his own earpiece, wriggling it around to get it in place. A voice was already speaking, clear as day: a woman with a cut-glass British accent, speaking with confidence in husky, low tones.

That would be Mother, then. The name seemed appropriate.

"Good evening, gentlemen," she was saying. "Please confirm membership."

"Sonny and Dash," Sonny said clearly. "Alpha. X-Ray. Four-one-two. Indigo."

"Confirmed," she said. "Welcome on board, Dash."

"Oh, I haven't got my phone," Sonny added. "But Dash has his."

"The signal from your phone is transmitting from Westminster Bridge," Mother said dubiously.

"Hah! Yes," Sonny said, a smirk on his face. "But it's indisposed. We'll have to use Dash's phone for the time being. Now, Mother, where am I going?"

"Charing Cross Police Station," Mother said. "They're expecting you. The prisoner is not."

"Excellent," Sonny said, shoving the key into the ignition. "He'll be chuffed to bits to see me." He set down the handbrake and began to slowly pull out onto the road, joining the traffic.

David had no idea where Charing Cross was. He sat back and let Sonny lead this mission, driving them down the nighttime London streets, some of which were narrow and dark.

"So, what's happening when we get there?" David asked.

"Okay, so, Mr Merritt is who we're picking up. Robert Merritt. We call him Merritt the ferret. Human scumbag and solicitor. That's lawyer to you. Learn the lingo."

David smiled. "Noted. What's his connection to our lead?"

"Merritt is a known associate of vampires, being their solicitor," Sonny explained. "One known vampire in particular that our department would really like to have a word with about all these vampire genes popping up on the black market lately. So, we grab Merritt, question him, see what shakes out."

"Got it," David replied. Seemed straightforward enough. "And he's definitely a human?"

"Well, he was last time we checked," Sonny said. "But this is why we're taking him from the civilian coppers. Our department deals with anything connected to the supernatural or otherwise inhuman. And it's all done as hush-hush as possible so as not to inconvenience the civilians."

David nodded. "Got it." He glanced over at Sonny. "I can deal with weird stuff, no problem. But...you are gonna *warn* me ahead of time if we tango with vampires again, right?"

Sonny grinned. "Absolutely. Don't fret, sunshine. The brass always plans jobs like that in advance. We can't go rushing in unprepared and have a big public cock-up. We're not allowed to sneeze in their direction without prior planning and several stamps of approval."

"Okay. Good," David said. "Just checking."

Sonny chuckled. "I know we threw you in at the deep end back there, but that op was the result of months of careful surveillance work, so we knew what we were walking into."

"Yeah, you knew, but I didn't," David quipped. "Now I know what to expect."

"Don't be so sure," Sonny told him. "This job has a funny way of surprising you. Oh! Quick pit stop." He indicated at the last moment, then shot across the street to a parking spot outside a late-night café. The van jerked roughly at his abrupt parking.

David grunted, then glanced up at the café outside. "Don't tell me you're getting snacks?"

"Not for me, innit?" Sonny brandished a twenty-pound note. "Pop in there and get four black Americanos to go."

"Four?" David questioned. "Wait, are you buying coffee for the whole station?"

Sonny smiled wryly. "It's a lot easier to blend in when you serve distractions. Watch and learn, sunshine."

*

Sergeant Trevor Howard was three and a half hours into his night shift, sitting on desk duty for the station.

Things were fairly quiet. Couple of chaps in the holding cells from a drunken brawl inside Leicester Square Tube station, and one seedy older gent in an expensive but dishevelled suit who'd made a nuisance of himself in a strip club on Brewer Street. Otherwise, all quiet at the minute, but things would certainly pick up later tonight, being the weekend.

The two drunk chaps would be released in the morning, once they'd slept it off. The suited menace, who insisted he knew his rights, would've been let off with a caution, but during processing his name was flagged on the system. He'd kicked up a right old fuss when Trevor had informed him that they had to detain him pending further inquiries.

Merritt, his name was.

He had to be dragged off to the cells by two uniforms, all the while screaming bloody murder. Merritt's profession was listed as solicitor. He was probably one of those know-it-all posh types that would insist on representing themselves if push came to shove. For the time being, Merritt was periodically shouting obscenities in his upper-class accent from his cell down the hall.

Well, he wouldn't be Trevor's problem for much longer. After being flagged on their system, a request from higher up had come in for a transfer. Merritt was soon going to be someone else's problem.

Trevor wasn't sure which department it was yet. When that sector code came up on the system, it usually meant Special Branch, Flying Squad, Vice, or one of the numerous and secretive arms of British Intelligence.

Whichever one it was, it would likely be the most interesting point of Trevor's evening, eventful detainees notwithstanding.

Just before nine PM, two chaps strolled into booking and up to Trevor's desk. He knew they would've been screened upstairs already, and he recognised the first guy. The Italian-looking one.

"Awright, mate," the man greeted. "Been a minute."

"Awright," Trevor replied, his gaze instantly drawn by the takeaway coffee cup the second man was carrying. Trevor didn't recognise him. Must be new. "New partner day, is it?" he asked, motioning to the new fella.

"Should be our day off, innit?" the Italian replied. "We rushed in. Thought you'd like a coffee."

Trevor was relieved the coffee was for him. It would no doubt taste better than the cheap instant crap he had in the staff kitchen. "I won't say no. Ta."

"We're here to transfer Mr Merritt," the guy said.

He was handed an ID card.

Sonny. Yes. That was his name. Sonny Smith, Vice.

"Oh, yes, Mr Merritt," Trevor said, turning his attention to his computer screen. He couldn't wait to whizz through this transfer, then begin sipping his posh coffee. "Been cursing up a storm, he has."

"Sounds about right," Sonny said. "I believe my superiors have sent in the necessary paperwork."

"Let's see," Trevor said, clicking the file. He wasn't used to vice being so efficient, but it appeared everything was in order. "Yeah, looks like you're good to go," he said, taking up his paper clipboard. "Please sign."

Sonny took the clipboard and leaned casually on the desk as he scrawled his signature in a flourish. "There we are." He handed the clipboard back.

"Do you want uniform down here to escort him?" Trevor asked.

"Nah, we're good, mate," Sonny replied. "Got the transport ready out back."

"Right, then." Trevor got to his feet and reached for the big bunch of keys. "Let's give Mr Merritt the good news."

He led the way down the hall to the cells, with the two young vice officers following behind him.

Merritt could be heard muttering and grumbling inside his cell, voice echoing slightly off the walls. The two drunks had to be asleep, as there wasn't a peep out of either of them.

"Mr Merritt," Trevor called, jangling his keys in the lock. "Please step back from the door. Your transport service has arrived."

"Transport?" Merritt shouted. "What the bloody hell are you talking about?"

Trevor cranked open the cell door, standing back to allow Sonny to position himself in the doorway.

"Hello, Mr Merritt," he greeted wryly. "Let's go an' 'ave a chat, shall we?"

Merritt clearly recognised Sonny, evident from his expression. "Oh, fuck it all," Merritt grumbled. "I haven't done anything!"

"An' you can tell us all about it," Sonny responded, gesturing for Merritt to get up and step forward.

Surprisingly, Merritt did as he was told with minimal swearing.

Trevor would be glad to see the back of Merritt. He was eager to see them all off, then get back to his desk and coffee.

Chapter Thirty-One

They loaded Mr Merritt in handcuffs into the cage in the back of their van and shut the door on him.

Sonny said farewell to the uniformed officer who'd opened the door for them, then pulled David aside once they were out of earshot.

"I have some advice," he said quietly, as they walked around the side of the van. "I don't trust Ferrett, and the less he knows the better. You're an unknown to him. He already knows me, which means I'll do all the talking. So, what do you say to being the strong, silent type in this scenario?"

"Works for me," David replied quietly. "And I don't mind playing bad cop if needed."

"I doubt it'll get that dramatic tonight, but good to know." Sonny winked at him, then walked around the front of the van to get to the driver's seat.

David tried his best not to smile. As far as work went, this was fun.

He opened the passenger door and got into the van. Mr Merritt was already talking, pleading his case to Sonny to let him go, offering bribes and then resorting to blackmail.

Sonny didn't respond other than to chuckle, as he drove them out of the police station. He'd fallen uncharacteristically quiet, which meant he was taking the job seriously. This left Mr Merritt talking to himself in the cage. David wasn't sure if the man was drunk or not, but his language sure was colourful.

All these British accents and Britishisms were still a novelty to David. While he caught Sonny rolling his eyes a couple of times at what Mr Merritt was saying, David found his cadence and words interesting. Upper class. A lawyer. Clearly intelligent and not afraid to throw in big words to show off, yet he swore a lot and resorted to degrading insults easily.

David kept quiet and didn't react.

Prisoner transport was no joke either. They needed to stay alert. David kept his eyes on the road and their surroundings through the windows. He'd experienced his fair share of ambushes during transports before. He half expected an attack; an armoured car ramming them, or vampires with big teeth flying down from the night sky, and his mind anticipated several of these scenarios, but ultimately none of those happened. Their journey was quiet, albeit with Mr Merritt complaining nonstop.

Sonny drove them into a quiet, industrialised area, and straight into what David first assumed was a car lot due to the automatic door, but then he realised that it was more of a private garage.

In his earpiece, Mother huskily gave brief, one-word instructions. Likely code words. "Nest" was probably code for the garage they drove into. Sonny obviously knew the way.

They were the only ones here, but David was willing to bet a security feed was monitoring them. The lights flickered on automatically. David followed Sonny's lead and got out of the van when he did.

They walked around the van and met at the back, but Sonny didn't want to open the van right away. He motioned to David to follow.

In the gloomy garage, David had a quick look around. There wasn't enough here to suggest it was a government facility; the place was sparse with minimal tools or shelves, just enough to enable it to pass as some legitimate garage, business or personal. A front. Off the books, most likely.

David knew the drill.

He was curious as to what Sonny's personal style of interrogation would be, but this was not a convenient time to be daydreaming about Sonny being a badass, so David forced himself to focus.

He helped Sonny prepare the scene: one wooden chair set under a bare light bulb. Nothing within reach of the suspect. Obviously, the plan would be to put Mr Merritt in that chair and question him.

Sonny wasn't in a rush. He checked his watch a couple of times, and when Mr Merritt began shouting audibly from the van for attention, Sonny grinned and tapped his watch. "Didn't even last five minutes," he murmured.

David smiled.

"Wait another five," Mother instructed.

Sonny glanced up at the ceiling, winking in a cheeky manner.

So, the security feed was up there, David thought.

They waited. Merritt kept shouting from inside the van. Sonny checked his watch casually. "Three more minutes," he murmured.

David nodded.

Once the five minutes were up, they opened the van and dragged Merritt out.

"Here we are, Mr Merritt!" Sonny said jovially. "Your new home for the foreseeable future!"

They shoved him down onto the chair. David went behind him and zip tied his arms and then his ankles to the chair. He wasn't moving anywhere without this chair strapped to his ass.

"You fucking cunts!" Merritt spat. "You can't do this to me! I have friends!"

"Hah!" Sonny barked in amusement. "Friends? A grimy li'l toe rag like you?" He stood in front of Merritt casually while David watched from the side.

"Yeah, friends in high places!" Merritt shot back. "You're going to wish you'd never..."

He trailed off when Sonny whipped a black metal rod from his belt, extending it with one expert flip as an audible electrical current sang in the air.

A taser. A very hi-tech taser, by the looks of it.

Merritt fell quiet. He was already damp with sweat, but David noticed bigger beads forming around his temple and collar.

"See this? This is a prototype," Sonny said, crossing one arm under the other as he held up the taser in a laissez-faire fashion, like one might hold a cigarette. "A normal taser emits fifty thousand volts and can zap you from a couple of inches away. This li'l beauty is seventy thousand and can zap you from over one foot away. I've been dying to try her out in the field. Imagine how it would feel on your ball sac, Mr Merritt. Seventy thousand volts."

"You can't fucking do that," Merritt said shakily. "You'll fucking kill me!"

"That is a high possibility," Sonny replied casually. "Alas, we don't really have the time for fun and games this evening. More's the pity. So, bearing in mind we are pushed for time, perhaps you'd be so good as to answer our questions quick smart, innit?"

As Sonny spoke, Mother also began to speak quietly but clearly in their earpieces, relaying figures and accounts.

Sonny kept speaking, not giving away that he'd received intel in his ear.

"You recently handled the liquidation of several assets," Sonny continued, "both here and in Europe, then transferred a considerable sum of money into an offshore account. An account that you are a named holder on, and which made a substantial payment to another account based in Mexico. Care to explain that, Mr Merritt?"

Merritt shook his head. "I don't ask what my clients do with their money. It's none of my fucking business."

"But it looks sus, doesn't it?" Sonny said. "Especially when the recipient of that money over in Mexico was found to be involved in some very illegal activities of the vampiric sort."

"Even if that's true," Merritt scoffed, "what my clients do in other countries isn't my concern nor responsibility. All I do is handle their legal business here."

"Bullshit," Sonny said calmly. "You're up to your eyeballs in this muck, Merritt. Who had you acting as their bag man? Which vampire from your sleazy little black book was it? Give me a name."

"It was anonymous," Merritt said. "I don't know who it was."

"Oh, I think you do," Sonny replied, waving the taser casually. "I told you we're pressed for time. Cough up a name, and we can go our separate ways."

Merritt didn't say anything. He was sweating though.

David felt his phone vibrate in his pocket. At the same moment, Mother said, "I've sent Merritt's savings account to Dash's phone. Threaten his money."

David said nothing as he removed his phone from his pocket. He offered it out to Sonny, who took the phone in his free hand. Sonny looked at the screen and chuckled softly.

"Thought you'd have more than that, Mr Merritt," he said, turning the screen around to show Merritt. "Vampires are stingy bastards, eh? Still, that's a tidy sum."

Merritt stared at the screen, his face turning whiter than it already was. "What the fuck are you doing?"

"Well," Sonny said, stepping back, "we are mere seconds away from seizing your assets, including this savings account of two hundred thousand, if you don't start talking."

Merritt gaped like a fish. "You...you can't do that!"

"We can, and we will," Sonny said. "So, you have five seconds to spill the beans before we bleed you dry. Vampire pun not intended. Five. Four..."

"Okay, wait!" Merritt pleaded. "Hold on!"

"I'm not hearing a name yet, mate," Sonny said breezily. "Three. Two..."

"Balogh! Balogh!" Merritt shouted. "It was for Balogh, you cunts!"

Sonny was quiet. David could tell by his face that the name meant something to him.

The silence lasted only a moment, the only sound Merritt's laboured breathing.

"You know Balogh's location?" Sonny asked him.

Merritt snorted, a grim smile twisting his mouth. "He never tells me that! And even if he did, what use would that be to someone who only takes physical form when it suits him?" Merritt spat out. "What do you expect to do, chase after him with a pair of handcuffs? Fucking pathetic, you lot are."

"Shut your pie hole, would you?" Sonny replied firmly. "How do you stay in touch with him? An address? A phone number?"

Merritt shifted in his bonds. "Yes, sometimes."

"Well, cough them up, then," Sonny said, a trace of irritation in his voice. "Before we drain all your funds and sling you out on the street."

David saw Merritt's hesitation. The threat of removing his funds clearly hit him where it hurt.

Although, he wasn't going down without a fight. "I can raise funds again," he said, a hollow threat. Feeling them out.

"Yeah, not impossible for a slimy li'l fellow such as yourself," Sonny replied. "But it would take a while, and at this time of night it would be terribly inconvenient for you. No bank account. No savings, no credit. Sure, you might be able to untangle the mess eventually, but it'll mean dossing it for a few nights, maybe more. Are you sure you have the energy for all that? Just give us an address."

David smiled. From the sour expression on Merritt's face, he knew Sonny had him.

"It's your funeral, you cocky little shit," he snarled. "Lockmill Estate, outside of Edinburgh.

"Scotland?" Sonny said, likely buying them some time as Mother confirmed in their earpieces that they were searching for the address.

"It's where all physical deliveries are sent," Merritt said. "That's all I have."

"The address checks out," Mother said. "A large estate in the countryside."

They had their lead.

Sonny met David's eyes and gave him the nod. The interrogation was over. He handed the phone back to David, then retracted his taser.

"See, Mr Merritt?" Sonny teased. "That wasn't so hard, was it?"

"Fuck you," Merritt hissed. "If Balogh finds out, my life is over anyway. Drop me back in Leicester Square. I'll spend my remaining hours smothered in the bosom of nubile young dancers."

"Yeah, I bet they can't wait to see you again," Sonny quipped. He motioned to David to untie Merritt.

"Drop Merritt off," Mother said. "Return to base for debrief."

"On our way," Sonny said.

Chapter Thirty-Two

They dropped Merritt on the outskirts of Leicester Square, near Chinatown. The streets were busier down here and Merritt soon slipped into the sea of pedestrians and tourists, scuttling away into the bustle of the street like a rat.

"C'mon," Sonny urged David, shutting the van's back door. "Hopefully I can squeeze us past traffic."

They got back into the front of the van, Sonny in the driver's seat.

"Where's base exactly?" David asked.

"Two miles across town," Sonny replied. "Dropped off the ferret," he said, for the comms benefit. "Headed to base now. Does anyone want coffee?"

"Confirmed," Mother's voice replied. "No, Sonny, don't stop anywhere. Guv wants to debrief ASAP."

"Copy that," Sonny replied. "I'll be quick." He removed the earpiece from his ear and the wristband from around his wrist.

David copied the motion, and dropped his equipment back into the case when Sonny held it out. When the case was shut, David suspected this was a cue for them to talk before they got to base.

"Dare I ask?" David began. "Balogh?"

Sonny smiled wryly. "Yeah, strap in," he said, reaching for his seat belt. He started the van and pulled out to join traffic, cutting down a narrow side street. "Once we're out of the centre, I'll take you on the scenic route. Buckingham Palace. Wellington Arch. Actually, it's the most direct route and just so happens to be scenic."

"Cool," David said, more interested in all the other stuff. "So, this Balogh guy? I take it he's a vampire?"

"Oh, yeah," Sonny replied. "Count Kristof Domokos Balogh."

"That's quite a mouthful," David quipped.

Sonny tittered. "You'll get used to it," he said. "We call him the Count, or Dracula."

David turned to look at Sonny. "*Is* he Dracula?" he asked dubiously.

Sonny shrugged. "So far, he's the oldest vampire known to us. I mean, the oldest one that's currently active. We suspect he has several aliases, but his most used alias is Count Balogh, a rich aristocrat of Hungarian descent. Allegedly."

"Right," David said. "What does he look like?"

"They can show you in the debrief, if you ask nicely," Sonny told him. "Although, that's neither here nor there. Balogh can change appearance at will."

"Huh," David said. "I see."

*

With Sonny dodging the congested roads, they made good time and were there in twenty minutes: Exhibition Road, a wide and quiet street with impressive old stone buildings on either side. Sonny pulled in alongside one grand building with stone pillars outside it, pointing the van at a downward-facing garage entrance on the street.

David watched him roll down the window and lean out to face a scanner. An infrared light beamed through the windshield, catching David off guard. Then the black garage doors automatically opened.

Sonny smiled at David. "Welcome to HQ, sunshine. Well, the basement, anyway." He put the van in gear and drove into the building.

Much of it looked like an underground car lot, until they left the van parked and went to a service door. David was given the bag to carry. Sonny entered a code on the keypad, then pressed his thumb to the brick wall. A concealed panel scanned his thumb. The door buzzed open.

"This way," Sonny advised, holding the door open for him.

They took the stairs down, bypassing the first level and continuing down to the next.

"Can't afford an elevator?" David teased. The stairwell was narrow and stark, brightly lit. No carpet.

"There's one on the other end," Sonny replied. "We're there now, princess. Hope you aren't out of breath."

"Hardly," David quipped.

Sonny buzzed them through another door, and they came out on a quiet hallway. No carpet here either, only tile. Easily scrubbed clean. The strip lighting overhead wasn't as bright as the stairwell.

David was expecting an office or tech setup of some kind.

Somewhere for a secure SCIF. The only signs on the walls were small panels showing numbers. No names.

Sonny led the way, turning right and walking down the hall. They passed a few doors, all closed. No windows. The doors could lead to rooms or stationary cupboards, no way of knowing what was on the other side.

"It's at the end of the hall," Sonny explained as they neared the final door.

A soft sound behind them drew David's attention, and he turned around. Down the other end of the hall, a slim woman in a white lab coat was exiting one of the doors. She held a small white box in her hands.

The sight of the lab coat was enough to give David a sharp stab of anxiety.

The woman didn't even look their way, she locked the door behind her and turned in the other direction.

"Is the lab here?" David asked, turning to Sonny. He wondered if he'd been duped into coming to the lab after all.

"No, floor above us," Sonny replied. He glanced at David, probably noting his concern, then looked behind them. "Those are storage rooms," he added. "And the elevators are further down."

"And which room are we going into?" David asked.

"Tech support," Sonny said. "Calm down, mate. It's not the lab. You might see some lab coats wander the halls, but they'll all be upstairs, innit?" He approached the door and punched in a code on the wall panel. It buzzed open, and he held it wide for David to get a good look inside before they entered.

David saw with some relief that it was an office.

A very expensive, hi-tech office, but not a lab. There were stations with computers, some single and some grouped together. The office chairs were modern, ergonomic and stark white; shaped to look like human spines. The lighting was low mood lighting, like a gaming room; the brightest lights came from the numerous computer screens and desk lamps.

David counted four people in the room, and they all turned their heads to look.

"Evenin' all!" Sonny called out, voice booming through the quiet. "Dash, this is the night watch. Come meet the team."

David recognised Kip, the blue-haired driver who'd dropped off the van earlier that evening. Kip was at an individual computer station, working on some complex-looking code. They nodded at David briefly, then went back to their work.

"Kip, you met," Sonny said. "Then this is Dev, and Owl." He indicated the other two agents at desks.

Dev, a skinny South Asian guy in a shirt and glasses, was probably somewhere between thirty and forty. He wore a headset and mic over short black hair and was nervously clicking a ball-point pen in his hand.

Owl, on the next station, was a younger, curvy White woman with a cherubic face and short, blonde curls. Her nose was pierced with a silver ring, and she smiled up at David. She was sitting in a matte-black electric wheelchair, which boasted stickers on the sides, including one that read "How's my driving? Dial 1-800-Eat Shit."

"Hello," Owl greeted, the only one of the agents to speak.

"Hi," David replied.

Down on the floor beside Owl's station was a bowl of water, a soft dog bed, and a little dog curled up there that looked like Nina.

"Hey, is that...?" David began, but there was no time to stand around chatting.

"And this is Mother," Sonny introduced, indicating the

statuesque woman standing in front of several bright monitors, casting an impressive silhouette. She stepped forward, and David saw she was around their age, thirty, with long chestnut hair. She wore a blouse and a long pencil skirt, sharp business attire.

"Hello, Dash," she greeted, her voice as husky in person as it had been over comms.

She didn't offer her hand.

"Hello," David replied, looking her over. She was taller than him, and unapologetically wore high heels, towering well over him and Sonny.

"The address Merritt gave you is up on the wall," Mother said, straight to business. "Kip has piggybacked off a weather drone for us to take a look. Could be abandoned. No activity yet."

The three stood in front of Mother's monitors, assessing the grainy nighttime images.

"What is that, a castle?" David asked.

"An old manor house," Mother replied. "Nearest traffic cameras are here, and here." She indicated on another screen. "We backdoored into their system and checked for vehicles headed toward the property. Several delivery vans over the last two months. We're trying to trace them now."

"That sounds promising," Sonny said. "Did you tell Guv?"

"Yes," Mother said. "He's dialling in shortly."

"Okay, good," Sonny said. "I think I should head up there."

Dev stopped clicking his pen. A hush fell over the room.

David watched Mother turn a concerned frown on Sonny. "And what will you do if Balogh is actually there?" she asked him.

Sonny shrugged. "Have a chat. Ask him some questions. That's all we can do, right? Unless you lot have come up with a vampire-catching trap yet?"

"There's not much we can do here," Kip called over. "You'll

have to ask the lab to hurry up the developments before we can create proper hardware."

"Yeah, you guys blame the lab for causing delays, and they blame you," Sonny said, teasing them. "Meanwhile, we got vampires running around setting up illegal labs. I'm getting annoyed with putting out the fires, I want to go straight to the source."

"With what, some garlic?" Owl called out, to a few titters from the other agents. "Good luck with that."

"All right," Mother said firmly. "Settle down. We work with what we've got until there's a new breakthrough. Sonny, you know you can't do anything unless Guv authorises it."

Sonny held up his hands. "I know. I'm just saying."

The monitor in front of them lit up with an incoming call.

"Speak of the devil," Sonny murmured.

Mother stood in front of the monitor, folding her arms. "Accept call," she said. The screen changed to what looked like an office video call. The office in question was wood furnished, and the man seated at the desk was an older Black man wearing wire-rimmed glasses, sitting with incredible posture and his shoulders back, a military bearing.

David's keen eye spotted a framed medal on the shelf behind him. This guy was high-ranking military for sure.

"Awright, Guv," Sonny greeted. "This is Dash."

Guv blinked slowly, the expression on his face not cracking one inch but David could sense he was annoyed. "Thank you, Sonny," Guv replied evenly. "I understand Merritt gave you an address?"

"It's in Scotland, Guv," Sonny said. "Mother was saying there's been deliveries going in. I thought I could pop up on a flight tonight and check it out. We got..." Sonny checked his watch. "About seven hours till sunrise."

David hadn't expected another mission right away. Unless Sonny planned to leave him behind? He had said I, not we. David glanced at him, and saw that Mother was doing the same on Sonny's other side. She didn't appear to agree with the suggestion.

Guv fell silent for a moment, appearing to think. "We have no means of capture, but there's no guarantee Balogh will be there."

"Right," Sonny replied. "I'll scope the place out. And if he is there, I'll ask some questions. We all know he likes to chat, and I'm the only one he won't bite."

Both Guv and Mother gave Sonny serious looks.

"Again," Sonny amended. "He won't bite me again. He learned his lesson."

David looked at Sonny with concern, and Sonny noticed.

"Vampires don't like alien blood," he stage-whispered, and winked at David. "Lucky us, right?"

David supposed that was lucky, in a roundabout way. Built-in vampire immunity.

Guv exhaled. "This is the best lead we've had in months. I don't want it to turn cold."

"We have to take it, Guv," Sonny said. "We already know Balogh hates phones, so there's little chance of him getting a telephone call, but the longer we leave it, the more chance Merritt has to warn him. It has to be tonight."

"I agree," Guv said, much to David's surprise. "Go on a flight ASAP for recon. Survey the property, see what you can find. Only engage as a last resort."

"Yes, Guv," Sonny replied. "Will do."

"Am I coming?" David asked, daring to butt in.

"No, I better head in alone," Sonny replied.

"But if we're both safe from being bitten?" David indicated

between him and Sonny. "Wouldn't it be better if you had backup?"

"No, I can handle it," Sonny said, shooting David a look he couldn't decipher.

"Quiet, the pair of you," Guv cut in. "I'm the one who decides who goes where. Understood?"

David fell silent.

"Sorry, Guv," Sonny piped up. "I just think, as I'm already known to Balogh, it'll be best if—"

"Quiet," Guv repeated firmly.

Sonny fell silent. He looked irritated about it too.

David wondered why Sonny didn't want him to come. Didn't he trust him?

"You take your orders from me," Guv said, his eyes raking over them both. "Dash is your backup on this, Sonny. But play it safe. Recon only. No unnecessary risks and do not try to engage. And, if Balogh is the broker behind all these new vampire genes on the black market, you will not do anything by yourselves. You will return to base, and you will hold fire while we will make the necessary arrangements before taking the next step. Are we clear?"

"Crystal, Guv," Sonny said.

David nodded the affirmative. "Yes sir."

He felt pleased with his little victory: he was going too. He wouldn't get left behind on this.

"All right," Guv said. "Get yourselves to Scotland. Night watch will support, and I expect a full report on my desk by 0900 hours tomorrow morning."

He signed off, and as soon as the screen cleared Sonny clapped his hands together. "So much for a night off!" he quipped. "Off to bonnie Scotland!"

"Dev," Mother said. "Get them some gear. Owl, book their flights."

"Yes, chop, chop!" Sonny called to the agents.

Amid the activity, David noticed the little Nina lookalike wake up and stretch. He went over to her, beside Owl's desk.

"Is this...?" He indicated the dog.

"The dog from Mexico?" Owl smiled up at him. "Yes, she is. Doc left her with me for the night."

David crouched down to say hello to Nina. "Buenas noches, Nina," he murmured, letting her sniff his hand before petting her. She seemed content, and too cosy to even get up. David wasn't sure if she remembered him, but after everything she'd been through, she probably needed a rest.

"Was everything fine with her?" he asked Owl. "The tests and stuff?"

"You'd have to ask Doc," Owl said. "She'll be back in the lab tomorrow morning."

The lab.

David realised at some point, he would have to go in there, but for now he'd rather avoid it.

"Okay, thanks," he said and got up to find Sonny. A trip to Scotland sounded good right about now.

He found Sonny in a small armoury with Dev, opening a box of gun clips. David entered the cage, nodding in appreciation at the firepower.

"Nice," he murmured.

"Oi, Dash!" Sonny tossed him a clip. "Take a gander at that!"

David caught the clip and opened it to look. The bullets were dark blue, and glowing. "Interesting," he said dryly.

"UV bullets," Sonny announced happily. "They're expensive, so be frugal with 'em."

David nodded. "Will they have any effect on Count Balogh?"

"Not really," Sonny said. "The bullets are for any other vampires that might be around. We have UV torches for Balogh."

"Torches?" David questioned. For some reason he expected fire, but when Sonny tossed him a thin black torch, he realised it was that kind of torch. "Right. Torches." Like the ones the team had used back in Mexico. He flicked it on to check, and a dark-blue beam with a white light centre shone out.

"You'll need the chargers as well," Dev said, pulling clunky charging boxes off the shelves. "Only take them out right before use, or you'll run out of battery."

That didn't sound great, David thought.

He watched Dev and Sonny transfer and arrange the equipment into a secure black case on wheels. A compact first aid kit, food pack rations, and small water bottles were also included.

"Quick question," David asked. "Is this all we got? What about crosses or holy water?"

Dev and Sonny both paused to look at him, then Dev sent a withering look to Sonny.

"Yeah, yeah," Sonny said, waving his hand at Dev. "I'll brief him about vampires on the way."

"That stuff doesn't work?" David asked, shocked.

"Vampires pre-date Christianity," Dev said, adjusting his glasses.

David looked at Sonny, who nodded. "That's true," Sonny said.

"Well, damn," David said.

Chapter Thirty-Three

To get to the airport, they had to take the Tube. Apparently, it was the quickest route.

David's first time on the Tube was eye-opening. He'd ridden the underground Metro Rail in Los Angeles a couple of times when he was much younger, but nothing of the sort since. The scale and age of the London Underground system was quite something.

He let Sonny lead the way, and without even looking at a Tube map, his partner got them through the pedestrian areas and onto the right platforms. When they sat down in a half-empty carriage, the train rattling noisily through the darkness, David felt in his pocket for the two cards he'd been given.

As well as arming him, PRISM had given him an ID card with his photo and the alias John Brown. The card read INTERPOL when held straight, and read PRISM when tilted at an angle, just like Sonny's. The second card was a red-and-white standard ID card, for the airport, Sonny had said. Same alias of John Brown.

"Are you gonna stare at those all night?" Sonny said, voice barely audible over the rattle of the train.

David smirked. He put the cards back in his pocket.

The train slowed, pulling out of the dark tunnel system and into a brightly lit station where passengers got on and off. Their carriage was still half empty, with nobody sitting in their immediate vicinity. David deemed it safe to talk.

"So," he said. "What happened to the part about careful planning before diving into a nest of vampires?"

"It's not a nest of vampires," Sonny replied. "It's Balogh, and he's known to us. He prefers dealing with humans, so the chance of any other vampires around is minimal."

"Right," David said, glancing down at their bags full of firepower. "Is that why you didn't want me to come?"

"I was gallantly protecting your downtime," Sonny replied, looking away from David to avoid eye contact. "I didn't realise you were so eager to work."

David opened his mouth to respond but held back his words. *I just want to be with you.* He couldn't say that. He'd sound needy. They'd only known each other a handful of days.

Yet, to David at least, it felt like they'd known each other forever.

He didn't want to say that either. He didn't want to appear vulnerable right now or overcrowd Sonny too soon.

David edited his thoughts before putting a fraction of what he felt into words.

"Where I come from," he said evenly, "being on the same team means having each other's backs."

Sonny looked at him, dark eyes searching his. He was quiet for half a moment, assessing David. Something burned in his brown eyes—a warning glint, perhaps.

When he spoke, it was with a levity that didn't match the intensity of his gaze. "There's no need to get dramatic," he said. "You're here, aren't you? Stop rattling your sabre at me, love."

David raised his eyebrows. He wanted to say more, but it was clear Sonny was on the defence, so he met Sonny down in the dirt and uttered one word under his breath: "Perra."

Sonny broke into a laugh at David's deadpan delivery of "bitch".

David smiled. This wasn't entirely resolved, in his view, but things were okay for now.

*

Exiting the Tube station, they remained underground and entered the labyrinthine airport terminus. Hundreds upon hundreds of passengers marched to and from the main exits in a variety of outfits, from business attire to colourful holiday clothes.

"Welcome to hell," Sonny quipped. "Otherwise known as Heathrow Airport."

They made a beeline for the travelator and kept walking. Their first stop was check-in, avoiding the queues of passengers and heading straight to the self-service computer screens.

"Hold that, would ya?" Sonny thrust the case at David and began tapping on the screen.

"How are we taking handguns aboard a regular plane?" he asked. Their handguns, and knives, were still holstered and concealed under their jackets.

Sonny ignored him, busy printing off the boarding passes. His face twisted into frustration as he read them. "Oh, those stingy bastards!"

"What?" David asked, peering over Sonny's shoulder.

"I told you they made us fly economy," Sonny said, furiously tapping the screen.

David could see he was trying to upgrade, but the system wasn't playing ball. No upgrades available.

"Shit," Sonny swore. "Look, wait here. I'm gonna go to the desk and flirt with someone for better seats."

"Can't I flirt too?" David quipped.

Sonny paused, turning round to look at him. "Actually, British birds love Americans," he said. "Change of plan. You go flirt. I'll wait here." He gave David the boarding passes and his credit card. "Take your hat off and leave the case. Now go on." He shooed David off. "Go work your American magic."

"American magic," David drawled. "Okay." He removed his hat and ran a hand through his hair, then headed off toward the check-in desks for British Airways. He did a visual scan of the queues for how fast they were moving.

"Oi!" Sonny called over to him. "Don't queue up, you ponce! We haven't got all night! Go to the special service desk." He pointed furiously at the far end of the desks.

"Got it," David said, trying not to smile. He didn't know what a ponce was, but Sonny's way of speaking always made him smile because of its sheer Britishness.

David bypassed the queues and went to the desk at the far end. Business class and special assistance. Only one other passenger stood in that queue, so David got in behind them.

He hoped this would work.

When it was his turn, he stepped up to the desk and assessed the woman sitting there. She was smartly dressed in British Airways uniform, with a full face of make-up. Blonde hair tied up neatly. She was older than David, maybe in her forties.

He noticed her eyes flick up and down, checking him out too. That was a positive sign.

"Good evening, ma'am," David greeted, laying on the charm. "How are you tonight?"

She smiled at him. "Fine, thank you," she replied. "What can I help you with, sir?"

"I have this booking here," David said, setting the boarding passes onto her desk. "We were hoping for an upgrade, if that's at all possible."

"Let me see," she said, and began tapping on her screen. "Hm. There are two seats in business class, but we reserve them for special circumstances."

"What circumstances might those be?" David asked politely.

"Certain business clients and diplomats," she answered.

"Well, that's a stroke of luck," David said. He took out his card, holding it in front of the desk to block her view. He glanced down to check he was tilting it correctly to show the INTERPOL angle.

This wasn't the smoothest he'd ever been, but he would get the hang of it next time.

David showed her the card. "We're travelling on urgent business," he told her. "Can we grab those upgrades?"

"Certainly, sir," she said. "I'll do that right now."

David counted this as a personal victory. "Thank you so much," he told her, and waited. When she said the additional price, David was surprised at how low it was. He'd expected hundreds for each seat, but it was barely one hundred for both. He used Sonny's credit card, waving it over the contactless machine. She handed him the new boarding passes.

"Do you have any bags to put in the hold?" she asked him.

"Er, I'm not sure," David replied. "I'd better go check. Thanks again." He left the desk to find Sonny. "Hey. Are we checking the bag into the hold?"

Sonny burst out laughing.

"I take it that's a no?" David quipped.

"Definitely not," Sonny replied.

"So, we're taking handguns into a cabin?" David asked. "And our knives?"

"Yes," Sonny said. "Like secret police or air marshals, but a more Rambo version. Keep everything holstered and hidden."

"Okay," David said, having to trust Sonny.

"You got the upgrades then?" Sonny asked.

"Yes," David said. "Business class."

"Well done, sunshine." Sonny took the boarding passes and credit card from him and slipped them inside his jacket. "Let's whizz through security and go grab a bite before take-off."

"No meal on the flight?" David asked.

Sonny laughed again. "It's barely an hour in the air."

"Oh," David said. "An hour? Doesn't really seem worth flying."

"Quickest option," Sonny said. "Even the fastest train takes four hours, and if you don't pre-book, it's more expensive than flying. We're on a tight schedule before sunrise."

"I see," David said. "Well, then, an hour is obviously the better choice."

"You catch on quick," Sonny teased. "Fancy a burger? I'd like a burger."

"Sure."

Sonny led the way, not to the main security processing area, but to a smaller security room that was clearly used by staff for the airport. David spotted an air stewarding crew and some duty-free retail staff being processed, setting all their bags and jackets through an X-Ray machine and then queuing at the body scanner.

Meanwhile, two White men in black business suits walked

around the body scanner, bypassing it without stopping. They held up their ID badges with an air of authority. Plain clothes police were David's guess, and they would be armed so their guns would set off the scanner, hence the bypass.

Visibly armed police were present too. Not stationary but strolling through the area in pairs. They wore navy-blue tactical gear with the word POLICE printed in white across their backs, geared up with automatic rifles held casually in the front.

The nearest pair of armed police glanced at David as they walked past the staff entrance, and his heart rate picked up from nerves. He knew armed police in airports were more of a visual deterrent than anything, and plain clothes police were always more of a threat. But seeing all these officers around in such a small, confined area was giving him anxiety.

"Hey," Sonny murmured to him. "Use the red card. And relax, we do this all the time. Follow me."

David nodded. He had to remind himself he wasn't on the run anymore. He was protected.

Sonny approached the staff desk and handed over his red card. His move was fluid, relaxed. Sonny gave off an ease like he was here to pick up the milk.

"Busy tonight," Sonny mentioned to the guard at the desk.

"Yeah," they replied, disinterested. They swiped his card through a machine, glanced at their computer monitor for barely a moment, then handed back the card.

Sonny had passed, now it was David's turn.

He was anxious, but managed to hold it together as he handed over his red card. The guard scanned it. That moment took forever, and when the guard looked up at David, he felt a twinge of guilt for the ruse. But then he was waved through.

He'd made it. John Brown was in.

Sonny motioned for David to follow him, and he led the way around the body scanner. They didn't stop, and they didn't offer the bag for scanning. Same as the plain clothes police, and the staff running the security check barely batted an eyelid at them passing by.

That was easier than David had anticipated.

"There you go." Sonny smiled at him. "Piece of cake, innit?"

No sooner had he said the words than they rounded a corner and immediately crossed paths with another uniformed police officer, this one with a sniffer dog; a brown and white mottled spaniel.

David spotted the dog. The dog noticed them too; it paused in its tracks, nose wriggling as it scented. David thought the dog would want to sniff them, or signal to its handler that it had discovered something unusual.

But the dog whimpered and turned away, hiding behind its handler's legs.

"Lizzy?" the handler said, as he was twisted up with the leash. "What's the matter?" He appeared more concerned with the dog than David or Sonny and didn't understand what the dog had detected.

This seemed to confirm David's theory. Since he'd been on the run, dogs all shied away from him. Only Nina, the little Xolo from the vampire lab, had been friendly.

"Oi," Sonny said in a hushed whisper, because David had lagged behind. "Come on, would you? We got maybe half an hour to shove food into our gobs before we have to make a run for this bloody plane."

"Did you notice the dog?" David asked, catching up to Sonny's side. "All dogs seem scared of us."

"Hm?" Sonny glanced round briefly. "Well, I'm not

surprised. Animals sense these things, don't they?"

"But Nina was fine with us," David said, wanting Sonny to see his point.

"So, what?" Sonny said, striding off into the departures lounge. "Ah! Burgers. There we go."

David could see that Sonny didn't care about the Nina revelation. Maybe it was nothing, but David made a mental note to speak to that doctor once they got back to base. He had a feeling that Nina wasn't as regular a dog as they'd first thought.

They sat inside a dining bar in the enormous lounge, within sight of the departure board. While they waited for the food to arrive, David asked for that briefing on vampire do's and don'ts.

"Oh, yeah," Sonny said breezily, like he'd forgotten to brief him at all. "Well, hopefully you won't tangle with anyone tonight."

"But," David prompted.

"But, just in case," Sonny continued, "here's the lowdown. Religious stuff, forget it. Crosses, prayers, Latin... None of that works."

"Fine," David replied. "Can we start with what does work?"

"Sunlight," Sonny said. "Always sunlight. UV light is also lethal. Any bright lights can be a deterrent, if you want to give them a surprise."

"Got it. And stakes?"

"Slows them down, but ain't lethal," Sonny said. "Same for regular ammo. Don't get me wrong, if you blasted one with enough bullets, they'd have a hard time putting themselves back together, but it wouldn't be lethal."

David tried not to visualise that. "Right. Anything else?"

"The invite-only thing is, surprisingly, true," Sonny said. "Or, so it appears so far. Personal dwellings, owned by you, with a ring of salt around the perimeter, and you're golden. They can't get inside. Or," he added, smiling, "they want us to think that. Personally, I don't take anything for granted."

"Right," David agreed. "Okay, so, daylight and UV light are sure things. Maybe salt. Nothing else is lethal or confirmed to work."

"That's correct."

The food arrived. David couldn't help noticing the little wooden pick that skewered his towering burger. Like a tiny wooden stake. He picked it out and twirled it between thumb and forefinger thoughtfully. "Why is the stake thing so prevalent in fiction?" he asked, musing aloud.

Sonny was already demolishing his burger and spoke around a mouthful of food. "In ye olden times," he began, "they would drive stakes into a corpse when burying it if they thought it, or its ghost, was at risk of rising again. There are one or two staked corpses under the roads in London, usually at an intersection. Old crossroads. Nobody wants to dig them up. Superstitious old lot, we are."

"That's interesting." David discarded the wooden pick. "So, it was a preventative measure only. When did it become associated with vampires?"

"This isn't a dinner topic," Sonny said, grabbing fries to put in his mouth. He continued talking as he ate. "Medieval Europe. Plague stuff. Corpses had some weird rot and would bloat out of their graves. Some had a rosy flush on their skin after death, blood on their lips. People back then thought it was the dead rising. So, they began staking corpses into the ground to keep 'em put. Sometimes they'd lop off their heads as well, or burn the bodies to scatter the ash."

"You're right, that isn't a dinner topic," David quipped. He picked up his burger and began to eat. "That's interesting though."

"Yeah, well, you can watch some documentaries when we get back, innit?" Sonny told him.

"I can't wait," David drawled. He chewed for a while, ruminating. "So, I'm guessing that none of those staking examples were actually vampires? If it's common knowledge?"

"Correct."

"And there's no common knowledge of the vampires we're dealing with?" David asked.

"Bloody hope not," Sonny said.

"Where do they come from?"

Sonny shrugged. "We don't know. Doc and my cousin have studied blood samples, and best they can work out is that vampire genes are some kind of parasite that need a host body to survive. Not entirely unlike us with our special guests, but a different breed."

That was a grim thought.

"Great," David said sarcastically. "This is precisely what I wanted to hear."

Sonny chuckled. "Look on the bright side. We actually know where our parasites came from."

"What, from space?" David said. "Yeah, that really narrows it down, Sonny."

He grinned in amusement. "We know way less about where vamps come from and been studying them for longer. Ironic, innit?"

"How long has your department known about vampires?" David asked.

"Decades, by all accounts," Sonny replied.

"And in all that time," David asked, "they haven't managed to recruit any?"

Sonny tilted his head. "Well, sort of. Balogh was on board for a while, but he's like a cat, he wants to go do his own thing."

"I see." David was starting to see why Sonny wasn't afraid to go see this vampire now. "So, he's an associate?"

Sonny tilted his head again. "My advice?" he said. "Don't try to get too cosy. He's unpredictable and unsafe."

"But you want to find him and, what? Interrogate him?"

"One step at a time," Sonny replied. "Find his base first. If he's there, which he may well not be, then I'll ask him questions. He may or may not play ball. Just have to wait and see."

"Right," David drawled. "Well, I trust you know what you're doing."

Sonny grinned at him and popped a fry into his mouth. "No worries, mate."

Chapter Thirty-Four

They made their flight in the nick of time and flew to Scotland without mishap. Business class was nice. Very nice indeed. David could see why Sonny had wanted the upgrade. In their cosy compartment suites, they had plenty of room to store the case safely.

The flight was under ninety minutes. They touched down, wheeling their cases as they followed the passengers streaming out.

"What now?" David asked, looking around the quiet airport.

Sonny pointed to the car hire by the exit. "Should be a car waiting."

A short and noisy line of people waited for their hire cars. Sonny instructed David to queue up while he went to make a call. David waited, listening to a family of Americans from Florida in front of him talk about their trip to Loch Ness. He gazed out at the airport and caught sight of Sonny by a payphone with his back to

David.

Odd. Why hadn't he used his burner or asked to use David's phone?

David was next up for the cars, and he gave Sonny's name. By the time he was being led outside to the car rank, Sonny had finished his call and came jogging over.

"Who were you calling?" David asked him.

"Hm? Just Rafe," Sonny said breezily. "Got the keys?"

"Here." David handed him the keys.

Their rental was a black Mercedes. Not exactly a car for rural roads.

"Is this thing gonna do the job?" David asked. "Aren't we going cross-country?"

"If you want to help, sunshine, check the map and hope it shows roads," Sonny told him. "Clearly there was no 4x4 for hire last minute."

"Clearly," David muttered.

They got into the car, with Sonny in the driver's seat. David used his phone and opened the maps app.

"Put it in," Sonny instructed, as David typed in the address.

"I know how to use the app, thank you," David retorted.

"So, if we get lost, I know who to blame," Sonny quipped back.

"No, that's not how it works." David tapped the screen to start the directions. The route was estimated at fifty minutes to the destination. "It'll be after midnight by the time we get there," he pointed out.

"Then I better put my foot down," Sonny replied.

They strapped in and drove off.

*

Once they drove into the countryside it was pitch-black outside. The night sky was cloudy here, so the moon and stars weren't visible. Sonny had the headlights on full as he floored it down winding country lanes.

David held onto the dash with one hand as Sonny took corners too fast, and his phone with the other. The maps guide announced, "Recalculating," three times when Sonny missed turnings.

"If you slow down, maybe you won't miss the exits," David chided him.

"All these hedges look alike," Sonny complained. He braked hard, then twisted in his seat to drive backwards until he found the exit they'd recently passed.

David hoped no second pair of headlights came up in their rear view. "Tell you what," he said. "I'm driving on the way back."

"Yeah? Don't forget which side of the road it is," Sonny teased him.

"I think I got it," David quipped.

Sonny made the exit, and they sped off down another dark, tree-lined lane.

As the time approached one AM, they passed by a turning for a place called Barakeith.

"Town?" David guessed.

"Probably a village," Sonny replied.

They continued the route, and the dirt track took them out of the trees and hedgerows, up a hill and toward a grand sprawling estate silhouetted against the sky.

"Guessing that's the manor," David said.

"Foreboding, innit?" Sonny said. "All you need is a witch flying around on a broom, and the picture is complete."

"Please don't tell me they're something to worry about?"

David asked.

"Flying broomsticks?" Sonny chuckled. "No, mate. No flying brooms."

"What about witches?"

"Obviously they exist," Sonny said, deadpan.

David exhaled. "Right. Of course. But will there be any up there?"

"Shouldn't think so," Sonny replied. "Most witches mind their own business. It's everyone else you gotta watch out for."

"Duly noted," David said.

"I'm gonna look for a lay-by," Sonny said. "We'll hide the car and continue up on foot."

David agreed with that approach. It was in their best interest to maintain stealth.

An old stone wall, only a couple of feet high, ran alongside a field. Sonny chose to drive inside the field, which allowed for the car to be partially hidden from the road. They were lucky it had been dry so the grassy ground was solid.

David turned off maps and set his phone on airplane mode. They got out of the car and went around each side, meeting at the rear. Sonny popped the trunk, and together they opened their case. Their handguns were loaded with UV bullets and strapped back into their holsters. UV torches and regular flashlights were slotted into pockets. Earpieces went in ears; receivers were strapped onto wrists.

"Gearing up," Sonny said quietly. "Preparing to infiltrate."

"Copy that," Mother's voice replied. "Satellite footage shows no movement, no heat signatures. But, as we know, that doesn't always mean no life forms, so watch your step."

"Copy," Sonny said. "We'll circle around and approach from the northwest corner together," Sonny told him. "Then make entry. You cover my six."

"Copy," David replied. That, he could do.

"Also," he added, "this is a good time for masks." He pulled up the black scarf to cover the lower half of his face.

David did the same.

Sonny locked up the car, and they set off in the dark.

Silently, they made their approach toward the manor house. Sonny hadn't drawn his weapon yet, so David didn't either.

The hill was quiet. No bird noise, not even an owl. There were no distant sounds from towns or traffic, nothing. Deadly quiet, only the faintest sound of the wind blowing clouds overhead.

No lights on. The place looked deserted. They circled around before reaching the outer walls of an old garden that had long fallen into disrepair. A forgotten fountain, overgrown with weeds, stood proudly at the front of the property.

Still no movement.

They went round, looking for a back entrance. Being a manor house, it was set up for a large kitchen complete with servant's entrance. Sonny signalled to David with his hand that they'd make their entry there. He led the way to the door. While he jimmied the lock with a pick, David kept watch. Silently, the door opened. Sonny checked for any burglar alarms but found none.

They moved into the property.

It was dark, so they both used their flashlights to see where they were walking. The lights cast eerie blue beams through the kitchen. It was simply enormous, David noted. Like Downton Abbey. Once it would have had numerous servants scurrying around, preparing feasts for the lord of the manor, no doubt. Now, it was bare and dusty. The wood-burning stove and range oven long since out of use, with evidence of mouse droppings on the surface. Nobody had cooked anything here for some time.

But evidence suggested someone had been in the kitchen. David and Sonny spotted it at the same time. A discarded bowl and spoon, empty. Recently used with evidence of something red staining the rim. Soup, or blood?

David glanced at Sonny, and their eyes met. They didn't speak. Sonny pointed with one finger, indicating they were to move upstairs. David nodded.

Silently, they continued their infiltration, walking up the steps and entering the manor house proper. David half expected Count Dracula, wearing a big cape like in the movies, to burst out from behind every door and jump-scare him.

But nobody was home.

As they cleared each room, finding nothing except old dusty furniture, it became clear that whoever that bowl belonged to, they weren't in the house right now.

"Anything?" Mother's voice asked.

"Negative," Sonny murmured. "House is clear."

"Satellite is showing images of secondary buildings outside," Mother replied. "Could be some garage space. Maybe old stables."

"Copy," Sonny said and motioned with his head for David to follow.

They made their way back outside. The clouds had cleared, and the moon was able to shine down on them, casting some light in the dark.

There were indeed extra buildings out on the grounds. Small, with solid brickwork. Probably they were once guest houses or servant's quarters. David could only guess. It looked like they'd been converted into storage space over the years. The first one they checked inside had had its inner walls ripped out. David saw the old markings of a staircase climbing up one outer wall. The space inside the dwelling was clear, but the stone ground had evidence of large items being stored on it. Markings, lines in the dust and muck. Big boxes, or crates, would be David's best guess.

Whatever had been here was long gone.

"Think we found a store of some sort," Sonny reported quietly. "Empty."

"Someone warned them?" David said.

Sonny nodded. "Seems that way."

"Is there a basement?" David asked.

"That's not really a thing here," Sonny replied. "Attics or garages. There's a chance whoever was here is out on delivery and is coming back. I'll set up some surveillance and we'll sit tight."

David kept watch while Sonny set up a series of tiny cameras in the outer dwellings, and inside the manor's kitchen. The cameras were no bigger than a button.

Once the cameras were set up, with visual confirmed back at base, they exited the property and made their way back down the hill.

David's adrenaline was still high, despite not having made contact with any bogeys.

Sonny paused on the hill, gazing down at the distant village below them.

"What?" David hissed.

"Just thinking," Sonny said, pulling his mask down. "Mother? Can you check for hotels or guest houses in a place called Barakeith. It's south of the property. If we hole up there, we'll have a direct view of the comings and goings of this place."

"Checking," Mother replied.

David perked up at the word hotel. This was fast becoming his favourite mission so far. No vampires. Possible hotel room sex on his horizon. All boxes ticked.

They continued walking, heading back to the car.

"No hotels," Mother replied at length, "but there is a B'n'B property available on short stay."

David looked at Sonny hopefully. He was relieved when Sonny smiled back at him.

"Yep, that'll do," Sonny said.

Chapter Thirty-Five

The B & B property was booked, but unfortunately the earliest check-in time was nine that morning.

That meant they had another seven hours to kill.

They returned to the car and drove a little way up so they could keep an eye on the manor and the road to and from it. No other traffic was seen. Sonny dictated a quick report to base, who were also monitoring the security feed from his hidden cameras. They didn't have much else to do except keep an eye on the dark road and watch the manor house silhouetted against the sky.

Base was still on the comms, but everyone fell silent. Surveillance could be a real drag, David already knew this so he shouldn't have been surprised it was no different for this department, vampires or no vampires.

David caught his own reflection in the wing mirror, and it reminded him of other vampiric legends. "What about mirrors?" he asked quietly.

"Hm?" Sonny glanced at him. "What about 'em?"

"For vampires," David said, making a motion with his hand to say, wasn't that obvious?

"Oh." Sonny shrugged. "Inconclusive. The younger ones seem to show up on film and in mirrors, but we don't have a wide enough field of test subjects to state definitively that they always do."

"And Balogh?" David probed.

"Sometimes," Sonny said. "It's not conclusive."

"So, all those security cameras you put up? There's a chance they won't pick up on anything. Is that what you're saying?"

"Correct," Sonny replied. "But they will pick up familiars. The humans helping vampires."

David nodded. He'd rather deal with a human than a vampire.

"Do you think those big square marks on the ground were coffins?" David asked.

"Who knows," Sonny replied.

David expected him to follow up with a joke, but he fell quiet.

"How long until sunrise?" David asked.

"O-600 hours," Mother replied.

That was another four hours. David settled into his seat, ready for a long night.

*

The first few hours they spent the time in near silence, which was normal for surveillance work, but David was new to waiting for vampires, and the silence made him antsy.

Daybreak came early, at five. With the gradual lightening of the sky in the prelude to dawn, and the distinct chirp of songbirds outside, the blanket of darkness lifted. So, too, did the tense mood of surveillance.

As the first rays of the sun rose over the horizon, Sonny spoke up.

"Think it's safe to say we won't see any vampires for a while."

"We're nearing the end of our shift here," Mother replied. "Auntie will take over. She's been briefed on your status."

"Copy that," Sonny said, grunting as he shifted in his seat. "I'm gonna stretch my legs. Wait here," he told David and opened his car door.

"What about my legs?" David asked, watching Sonny rise in one fluid motion.

Sonny turned around and leaned down to smirk at David. "You can stretch your legs when I come back."

He shut the door before David could ask him how long he was going to be. Maybe he was going to relieve himself in the field. David planned to do that when he had the chance.

He was alone in the car for another fifteen minutes until Sonny came back.

"How much stretching did your legs need?" David teased.

"Said the bishop to the priest," Sonny quipped back.

The joke caught David off guard, and he had to stifle a laugh so it didn't ring out loudly.

"I cut across the field and had a look for any back roads," Sonny said. "There's a bridle track, but nothing's been down there other than animals for a few days. No tyre tracks."

"Right," David said. "But that's assuming a vehicle was used?"

"Yeah," Sonny agreed. "Well, tech can usually find vehicles on traffic cams," Sonny said. "Not a guarantee though."

They swapped over, Sonny getting back into the car and David taking a walk outside. He was grateful to see the sun, felt protected in the daylight. The sunrise showed hues of gold and pink, getting stronger as the minutes went by. Birds sung happily, perched in distant trees or nearby hedgerow. The quietness of nature felt very different in the morning sun.

After a few minutes, David went back to the car and got in.

"You can remove the earpiece," Sonny told him. "The morning team is in now, and we've agreed they'll keep up the surveillance while we get some rest."

"Sure." David removed the earpiece and the receiver. "I thought the B & B check-in was nine? We still have over two hours."

"Yeah, and we'll use that time to go find a supermarket," Sonny told him. "Or whatever counts for a supermarket in these parts."

"A Scottish supermarket," David mused. "We can buy haggis."

Sonny paused halfway through putting on his seat belt and looked at David. "Do you like haggis?"

"I haven't tried it," David replied.

Sonny was clearly fighting a smirk. "Do you know what it is?"

"It's like a brisket, right?" David guessed. He couldn't remember exactly.

The smirk teased the edge of Sonny's mouth. "Not quite, sunshine," he said. "You look out for one when we get to the store. See what you think."

"Okay," David agreed.

*

They drove for thirty minutes. Thanks to the maps app, they made their way to a minimart of some kind. It wasn't a chain David recognised, but it looked well stocked.

Sonny parked the car in the dinky car lot out front, and they walked in as the front doors were opening for the day. The only other customers there at that time were a pair of very old ladies with long raincoats, sensible shoes, and warm hats and scarves over their grey hair. They both trailed squeaky-wheeled shopping trollies.

One of the women stopped dead and looked David and Sonny up and down.

"Aye, yer not local, are ye?" she barked in a Scottish accent.

David expected Sonny to reply, but when he glanced at his companion, he noticed Sonny biting his lower lip like he was trying not to laugh.

David replied for them. "We're sightseeing," he told her, and tried his best to smooth down his own accent to blend in. He was hoping he sounded British, but judging by Sonny's reaction, his face twisting up in amusement, David had probably screwed it up.

"Sightseeing?" the old woman questioned. "What sights are there here?"

David had to scramble for an answer. How the hell should he know? He'd only been on this continent for a couple of days.

"Er, well," he said, "we passed by a spectacular-looking manor house on the way here."

This was risky, but local knowledge was always useful in surveillance, and David's gambit paid off.

"Oh, aye, I know it," she replied. "Rented out to some rich eccentric. Has swinging parties, so I heard."

"Oh?" David said, surprised.

Sonny had to turn away to smother a noise of laughter.

"Er, that's interesting," David said, covering for him. "Local eccentric?"

The woman looked him up and down. "Yer not one of his

fancy boys, are ye?" she demanded.

Sonny was still plastering himself into the nearest wall, shaking with silent laughter. It was all David could do to keep a straight face himself.

"I'm not currently anyone's fancy man," he replied, deadpan. "But if there are any openings, let me know," he added with a smile.

His American accent had snuck out, and the woman noticed. Her whole face lit up, blue eyes sparkling behind her glasses. "Och, yer American?" she said. "Been nae Americans here. The ones that go in for the swinging parties—they're all Europeans."

"I see." David nodded along. "When was the last time they had a party?"

"About six months ago, aye," she told him. "They come in here sometimes. Long black coats. A lot of hair and make-up on the women. On the men, too, aye. They buy so much alcohol and olives. Must be making martinis, like James Bond. Best of them was Scottish. Sean Connery."

This conversation was taking twists and turns. David would've continued plying her for more information, but Sonny interjected. He got hold of himself and excused them both before dragging David away.

Once safely ensconced in the fruit and vegetables aisle, David said, "I thought you'd want more intel? Sounds like Balogh's been busy."

"All that tells us is that there's activity," Sonny replied. "Our objective is still the same, and we don't have time to decipher how much of what some bonkers old lady is telling us is true or not."

"Yes, but," David said as Sonny walked away. "Isn't it worth gathering anyway?" he asked, hurrying to catch up. "And why were you laughing?"

Sonny smirked. "Because she sounded like a character in an old sketch show, asking if we're local. I can't wait to tell Rafe." He grabbed a basket from a corner pile, and walked out of fruit and veg, not picking any up.

David raised both hands in defeat. "Okay, well, excuse me for wanting to get some useful intel."

They went into the dairy aisle, and Sonny picked up a pint of milk.

"All you found out from that amusing exchange is that a month ago there may or may not have been a party attended by some European goths," Sonny said. "So what? It doesn't help us one bit."

David didn't understand why he was being so dismissive, but he wasn't going to argue right now. He was lagging, and he could use some coffee.

"I'll be in the hot beverages section," he said, and walked away.

"Don't forget your haggis!" Sonny called after him.

Twenty minutes later, they'd circled around the store twice and picked up essentials for a couple of days. (Well, David had picked up essentials. Sonny had picked up junk.) David hadn't spotted any haggis until Sonny pointed it out under the meat counter. He wasn't sure what he'd expected but it certainly wasn't some large, sausage shaped item. An even darker meaty sausage laid near it.

"So, they're all haggis?" David asked, staring at the sausages.

"No, that's a black pudding." Sonny pointed on the glass. "The bigger one is haggis. Similar thing, but black pudding is pig's blood, and haggis is sheep offal. Liver, heart, lungs. And spices, obviously."

"Oh, obviously," David drawled.

The person behind the counter in a white coat, hat, and face covering glanced at them with interest. Their outfit reminded David of lab coats. This wasn't a lab, and the person was handling cuts of meat, not needles, but David felt uneasy.

"I think I'll pass," he said, turning away from the meat counter.

"Sure you don't want haggis?" Sonny asked, following behind him.

"Quite sure."

It was too early in the morning to be thinking about red meat. David remembered that red-stained bowl in the manor's kitchen. Had that been blood?

"Let's go pay for these, then," Sonny said. "By the time we drive back, it'll be nine."

"Okay."

They went to the cash desk, the only one, with one person serving. Sonny unloaded the basket onto the small conveyor belt and produced a reusable bag from his pocket.

David happened to glance at some notices pinned to the far wall and spotted a colour printout for a missing person.

MISSING: Susan McBride. Last seen...

The date it gave was six months ago. The same time as the alleged swinging party.

David nudged Sonny to get him to look at the poster, but he didn't appear too concerned. He merely nodded in acknowledgement.

To David, missing persons and vampires in the same area was a huge red flag.

*

Groceries in the car, they drove back through the country lanes. Traffic was minimal here. David saw two, maybe three cars total out on the roads.

With the manor in the distance, they turned into the village of Barakeith. It was a small, picturesque collection of cottages, barely half a mile from end to end. The details of the B & B booking had been sent to David's phone, and Sonny cruised slowly past cottages and an old Norman church as they looked for their house.

"It's cute here," David mentioned.

"Have you gotten over your horror of haggis?" Sonny quipped.

"Why did you have to bring that up?" David said. "I'd almost forgotten about it."

Sonny snickered. "You went white as a sheet."

"I don't want to talk about it," David told him. He didn't want to explain that it was less about the haggis and more about the person in a white coat giving him bad memories.

Well, a bad memory was putting it lightly. PTSD was probably more accurate.

They pulled up outside their rental cottage. Sonny parked on the loose gravel drive, and they got out. The cottage was painted white, with a red-tiled roof. A pretty garden grew around it, with roses lining the door and front windows, picture perfect.

Sonny strode up to the front door and knocked using the brass door knocker shaped like a stag. David waited close by, not standing too close because it was probably safer to not give the impression that they were a couple.

Not that they were a couple, he admonished himself. He was all too aware that he had a habit of standing close to Sonny. Easier to go unnoticed in crowds or cities, but out here in the middle of nowhere, less so.

The door opened, revealing a middle-aged White woman in jeans and a sweater, with brown hair tied back.

"Hello, are you Morag?" Sonny said politely. "We booked the B & B."

"Aye, come in," she replied. "I was doing some last-minute dusting. Didnae expect a booking when I woke up this morning."

"Oh, we don't mind a bit of dust," Sonny said. "We're just two blokes, so we won't even notice."

Morag clearly enjoyed the banter, chuckling with amusement. "I couldnae let ye stay in a mess," she said.

David looked around the hallway, decorated with flowered wallpaper, ornate picture frames, and antique side tables. The place looked spotless.

And this hallway was even narrower than the one in Sonny's house.

"Let me show you the kitchen first," Morag said, leading Sonny through. "Now, this bottom oven can be a bastard to work. The top one is more reliable."

"I do appreciate a reliable top," Sonny said, deadpan.

Morag didn't get the joke and continued talking about kitchen appliances. She didn't catch Sonny glance at David and wink, nor David trying not to smirk.

She asked them what they were doing here, and instead of claiming sightseeing like David had, Sonny rattled off a mundane cover story involving land surveys and mud samples.

"Probably won't be too long," Sonny told her. "A night or two. Depends how good the sample collecting goes."

"As long as ye don't track mud into the house," Morag replied. "I'll be happy for the business. Stay as long as ye need."

"Thank you so much, Morag," Sonny said. "We'll be pleased to get some rest; it's been a long journey."

"Aye, ye must be tired. I'll leave you to it, then."

She handed over a key for the front door and told them she lived in the house across the road if they needed anything. Her contact number was on the booking form, and on the list of house rules and information pinned to the fridge door.

David read the list and noticed that the name was McBride. Morag McBride.

Same last name as the missing woman.

She was already out of the front door. David beckoned Sonny over to look at the list.

"What?" Sonny did not appear interested. "What am I looking at?"

"The name." David pointed with his finger. "The missing persons poster? McBride."

"Oh, God." Sonny rolled his eyes. "Calm down, Agatha Christie. Do you know how many McBrides there must be in Scotland?"

"But how many in one small town?" David replied. "We could be staying in the missing woman's home."

"Well, if that's the case," Sonny said, "let's hope she doesn't come back while we're in the middle of anything naughty." He raised his eyebrows, then exited the cottage.

David went after him. "Hey," he said, looking around to make sure they weren't overheard. "What sort of naughty are we talking about here?"

Sonny was unpacking the car and handed David a grocery bag. "Well, sunshine, we have a whole day to kill. So, I'd say the sky's the limit."

As much as David itched to solve all the mysteries unfolding around him in this village, he also itched for something else.

Mysteries could wait.

*

David was tasked with unpacking their groceries.

He would've rushed the job, but when Sonny produced a small radio transmitter and began sweeping the house for bugs room by room, he decided to take his time.

So, despite Sonny's disinterest in the locals, he clearly didn't trust the woman renting the cottage. Unless sweeping for bugs was standard practice.

David left him to it. He unpacked their food, and while he was doing so, he peeked into every cupboard, every drawer. What he found in one drawer were some old utilities letters, including a boiler service certificate. The name it was addressed to was Susan McBride.

This was the missing woman's home, and Morag was renting it out.

David took the letter and went to find Sonny. "Look," he said, brandishing the piece of paper.

Sonny was in the lounge, waving his gizmo behind the television set. He glanced around casually. "What are you upset about now?"

David showed him the paper and pointed to the name. "This proves it," he said. "The missing woman. Susan McBride. This is her house."

"People go missing," Sonny said flatly. "It happens.

"So, why are you doing a sweep?" David hissed, keeping his voice down. "Could Morag be working for someone?"

"Doubtful," Sonny said. "I'm checking for cameras. You know how many pervy civilians rent out homes to watch people have sex? A lot, that's how many."

"I...what?" David couldn't believe it. "That's what you're worried about?"

"I'm being realistic," Sonny said. "You, on the other hand,

are trying to be the next Miss Marple. Finding clues to crimes everywhere you look."

"Who's Miss Marple?"

"Agatha Christie," Sonny said. "Miss Marple. Hercule Poirot. Detectives. Next thing I know, you'll be gathering the entire village in the drawing room and telling us it was Colonel Mustard in the library with the candlestick."

David exhaled through his nose in frustration, watching Sonny carry on his sweep. "Why aren't you interested? Do you know something I don't?"

"About what? The village?" Sonny chuckled. "I know as much as you do. I want you to unclench and stop trying to create extra work to do. You utter newb."

"Okay, okay!" David waved the paper in defeat. "I thought this was a clue to finding Count…you-know-who."

"And your enthusiasm is noted," he said. "We can follow up on breadcrumbs if we get no joy at the manor tonight."

"Thank you!" David raised both hands. "That's all I ask."

"Are you gonna pipe down now?" Sonny said teasingly.

"Maybe," David replied, smiling. "I'll see what else I can find." He turned and exited the room.

"As long as it isn't Miss Scarlet with the monkey wrench," Sonny called after him.

*

There were no bugs or hidden cameras in the cottage. Not that Sonny found anyway.

David hadn't found anything else of note either. Personal items had been cleared away. Individually wrapped soaps sat in a dish in the upstairs bathroom, like a hotel. They had migrated upstairs, sans their boots and jackets. There were two bedrooms, one master with a double bed, and one tiny room with a single.

David sat on the double bed in the master. The duvet cover was puffy and continued the floral motif as in the rest of the cottage. He opened a search app and social media on his phone so he could look up McBrides in this area.

Sonny appeared in the doorway. All the doorways in the cottage were low and crooked and made Sonny appear tall.

"Right," he announced, looking at David with an indecipherable expression on his face. "I'm having a shower."

"Okay," David replied, looking back at his phone. "Have fun with that."

"I will." Sonny smirked. "I brought *things*."

His tone implied something interesting. David looked back up. "Oh, yeah?"

"Yeah." Sonny grinned. "So, don't go anywhere. And lose that." He nodded at the phone in David's hand.

"Oh," David said, realising. "Right. On it."

Sonny shut himself in the bathroom, while David hurried back downstairs in sock feet. He turned on the television, pausing only briefly to watch a Scottish news broadcast about the economy. He left the TV on and placed the phone on the couch under a cushion.

It would mean anyone listening in would have a hard time hearing anything going on upstairs.

David hurried back up the stairs. He heard the water running in the bathroom. Sonny could be a while, if he was doing what David guessed he was doing for prep, but he excitedly pulled his clothes off anyway.

Belatedly, he also pulled the drapes shut. They had flowers too. The daylight was bright behind them, casting the room into hues of pink from the material.

David hopped into bed naked, pulled the covers up, and sat against the headboard to wait. He was excited, stupidly so. His cock firmed up the more he anticipated what was about to happen next. David counted the minutes.

Eventually the water shut off. A few minutes later, the bathroom door opened. David listened for any telltale soft footfall on the creaky floorboards.

"Are you ready for me, Colonel Mustard?" Sonny's voice called out softly.

David laughed. "Standing to attention," he replied.

He heard Sonny titter, then saw his dark head of curls around the open doorframe.

He peered into the room. "Show me?"

David whipped the covers off, revealing his erection.

"Right here," he said.

"That's quite the candlestick, Colonel Mustard," Sonny replied, moving to stand in the doorway. He was naked, his own cock at half mast.

David was distracted from answering with any wit. He really wanted sex.

"Are you Miss Scarlet in this scenario?" he asked, making Sonny grin.

"If you like," he answered, padding over to the bed.

"Well, then, let me kiss you, Miss Scarlet." David reached for him, pulling Sonny down into the bed.

They hadn't kissed properly yet. Their first time had been too urgent, too rough and focused on the act of fucking alone. Now, they had more time. David made time for a kiss. Sonny leaned over him and pressed his body against David's as their mouths met. David loved to kiss, and he knew he was good at it. He kissed the hell out of Sonny until they were hot and sweat dampened their bodies.

"I can't wait any longer," Sonny murmured, breaking away. He pushed David's shoulder with one strong hand, shoving him back against the pillows. "I want you inside me."

"I'm all yours," David promised. "Did you prep?"

"Yes, that's what I was doing in the bathroom." Sonny straddled David's hips, one thigh on either side of his body.

"What about a condom?" David asked.

Sonny shook his head. "You'd burn through it."

No condom, then.

David held Sonny's slim hips with one hand and reached for the base of his cock with the other. Sonny rose up on his knees and reached behind him to guide David's cock to his hole, lubed and open.

This was their first time with penetration; the previous time in Chinatown they'd done everything but. And it felt glorious as David slid inside. He let out a groan, gazing up at his partner as Sonny lowered himself slowly down. He looked magnificent like this. David was half in love already.

He let Sonny set the pace, forcing himself to not move. Sonny's mouth quivered, lips parting. He slid down David's cock until he was fully seated and drew in deep breaths.

"Tan bueno," David purred. He held onto Sonny's hip, digging his thumbs into his skin. David fantasised about holding him and pounding in hard. Later, later. For now, they'd take it slow.

David moved one hand up front, closing it around Sonny's cock. David swiped his thumb across the head and started to jack him slowly. He inched his hips up the tiniest bit, rocking Sonny's in his lap.

Sonny grunted, stuffed full with David's cock. But he clearly wanted to be in the driver's seat, snatching his hand around David's wrist firmly.

"Let go," he growled.

David opened his hand, releasing his grip. Too sensitive, perhaps.

Sonny moved David's hand away. Then he adjusted himself, settling in. He splayed his knees out, driving David's cock in deeper. With one hand he reached around to hold onto David's thigh like an anchor. His other hand came down on David's chest like a warning not to move.

Oh, I have a power bottom!

He laid back and let Sonny do the work, grinding in his lap, riding his cock slow and deep. David enjoyed the view, listening to Sonny's breaths rasping out, watching his naked body roll and move.

David groaned in pleasure. "Fuck, that's hot," he praised. "I wanna turn you over and smash you into the mattress."

Sonny's eyes flashed, and the pupils shifted from round orbs to long slits. He stared down at David with a hazy look of desire.

"Your eyes," David gasped, his orgasm sneaking up on him. "Fuck."

He came, surprised by the ferocity of it. He emptied himself inside his partner, swooning with the feeling of an intense orgasm.

He wondered if sex with Sonny would always feel this amazing. David couldn't remember feeling such intensity before.

Round one complete, they collapsed side by side in the bed.

"Hey," David mentioned, "your eyes change when we have sex. Did you know?" He searched Sonny's eyes, but they had already shifted back to normal.

Sonny didn't say anything. The two of them lay quietly for a long moment, the only sound in the room was the sound of them breathing.

"My eyes don't do that?" David asked.

"No."

"Weird," David murmured. "Wonder why not?"

"Haven't you noticed any changes at all?" Sonny asked him. "Anything unusual?"

"No, I don't think so," David replied. "Just the dreams. That...raspy noise."

Sonny nodded. "Back in the lab, my nails grew fast. Hard too. This was before they decided to do chemo on me to slow down the process. Contain whatever was making those changes to my body."

"Fuck," David uttered, picturing it. Slitted pupils, unusual eyes. Long claws. The trauma of more medical testing. "Are we gonna wake up one morning and turn into werewolves?"

Sonny chuckled lightly. "Werewolves aren't morning creatures, love."

David looked at him dubiously. "You're saying that like it's a fact?"

"It is," Sonny replied. "Werewolves don't get up in the mornings. They like the night, innit? The moon."

"Are there werewolves out there too?" David asked.

"Historically, yes," Sonny told him. He rolled onto his front and leaned up on his elbows, smirking at David like he had no care. "I told you, we aren't the only weirdos around, mate. Get used to it."

Despite it all, David found himself smiling. "Great," he drawled. "I'm so thrilled to hear all this."

"PRISM will give you the introductory briefing," Sonny said, back to being blasé. "Slideshows, the whole shebang."

"Aren't you worried?" David asked him. "About what we are?"

"What use is worrying?" Sonny asked in turn. "Keep calm and carry on."

"Hm." David hummed, unconvinced. "And what'll you do if you wake up and find I've turned into God knows what in the bed next to you?"

"Cross that bridge when and if we come to it," Sonny replied. "Look, are you always this anxious? If I gotta fuck you twenty times to make you shut up and go to sleep, I will. I'll take one for the team."

David laughed. This conversation was absurd. Still, more sex would be nice.

"Okay, let's aim for twenty," he quipped, rolling over to tackle his partner.

Chapter Thirty-Six

David took out some of his frustrations on Sonny's ass, pounding him into the mattress during a variety of positions. They both had the stamina, so they kept going.

All in all, it was a morning well spent.

Afterward, they lay together in the bed, David holding tight to Sonny's body as they both regained their breath. They didn't have to leave; they could lie here all day if they wanted. David wanted that.

Unfortunately, the rumbling of both their stomachs was becoming hard to ignore.

Sonny nudged David aside. "I'm gonna shower, then I have to eat. Sounds like you need to eat as well."

"Yeah," David agreed, albeit reluctantly.

"Take the shower after me, and I'll make you breakfast," Sonny promised, sliding out of David's grasp.

"We could shower together?" David suggested.

Sonny laughed; an amused bark. "Not enough room, sunshine. That shower is one low-pressure dribble over a tiny bathtub. I can barely fit myself in there."

"Oh," David said. "That's disappointing."

"I won't be long," Sonny told him, padding across the carpet. "Come down to the kitchen when you're done."

"Okay," David agreed.

Sonny left the room, and David laid in the bed listening to the sounds from the bathroom across the hall. The cottage was so small, it was easy to hear. As he pictured Sonny taking a shower, a smile bloomed on his face.

Despite having been awake for twenty-four hours, David was buzzing. Finally having some time to themselves, time alone, was just what he'd needed.

He waited while Sonny took the first shower, then softly made his way downstairs. Kitchen sounds downstairs indicated the promised breakfast. Like any normal couple waking up on a lazy morning.

David's smile grew, and he went to take his own shower.

Sonny hadn't been kidding; it was rather small in the tub, and neither of them were large men by any means. David took a careful shower and used the shampoo and soap products from the tiny bottles on display.

This cottage was a trip.

He didn't want to take too long, eager to get back to his partner, so he hurried the shower and got out to towel off.

He couldn't find a hairdryer, and had no hair products for short hair. David rough dried his hair, then combed it back. The cut still looked good when wet. David wiped steam off the mirror and smiled at himself.

Today would be a good day.

They hadn't brought a change of clothes, as they hadn't had time to pack for an overnight stay. David found a pair of white towel bathrobes, so he selected one and put it on.

Hopefully, they'd be going back to bed after breakfast. Or, lunch.

He padded downstairs barefoot. The sun was shining into the cottage through its front windows, lighting up the roses outside to a dazzlingly bright pink. Small and delicate flutterings by the lounge window drew David's attention—songbirds in the rosebush outside. They were unaware of any occupants inside observing them. David imagined how peaceful it must be to sit in that quaint little lounge, with its soft furnishings, and watch the birds hop about by the window catching bugs.

Idly, he wondered if he would ever have a life like that. Something quiet and peaceful. He stood in the open doorway to the lounge, looking in on it like a stranger viewing a different world.

Just for today, at least, this peaceful world was his.

David followed the smell of toast into the kitchen. He saw Sonny by the counter, wearing only a T-shirt and his underwear. His legs were bare, the curly hair on them dark.

He was busy preparing food, his back to David. He'd washed his hair, but without access to a hairdryer, it wasn't styled. David saw it was curlier when wet.

In fact, Sonny with his dark colouring was the darkest thing in the bright, homely kitchen, its decor in soft shades of duck-egg blue, off-white, and wood that was naturally light in colour like honey.

Strange to see him in such a setting. Strange, but not unwelcome, only an interesting contrast. A soldier of hard lines and too much knowledge of the world in an everyday kitchen, cooking breakfast.

It was exactly the kind of domestic boyfriend fantasy that David secretly longed for, which was probably what drove him to cross the kitchen floor with the intent of plastering himself to Sonny's back and kissing his neck.

But David never got that close. With only a hair's breadth between them, Sonny whirled around and held a knife to David's throat.

"Whoa," David uttered, freezing on the spot. He realised now he'd made a mistake, catching Sonny off guard. "Easy," he whispered, with the cold blade of the knife under his jaw. "It's me."

Sonny's eyes blazed intensely, but as quickly as the fire burned in them, it then retreated. His body relaxed, and he eased the knife back while still holding it out in a defensive position.

"You should know better than to sneak up on a fella when he's got a knife in his hand," Sonny said, his tone clipped.

He seemed extra prickly. Perhaps it was being in someone else's house that had him on edge.

"I apologise," David said, forcing calm into his voice. "I thought you knew I was there."

"Why would I know?" Sonny snapped. "You don't make any noise, creeping about like that."

He was mad. David found it attractive.

"I honestly hadn't intended to creep," he said evenly. "Shall I whistle next time? Perhaps a song?"

"I'll tie a bloody bell around your neck," Sonny grumbled. He lowered the knife, finally.

David took the opportunity to gain the upper hand, reaching out to snap his hands around Sonny's wrists. The move caught Sonny off guard, and he tried to twist his hand out of David's grasp to turn the knife on him again. They grappled with soft grunts. David was determined. When Sonny hooked a foot around David's knee to bend his leg, David anticipated it and spun them around to shove Sonny back against the fridge.

Knife still dangerously close, David risked the proximity and stole a kiss, covering Sonny's mouth with his. He felt the tension ebb out of Sonny's body as the kiss deepened, Sonny giving in. He didn't release the knife but relaxed his grip.

David was turned on and pressed his body close to let Sonny know it. As their bodies bumped together, David felt a growing interest in his partner too.

Sonny broke the kiss. "I could cut your dick off right now," he threatened, but there was no heat to it.

David smiled. "And then where would you be? No more sex."

"I'll keep your dick, get rid of the rest of you," Sonny retorted. He nudged David away and faced the counter. "Go sit down, you knob. Stay out of the way."

David chuckled heartily. "You're crazy, but I like it."

"Fuck off," Sonny muttered, but David saw him smirking.

David sat at the table, with its blue and white criss-cross tablecloth and pristine bowl of fruit. That domestic boyfriend fantasy was making him a little punch-drunk.

Even when Sonny deposited a plate full of disaster food, the fantasy didn't lose its sparkle.

"What's this?" David asked him.

"It's beans on toast," Sonny said, sitting next to him at the table. "With grated cheese and Worcestershire sauce on top."

"I can see that," David said wryly. "What I meant was, why?"

"Why, what?"

"Why are we eating this?" David asked. "We bought so much other food."

"Look." Sonny pointed his butter knife at David. "If you want to make your own, sunshine, you go right ahead. But don't knock beans on toast till you've tried it."

And with that, he dug in furiously.

David didn't want to offend him, so he ate and it wasn't too bad.

"I have a question," David said. "You're half White, aren't you?"

Sonny lowered his knife and fork with a clatter and sent David a withering look. "Are you gonna complain about my cooking?"

"No, I was merely curious," David said. This was a risky conversation, and he knew it. "You know I'm half White. My dad was Mexican, my mom is White. I was curious about your parents. Was it hard growing up here?"

Sonny looked at him, searching David's face. "Was it hard growing up there?" he countered.

"America? Yes and no," David replied, willing to be open if it meant Sonny felt more comfortable opening up. "I felt like I never fit in anywhere. To White people, I'm Latino. My dad looked Mexican; he was a lot darker than me. He had an accent. Other kids at school noticed that. But to other Latinos, I'm White. On top of that, I'm bisexual. To straight people, I'm gay. To gay people, I'm straight." David exhaled. "Sometimes people think I'm one of them until I do something or say the wrong thing, then they make sure I know that they think I'm different to them."

Sonny's eyes had flicked down and now rose to meet David's again. "Did I do that?" he asked hesitantly.

"No." David smiled. "You make me feel like I fit in. I feel like you get it."

"Well, we are the only two humans with aliens inside them," Sonny said, breaking eye contact again.

"No, it's not just that," David told him. "It's all of it. Can you tell me a little? About your parents?"

"Christ," Sonny muttered. "All right. My Iranian grand-parents were both from Tehran, came here as students and applied to stay because they were Bahai. It's a persecuted religion in Iran, right? So, they stayed in London, had kids: my mum and my aunt, Farah's mum. They weren't strictly religious, not exactly. They were fine with my mum marrying Dad, an English lad from the East End. No religion except the pub. Dad smoked, drank, swore a lot. But don't get me wrong, he was reliable. Everyone liked him. He held down a job. Car mechanic." Sonny paused, the ghost of a smile on his lips.

"Do you still see him?" David asked. He sounded like a real character. David guessed that was where Sonny got it from.

"No, he died," Sonny said, avoiding eye contact. "I was ten. It was the smoking. He got pneumonia before Christmas, and he was gone by New Year's. Just like that." He cleared his throat. "Mum remarried a year later, needed the support; two little kids on her own. But he was Iranian and religious. She put a headscarf on for the first time in her life. Me and my little sister were suddenly expected to go to mosque and all that, as I'm realising, 'oh, shit! I think I'm fucking gay!' So, I said, nah, I'm gonna go live with me gran and granddad. Dad's parents. White, working class, East End. Real friendly, just like dad. They used to run a pub before they retired. We lived above it. Granddad pulling pints at the bar, Gran in the kitchen cooking pub grub. Pie and mash, mostly, or chips. She didn't know how to cook much else."

David now regretted teasing Sonny over his cooking skills. He didn't interrupt Sonny while he was still talking; it all tumbled out at once, like a confession of sorts. It was clear he didn't talk about this often.

"So, my grandparents were basically my parents for longer," Sonny said. "I lived with them since I was eleven. They're the ones who came to see me on parade when I joined cadets, then the service, and sent me birthday cards and mail to my barracks. I should've picked another bloody job though. Or got out early." Sonny raised his glass of juice to toast with. "Cheers to messing it all up." He took a gulp and set down his glass with a bang.

A beat of silence followed, indicating that Sonny was done talking.

"I don't think you messed it up," David told him. "You did a lot better than me. I was on the run from my own government, stripped of my identity. A walking lab experiment gone wrong."

"I'm no different, sunshine," Sonny said. "I'm a lab rat on a tight leash like I told ya. The only perk of the leash is that it's long."

"What are the alternatives?" David asked, thinking aloud.

Sonny shrugged, but he looked David in the eye for a long moment. It was a warning look. David guessed that this wasn't a safe conversation to continue out in the open.

He took the hint and raised his own glass. "Here's to long leashes," he said. He looked at Sonny as he silently mouthed the words, "For now."

Sonny nodded once and raised his glass again. "And here's to not fucking up."

They were done eating and cleared the plates away together.

"Hey," David said softly. "I'm sorry about your dad. I didn't know."

Sonny shook his head in a dismissive gesture, busy washing dishes.

"Are your mum and sister still around?" David asked.

Sonny nodded. "East End. And Toff's family is south or West End, which is why I chose to live in north London to give 'em all a wide berth."

David smiled. "And your grandparents?"

"The Iranians popped off years ago," he replied. "And my White granddad, too, but Gran's still kicking. Dad didn't have a large family, so I'm footing the bill for her care home." He glanced at David pointedly.

Now David understood. Sonny was sticking around for the sake of his gran. At least, for the moment.

"Is she okay?" David asked.

"Not too bad," Sonny said. "Arthritis. She needs help with stuff. I'm not always around, so I picked this care home with a rose garden out back. She loves roses, she does. And they look after her there. The staff are good."

"It's nice of you to do that," David told him.

"She was like a mum to me," Sonny said. "When I was on leave, I'd go home and see her. When Granddad died, it was only me and her, but I did long hours and had to go away at the drop of a hat. I should've been there more."

David nodded. He understood.

"I feel like I didn't have anyone after my dad passed," he explained. "My sister and my mom are in San Diego, but... Well, they're homophobic, so I never felt safe with them. They would only tolerate me if I never mentioned my personal life."

"Relatives," Sonny muttered.

"Yeah."

They were quiet a beat, then David asked, "Did your grandma...?"

"Know I was gay?" Sonny smiled wryly. "Oh, yes. We used to look through the magazines together and talk about which men we fancied."

"What, porn mags?" David asked, shocked.

"No!" Sonny snort laughed. "Get your mind out of the gutter! No, I mean those celebrity magazines. Actors and that. She loves perving over actors, she does. Films too. She wants films where the men are shirtless and preferably sword fighting. Those are her favourites."

"I see." David smiled. "That's cute though. She sounds like a pistol."

"Yeah." Sonny smiled back. Then he asked, "Did your dad know?"

David nodded. "I mean, we didn't speak on it at length, but he was pretty cool generally. He was the most chill person, never had a bad word to say about anyone. I went to live with him when my parents separated. I don't know, maybe that's why my mom and sister thought I wasn't on their side, because I wouldn't stay in the house with them. But..." David shrugged. "They're both mean."

"How old were you when they divorced?" Sonny asked.

"I was young when I knew they weren't great at being married, you know?" David replied. "But they didn't start proceedings until later. I was around twelve or thirteen."

"And when did he...?" Sonny asked, trailing off.

"He died when I was almost nineteen," David said. "Accident at work. Two other guys were killed along with my dad. He did construction. And, no, there wasn't any compensation."

"Fuck," Sonny muttered.

"Yeah, so..." David shrugged again. "I signed up. Thought it would be a way to stand on my own two feet. Dad was only renting a place; I couldn't afford it after he was gone. I certainly wasn't going to move back in with my mom."

"Nah, I get it," Sonny said.

"In hindsight," David added, "I probably should've moved to Mexico. I like it there."

"Yeah, I can see why," Sonny said. "Great food too."

David smiled. "La mejor comida," he agreed. "The best."

They fell quiet again, and the mood felt sombre but with a ray of light piercing through the shared sadness. Camaraderie.

David felt good about where they were. He hoped Sonny felt the same.

"C'mon," Sonny said, breaking the silence. He set the last plate to dry with a decisive thud. "That's enough feelings and shit. Let's go and be homosexual."

David chuckled. "Love to."

*

They retreated to bed for more sex, slower this time, unhurried, tender. Not just sex, but making love, at least from David's perspective. He could do this for the rest of his life. He knew that with an unnerving certainty. Looking into Sonny's eyes when he came, whether they shifted shape or not, David knew he wanted them to stay together as lovers.

Was this moving too fast? Maybe. But it felt right. Everything else in David's life was kind of a mess, but this part at least felt right.

Afterward, they lay side by side, tangled together amid the sweat-stained sheets. "What would you be?" David asked softly. "If you could do it all again? What would you do? Where would you go?"

"Fuck if I know," Sonny murmured. "Anything but what I chose. Maybe something at sea? I like boats."

"I like boats," David agreed. "Being on the sea feels like being free. International waters, too, that's a plus."

Sonny hummed, then scooted away, trying to escape David's embrace.

"Hey," David complained, holding on.

"You're too hot," Sonny grumbled. "I'm getting all sweaty."

"Okay." David let him go, and they lay side by side instead.

Sonny huffed audibly and wiped the back of his hand over his brow. "I'll need another fucking shower. You're like a furnace."

David snickered. He was content to share a bed, at least for now. Baby steps. "I can go fetch some ice?"

Sonny smiled, gazing up at the ceiling. David could stare at him all day. Sonny noticed and sent him a confused look.

"What?"

"Will you tell me your name?" David asked him. "Your real name."

Sonny let out an exhale. "Nobody calls me that name," he said in a petulant tone.

"I won't use it," David protested. "I just want to know it. If you tell me, I'll tell you my full name."

Sonny's brows bunched together as he looked at David like he was slow. "I know your name, sunshine. It was on your file."

"My file probably has two parts of my name, three at most," David replied. "My full name is four parts, and the correct spelling for Cortés is with an S. At some point Dad got American ID with the spelling wrong, with a Z."

"All right," Sonny said. "Tell me your name, then."

David smiled. "You first."

Sonny groaned softly and looked away.

"Hey," David said, reaching for his hand. "It's okay. You don't have to. I wanted to know your name. But it's okay. Forget it."

"I'll tell you if you promise to shut up," Sonny said, pulling his hand away. He was trying to sound mad, but David heard the smile in his voice.

"I promise," David said, smiling in anticipation.

"It's Nushur," he said. "N-U-S-H-U-R."

"That's cool," David said. He leaned up on his elbow. "What

about your last name? Is it the same as your cousin's?"

"No, Mum took Dad's name," Sonny said. "King. Nushur King. Just so I'd have the most out-of-place name in the classroom at school."

"Nushur King," David mused. "He sounds like a badass boxer."

Sonny rolled his eyes with a grin. "Yeah, maybe in another life."

"You said you had a sister?" David asked. "What's her name?"

"Samira," Sonny replied. "But she got off lightly, 'cause everyone at school called her Sam. Whereas the White kids in my class all said my name sounded like the noise you make when you sneeze."

"That doesn't even make sense," David said. He shook his head. "Kids are stupid."

Sonny chuckled. "I know! But that's why it was easier to use a nickname. Dad always called me Son or Sonny."

"I thought your teacher started it?" David asked.

"He did," Sonny said, the ghost of a smile teasing his lips. "Mr Dougan. Called any lad who got on his nerves Sonny Jim. Just so happened I got on his nerves a lot, so the name stuck. It was easier to use back then."

"Were all the kids White?" David asked.

"No, we had one or two Muslim kids in class," Sonny said. "Their names could get shortened to Mo, or easy nicknames like that. All right for some, innit?"

"There were a few Spanish-speaking kids back in school," David said. "In San Diego. When their parents found out that mine weren't religious, I didn't get invited to their houses much. Got the cold shoulder."

"Yeah, that happened to me and my sister," Sonny said.

"Although, once Mum remarried, our stepdad wanted us to go to mosque. Sam started going and got to fit in with her Muslim friends."

"Did you go?" David asked.

Sonny shrugged. "Only once or twice, but I really wasn't in the mood for it at the time."

"No, I can imagine," David said quietly.

"Now it's your turn, amigo," Sonny said. "Share the full name."

"Okay." David drew in a breath for dramatic effect, then recited his name, "David Luis Guerrero Cortés."

"Oh, okay," Sonny said, smirking. "That's the full lot?"

"That's it." David smiled back.

"I thought it would be longer," Sonny said, clearly teasing him.

Not missing a beat, David replied, "Said the bishop to the priest."

Sonny tittered. "That was good, Fresh Meat. Not bad at all."

"Back to that?" David teased. "I thought we'd dropped that one."

"You're still green."

"I prefer Green to Fresh Meat," David said.

"We don't pick our nicknames," Sonny retorted. "They happen organically. Organic fresh meat!" He chuckled. "Hey, I should call you haggis from now on. Ah!" He let out a yelp when David pinched his ribs.

"Oh, somehow I knew you'd be ticklish," David drawled, reaching out to pinch flesh again.

"Don't you fucking dare!" Sonny laughed, wriggling away as David tickled him. "I mean it. I'll break your wrist!"

David chuckled. "Okay, truce. Stop running your mouth, and

I won't tickle you."

"It's an assault on my rights, my freedom of speech," Sonny teased.

David leaned over him, pressing Sonny against the pillow. "Then I'll keep your mouth occupied another way." David tilted his head and kissed him. Sonny kissed him back, but as they kissed David felt Sonny's fingers slide around his middle and dare to pinch.

David smiled into the kiss when Sonny's pinching got no reaction.

"Mmph?" Sonny pushed him back. "How are you not ticklish?"

"I don't know," David said. "Grew out of it, I guess."

"Jammy git," Sonny complained.

David didn't know what that meant, but he understood the sentiment.

They settled down into the bed, not touching but lying close. David nudged his hand nearer to Sonny's outstretched fingers, brushing them together. They fell asleep like that.

David dreamed. Sex dreams, and that was to be expected. He was happy, elated at finding a mate who he fit with so well.

The dreams morphed and shifted into other random things, as dreams tended to do. David let himself float through them. He dreamed of airports, of trains, and dark, haunted castles. Sonny was with him sometimes, and at other times when he wasn't, David had a strong sense that he was wandering around looking for Sonny. Looking for his mate.

In the dark corners of his dream, a raspy chittering noise filtered out, catching his awareness before fading out again. Whenever David looked around for the source of the noise, he saw nothing but darkness with an uncanny sense that something watched and waited within that void.

Chapter Thirty-Seven

When David woke, Sonny wasn't in the bed.

He had some vague memory of Sonny getting up and going to the bathroom. David had assumed he would come back to bed, but maybe he was doing something else.

Curious, David got out of bed. He pulled on his shorts and wandered out into the hall. It was still daylight, and brighter out here than in the bedroom. He squinted, padding along the carpet to the second room. The single bed was unoccupied. Sonny must've gone downstairs.

David had a hunch why.

Softly, he walked down the stairs. The kitchen was empty, so was the downstairs water closet. David reached the sunlit lounge and peered in.

Sonny was curled up on the couch with a comforter. He appeared fast asleep. One bare arm and both bare feet were poking out from beneath the comforter. He'd put his pants on at some stage, but nothing else. Either he'd been too hot in the bed, or he slept better on couches.

David could understand. It was simply one of those things.

He left Sonny in peace and tiptoed back upstairs. He got back in bed, right in the center, lying on his side. He closed his eyes, and let sleep envelop him once more.

It felt like he'd barely shut his eyes when David heard that strange chittering noise again, raspy and close by. He woke up with a start, looking every which way to catch what made the noise.

There was nothing in the room. To make sure, he got up and walked across the carpet, performing a visual check from different angles.

Nothing. It must've been a dream.

David sighed and turned back to the bed. He got the shock of his life to see the figure of a man in bed already, lying under the covers. David only just managed to stop himself from yelling in surprise. He backed away, and rounded the bed to get a look at the man, who appeared to be fast asleep. It wasn't Sonny, it was...

David stared at the person in bed.

This was crazy, but it looked like him. The face was turned up, eyes shut. That was David's face.

What? David thought. Was that him? Was he still asleep?

He looked down at himself where he lay. He appeared to be fully clothed, in combat pants and boots, and a green top—US Marines gear. David brought his bare hands up to his face to look at them, noting that there were more fingers than there should be.

"Am I dreaming?" he said. He looked at his hands, wriggling the fingers. The image shifted from in focus to blurry when he stared too long.

This was strange.

Should he get back in bed?

Voices downstairs drew David's attention. He turned and left the bedroom, walking down the hall. Everything looked the same; it was the same cottage. The colours were a little muted, like a dark filter had been laid over the original. David walked to the stairs, listening. The voices were still audible. One was Sonny's. One was another man's. They were speaking together with familiarity, in English, having a full-blown conversation without him.

Jealousy stabbed and twisted into David's gut. An overreaction, perhaps. Maybe this was a colleague. Maybe it was an enemy, and Sonny was in trouble.

It better not be a boyfriend, David thought, as he stalked down the stairs.

The voices came from the lounge, where Sonny had been sleeping. David listened carefully as he approached the open doorway, but it was hard to make out their words. They were speaking in muted tones so as not to be overheard. David couldn't pick out the other man's accent, but it was close to British. *Possibly* accented. The two spoke quickly, and it was hard for David to understand it all, but he heard some of it.

"They got the gear out in the nick of time," the man was saying. "Thanks to you, dear boy," he added with a drawl.

"Better not be anything dodgy." Sonny's voice.

"Define dodgy?" A chuckle. Tone mocking. "The crates were storing sensory deprivation tanks. A little business venture that held some irony for me. Humans with more money than sense buying what essentially amounts to a plug-in coffin. Oh, it did give me cause for amusement, I can tell you."

"Scrub it," Sonny replied. "No leads back to you."

"It's already scrubbed, as you put it," the other man said.

"I mean it, Balogh," Sonny said. "I stuck my neck out for

you."

"Such a pretty neck," the other voice replied.

Wait. Balogh?

David felt himself tense. Balogh the vampire was in there with Sonny? Worried for his safety, David burst into the room. He wasn't sure what he expected to find; some Count Dracula type dipping Sonny back in a neck biting meets *Dancing With The Stars* manoeuvre.

But the scene before him wasn't what he expected. There were three men in the room. Sonny was still fast asleep on the couch as the other two talked. One standing, with the other sitting on the corner chair, one leg crossed casually over the other.

The two who were awake turned to look at David. That's when he saw one of them was Sonny...a different Sonny. And the expression on his face showed surprise.

David looked at him, his eyes tracing his figure. Sonny was also fully dressed, wearing his black combat gear. But the curious thing was there were more images on and around him, drifting in and out of focus. A man who looked very much like Sonny, wearing flowing patchwork white robes and a turban on his head, spinning around and around in a graceful dance. And another man in all black, wearing a black turban and cloth covering most of his face, in the style of those *Assassin's Creed* video games.

Whenever David tried to focus on one of the images, it blurred and faded away as the other came into focus. Like negatives superimposed onto the same space but revolving around and around like a carousel.

"David?" Sonny prompted. "What are you doing here?"

"I could ask you the same question," David replied. "What's going on?" He looked between Sonny—all three Sonny's—and Balogh.

Balogh was calmly sitting in his chair but grinning toothily. He was clearly taking great pleasure in this.

Balogh was a solid, single image. He appeared to be a light-skinned, middle-aged gentleman in a black suit and tie, like he was on his way to a funeral. His hair was dark, clipped neatly into a short style. He was clean-shaven, and his eyes were pitch-black, hardly any white showing, with two bright pinpoints at the center. Like wolf eyes in the dark.

"Is this him?" Balogh asked, staring at David with a smile. "Nushur, darling, you didn't tell me your new pet was so *interesting*."

David frowned, still tensed for a fight. Yet...this was not what he'd expected some powerful vampire to be; a mean gay taunting him for fun.

"What's going on?" David repeated, looking at Sonny. The men in robes, one in black and one in lighter colours, were still swirling around Sonny. It was starting to make David dizzy.

"David, listen," Sonny pleaded. "Go back upstairs. Everything is fine, but you shouldn't be here. Go back upstairs."

"Like hell," David replied. "Not until you explain what's going on. And who...or what are those on you?"

"Oh, those are his past lives," Balogh interrupted. "One might also call them ancestors. Marvellous, aren't they? You know, our dear Nushur has a direct line back to Hasan-i Sabbah's first order of assassins."

"Balogh," Sonny warned.

"And the one in white, twirling around?" Balogh continued, heedless of Sonny's warning. "Prominent Sufi. You know, those famous whirling dervishes? Spinning around and around to imitate the orbit of heaven, inducing a trancelike state, and all that? It's interesting, wouldn't you say?"

"Balogh, not now," Sonny said, tone clipped. "Chrissakes."

David watched Sonny. If he was comfortable enough to be on familiar terms with Balogh, then they probably weren't in immediate danger. Which meant... David wasn't sure what it meant. Was Sonny in some sort of relationship with this vampire?

"Oh, ha, ha, ha!" Balogh started to laugh, bold and bright. "Oh, my. No, no, my dear David, we're not in *that* sort of relationship. Are you jealous already?" Balogh glanced at Sonny. "He must be fire in the sack, Nushur. These Latin boys. No wonder you wanted to keep him all to yourself."

"Oh, my God," Sonny groaned, rounding on Balogh. "Can we not do this now? I still need answers!"

"All in good time," Balogh replied. He had a lilt to his accent, David noticed now, but he still couldn't place it. He hadn't heard Hungarians speak in English before, so he didn't know if this was what their accent sounded like, or if it was from somewhere else.

As he stared at Balogh, David noticed another image begin to appear over him. A younger Balogh, with dark facial hair and a longer, shaggy haircut. He was dressed in fur-lined leather clothes and metal armour, like some medieval warrior of old. The furry hat on his head looked Russian to David's eyes.

"Balkan," Balogh corrected. "I'm not a Russian, dear David."

David realised he hadn't spoken a word, yet Balogh had still answered.

Balogh raised one long pale finger and tapped it to his temple. "I know what you think, my boy."

"David, he can read minds," Sonny interjected. "This is why I didn't want you to meet him right away. Will you please go back upstairs?"

Oh.

"Now, now," Balogh said, rising to his feet. The motion was

fluid and inhuman; like wires raising a weightless marionette. "Let's not be so hasty," he purred. "David...Cortés, isn't it?" Balogh addressed him directly. "Wouldn't you like to see what we are seeing now? The lives you've brought in with you?"

David hesitated. "What?"

"Here." Balogh raised his hand, like an orchestra conductor commanding music to rise, and with the motion a full-length mirror appeared. The mirror had no edges. It wasn't a normal mirror.

"David, we're in a dream," Sonny's voice reassured him.

"That is true," Balogh said. "To be more specific, we are in Nushur's dream. He invited me in."

That didn't fill David with confidence. Still, he couldn't help turning to the mirror, couldn't help looking. He saw himself standing there, in the muted hues of the cottage lounge. He was dressed for combat, in Marine Corps camouflage. There were more figures sharing the same space as him, ghosts vying for the same spot. David saw several different silhouettes, but the clearest and most prominent man was a Mexican-looking cowboy, with a long black moustache. David knew instantly who he was: that was his great-great grandfather Juan Havier Cortés, who fought against the US invasion in the Mexican-American war.

And the other image... David could hardly believe it. A brown-skinned man with long black hair wearing a brightly coloured feather headdress, a pleated skirt and little else save for more feather adornments on his ripped body.

David didn't know who this was.

"Yes, he's harder to place, I'll admit," Balogh said. "Not Aztec. Older than that. Toltec. He's a Toltec high priest, or shaman. Yes, that's it."

The hairs on the back of David's neck stood on end as he watched the mirror, watched the Toltec ancestor before him.

David wanted a closer look, but the mirror faded away.

"Fascinating, isn't it?" Balogh watched him with hungry eyes. "It's faint sometimes, but the stronger the ancestor, or past life, then the clearer the impression. I can read the DNA in your blood as easily as a computer programmer reads code. Now, I'll tell you what piques *my* interest." He half turned to Sonny. "If you want to know how your new pet waltzed into your dream so easily, breezing past the first two gates of dreaming without so much as a knock on the door, I'd wager it's down to the Toltec line. Toltec dreaming. Look it up."

"All right, all right," Sonny said, sounding exasperated. "We do have other more pressing matters at hand. Who brokered vampire genes to that lab in Mexico?"

"Well, isn't it obvious?" Balogh scoffed. "That weasel of a lawyer, Merritt, tossed me under the proverbial bus to throw you silly boys off his scent. I'd bet any money he's your broker. I mean." He snorted with distaste. "Why would I want more competition? It's hard enough to find a decent meal these days with all this digital surveillance, I certainly don't need to add rabid young vampires into that mix."

"Fuck. It's Merritt." Sonny groaned with annoyance. "That little shit."

"This is why I don't keep familiars around for too long anymore," Balogh said. "They get greedy. They want to become immortal, yet they have no idea how tricky life, or should I say death, is these days."

"We have to go," Sonny said. "We wasted twenty-four hours. Merritt's probably in Europe by now."

"No, he hasn't left England yet," Balogh replied. "He's too cocky and thinks he has plenty of time. He doesn't know about our little arrangement." Balogh smiled toothily at Sonny. "He probably thought you'd get on my tail and annoy me enough that I'd dispose of you for him."

"Yeah, it's obvious now," Sonny said.

"Wait, wait," David said. "Back up. What is your arrangement, exactly?"

"Oh." Balogh turned to him with a charming smile. "Would you be interested in coming on board? I'm always open to new arrangements."

"Back off, Balogh," Sonny warned. "David," he added, coming to stand in front of him to draw his full attention. "Wake. Up!"

The dream cut off quite abruptly.

David found himself blinking his eyes open, back in the bed. At first, he assumed that was nothing but his own dream. A crazy dream, but his own. Just his mind having a wild time. He almost turned over to fall back asleep.

Then he thought, what if it wasn't a dream?

David opened his eyes. He sat up in bed. Where was Sonny? He would check where Sonny was, then he'd go back to sleep. David got up and walked out into the hall. It was still daylight outside.

As he approached the top of the stairs, Sonny came into view at the bottom; shirtless, wearing pants only. They locked eyes, and from the look on his face, David knew that it hadn't been a dream.

"What," he started to say but paused when Sonny put a finger to his lips.

All their equipment was in this cottage. They could be overheard. David nodded. They could have this conversation elsewhere.

Chapter Thirty-Eight

They got dressed and went outside for a brisk walk, away from the cottage.

Down the quiet, narrow village street lined with little cottages, they could talk, albeit in hushed tones.

"That was all real?" David hissed, trying to keep his voice down.

"Yeah," Sonny said. He seemed uncharacteristically at a loss for words.

"I thought Balogh was a wanted and dangerous vampire?" David hissed. "Why are you working with him? You're a double agent, aren't you?"

"Let's go in there." Sonny motioned to the tiny stone church up ahead. The ivy-laden gate to the graveyard was open, and nobody was about.

They went inside, standing among the quiet gravestones.

"Look, it's complicated," Sonny said, resting his hands on his hips. "Like I told you before, Balogh used to be an asset for PRISM. It was well before I came on board, before I'd ever heard of PRISM. They would give him vials of blood from suspects, stolen samples, and he'd drink it to gather intel for them. You've seen what he can read just from being close to you. One sniff of your blood, or one drink, and he knows your entire life's history. They thought that's how he reads minds too. Blood scent and some psychic power mixed together. Who the hell knows, but he can read anyone like an open book. PRISM used that, weaponised it. Nobody was safe from having even a drop of their blood being stolen without their knowledge and handed over to a vampire asset to read. Until Balogh got bored and went off grid."

David exhaled through his nose. "Wow. Bet that ticked off the brass."

"Course it did." Sonny smiled wryly. "That was a little before I came on. I was told all the horror stories about Balogh, how dangerous and manipulative he is. PRISM can't hold him, because the guy can turn to mist or vanish whenever he wants. They don't really know what he is, but Doc thought probably some entity like a spirit or parasite inside a human host body. She thinks the spirit is old and changes bodies when it wants a change of identity, but these are all guesses. Balogh will never tell you the truth. He's a slippery old fish."

"Yeah, I got that." David tilted his head, looking at Sonny thoughtfully. "I have a question. Back in Mexico, when I brought up reverse engineering a cure for you to free you from PRISM, you had a look on your face like you were already working on it. Balogh is helping you, isn't he?"

Sonny nodded, looking away. "That's right. He's been studying blood diseases and DNA for longer than either of us have been alive. If anyone's going to get a working antidote, it's him."

"You trust him?"

"Only as far as I can throw him."

"He likes you," David said. And, he thought, maybe not in a traditional sense, but maybe like a mentor liked his mentee.

"He seemed to like you too," Sonny pointed out. "Look, you've met him now. You can see he's nosy. He's probably bored. We're playthings to him. Like mice to a cat. The first time I tracked him down for PRISM, he got the drop on me and bit my neck. Luckily for me, my blood makes him sick. I watched him have a very violent reaction to feeding on me. After he recovered, he came to speak to me privately and asked me about this alien thing. He was curious. Still is. That's probably the only reason he's agreed to help me."

"So, he's making an antidote for you?" David asked.

Sonny shrugged. "He's looking into it, but someone like that's never gonna do something out of the goodness of his heart. He's sneaky. You have to be more careful with Balogh next time, sunshine. He can read your mind. He'll play with you for fun. I'll show you how to shield your thoughts before you face him again. All right?"

"Yeah, okay," David agreed. He'd be interested in that. He also wanted to ask about those ancestors he saw, but for now it would have to wait. "So," David said, "Balogh's not our broker?"

"He's not." Sonny shook his head. "He's not even in Scotland, I asked. He uses that house as a storage spot for UK buyers and uses human associates to make the deliveries. Are his goods hot? Yes, most likely. But they're run-of-the-mill human goods, not vampire genes. Merritt fingered him to throw us off the scent, and now I need to figure out an excuse for us to track down Merritt again without giving away how I know."

"Okay." David let out a sigh. He couldn't think up some great excuse for pivoting back to Merritt with everything else on his mind. "I have a question," he said. "If Balogh can read us through our blood? Does he know what our...you know, the aliens inside us, does he know what they look like? Or what they are?"

"Careful," Sonny warned. "That isn't a door you want to open with him."

"Why not?" David asked. "He showed me a great-great ancestor that I recognise, so I know it's legit."

"That's not what I meant." Sonny's expression was serious. "Yes, he *would* be very interested in finding out as much as he can about the alien DNA. He calls them alien cuckoos. Now, use your brain. *Why* do you think he's interested?"

David felt like he was missing something. "You said he studies blood?" he guessed. "Is he, like, a scientist?"

"Yes, but for purely selfish reasons," Sonny replied. "Remember what I said about Doc's theory? That inside the human shell you saw of him there is what we suspect to be a much, much older parasite using that body as a host. We think this parasite changes bodies over the years. Assuming an identity when it finds a suitable host. That's how it survives for so long."

"Oh." David got it now, and he had a sinking feeling as the realisation settled over him. "He wants to use us."

"Precisely," Sonny said. "You keep forgetting that you're carrying around important DNA now. You're an asset. Everyone is gonna want a piece of that, even if they don't fully understand what you are yet. And this is why, sunshine, you simply cannot trust anyone."

"Including you?" David asked.

The question appeared to catch Sonny off guard, judging by the surprise flitting across his face.

His hesitation before answering didn't do anything to dispel

David's doubts.

"Learn to put yourself first," Sonny replied, effectively dodging the question. "We better get back. I'll think up some reason to point the finger at Merritt, and we'll pack up."

"Okay," David said. He didn't know what else to say.

So much for their nice day off.

They left the little churchyard and walked back down the street. On the way to their cottage, they passed by Morag's house. It reminded David about all the other mysteries in the village.

"What about those missing people posters?" David asked. "And I saw a bowl with red stuff in the kitchen of that manor. Don't you think there's a connection? Something Balogh isn't telling us?"

"Red stuff?" Sonny said wryly. "Probably tomato soup. Vampires don't drink blood from bowls, they drink from the source."

That made sense, David thought.

"Okay, but the missing people?" he pressed.

"I don't think it's connected," Sonny told him. "I mentioned it to Balogh, but he said he hasn't been to Scotland in years. The parties and the missing people sound like it could be human crimes, if they are crimes, and totally unconnected."

"Huh." David thought about it. Who had opportunity and motive to do away with Susan? He was no detective, but Occam's Razor would suggest that whoever had the most to gain from her disappearance was a suspect.

"Do you think Morag wanted her relative out of the picture in order to rent out her house for cash?"

Sonny shrugged. "Possibly."

"Are we going to do anything about it?" David asked him.

"If it makes you feel better," Sonny said, "I'll add it into the report that local cops should look into her. But we don't make those decisions, sunshine, only PRISM does. They usually don't want the local law sniffing around anywhere we've been, so don't hold your breath."

"So, that's that?" David asked. "This poor woman whose home we've had sex in stays missing and gets no justice?"

Sonny's eyebrows flicked up. "Don't get out ya pram, love. We aren't local law enforcement. Human business isn't our business."

"But it should be," David argued.

They approached their cottage, gravel crunching under their feet as they walked up the drive.

"No one pays us for human business," Sonny said quietly. He dug in his pocket for the front door key. "And you'd do well to remember that."

"When I joined the marines," David replied quietly, "I swore by an oath of conduct, and that means having respect and concern for other people."

Sonny looked at him with a vaguely disinterested expression. "You're not in the marines anymore, love. This is Intelligence, a community that would sell its own mother and stab you in the back at the same time. This is your life now. Remember that."

"Sounds pretty bleak," David said, unwilling to let it go.

"And that realisation is your first step to acceptance, and later, apathy!" Sonny said jovially, like this somehow won the argument.

But, luck was on David's side, as Morag herself appeared at the end of the drive.

"Hiya!" She called, waving to them as she approached. "I saw ye walking past. Did ye have a nice wee walk there?"

To David, this was a perfect sign. He looked at Sonny and raised his eyebrows as if to say, see? She's right here.

Sonny looked at him, then rolled his eyes. "Fine," he groaned, pushing open the door. "I'll ask her some questions if it gets you off my back."

"That's all I ask," David replied, then turned to Morag with a smile. "Hi, there. Would you like to come in for a quick coffee?"

Morag's face lit up. "Oh, aye! Thanks! I'd prefer tea though."

Sonny grumbled under his breath, but David had won this round.

They all went inside, making polite small talk, and migrated into the kitchen.

"There's tea bags in that cupboard there." Morag pointed out. "I like mine strong."

Sonny turned to David and waved his hand at him. "Go on, then. Make some tea."

"No problem," David replied. He went to the cupboards to look for a tea kettle or a pocillo cup to fill with water.

Morag and Sonny fell quiet and watched him.

All David could find was a pan, so he took it to the sink. Before turning the tap on, he glanced at them both. "What?" he asked.

Sonny was clearly fighting a grin. "You all right there, son?" he asked, his voice a few octaves higher in obvious amusement.

David paused. "Yes?" he replied. Was he missing something?

Sonny tittered a laugh but didn't elaborate.

Morag, fighting a smile, was kinder. "The electric kettle on the counter over there would be faster."

David looked around, spotting a sleek white machine he hadn't realised was an electric kettle. That explained why there was no kettle on the stove top.

"Right," he said, and went to put the pan away.

Sonny was still tittering, wiping a tear from his eye. "Ah, that was brilliant. I wouldn't have even told you; I would've let you boil water from scratch."

David rolled his eyes. British kitchens made no sense to him. He made the tea, three mugs, and delivered Morag's and Sonny's to them at the table.

"Thank you," Morag said.

David went to lean on the counter, more interested in watching Sonny and Morag than he was in drinking tea.

Now Sonny had gotten hold of himself, he began conversing with Morag over a cup of tea, casually at first. David understood that this fake-nice persona was Sonny's prelude to interrogation.

David watched closely.

"Now, Morag. Can I call you Morag?" Sonny said. "I'm afraid I have to ask you some questions. It's about Susan."

David watched Morag's face as her smile fell away and a look of blank surprise took over. Whether she was innocent or not, this woman wasn't used to lying, David thought.

"What about Susan?" Morag asked.

"My associate and I are private investigators," Sonny said, his tone serious. "We've been hired by a third party who wishes to remain anonymous, to look into Susan's disappearance. We rented out this place to perform a search, dust for fingerprints. But before we hand over our findings for forensic analysis, we wanted to get your side of things. So do you know where Susan is?"

"Did Roger hire you?" Morag demanded, a pink flush staining her cheeks. "That bawbag ex-boyfriend of hers? You cannae listen to a word that man says. He's the one putting up those missing posters, the one who's been stalking her ever since she left him. He's a shite of a man."

"Unfortunately, I can't disclose our client's details," Sonny replied calmly. "However, I can assure you that Susan's welfare is our top priority. It's a..." He paused before continuing. "A code of conduct we have."

David schooled his features so that he didn't smile, but inside he was smiling.

"Aye, she's fine," Morag spat, clearly emotional over this. Her face was flushed but she had a fire in her eyes and her voice was firm. "She's trying to make a fresh start of it, away from here and away from him. And if you have any moral decency, you won't follow her. Not for Roger."

Sonny didn't reply but looked around at David, flicking his eyebrows up in question. He was asking if David was satisfied with this.

David nodded. He believed Morag.

Sonny turned back to her. "Thank you, Morag. I want to assure you that we won't be following up on this, and as far as we are concerned the case is closed."

Morag nodded. "Good," she said shortly, then pushed her chair back and got to her feet. "I should be going."

She marched out of the cottage but didn't slam the door. That last act showed she had care for the place in Susan's absence.

Sonny twisted around in his chair, crossing one leg over the other as he looked at David smugly. "Happy now?" he asked.

"Yeah, I suppose," David said. "Thanks for doing that."

"Oh, no trouble at all," Sonny said, a note of sarcasm in his voice. "It's not like we have anything more important to do, is it?"

David tried not to grin. "I thought you needed more time to..." he trailed off, not saying the words, but waving his hand beside his head to indicate thinking.

"Yes, well," Sonny said. "No lightbulbs yet, I'm afraid." He drummed his fingers on the table. "Maybe food would help."

David held out a hand so Sonny wouldn't get up. "Okay, but

this time, I'm making it."

Sonny grinned. "Don't you want more beans on toast?"

"Leave the food to me," David told him firmly.

Clearly, he'd have to be the chef around here. David whipped up a quick chilli con carne with rice, a few wedges of lime, and a generous dollop of sour cream on top.

They sat down to eat. Sonny made humming noises of approval, so David counted the meal as a win.

It was still daylight outside, but the sun would set in a few short hours.

The ringtone from David's phone chimed in the lounge. He got up to go answer it, removing the cushion he'd placed on top.

Sonny followed him, waiting to see who it was.

The screen said Guv. David turned the phone to Sonny to show him, thinking he'd want to take it, but Sonny gestured for David to answer.

David accepted the call. "Hello? I mean, yes, sir?"

Sonny placed a hand over his mouth as he shook with silent laughter.

"Any new leads?" Guv asked.

"Not yet," David replied.

A beat passed, then Guv asked, "Is Sonny with you?"

"Yes, he's right here," David said, tilting the phone out so Sonny could listen in.

"Tell him I want you both back in London," Guv said. "Surveillance picked up Merritt purchasing a ticket for the Eurostar this evening. That strikes me as suspicious."

"Like he's trying to skip town?" David guessed.

"Yes. I want you two to go pick him up. Bring him in this time," Guv said. "He's hiding something."

"Yes, sir," David said.

"Get to the airport ASAP," Guv said. "I'll have the tickets sent to your phone and a car waiting in London."

"Yes, sir," David repeated. The call ended. David pocketed his phone. "Guess we better pack?"

Sonny raised one hand in a clenched fist, a silent air pump of victory. "Yeah, reckon so," he said, his tone nonchalant. "Looks like we came up here for nothing." He smiled and winked at David. "You didn't even get to try haggis yet."

"And I'm fine with that," David quipped. "Let's get going."

Chapter Thirty-Nine

They had to hurry.

And, with the earpieces going back into their ears, conversation between them had to be restricted for a listening audience. Everything on David's mind, everything he wanted to discuss with Sonny, had to be tabled for now.

They had a man to catch.

They packed up their gear, locked up the cottage, and dropped the key back with Morag. Then Sonny drove them to the nearest airport, flying down the winding country roads and making David wince every time they took a corner.

"Merritt's train is scheduled for departure at 19:05," Mother explained via comms. "He should be inside the terminal ninety minutes before."

David checked the time. It was nearly five PM. "So, very soon?" he said. "Are we going to make it?"

"You're booked on the 17:20 flight to London City Airport,

which is seven miles from St. Pancras station. It'll be tight, but…"

"We'll make it," Sonny said, increasing speed. "Easily."

David put his hand onto the dash as they took another sharp bend at breakneck speed. "Wouldn't it be easier to get agents closer to London?" he asked.

"We'll make it," Sonny repeated. "We might break a sweat, but there's plenty of time."

"There's a siren car already waiting for you at London City," Mother informed them. "If you cut around congested areas, you'll get through in no time."

"We'll be there," Sonny replied.

They made it to the Scottish airport and got out of the car. As it was a small airport, the car rental assistant was in sight by the exit, so Sonny simply tossed him the keys. Then they grabbed their bags and took off at a jog, heading to security.

They were lucky, making their plane within moments of the last boarding call. As soon as they boarded, the doors closed.

Sonny was annoyed to discover they had been placed in coach, but luckily for them they had a row of three seats all to themselves. They stored the bag securely in the overhead, then sat for take-off.

"Merritt has entered St. Pancras station," Mother reported softly in their earpieces. "We have him on CCTV, along with a tall unidentified White male walking close beside him."

"Bodyguard?" David asked.

Sonny nodded. "Sun still up, Mother?"

"It's setting, but it's in the sky," Mother replied.

"Human bodyguard?" David said. That was fine; he could handle humans. "Can they slow them down at immigration?" he asked.

Sonny shook his head. "Better not to flag persons of interest to the civilians.”

David nodded. It was just him and Sonny, then.

“You have more teams for this sort of thing, right?” he asked. “Or are we the only team?”

“We’re the A team,” Sonny said with a smile. “There is a B team and C team.”

“And they are currently unavailable,” Mother interjected.

“The A team,” David mouthed silently. He nudged Sonny. “Does the A stand for…?”

Sonny looked at him. They were sitting side by side, close enough that if David leaned in a little more they could’ve kissed. It crossed David’s mind, but he got the impression that Sonny wanted to keep things between them on the down-low, at least for now.

“What?” Sonny asked.

“You know,” David whispered. “A for…alien?”

Sonny snorted. “No,” he said flatly. “A for alpha, you plum.”

“Oh,” David said. “Well, it could, right?”

“Shut up and look out the window,” Sonny told him, fighting a grin. “I gallantly gave you the window seat both ways, and you’re not even looking out of it.”

“There’s clouds at the moment,” David replied. “I’ll switch if you want.”

Sonny didn’t reply, just wiggled his eyebrows until David realised the unintentional double entendre. He had to curb his chuckle so nobody would hear.

How was he going to keep things between them a secret if Sonny was going to make him laugh without warning?

That was a problem for Future David. Present David needed to focus on the mission at hand.

*

They landed into a dark pink sunset, at a small airport. London City.

Sonny grabbed the bag, and they were first off the plane, running at a jog to get to the exit with Mother guiding them on comms.

Using a staff exit door that opened directly onto a side road, they saw a sleek black car parked. Kip, the blue-haired agent from night watch, was waiting for them.

"I suppose you wanna drive?" Kip asked, tossing the keys to Sonny.

"I was hoping not to go through that experience again," David teased.

Kip cracked a smile at his joke.

"My driving is impeccable," Sonny retorted.

David glanced at Kip over the roof of the car for confirmation. Kip tilted their head side to side, as if to contest this claim.

David smirked. "Uh-huh," he drawled.

He and Sonny got into the front, Kip in the back seat.

"We have less than twenty minutes until Merritt's train departure," Kip said, tapping on their phone. "CCTV confirms he's through security and went to board the train."

"Strap in," Sonny said. "Said the bishop to the priest." He pushed a button for the concealed blue lights and siren. Then he put his foot down and peeled away from the curb. Soon they were hurtling down a busy dual carriageway.

"Have we got a visual?" David asked Kip.

"I'll send them to your phone," Kip replied.

David's phone vibrated, and he got it out to check the pictures. Security footage stills of Merritt in a dark coat, carrying hand luggage, and the larger gentleman beside him holding no luggage.

That big White guy was bodyguard material, David thought. He'd been in a few fights, from the looks of him.

"Do we know anything about the other guy?" David asked.

"Ran him through facial recognition back at base," Kip said. "Terry Watts, resident of south London. A few priors, mostly theft or burglary. Nothing to suggest he's involved in supernatural activities, but Guv wants them both brought in for questioning. Separately."

"That means," Sonny told David, "the unknown is likely just a random guy Merritt is paying to have around. Try not to say anything confidential in his earshot. We have the power to bring Merritt in for more questioning, and we don't have to explain why."

"Copy that," David replied.

*

They made good time. The siren helped, and traffic parted for them where it was busy. Sonny took a lot of back streets and narrow brick-lined passageways to avoid congested areas.

"Almost there," he said, turning off the siren. He came out from a side street and screeched to a halt at a taxi rank outside a glass exterior building nestled between older red-brick buildings.

"Leave everything with me," Kip told them. "And try to keep things low-key."

"Low-key is my middle name," Sonny said, as he handed over his gun.

David did the same.

They got out of the car and left Kip with the keys. Sonny took off at a jog toward the big building, heading to the entrance. David glanced up at the enormous glass structure as he followed Sonny in.

"Is there a shortcut?" he asked. This place was *busy*. It would be difficult to run through the crowds here without causing mishap.

"Take a left," Mother's voice instructed in their ears. "I'm opening a service door. You can take the stairs to the upper level."

"Copy," Sonny said. He ran, leading the way.

David followed him. They found the service door, which unlocked itself for them to pass through. Inside was an empty, stone-step stairwell.

"Top level," Mother instructed.

They ran up at least three flights of stairs by David's count. When they came out the door at the top, it was like stepping out into an entirely different building. The curved roof was transparent glass, showing the last of the pink sunset across the sky. Inside the terminal of sleek trains, passengers walked up and down platforms with their suitcases. The station was huge, and sound echoed here. The walls on either side were made of old red brick, with beautiful arches and detail built in.

It was such an interesting building, with the old meeting the new, but they had no time to stop and gawp. David had to take it all in within seconds and get his bearings.

"Which train?" Sonny asked as they jogged to the platforms.

"Platform seven," Mother said. "I have visual of you on my screen. Take a right, and it's two trains along."

Sonny jogged away, David running alongside him. They had to be careful they didn't smash into the passengers wandering around, ducking and diving around them as they ran past.

"Seven." Sonny pointed, as they came upon the correct train. "Which carriage?"

"Carriage two," Mother said. "Front of the train."

"Oh, fuckin' 'ell," Sonny grumbled, and picked up his pace to jog faster.

David kept pace with him, and they ran alongside the shiny white train.

"The bloody twat put himself in first class," Sonny muttered.

"The guy has aspirations," David said.

"He fuckin' does," Sonny agreed.

The train was long. They ran all the way to the other end of the platform, counting down the carriages, dodging passengers.

"Four...this is three," Sonny said, slowing down to a stop outside carriage number three. "Dash, get on here and move up to two. I'll distract Merritt while you neutralise his bodyguard. I've got Merritt. Remember to let me do the talking. Keep civilians safe."

David was pleasantly surprised that Sonny was letting him take point on this.

"Copy that," he said.

*

Robert Merritt felt suitably smug this evening.

He had successfully tied up his loose ends in London, vacating his office today. Any important paperwork was in his briefcase beside him, the rest shredded. He had booked two business premier seats on the Eurostar, due to leave any minute for Paris, one for himself and one for Terry.

Terry was a nobody. Fists for hire, should the need arise.

But this was why Merritt felt smug. He didn't anticipate any need for a bodyguard, as he'd already sent those interfering PRISM agents off on a false lead to Scotland, siccing them on that creepy old git, Balogh.

If all went according to his plan, PRISM would seize control of Balogh's business and holdings, and the old bastard would be forced out of hiding.

Merritt didn't care if PRISM or Balogh came out on top, he just needed them to fight each other long enough for him to slip away.

In a couple of hours' time, he would be in Paris, and he could disappear into Europe from there. Merritt gazed out the window. They had a four-seat table for the two of them. Terry was big enough to need one and a half seats, sitting opposite Merritt and currently engrossed on his phone. Not the smartest bodyguard in the world, but his mere presence was deterrent enough.

Passengers walked past the window, heading to the first carriage. The last stragglers to board. Merritt looked at them for a moment, then gazed around at the carriage when the announcement in first English and then French began. Other passengers were taking their seats, storing luggage, and settling down for the journey.

They were soon due for departure. He was going to escape scot-free. Merritt smiled. He'd made it.

He was still smiling to himself as he turned back to the window. A passenger walked by outside, very close to the window. Merritt almost looked away, then did a double take when he recognised the dark head of curls, brown skin, and the fitted leather jacket.

Merritt stared in surprise as Sonny leaned in close to the window. The bastard was grinning.

"Oi," Sonny said calmly, muffled behind the glass. "I want a word with you, Merritt."

It was only one agent. In that split second, Merritt made the decision to sacrifice his bodyguard.

"Terry!" he hissed. "That man outside is a threat to me. Go and deal with him."

Poor, oblivious Terry put down his phone and looked up. "Him?" he asked, looking at the window where Sonny was smiling and waving at them.

"Yes!" Merritt hissed. "Go deal with him!"

"Got it." Terry made to get up, having to shuffle his bulk through the small gap between table and chair.

A passenger walking past their table, a man, swept down upon Terry and in one fluid motion pinned Terry to the table face first, twisting Terry's arm behind his back. "Stay down," the man said quietly. His accent hinted at American.

Merritt stared in shock. Not only had Terry been taken down in mere seconds, but now the two men were blocking Merritt's exit from his seat. He was pinned down. If he wanted to escape, he'd have to clamber over the table and go past them, and Merritt knew he wasn't agile or quick enough for moves like that.

Other passengers stared and gasped in shock. Even if one of them called for the British Transport Police, Merritt knew that PRISM had authority over them.

He was cornered.

Sonny boarded the carriage. "Everyone, remain calm," he called out. "We are Interpol. Apologies for interrupting your journey, this will all be over momentarily."

Then he repeated everything in French to show off.

Merritt rolled his eyes. "They're not Interpol!" he protested, but he was drowned out when Terry began his own protests, face mashed against the table.

"I ain't even done anything!" Terry shouted.

"You're both coming with us for questioning," Sonny said, taking out black matte handcuffs. He tossed one set to his partner. "You have the right to remain silent."

"Merritt, what the fuck?" Terry shouted. "I'm not going down for you, you arsewipe." He stopped struggling and allowed himself to be cuffed.

"They're not Interpol!" Merritt repeated. "They're a fucking government conspiracy, is what they are!"

"Take this one outside," Sonny told his partner.

Terry was taken away, his big shoulders drooping. He'd folded like a napkin.

Merritt was on his own, having to face down Sonny with the entire carriage watching and murmuring in shock.

"Are you gonna come quietly?" Sonny asked, standing beside the table.

Merritt reached inside his jacket for his flick knife. He pulled it out and pressed the blade open. "Get out of my way, you little shit!"

"I'll take that as a no." Sonny raised his hand, whipping out a concealed taser stick like some cheap magician.

The shock hit Merritt quicker than he could react.

"Ack! Argh!" Merritt grunted, as electricity jolted him. He dropped his knife. "You...fucking...cunt!" he gritted out.

"Takes one to know one, mate," Sonny retorted, just before Merritt lost consciousness.

Chapter Forty

David had assumed they'd return to base with their detainees, Merritt and Watts, but instead Sonny drove them to an unassuming brick building in the south of the city, within sight of the River Thames.

It was probably an off-site holding. David saw a few people staffing the building: none in uniform, all plainclothes with Metropolitan Police ID cards on lanyards around their necks.

Sonny signed them in at the desk. The clerk there, an older White woman with a short bob, seemed to have been expecting them. She escorted them all down the hall, swiping through locked doors, to two different interview rooms on opposite sides of the hall.

David was directed to escort Watts into one room, while Sonny took Merritt into the second. Inside the room was one table and three sets of chairs, set up in a typical interview style of two on one. David cuffed Watts to the shackle at the table, as instructed, then left him.

The clerk shut the doors, then showed them the keypad code to unlock them. "Let us know when you're done," she said casually, like these weren't serious interrogations.

"Will do, ta," Sonny replied. He motioned with his head for David to follow him. "Fancy a drink?"

"Sure."

He led David down another hall, its strip light in the ceiling flickering on and off at one end. They entered a small break room, barely enough room for a counter boasting one kettle (the electric kind), a sink with a mug inside it, and one vending machine of soda cans and other snacks.

Sonny tapped his ID card at the machine's reader and swore under his breath when it didn't respond.

"What's wrong?" David asked.

"This piece of shit ain't working. It won't give me my comp," Sonny complained, getting out his wallet. He tapped his bank card instead. "Fucking cheek of it," he muttered, punching buttons to select his drink.

The machine spat out a soda can.

They waited in the break room, sitting at a tiny table with their knees brushing together. David didn't move his knee. He got the feeling Sonny was nudging his into David's on purpose; a subtle PDA under the table. Or that's how David interpreted it when they shared a smile.

"How long do we wait?" David asked at length. He was hungry, despite the couple of protein bars from the vending machine they'd just wolfed down.

"Let_'em stew for a bit," Sonny said. "Can't start without the Guv's say-so anyway."

"Is he coming in?"

"Might do." Sonny shrugged. "There's observation windows. But he might just watch the feed instead. Depends."

"Where's he based?" David asked.

"Just over the road from base," Sonny said. "Next to the Consulate of Venezuela." He looked at David with a knowing smile, like he could guess that Venezuela would be top on his list of places to hide out.

David kept his face neutral. "Good to know." He shifted in his chair and decided to change the topic. "Is Kip back at base?"

"Probably." Sonny checked his watch.

"Who will you take a run at first?" David asked.

"Bodyguard," Sonny said. "Odds are he's just a hired hand. Guv will probably want to cut him loose while we focus on Merritt."

David nodded. He would do the same if he were in charge.

*

After a forty-five-minute wait, they got the word from Guv to go ahead. He would be watching the security feed and instructing via earpiece.

"I'm still strong and silent?" David inquired.

"That's right, sunshine," Sonny replied. "Do your best to look menacing, innit? Leave the talking to me."

David was fine with that. He was still new to this, and he didn't want to mess up an ongoing investigation by saying the wrong thing.

They entered Terry Watts's room first. After the long wait, he was clearly sweating and started singing right away, confirming their suspicions that he'd been brought on as muscle but had no clue what Merritt was up to.

Watts said that Merritt had gotten him off on a drunken

assault charge a few months back, waiving his usual fee. Watts claimed that Merritt requested a favour in return: that Watts accompany him to France as a bodyguard.

"Cut him loose," Guv's voice said firmly. "I'll have surveillance track his movements, but I doubt Merritt would've told him anything."

Sonny nodded. "All right, Mr Watts," he said. "Thanks for your cooperation. We'll see that you get released within the hour. However, you might want to stay in the country in case we have any further questions."

"I didn't even wanna go to bleedin' France in the first place," Watts grumbled in reply.

David caught a small smirk on Sonny's face as they wrapped interview one.

Now it was onto Mr Merritt. (Again.)

They had a quick break in between to use the bathroom down the hall, and eat another protein bar from the vending machine.

"I'm bloody hungry," Sonny complained. "Curry after this?"

David perked up at the word curry. "Yeah, sounds great."

"If Merritt doesn't break right away, I propose we go have dinner," Sonny went on.

"Sonny," Guv's voice said firmly. "Get on with it."

"Sorry, Guv," Sonny replied, tossing the last of his protein bar into the trash. "Let's 'ave at it."

David followed him into Merritt's interview room, where Merritt was cuffed to his table. He began yelling at them the moment they entered.

"It's about fucking time!" Merritt shouted. "I need the toilet! I'm gonna piss myself."

"Wouldn't be the first time, I'm sure," Sonny said casually.

He sat across the table from Merritt.

David resumed his stance at the side of the room, arms folded and staring at Merritt in his most intimidating pose.

"I mean it!" Merritt insisted. "I'm gonna piss myself!"

"Better make this quick, then," Sonny retorted. "Stop beating around the bush and tell us who you're working for. And no fibs this time."

"I can't do that," Merritt said. "I value my life."

"If your information is of value, you'd be offered protection," Sonny said.

"Fuck off," Merritt replied.

Sonny clicked his tongue and shook his head, like one might do to a child having a tantrum. "Well, we've got all night," he said, picking up the plastic cup of water from the table. Holding it aloft, he began pouring drips of water into the second plastic cup. It made loud sloshing noises.

Merritt squirmed in his seat. "Stop doing that."

Sonny smiled. "We've got all night." When the first cup was empty, he set it back on the table and picked up the other cup to repeat the process.

Merritt groaned and wriggled uncomfortably. "I really need to piss!"

"I'll take you to the bogs if you start talking," Sonny replied.

Merritt glanced up at the security cameras, just a quick flick of his eyes. He was aware of being watched, and he looked shifty.

Surprisingly, he agreed to Sonny's terms.

"All right," he said. "Fucking hurry up, I'm going to burst."

Sonny sent David a look, motioning for him to get the door. While David did that, Sonny uncuffed Merritt from the table and led him by the cuffed hands out of the room.

"If you piss on me," Sonny said in a low tone, "I'll give you such a slap."

"I'm not into water sports," Merritt replied, chortling a dirty laugh.

Sonny marched him to the men's bathroom at the end of the hall. David opened the door for them, checking it was empty before they entered.

Though Mr Merritt was one of the more interesting characters David had questioned, he hoped they wouldn't have to see him again after this.

"Go on, then." Sonny shoved the older man toward the urinals. "Now, talk."

"Just a bloody second," Merritt complained, struggling with his belt and zipper as his hands were cuffed. He managed it, leaning into the urinal and letting out a loud groan of relief as he began to urinate.

David glanced at Sonny, and they shared a look of amusement.

"I'm not hearing names, Mr Merritt," Sonny prompted.

"Hang on." Merritt continued the longest piss ever, then finally zipped himself up. "Can I wash my fucking hands first?"

They guarded him closely while he went to the only sink, with a small mirror above. David was starting to wonder if he was yanking their chain again. Merritt rinsed his hands with soap and water, then ran the hot tap into the empty sink.

"I'm getting impatient," Sonny commented. "I could give you a bog wash while we're here."

"Just watch," Merritt hissed. He raised his hands, right index finger extended. On the partially steamed up mirror, he drew something. A circle with one dot in the middle.

David didn't understand what it meant. It looked like one titty. Or perhaps a crude eyeball. He glanced at Sonny to see his reaction; though his expression was neutral, David saw something hard in Sonny's eyes.

Whatever the symbol was, he knew it.

"There," Merritt declared, using his hands to scrub the drawing away. "You've got what you wanted. For all the fucking good it will do. Now let me go."

"Not so fast, Merritt," Sonny replied. He appeared to be stalling, perhaps waiting for instruction through his earpiece.

David listened but heard nothing yet.

They were interrupted by the bathroom door opening, and two plainclothes policemen filing in. David spotted their ID badges on lanyards around their necks, watching them in the mirror.

As the two men stopped short and reached inside their jackets, David felt his stomach drop.

Oh, shit.

Sonny reacted first, shoving Merritt toward David and effectively pushing them both into an open stall. "Get down!" he ordered.

The two men opened fire with automatic pistols. Bullets rained down around them, lodging into the tiled wall and sending ceramic pieces and dust flying. David pulled Merritt onto the ground for safety. His instincts told him that these guys had been sent to silence Merritt.

From the open door of the stall, David watched Sonny duck down to avoid the spray of bullets. He pulled throwing knives from his belt and launched them one by one, finding their mark. The gunfire paused. Sonny charged forward to engage with their assailants.

David couldn't just sit there, he had to help.

"Stay down," he told Merritt, then clambered over him. He rushed to join Sonny, but he'd already dispatched the two men;

the men lay on the ground with broken arms and necks at odd angles, staring up lifelessly. Sonny hadn't got off scot-free, he was bleeding from his leg from a bullet graze.

"Who are they?" David demanded.

Sonny went to the door and looked out into the hallway, checking the coast was clear. "If we get out of here in one piece, I'll tell you," he replied. "Get Merritt."

David went back to the stall to fetch a quivering and scared Mr Merritt.

"They're going to kill me!" Merritt said shakily. "This is all your fault, you fucking cunts!"

David hauled him up, glancing down at the two dead policemen on the floor. "They knew we didn't have our guns," he said to Sonny.

Sonny didn't respond. No quip, no jokes. That meant this was serious. He hustled them out into the hallway, speaking into his earpiece. "Guv?" he said. "Guv? Can you hear me? We—"

Men spilled into the hallway from a service exit. Not police this time, but White guys with a biker look. Mercs was David's guess. One of them produced a sawn-off shotgun from his coat, the others brandished handguns.

David realised they were trapped. Those armed men were blocking the exit.

"Back, back, back!" Sonny urged, and the three of them fell back into the bathroom.

Merritt crumpled to the floor whimpering and crawled off on his cuffed hands and knees to hide in a stall. David looked for windows, but there were none in here. Sonny moved the metal trash can against the door, then stood behind it to get the drop on whoever came in first.

"Hey," he said to David, taking the taser from his jacket. He tossed it over. "Use it."

David caught it by the handle and held it firmly. He flicked it once to extend the baton, and felt the electricity pulsing faintly. "I've never used one of these before!"

"Just point it at whoever you want to zap!" Sonny replied, setting push daggers into his palms blade out.

"What if I zap you?" David protested.

"Well, try not to!" Sonny shouted back.

Merritt repeated, "Fuck, fuck, fuck, fuck, fuck."

David heard voices on the other side of the door, speaking in a language he recognised but didn't understand: German.

He readied himself, catching Sonny's eyes for a moment as they shared a look to say "Let's get the bastards."

The door was kicked from outside, but the trash can partially obstructed their entry. The voices raised, annoyed, and a stronger kick followed. The door swung inwards, and the mercs poured in. Sonny grabbed the first guy from behind, dagger plunging into his neck. He screamed and fired his gun, shot going wide at the ceiling. David pointed the taser at the second guy and shocked him with seventy thousand volts. The merc froze up as he was caught, causing the third guy to bump up against him and they shook together in electric shock. Their prone forms blocked the entrance for a moment, but David had to duck for cover when the men behind them opened fire.

Sonny dropped his first victim and kicked the door back, squashing several of the mercs in it.

David had caught a stray bullet on his arm, and dropped the taser as he hit the floor. The baton clattered off under the stalls. He still had his knife, and drew that as he picked himself up again.

Sonny was struggling with the door trying to get it closed. David went to help him.

"Where's our back-up?" David gritted out, using his back to push against the door, feet planted firmly on the ground.

"Signal must be jammed," Sonny replied. "We have to hold out."

They'd almost gotten the door closed, but there were several *strong* men behind it wanting to get in.

"Can you reach that gun?" Sonny asked him, glancing round to check on the one dead guy with a gun still in his hand.

"Not without leaving the door," David answered.

"Fuck," Sonny murmured, then shouted, "Merritt! C'mere and get that gun! Merritt! Oi! Move your arse!"

Merritt gingerly poked his head out from the stall, still on all fours. He looked terrified.

"There, on the floor!" Sonny shouted at him. "Crawl over then slide the gun to me."

David watched Merritt debate the situation and knew this was taking too long. The mercs outside got tired of pushing and decided to open fire on the door instead. Merritt let out a whimper and retreated inside the stall.

The door was thick, so not all of the bullets got through. David felt one graze past his shoulder and knew that Sonny was probably catching the same. They couldn't keep this up.

Then he heard the telltale click of the shotgun. He shared a look with Sonny and they both jumped away a split second before the door blew open. The mercs spilled into the bathroom. David and Sonny turned to face them.

Round two.

David had to fight off three at once, while also dodging bullets from their handguns. Sonny engaged the rest, and the fight took up the entire space of the bathroom.

"Get the gun!" Sonny shouted at David, as the gun in

question was kicked across the floor by an errant boot.

"Merritt, get the gun!" David answered, followed by a grunt as he got a punch in the gut.

He almost got the barrel of a gun in his gut next, but he managed to pull one merc in front of him as a shield before his assailant fired. Blood speckled the floor, making the ceramic tile slippery to stand on. The mercs he knocked down stumbled into the ceramic sink unit, and David followed with a stab and a punch.

Sonny stabbed a guy several times in the neck in quick succession, blood squirting out in a jet of red. Another guy charged at him, yelling in German, and grabbed Sonny by the jacket. Sonny in turn grabbed the guy's arms then spun him around, tossing him bodily at the stalls. The flimsy structure crumpled like dominoes.

A panicked Mr Merritt came scuttling out on all fours, right into the line of fire.

"Merritt, wait!" Sonny moved toward him.

David was pinned down, and all he could do was watch in what felt like slow motion as the shotgun merc fired at Merritt and Sonny stepped in the way. Sonny was blasted backwards, blood and guts flying outward like a bursting star.

David's world narrowed to a pinpoint as time slowed down. He watched Sonny fall to the floor, and not get back up. His stomach was blown apart. That was a kill shot and David knew it.

In that split second of hesitation, David let his guard down and one of the men he'd been grappling with took a shot. David barely registered the bullet going into his chest. He was still staring at Sonny spread out on the floor.

Everything that happened in the following moments barely registered, sound muted as the blood in his ears pounded. The mercs had won. They shot Merritt next, filling him with bullets, then they exited the bathroom, pausing only to pick up discarded guns and the taser. They left their dead.

David slid down to his knees on the floor. The bullet had missed his heart, he knew that much, or he would be dying a lot faster. It was lodged somewhere in his chest, and there it would probably have to stay for the rest of his life. He absently put his hand over the wound, gushing blood. If he didn't get medical attention soon, he could bleed out, and "rest of his life" wouldn't be very long at all.

He didn't care.

Slowly, he crawled across the floor to Sonny's lifeless body. David leaned over him, looking into his open, glassy eyes.

"I...I thought you couldn't die?" he whispered, voice hoarse. "Sonny? Sonny?"

No answer. No more quips, no more banter. David felt this loss harder than the bullet in his chest. Tears pricked his eyes. If he survived, he'd be on his own again.

Alone.

"No," he choked out. "I just found you! You can't do this!"

Silence.

Maybe if David could get him to the lab, they could fix him? He'd have to go get help. Maybe then, there was a chance.

David was about to move, then paused as he noticed something odd. The veins on Sonny's neck and face were turning strangely blue. David peered closer, unsure if it was a trick of the light.

No, his veins were turning blue...and glowing.

Then he got the shock of his life as Sonny drew in a raspy breath, his body jerking with the motion.

David held his breath. Could this be the throes of death? Sonny's back arched on the floor like a string of beads pulled taut, and his mouth was open with a strange raspy sound escaping from his throat.

"Sonny?" David uttered, then looked at the wound on his stomach. "What the fuck?" The slick red of his open guts began to glow blue and knit themselves back together.

David was torn between mute shock and the urge to be sick. It was disgusting, yet fascinating. Before his very eyes, Sonny came back to life. His wound closed up, and his body sat up jerkily.

Sonny heaved in gasping breaths and looked around in confusion. His eyes weren't normal, the pupils were slits and faintly glowing.

Nonetheless, David exhaled a sigh of relief. "Man, I thought you were a goner."

"Not yet," Sonny replied, voice still a little raspy. He twisted round to look at Merritt, dead on the floor. "He definitely is though."

"The fuck you jump in front of him for?" David demanded. "You could've been killed. You *were* killed!"

"Well, I won't be doing it again," Sonny said, sounding contrite. He noticed David clutching his chest. "Are you hurt? Let me see."

"It missed anything vital," David assured him. He moved his hand cautiously, letting Sonny inspect his wound.

To David's surprise, the bleeding had stopped. "What the hell?" he muttered.

The skin was almost intact again. If the bullet was still inside, it would have to remain there, but it wouldn't be his first.

"You're healing," Sonny said. "That's good." He looked up, meeting David's gaze. His eyes were shifting back to normal.

It was then David realised those slits were more like cat's eyes.

A cat with nine lives.

"Oh, my God!" said a woman, as the two of them looked up at her arrival.

The clerk from the front desk. She stared open-mouthed at the bloodbath of the room. "What happened in here?"

"Long story," Sonny replied as he eased himself up off the floor, pulling David with him. "Do me a favour, love? Call extension one-oh-one. They'll send a cleanup crew."

She nodded mutely, then left.

David cast one last look at Merritt. "They got him, whoever they were. We'll have to find out."

Sonny sighed. "I've got a pretty good guess who."

*

When the cleanup crew from PRISM arrived, so did Kip with the car and a portable medical kit.

"Christ, Sonny," Kip muttered, as they patched up his still healing wound. "I've brought spare shirts."

Sonny's shirt and jacket had both been blown to smithereens. David's had fared better, with only a couple of bullet holes, but was a bit bloody, so he opted for a clean shirt too.

Kip bagged up David's bloody shirt. When they noticed David watching, they said, "For the lab. The sample isn't ideal, but they can work with it for now."

David said nothing and nodded. If it kept the lab off his back for a while, he'd let them keep the shirt.

Kip drove them back to base, and they all returned to the tech room. Guv called in and gave Sonny a serious dressing down for screwing up the interrogation. Their witness, Robert Merritt, was dead. So was Terry Watts, found two blocks away in a back alley with a fatal shot to the chest. And to top it off, a prototype piece of equipment (the taser) had been stolen.

Sonny appeared uncharacteristically contrite about it all.

David kept quiet, as did everyone else in the room, but he didn't think the situation was entirely fair. If they'd had their guns on them, they might have stood a better chance. As far as he understood it, there seemed to be some red tape issue around them taking guns to interview rooms used by the Metropolitan Police.

"We won't use Met sites until I say otherwise," Guv ordered. "Someone leaked your location, probably a mole inside the Metropolitan Police. From now on, we're keeping our ops within our own organisation, on our own sites."

"Yeah, and someone must've jammed the signal in the building," Sonny said. "I take it you didn't get anything said in the bogs? Merritt drew a symbol we're familiar with. A circle. That's all we got, Guv, but it's a start. Could be the Illuminati."

David didn't know exactly who those guys were, but he recognised the name.

Guv nodded in silence, then replied, "Leave it with me. I have a detail following the mercs. I've let them leave the country so we could track them, but until we get clearance, all we do now is observe and wait for intel. Understood?"

"Yes, Guv," Sonny said, a sigh in his voice.

"Go home. Recover. That's an order," Guv said. "I'll be in touch."

He signed off.

Dev stepped up to Sonny and delicately cleared his throat. "Um, Guv asked that I give you guys some bulletproof vests to take home?"

Sonny let out a long groan. "Ugh! One little fuck up, and he's gonna make me wear those bloody things now?"

"They'd probably be useful to have," David said.

Sonny sighed. "Fine! Put 'em in a bag, and I'll take them."

While Sonny was busy with Dev, David noticed that Nina the dog was once again sleeping under Owl's desk.

He went over to pet her, craving a little normality after a bad day. This time, Nina woke up and greeted him, enthusiastically wagging her tail.

"Aw, you remember me," David murmured, petting her ears. "Should I take her for a walk, or something?" he asked.

"Doc said she can't leave the building yet," Owl said. "We're taking it in turns to walk her around base though. She's enjoyed sniffing all the things."

David chuckled. "I bet you have, Nina."

"Dash?" Sonny called to him. "Stop smooching the dog. Unless you wanna stay here all night."

"Wait. I'm coming," David replied. He scritched Nina's ears one last time. "I'll see you soon," he promised her.

As they walked out of the room, David caught Sonny shaking his head.

"What?" he asked.

"You and that flippin' dog," Sonny said with a wry smile.

"What? Don't you like dogs?" David asked. The memory of Sonny pointing his gun at Nina flashed in his mind. Sonny had tried to shoot him, too, but he hadn't, and now they were good. Maybe he'd warm up to Nina.

"Have you ever had a pet?" he asked.

Sonny smirked. "Do you count?"

"Wow," David drawled, feigning offense. "You're gonna pay for that later."

"Threaten me with a good time," Sonny teased.

They got into the elevator together. Despite how easily they fell back into their banter, David fought with a growing sense of dread.

"Are we safe walking out of here?" he asked. "Shouldn't we put those tac vests on?"

"You heard Guv," Sonny replied. "Those mercs are long gone."

"But whoever hired them clearly has moles in the police," David pointed out.

"They wanted to silence Merritt, love. We weren't the targets, we were in their way."

David hummed in consideration. "But even if they think we're dead now, they'll soon figure out we survived."

Sonny shrugged. "Good time to lie low, then."

David couldn't argue with that. He made a mental note to start sleeping with a loaded gun in easy reach again.

So much for a new start.

The elevator opened, and they walked out. This was his first time exiting HQ on foot. He followed Sonny out of a service door at street level, down a gloomy side street and onto the main street. Stepping out here was like walking slap bang into the city center, with bright street lights, busy traffic, and pedestrians on all fronts.

When David glanced back at the building they'd exited, he saw this side of it was a world away from the service side he'd seen previously. He wasn't even sure what this building was; it looked like a toweringly tall, gothic castle to him. There were pointy turrets and gargoyles and decorated windows.

"Hey," he said to Sonny. "What is this place?"

"Hm? Oh," Sonny said. "It's the Natural History Museum. That's the public entrance."

"Oh," David said, staring up at the building. "It looks like a castle."

"Guv's office is over there," Sonny said, pointing across the street.

The buildings that side were grand also, but in a more understated fashion. David clocked the Venezuelan flag outside one building; that had to be the Consulate of Venezuela Sonny had mentioned. A few buildings down on the same block was a French flag, probably the French Consulate.

A lot of institutions here.

The now deceased Mr Merritt had mentioned the Illuminati, the notorious secret global order, but how was PRISM any different? Operating secretly while in plain sight. David was just starting to realise he'd entered an entirely new world, a world of underground organisations.

"Come on, mate," Sonny said, nudging David with his elbow. "Tube's round the corner 'ere. I'll call Rizwan and tell him to get our curries ready to go. We can eat at home."

"Okay," David agreed. He was hungry. "And can you maybe explain to me what this Illuminati is?"

"Sure you don't want to wait for the office slideshow presentation?" Sonny quipped.

"No, I'd rather hear it from you," David replied.

"All right. The short version?" Sonny said. "The Illuminati started in Bavaria, eighteenth_century. There's still an underground faction of them left in Europe. Rich man's club, secret ceremonies, political favours, that sort of thing. Been on PRISM's radar for a long time."

"Okay," David said. He got the feeling Sonny was holding something back. "And they're human?" he questioned, thinking of the mercs they'd recently taken on. Some of them had been *strong*.

"Well." Sonny tilted his head side to side. "Bit of a mix. But isn't everyone these days? Come on, let's go eat." He took David's elbow and made him walk along the street. "Just relax, innit?"

"I'll relax once I know what we're dealing with," David

argued, but he relented and walked beside his partner.

Epilogue

In the shadowy space between dreams and awake, a space that wasn't quite one or the other but its own realm, Sepehr stirred.

He sensed his host was falling asleep. And that wasn't all; the other host was also falling asleep nearby. Close enough that their dreams overlapped, with the doors of dreaming carelessly left ajar.

Through the doors, Sepehr sensed him.

Amon.

Sepehr unfolded himself, stretching his long limbs and rising to stand tall in a realm that was too small for him. A realm he was currently stuck inside.

But he wasn't alone, not anymore.

Sepehr rolled his shoulders, a minute action to set off a wave among the sensitive feelers on his head and arms, rippling like lit-up sea anemones in the tide. His feelers created sound, a soft chitter, and he used the sound like an echo location to find Amon.

He walked toward the sleeping form of his mate, tucked up

small in his dormant state. Sepehr stooped down, crouching beside Amon. In their private, ancient tongue, he spoke to his mate to revive him.

Wake up, my love.

Amon stirred, rumbling softly. *Sepehr?*

Yes, Amon. I am here. We are together again. He reached out his claw-tipped hands, using the backs of his long fingers to gently caress his mate's face.

Amon tried to move, but he was still weak. He managed to unfurl his form enough that Sepehr could spoon in beside him and, for the first time in many, many years, they embraced each other. Not strong enough yet for their swirling dance, but the embrace was heaven.

Where are we? Amon asked.

Dormant, Sepehr answered. *But soon, my love, we will grow strong again. We will rise.*

Acknowledgements

Thank you NineStar Press for making my publishing dream come true! Huge thanks to BJ, my wonderful editor, and thank you to Raevyn.

Thank you to my cover artist, HolBat (linktr.ee/sibeliusbertolini) who drew such an amazing illustration.

Thank you, G, for the help with Spanish.

Thank you, Moss, for your support.

Thank you, Leyla.

Thank you, H.,

Thank you to my patient cats, who missed out on a lot of lap time while I was writing this book.

About the Author

Quince is a MENA-British author who lives in England, enjoys sci-fi and fantasy, history, and Halloween.

Website
cquince.carrd.co

CONNECT WITH NINESTAR PRESS

WEBSITE: NINESTARPRESS.COM

FACEBOOK: NINESTARPRESS

X: @NINESTARPRESS

INSTAGRAM: NINESTARPRESS

BLUESKY: NINESTARPRESS

THREADS: @NINESTARPRESS